TRAIN WRECK

T.GEPHART

Train Wreck
Published by T Gephart
Copyright 2017 T Gephart

ISBN-10:0-6480231-0-9
ISBN-13:978-0-6480231-0-4

Discover other titles by T Gephart on
Facebook, Twitter, Goodreads, or *tgephart.com*

Cover by Hang Le

Editing by Insight Editing Services

Formatting by Type A Formatting

TRAIN WRECK

EVE

"YOU ARE A LYING PIECE of shit!"

I tossed my Chanel handbag at him even though I knew it wouldn't do any real damage. You needed a good-sized LV for that. And I really wished I had more vases or decorative stuff lying around, it would have made it easier to hurt him.

"Eve, baby. It's not what it looks like. I don't even know her." He held his hands up defensively trying to pretend that the woman he *barely knew* wasn't just giving him a blowjob in *my* apartment. "It was an accident, I swear."

Oh. My. God.

He did not just say that to me.

I was seething. So tied up in rage that in that moment I totally got the rationalization for murder. Ten years behind bars didn't seem so bad.

"An accident!" I pulled off one of my Louboutins and aimed for his head. The heel could be deadly even if it was just a shoe.

Sadly it missed.

"Your penis just accidently *fell* into her mouth? Come on, you went to Harvard, don't embarrass yourself by acting stupid."

The other shoe went sailing, and like its predecessor was also off the mark. Damn it. I really needed better aim.

Of course, while Oliver was playing dodge ball with my wardrobe, his little *friend* looked on with wide-eyed terror, frozen on her knees, silent.

"You know him?" My eyes scanned the room for something else to hurl at Oliver.

The blonde nodded, slowly her mouth opening and closing a few times before she finally found her voice. "We work together. I-I didn't know—"

And that was as far as she got.

"Look, I'm assuming the asshat didn't tell you he had a girlfriend or that he actually lives in *my* apartment." And judging by her shock, she was either a stellar actress or had likewise been deceived. "And trust me when I tell you this, but I did you a favor. He only lasts about five minutes when it actually counts. I've had to finish myself off more times than not, if you know what I mean."

I was lying of course. Oliver was great in bed and sex with him was better than average if I was really honest. But I wasn't about to give him that kind of credit. And while I hated he had cheated on me, there was no point being angry at Little Miss Fellatio, it wasn't *her* I was in a relationship with.

"Baby. Evie," Oliver started, his pants still unzipped. "It was a moment of weakness."

To be fair, I didn't care if it was the first time or he'd been seeing her for six months.

He had cheated.

He, the man I thought cared about me, who I'd come home to on what had been one of the worst days of my life, had betrayed me. And as horrible as it was to admit, *that* was what I was really mad about. That I had needed him, hoped to come home and find some refuge, and it was taken away.

Because he cheated.

"Get out, Oliver," I screamed, no longer willing to have to look at him and the reminder of his infidelity. "We're done."

There wasn't a doubt in my mind that we were over. No room for second chances. And if I was honest with myself it was because, as much as I enjoyed Oliver's company and loved the orgasms he provided me, I didn't love him.

No. We were glorified friends with benefits, convenient fuck buddies and someone to take whenever a plus one was required.

But I didn't love him.

Not like I thought I should.

Which is why instead of being devastated the relationship was over, I was more pissed off that my pride had taken another battering.

Damn it.

Couldn't he have kept his dick in his pants for one more freaking day?

"Evie. Buttercup." He looked to me and then to the woman whose knees were still planted on my Aubusson rug. "Kitty?"

Kitty? Her name was *Kitty*? Great how very appropriate.

So much for not knowing her.

The petite blonde shook her head, doing her best to remain as still as possible. Oliver, it seemed, was shit out of luck with both his women.

"Get out, Oliver. Now, before I call the police."

He looked like he wanted to argue—to reason—say something to persuade me, but he didn't. Slowly, backing away from us, he zipped up and made his way to my front door.

He hesitated at the door, grabbing his keys from the crystal bowl that sat on the bureau in the entranceway. Damn, *now* I remembered the crystal bowl. It would have been perfect to throw earlier.

"I'll call you tomorrow," he coughed out uncomfortably.

I wasn't sure if that was directed at me or to Kitty.

"Don't bother." I waved after him. "I'll have your things boxed up and delivered, expect the bill." *If I didn't burn them first.*

He didn't speak as the door closed behind him, no doubt hoping a good night's sleep would let me cool off. Because he was delusional like that. And had he been less of a jerk face and a better boyfriend—the cheating in my apartment aside—he would have known that one night's sleep wasn't going to cut it. No, I could sleep for an entire year and it wouldn't make a difference.

Kitty coughed awkwardly, either to clear her throat or alert me she was still there.

And then there were two.

While Oliver had vacated my apartment, Kitty—the blower—had been sort of trapped. Probably wondering if her sudden movements might redirect my anger—or projectiles—to her. She'd abandoned any association to the douche canoe that was my *former* boyfriend and so remained. And he had left without a second thought about her safety.

He really was a gutless piece of shit.

There was no protocol for this, well none that I knew of. It had been a while since I consulted Emily Post, but was pretty sure she didn't have any handy hints that would cover it. Guess I was on my own.

"So, Kitty, you feel like a drink? I sure as hell could use one." My bare feet padded to my kitchen.

Wine. This would definitely be easier with wine.

"Ah. Um," she stammered, slowly rising to her feet. "I-I should go."

Unlike Oliver—who while having his cock out had been mostly dressed—Kitty had been wearing all her clothes. Perhaps their interlude had been destined to be one-sided, or maybe they hadn't gotten to the good part yet. But it helped that neither had to perform an undignified redressing with an audience; I was especially glad to be spared the visual.

"Okay, do you need me to call you a cab?" I pulled my head out of the refrigerator long enough to answer. "Or did you drive?"

I stopped for a minute, processing that I was genuinely concerned about how she got home, which I guess was sort of weird. I was acting weird. This whole scenario was really freaking weird.

This must be what shock feels like.

Or maybe I had truly lost my mind.

I probably was only remaining upright because of anger. Adrenaline was a powerful thing. Sometimes it gave you super strength, the ability to lift a car or something like that. Or obviously in my case, the ability to have a rational conversation with the girl my boyfriend was cheating with. At least I was still functional even if I had no idea what the hell I was even looking for any more.

Oh, that's right.

Wine.

I pulled out a chilled bottle of Riesling and wondered if I should even bother with the glass. There was no point denying I was going to be finishing it.

"Why are you being so nice to me?" She approached slowly, her careful green eyes floating between me and her exit route, and probably wondering whether I was clinically insane.

I didn't blame her.

I wondered too.

"Because today my world came crashing down and the worst of it wasn't finding the two of you." The desire for wine discarded as I placed the bottle on the counter and I sunk to my butt on the floor.

God, I didn't want to do this with an audience.

I had been strong the whole time.

All morning I had kept my shit together. The smile on my face fixed in place as people at the gallery looked at me with pitiful glances. Didn't even crack when I heard their *discreet* hushed conversations. Then there were the calls from my parents and my friends. But there were only so many "I'm fines" I could stomach before I felt compelled to pull a *Van Gogh* and slice off someone's ear. And clearly I wasn't a dedicated enough artist for it to be mine.

So imagine my surprise when I came home at lunchtime hoping to get naked, drunk, and call my boyfriend for angry—not at him, but that soon changed—sex and found him already home.

With his dick in someone else's mouth.

Damn him! This was supposed to be my day to have a breakdown, to plot my revenge for all those uptight assholes, and now I had to plot against him too. It was very inconvenient. Very selfish of him.

Crap. I wasn't even sure if I wanted to cry, vomit, or slice those Salvatore Ferragamo loafers he liked so much. That was the second time I'd mentioned cutting so I should probably hide the knives.

"Go home, Kitty. I need to be alone."

Or at least take away the possibility of a victim. A living one. I didn't hold out much hope for Oliver's fancy suits.

"I'm really sorry, I honestly didn't know." She mumbled apologies as she joined me on the floor. "I thought he was single. He didn't tell me about you."

The situation was ridiculous.

There I was sitting on the floor of my kitchen. My refrigerator obnoxiously beeping, warning me the door was still open. With the woman my boyfriend cheated on me with. What's even worse is that scenario wasn't what was making my heart hurt the most.

"I'm a failure, and I cannot be a failure." I said the words out loud, words that had been looping in my head since the morning. "I put everything into that collection, everything . . . why would they be so cruel? I bled on those canvases."

Poor Kitty. What she thought was going to be a lunchtime quickie had turned into a therapy session. Which I felt was fair considering A. She was still here and therefore fair game and B. I had been more than reasonably empathetic to *her* dilemma.

"Ummm, you bled *where*?" she asked bewildered, reaching across and thankfully silencing the incessant beeping by closing the refrigerator door.

Yep, she wasn't to have known that this morning critics had unapologetically torn me to shreds with scathing reviews. That my first ever solo art exhibition had been called a train wreck and me—its creator—a soulless socialite with zero talent and even less skill.

It wasn't just a critique.

They had annihilated me.

"On the canvas!" I exclaimed, making no more sense despite my added passion—insanity well and truly settling in. "They wouldn't know art if it bit them on the ass. They didn't even bother to interpret the pieces." My hands waved around furiously to illustrate the point. "I'm a smart person, it's smart art. I can't help it *they* are boring and have no fucking vision."

Denial.

I think that was the stage after anger. Or maybe I had mixed them up. Lord knows I wasn't an authority, but the idea it was normal made me feel a little better so I went with it.

Yeah, this wasn't *my* fault. There was nothing wrong with *me*. This was all *them*.

"Art is subjective and who are they to judge what is good." As the ideas tumbled in my head, I felt the need to share. "I'm sure everyone thought Picasso was dropping acid at first too." A very reasonable assumption, the amount of artists originally panned to be later revered was astounding. "That must be the problem here, clearly I am too progressive and not appreciated for my genius."

This was logic I could hold onto. Important and intelligent thoughts that explained how it all could have happened.

I had to hand it to Kitty, she was a good listener. She didn't try to interrupt or interject, just sat there and listened which was obviously what I needed.

And while the sting was still fresh and part of me still raw, I was definitely feeling better for talking about it.

"You're an artist?" she asked, her head tilting to the side like she wasn't sure. "A painter?"

"Yes, I'm an artist." Slight agitation bit at my voice. Wasn't she paying attention? She had looked like she had been listening so intently. "I predominately paint and sketch but sometimes I'll use other mediums. My professors at Yale always said I was very versatile."

"So like a professional?" Her head tilted again, I could see this was her thing when she didn't understand. "As in people *pay* you to do it?"

Oh, poor misinformed and naïve Kitty.

"Yes, artists get paid despite everyone believing they should starve and work for free. I'd like to go into someone else's place of business and tell them to work *for the love of it.*"

Okay, slight sore point, but it wasn't the first time I had to defend what I did as a legitimate career. I had a fine arts degree from Yale for Christ's sake and yet a waitress at Hooters got more respect. They had a "real" job.

"I'm sorry." And she looked it. "I've just never met a *real* artist before. There was a guy I dated in college who said he was, but he mainly got high and occasionally graffitied a mini mart. No one paid him, and he sure didn't go to Yale. I don't even think he graduated to be honest." She laughed, her voice easing for the first time since I'd met her.

It was a common misconception that "artist" wasn't a legitimate job description, and one of the reasons why I had hoped to finally get validation. To be praised in *The Times* or *The Village Voice*, seeing my name in those publications would be a dream come true. Hell, I'd settle for a polite and honorable mention in *Time Out*. Well, I got my wish. My name had appeared in all of them. Just not favorably.

"It's okay." I shrugged, my mood still swinging wildly. "I had my first art exhibition. It wasn't received well."

"Well, like you said, maybe they didn't get it." She smiled. "I saw this exhibit that everyone loved, and it made no sense at all. My friends kept telling me how fantastic it was but it looked like an old drop sheet someone had dripped paint all over. It was a mess. Some Polish dude, I think." She lowered her voice to a whisper even though it was just the two of us. "It wasn't very good. I don't know why anyone would pay millions for it."

Dripped paint? Polish? Millions?

"Do you mean Jackson *Pollock*?" Great, now I was doing the head tilt, I hoped this wouldn't become a thing.

"Well, I mean," she shifted, uncomfortable, "I'm not sure it's PC to call him that."

"No, that's his name, he's not Polish."

"Well, whatever. It was bad." She waved her hands around. "I like my art a little less weird. More classical. Actually, let me show you." She stood up excitedly and moved her hands to the back of her black fitted sheath dress.

What the hell?

Sure, it had been *far* from an ordinary day. And under normal circumstances—had my professional life not been in the toilet—I wouldn't have entertained saying two words to a woman who was about to fellate my boyfriend, let alone share a conversation.

But it was strange times, and strange times called for desperate measures and all of that. BUT even with all of the extenuating circumstances, I had my limits.

"Kitty, what are you doing?" My eyes followed her fingers sliding down her zipper at the back of her dress.

Firstly, holy shit was she a contortionist? I could only get about halfway before I had to whip the other hand around and yank from the bottom. But Kitty didn't suffer from the same limitations, twisting her hand around and slowly moving it down her back in one smooth movement.

And secondly, surely we'd filled the quota for weird? We didn't need to introduce nudity into it.

"It's fine, I'm not shy." She let her dress drop to the floor, revealing her incredibly perky breasts and a barely there lacy thong. "Honestly, I'm more comfortable wearing less."

And the mystery of why my dumbass boyfriend invited her back to my place was solved.

Kitty was stunning with her clothes on. Beautiful face, great hair, and a lithe toned body that by the looks of things could twist itself into all sixty-four positions in the *Kama Sutra*.

Oliver—the bastard—like a lot of men, was a simple creature. He could get hard by simply looking at a Victoria Secret catalogue. Of course, I never suspected he'd actually act like a dog even if he had the libido of one.

Not that any of that mattered now as I was confronted with skin. Lots of it, and a pair of breasts that were too fantastic to be real.

"See, look." She lifted her hair as her body twisted, her fantastic boobs no longer visible as she revealed a large and incredibly intricate back tattoo.

"Wow." It escaped my lips as I climbed to my feet. "It's stunning." My eyes squinted in disbelief.

I'd seen decent tattoos, lifelike pinup girls and pretty butterflies. Hell, a few of my friends even had a couple and they were better than just good.

But to say Kitty's was just a good tattoo was incredibly arrogant.

It was an extraordinary piece of art.

Across her shoulders and down her spine was Botticelli's *The Birth of Venus*, so clean, crisp and perfect it looked like Botticelli had painted it on her himself.

To achieve that level of excellence on a page or canvas was difficult. So many nuances—the positioning of the hands, creating the movement in her hair and fabric, the softness in the curves of her body.

On human skin?

It was impossible.

"No, not impossible." Kitty laughed, my silent thoughts not being so silent. "Josh is amazing. You should see his original work. I'm going to get him to do something else for me too."

"One man did all this?" I gave up fighting the urge to touch it, my fingers sweeping across her back. She had said she wasn't shy. "It must have taken months."

It was as if the image leapt off her back and spoke to me. Every color, every line—it told the story as clear as someone whispering it in my ear.

"I lost count after twenty hours." She turned to face me. "Not all in one session obviously, he worked on me for as long as I could take and then I'd go back. He was so gentle."

"Gentle? He was jamming a needle in your skin. How can someone be gentle?" My brain couldn't comprehend it, but that level of skill . . . in a tattoo?

Wow.

He must be a god.

Some kind of deity under the guise of a man put on Earth to live among us. Dazzle us with his talent. The tattoo artist part was throwing me, but Jesus had been a carpenter, right? Who was to know that if the second coming had happened now that the Son of God wouldn't have traded the long flowing robes for a black T-shirt and tattoo gun. I was in no position to judge.

"I don't know, he just is." Kitty brought me back to the present. "He's amazing." Her voice got breathy.

See, maybe there had been some divine intervention.

"Please tell me you got this *here*. In New York." My hand grabbed hers and squeezed.

The tattoo had taken hours, which meant there was a promising chance it had been local. But who could be sure? After all, I knew pretty much *nothing* about the almost naked woman whose hand I was clutching.

"His studio is in Queens." She laughed, her perky boobs shaking with the rest of her. "Same place he's always been."

And praise the Lord, hallelujah! Tattoo Jesus lived in Queens. It was definitely a sign of divine intervention.

"Could you introduce us?" Not sure what I would do or say when I met him or even if he could help me, but mental clarity was not the flavor of the day, clearly. In any case, I needed to meet the man who was capable of that level of excellence. Awed didn't even come close to it.

"I don't really know him like *that*." She blushed. "I mean, I wish. He's gorgeous. I'd throw myself at his feet if I thought I had a chance." Cue the dreamy eyes and wide smile—enraptured like a blonde, naked, tattooed Mary Magdalene.

It had to be a sign.

"Yeah, I'm sorta not interested in how gorgeous he is." Firstly, because I'd been single for less than an hour and dating wasn't really on my agenda. And I doubted that he—while talented and magical by Kitty's reports—would be my type. "I still need to evict Oliver."

"Oh, yeah." A nervous laugh escaped her lips. "I forgot."

Ah Kitty, she wasn't the sharpest knife in the drawer.

My mind spun. All of it had to have happened for a reason.

Surely me coming home early and finding Oliver and Kitty was part of a bigger picture. And who was I to deny the method to the madness.

And while it was incredibly hard to admit, maybe—and I'm not saying I was sure, but there was the *possibility*—some of those things that had been said about my work, were true.

Not the part about me not having talent, because that was bullshit. Sure, my family had money and I wasn't eyeball deep in student loans. But I was not being drunkenly evicted from nightclubs with my photo splashed on TMZ either. They could shove the socialite tag up their ass; my last name did not disqualify me from having actual ability and talent. Those grades I'd earned—fair and square.

But there was a—very small, tiny even—*possibility* that there was some flatness to my work. Not anything I could put my finger on exactly, but it was missing *something*. It didn't have the same magic I saw when I looked at this tattoo. I didn't get the feeling in the base of my throat and my skin didn't tingle when I looked at my pieces like I did when I looked at the back of my naked "friend".

And I wasn't sure I knew how to fix it.

Maybe at some point I'd been so preoccupied with being good, it got lost in the translation. Where my strokes became robotic, and instead of emotion it had been my ego leeching out.

Oh, crap.

What stage was this?

Acceptance?

No, no. I wouldn't accept I was bad. I would never accept that.

I could be wrong, have room for improvement but I wouldn't allow myself to accept bad.

"Here's an idea." My head dipped to the direction of the floor, the pool of black fabric still at Kitty's feet. "Why don't you put your dress back on." Because there were currently more boobs in my kitchen than on HBO. "And you can tell me everything you know about Josh." *Aka Tattoo Jesus.* Oh, and that wine that I had intended to drink, was totally happening. Because if ever there was a conversation that needed some feel good juice, this would be it.

"Okay." Kitty nodded, smiling brightly as she gathered up her dress and pulled it back over her head. "Are you going to get a tattoo?"

"Me? No, I'd never get something that permanent." The thought of marking my skin made me shudder. "But if this Josh is as good as you say he is, then I think he can help me."

I mean it was worth a try, right? If this tattoo guy from Queens could replicate one of the most famous renaissance paintings of all time, and translate that much emotion into skin, then I at least needed a conversation with him. And maybe find out where the leprechaun was he captured or if he had any other neat tricks, like turning water into wine. We *needed* to be friends, and he would soon see that.

And just like that, on the day where my life had been spinning out of control, I had enlisted the help of a stranger so I could meet another stranger. Neither of which was guaranteed to help the situation I was in.

Either I had totally lost my mind or I was on the road to greatness.

Time would tell which it would be.

JOSH

"YOUR TWO O'CLOCK IS HERE," Dallas called from the door, looking less than pleased at having to play secretary.

Two o'clock already? Wow, morning had really gotten away from me.

"Thanks, I'm just finishing this sketch then I'll get to it."

I hated leaving shit unfinished but it had been session after session and I'd barely had time to scratch. Still, being busy was not the kind of thing to complain about. And business was definitely good.

"You know since that feature in *Ink Magazine* we've been getting slammed." Dallas pulled a mind reader, echoing my thoughts. "Both of us are booked solid for six months and I think our phone disintegrated with all the unanswered messages."

This was his version of polite, probably because I had an appointment waiting at the front of the shop and not because he was being tactful. I fully expected that the minute I flipped the closed sign he would be saying it a little different. More *fucks* would be used for sure.

"I know, dude." I pushed back from my desk, my chair rolling out. "We need at least one other artist, and someone to man the front desk." One artist was bare minimum, I could hire three and we'd still have to turn down work. "But it's just not something I want to get from Craig's List. It takes time to go through portfolios and even if they are decent, I want them to gel with us as a unit."

The shop for me was an extension of myself. It was more than a job; it was my life. With my mom following my sister down to Florida to live, I overlooked the lack of family by putting all my energy into my dream. Built up with a high interest loan from the bank and a small inheritance when my pop died, I had even slept on the floor in the early days. Not that the health inspectors would be pleased to hear that. And now that I'd finally built a rep and business was good, I wasn't going to hand it over to some half-rate hack to destroy. Fuck that noise.

"Yeah, whatever." He rolled his eyes knowing the whys better than most. "But at least get someone for the front desk. They don't have to be a rocket scientist, a trained monkey will do."

"Isn't that *your* job description?" I laughed. Couldn't help myself, Dallas was too easy a target.

"Fuck you, man." He flipped me off, shaking his head as he smirked. "Don't think for a second I won't leave your ass and go elsewhere."

Dallas was full of shit. He wasn't going anywhere, and he knew it.

Not only was he one of my closest friends—we'd know each other since junior high—but there weren't too many bosses who gave him the kind of freedom I did. He wouldn't last two days in someone else's shop. Besides, he watched my back and I had his, so as much as he was a pain in the ass at times, I liked having him around. And when it came to business, he respected my decisions and deferred to me, even if it sometimes came with a soundtrack of bitching.

"Well buddy, you know where the door is anytime you get a

better offer." I rose to my feet wearing a smirk of my own. "Probably cost me a lot less in liability insurance, and I won't have to worry about you hitting on everything that's wearing a skirt."

"I only hit on girls when they aren't customers anymore," he argued, the smile he wore telling me he knew it was straddling the line. "Once they've paid, dude, there's no conflict."

Like I said, he was right there on that line. Something I may have done in the earlier days too before I wised up and realized I could be screwing up my career. Still, I wasn't going to waste my breath arguing considering most of those girls had no problem with it.

"Go do some work or something, monkey." I laughed, walking out of my room and into the hall.

The shop was a pretty sweet lay out. Not huge, but a decent storefront and Dallas and I had hung sheets of dry wall to section us off. It wasn't completely soundproof, but we insulated as best we could and it gave us the illusion of personal workspace and of course privacy. Important when some tats required more skin than others.

Not that it was a problem today—my two o'clock was a forearm piece on a dude called Matt.

"Ten to one, he flinches on the outline," Dallas coughed under his breath from behind me. "He looked like he was hyperventilating in the foyer," he added with a chuckle.

"It wouldn't be the first time." I laughed as I punched him in the arm. "Make sure you answer the phone if it rings."

"Answer it your damn self," Dallas smirked, "I won't be able to hear it wearing my headphones." He pulled the wireless Beats that were hanging around his neck and situated them on his ears. "Can't hear a thing." He tapped them to illustrate the point.

"I definitely need a new monkey." I shook my head as I watched him disappear into his room. "One that follows instructions." Said for my own benefit as my boots took me down the hall to the front of the shop.

Whoa.

That was *not* Matt.

Standing on the other side of the counter was a knockout brunette with insane curves. Dressed in clothes I could tell were expensive, and shoes that went beyond stiletto territory and into stilts. And her eyes were the lightest shade of brown I'd ever seen. Like caramel or whiskey.

Two things were obvious.

She was gorgeous, and she was lost.

"Can I help you?" I tipped my head, wondering if she perhaps needed directions. The idea of playing GPS was suddenly very appealing.

"Are you Josh Logan?" She rolled her lips with her teeth in a move that was straight up sexy and I had to remind myself to be professional.

And huh, she knew my name, didn't expect that. Still not hard to read the accreditation on the walls, my name plastered all over them. She was probably here to sell me something even though the sign on the door clearly stated no solicitation. But unlike most door-to-door salespeople, I had no desire to toss her out. Maybe I needed a new bible, phone company, light bulb—or whatever the hell she was selling.

"Yep, that's me." I gave her a smile and a nod, trying to discreetly look around for Matt. The front of the shop was empty except for the two of us.

"If you're looking for the guy who was here." Her mouth spread into an amazing smile that made my dick take notice. Yep, was definitely buying something today, especially after a smile like that. "He left."

It might have been a few months since I last dated, but all the parts still worked. And if we'd been in a club, I would have definitely offered to buy her a drink. But I hadn't completely lost my train of thought, my two o'clock pulling a disappearing act.

"He just left?" I didn't hide my surprise. "Is he coming back?"

Matt had made the appointment three months ago. And sure he was a little nervous when we spoke on the phone yesterday, but he gave me no indication he was going to punk out.

"I paid him two hundred dollars to reschedule," she said with zero hesitation and even less regret. "I tried calling you two days ago but no one's returned my call."

"Okay, look." She might have been the hottest woman I'd ever seen but she didn't get to walk into my shop and order people around. "Yeah, we may have had some issues with the phone, but you can't just pay people and take their appointments. That's *not* how it works."

To say I was annoyed was putting it lightly. And underneath the beautiful face and knockout body she was probably like some of the other entitled people who believed their shit didn't stink. She wasn't the first person to walk through the door who thought a fist full of bills got her priority. And while I appreciated that in other places lubricating a palm or two got her what she wanted, I had more integrity than that. And I sure as hell had more business ethic.

"Trust me, the way he was pacing he would have passed out on the chair so I was just saving you time." She smiled, no apology offered. "Besides, he was very happy to take the money. He didn't even try to talk up the price."

Can you believe the *nerve* on this girl?

I might not be tossing her out the door—something she totally deserved—but tattooing her probably wasn't happening either. My name on the door meant I got that choice.

"That's great." I gave her a tight smile and swallowed down the *who the fuck are you* I wanted to say. "But I don't have time to do a new sketch and do the work." Not a lie, I needed at least one consult before machine touched skin. "So let me know what you were thinking about getting," I forced myself to keep it sweet, "and I'll see when I can fit you in." I grabbed the appointment log and flipped to the end. "I think I have an opening around the first of December. Might be a nice Christmas present for yourself." I glanced up at her and grinned. Six months away. No way she'd wait that long. Not when she couldn't wait two lousy days for someone to return her phone call.

"Oh, I'm not here to get tattooed." Her head shook as she laughed, the sound going right to my balls even though I was annoyed. "Sorry, I should have said. Let me start over, I'm Eve Thorton." She stuck out her hand.

"Josh, but you already knew that." My hand clasped hers and shook. "So, Eve." I'm assuming using her first name was fine. "What brings you to Ink Addiction?"

"Well, *you* actually," she said, her shoulders shifting back. "I saw the back piece you did on my . . . er . . . friend, Kitty. Botticelli's *Birth of Venus*. It was absolutely stunning and I want to work with you. I'm an artist."

Huh?

What?

My mood shifted gears as I processed the words and tried to connect the dots. And while I remembered the back piece, and the girl, I was a little foggy on the name. But *that* wasn't what I was scratching my head over.

This woman was a tattooist?

Maybe I was profiling, judging a little, I'll own that. But apart from the fancy threads she was wearing and the immaculate hair—her arms, legs, neck and face were bare. Not one black line or flash of color unless you counted her bright pink lips and thick black eyelashes.

So unless she was hiding her ink underneath her dress—and there wasn't a lot of it—she had virgin skin.

And call me pedantic, but I didn't know of any decent artists who hadn't taken a machine to their own flesh at least once. Not to mention the other pieces that accumulated over the years. It wasn't the sort of thing people dabbled in. And other than a diamond stud in each ear, there weren't any piercings either. Nothing to even *hint* that this wasn't her first time inside a tattoo shop.

"Huh?" It fired out of my mouth as I squinted in disbelief.

I wasn't usually wrong when I got a read on people. It's why I was as successful as I was. Feeling out what people wanted and putting it into the art. Which could only mean that *someone* was having a little fun at my expense.

"Did Dallas send you?" I folded my arms across my chest as I watched for a reaction.

This had him written all over it. He probably fucked this poor girl and like the others, she'd gotten attached. Not sure why they didn't see him for the crotch hound that he was. Instead they worshiped the ground he walked on. Until the one day when they suddenly woke up and had a freaking revelation. Then it usually turned ugly.

And if I were a betting man I'd assume that my good friend with questionable morals had seen doe-eyed Eve and figured he might as well use it to his benefit. To illustrate his point that we needed another artist, sending me the least suitable candidate and hoping it would prompt a reaction. More creative than I gave him credit for, and had she dressed more appropriately—the fancy dress a dead giveaway—he might have had me. Although Lord knows what a woman like her was doing with him, she was waaaaay out of his league.

"Dallas?" She scrunched her brows in confusion. "I don't know Dallas."

Well, she was convincing, I'd give her that. Her eyes didn't cut away and there was no glancing at the floor. And when I mentioned his name there wasn't the usual pinking of the cheeks that came from a girl who had been *there*.

"Okay then." I decided I'd play along, curious to see if she was an award winning actress or something else. And as my two o'clock had walked—albeit assisted by the woman in front of me—it meant I had a couple of hours free. "So you're an artist, huh?" I gave her a warm smile to give her the illusion I was buying it. "Did you bring your sketch books? Some photos of your past work."

"No. I didn't think of that." She grimaced. "Shit."

The word, while unexpected, looked incredibly natural coming from those pink perky lips. She might not look like someone who cussed, but I had feeling she probably wasn't as prim and proper as she appeared. I'd be lying if the thought didn't excite me a little.

"Should I have brought them?" Her whiskey eyes flashed slightly in panic. "I thought we would just talk first, get to know each other."

Dallas hadn't come out of his room at all. Which was usual when he worked with his headphones on. He also didn't have a great sense of time. So it was plausible if he'd been in on it, he'd forgotten, had his head buried and missed her arrival. Still, his lack of appearance was a head scratcher.

And fuck me, but I still hadn't worked her out.

"Yeah, we can do that if you like, I'm happy to chat." Talking to a beautiful woman was never a hardship even if it turned out to be bullshit. "I just wanted to get a feel for your style." *Or the lack of it.* "But that's cool, we can get to the show and tell a little later." *Or not,* because I wasn't sure how much longer this was going to play out.

"I didn't even think to bring it." Her hand tapped her head adorably as she shook it, genuinely apologetic. "My mind has been a little scrambled the last few days. I'm really sorry, I should have been more organized."

There was something that flashed through her eyes—hurt, regret, maybe sadness? The smile slipped a little too and I got the feeling she didn't like disappointing people. Weird considering I was a nobody to her.

"I can go get it," she offered when I didn't answer right away. Great, now *I* felt bad.

As a rule of thumb I didn't like to be an asshole, especially when it hadn't been warranted. And other than wasting my time—Matt had been paid, but I hadn't—Eve really hadn't done anything wrong.

"No, you don't need to do that."

I wasn't ecstatic she'd paid off a customer but he'd been the dumbass who took the cash. He could have argued, but he didn't. Probably thinking he'd hit the lottery being paid to bail by a beautiful woman.

And had he stayed like he was supposed to, he probably would have passed out in my chair like she'd suggested.

So, apart from being stunning, she was also pretty perceptive, which was weird considering her taste in men. That was assuming I was right about her and Dallas, which at this point still seemed likely. I seriously doubted the tattoo fairy dropped her on my doorstep, as much as I would have loved that scenario.

"I do have one." She cut her eyes to mine, like she was trying to convince me she wasn't lying.

"Like I said, no problem. We'll get to it later." I tried to reassure her with a smile as I pointed to the back of the shop. "Why don't we go back to my room where we can talk more comfortably?"

"Sure, that sounds great." She nodded, big enthusiastic smile following.

And that smile was contagious, one of my own making an appearance as I extended my arm and directed her down the hall. My mood improved for a few different reasons.

For one, Dallas was going to be annoyed as fuck when his dumbass trick backfired.

And now that I had remembered my manners, I was curious as fuck about this woman.

Not to mention, I also had an unexpected itch to see if she knew what to do with a machine in her hand, the thought alone was sexy as hell. Not going to lie, if she was in fact the real deal, I'd be very surprised and very much aroused.

The view was pretty spectacular as I followed her down the hall, her heels echoing off the floor as we walked to my room.

It was hard not to notice those legs and just how freaking awesome her ass was. The dress she wore clung to every curve of her body like an advertisement for all the best parts. And no matter how much I told my eyes not to look, they ignored me and stayed exactly where they wanted.

Get it together, dipshit.

My head was not in the game as I followed the soft sway of her hips.

I could *not* go there.

Besides, whatever her reason for being here was, I didn't take Dallas's hand-me-downs. So asking her out on date wasn't going to be an option. And that, my friends, was a crying fucking shame.

She stopped short when she got to the open door of my room, waiting for me to nod and give her the okay before she stepped through. It seemed both of us were now using our manners. And didn't that just make her even more attractive.

My room wasn't huge, but had two very distinct parts. Having it set up that way made it easier to operate.

The first section, and by far the largest, was where I did most of my work. It had a massive hydraulic chair that could tilt into a bed so I could tattoo whatever part I needed at varying angles comfortably. Right beside it, my various machines were already set up, covered and ready to go. As were the little pots of color on the workbench assembled along the wall. After all, I had been expecting to get some ink in skin today so I'd already taken care of the prep.

But her long sexy legs waltzed right past all of that to where I had my drafting desk, stopping once she got there and surveying the paper covering most of it.

"Wow, is this what you've been working on?" She picked up

the stencil of the Koi that had been destined for Matt's forearm. "In the traditional Japanese style too." She looked at the colored sketch beside it. "It's very beautiful."

"Thanks." I closed the door behind me, not sure why the sudden need to have this conversation in private. Maybe it was to make it last a little longer, which didn't make sense considering it was all probably a joke.

She didn't pay any attention or concern to the closed door, her thoughts apparently on the sketch.

Ironically, she seemed to genuinely admire the work, which I didn't expect. And just like any guy, I didn't mind my ego stroked every once in a while.

"It was for Matt. You know, the guy you paid two hundred dollars to." I couldn't help reminding her of how she'd got back here in the first place.

"Really? He was going to get Koi?" She grimaced. "I would have pegged him more a *I heart Mom* kind of guy. Or I don't know." She tapped her chin deep in thought. "Maybe a tribal band or something. Huh, I guess you just never can tell."

I couldn't help but laugh. Her measure on Matt had been dead on. He'd originally come in looking for some abstract, heavily saturated tribal pattern on his arm and it wasn't until he saw some of my color stuff that he'd considered a Koi.

"Yeah, you never can tell." I chuckled, the tension easing out of the room a little. "Sit down, Eve." My head tipped to the stool behind her while I rolled over another.

She lowered her ass onto the stool as her eyes roamed restlessly across the walls where pictures of some of my previous work hung. She paused over each piece, like she was cataloguing it before realizing we were sitting in silence and looked back at me.

Funnily enough, I had my own distraction so the silence wasn't awkward, and I'd have happily sat there a little longer just looking if she needed a minute or two.

"So this is probably weird, right?" She eyed me cautiously, and if I had to guess I would say she was starting to lose her nerve. "Honestly, I'd like to say this is out of character for me, but I'd be lying. When I want something bad enough, I just go out and get it."

Not what I was expecting her to say, her statement confusing me a little. Was she genuinely looking for a job, or was the thing *she wanted bad enough* the moron a door down from me?

"Yeah, I'll admit." My hand rubbed the back of my neck. "I get artists who stop by from time to time, but they aren't so . . ." *Beautiful.* Is what I wanted to say. "Structured." Is what I went with.

"Oh, I know I look that way, but I am not uptight at all." She waved her hand casually in an effort to convince me. "I'm not. I'm as loose as they come."

Uh-hm. A cough made its way up my throat and I bit my lip trying to not to smirk at her choice of words.

"I don't mean like that," she mused sarcastically, my effort failing as she realized what she'd said. "Relaxed. I'm as *relaxed* as they come," she amended, her eyes not showing any embarrassment.

"Well that's good, it's important to be *relaxed*," I used her word, "especially when you're working. Emotion translates into the piece so you need to think about what you're trying to say. You want the art to show the mood, if you're holding back, it shows."

No idea why I felt the need to spill that, but I did. Maybe because I didn't get the opportunity to talk about it enough and seriously, what did I have to lose. Or maybe I was more like Dallas than I thought, easily getting distracted by a sexy woman.

"That's why your work is so beautiful." Those whiskey eyes looked at me with such hope.

"Thanks, but I thought we were going to be talking about you." I grinned. And as much as I enjoyed the admiration, I'd rather hear about the mystery that was Eve.

"Yeah, I know. Well, what can I say. I've been drawing in one way or another . . ." She paused, taking a deep breath, her perfect tits heaving up and down as I tried unsuccessfully not to notice. "For as long as I can remember. Art has been my life. I don't know anything else. And yeah, I get it." She laughed, her hands jazzing either side of her. "People see me—the outside anyway—and assume that I will cry or something if I chip a nail. But seriously, that's not me, I'm not that precious."

Maybe I had been completely wrong about her.

After all, I was no stranger to assumptions. In the past, people had seen me and my tattoos and expected me to either start a fight or steal their car. Not sure why ink equaled felon, but it was bullshit. I paid my taxes, was a business owner and the only fights I generally started were with the copy machine when it ate my transfer paper.

But I guess I'd made a similar assumption about her, only in reverse. Assuming that because of the way she looked, she couldn't be one of us.

Guess I was more of a judgmental asshole than I thought. Even after I'd told myself not to be.

"So, what do you like to draw?" It came out of my mouth as I continued to curse myself out. "What things do you most gravitate to?"

"That's just it." She shrugged, a small laugh bubbling up her throat. "I love portraits, as much as I love flowers. Abstracts, as much as that Botticelli you did. There isn't a style that I feel most comfortable with, and as long as my hand keeps moving, I'm happy." She laughed again, louder this time. "I know, I sound ridiculous, and I probably am but I can't think of anything else I'd want to do. Conventional jobs? They just aren't for me."

Her words struck a nerve, stirring the same sentiment up in me. I'd been inking my own skin with black markers for as long as I could remember. And while other kids played with blocks, I was happier scribbling on paper. There wasn't a chance I'd walk away from my shop and do something else. Fuck, I couldn't even imagine another scenario.

"Okay, here's a radical idea." More like insane but hey, it was a crazy afternoon so what the hell. Plus, this would solve the mystery about whether this was Dallas's handy work or if this girl was for real. "Why don't you show me something."

Without giving it much more thought, I rose off my stool and walked to the chair. She watched me curiously as I turned and settled in, letting my arms hang loose on the armrest. "You feel confident doing the Koi on my forearm?"

I figured she could squeeze it in on the left inner side and the stencil was already done. It would be a good test in shading, and we'd be able to see how clean her line work was. Like a job interview on steroids, and it had been a while since I'd added anything new to my arm, so why not now. If she choked and screwed up the outline, I'd stop her before she got to the color. And if shit looked too jacked up, Dallas was pretty decent at a cover up. I mean, how terrible could it be? She said she'd been doing this for a while so she had to have the basics down. She sure sounded like she knew what she was doing; the passion was definitely there.

"What?" Her eyes got wide as she looked at me in the chair. "What are you talking about? I can't tattoo you."

I got that she was nervous. First time I'd tattooed my boss I'd had to take a shot of tequila just to even out. But lucky for her I wasn't a mean son of a bitch like Big Gus.

"Sure you can. I assure you, I can handle it," I laughed. The buzz of the needle was almost a turn on. "Grab the stencil and roll on over."

She looked at the transfer paper and then back to me, obviously giving it some consideration as she looked at the bench where everything was set up and ready to go.

"You really think it's a good idea?" She reached over and grabbed the paper and rolled over toward me. "I'm nervous, what if my hand shakes?"

"Yeah, that isn't cool." I laughed, slightly worried my bright idea wasn't as good as I first thought. "Center yourself, take a few deep breaths and then start. Get the outline done. You can go slow but be confident, and if at anytime you're not feeling it, we can stop."

Her eyes shot up to me and I had a fairly good clue I knew what she was thinking.

And yeah, it was sort of like *sex*.

You had to put a lot of trust in the person on the other side, and respect needed to go both ways in case someone needed to tap out.

"Gloves are behind you." I tipped my chin to the stack of boxes, not sure if I had any in small.

"Okay," she said more to herself as she took a deep breath. "Okay." She spun around and grabbed a pair of nitrile gloves. "I can do this."

I'll be honest, her pep talk wasn't making me feel warm and fuzzy with confidence. If she was saying that out loud, who knows what she wasn't saying.

This was probably not one of my best ideas, stupidly getting caught up in the moment.

"Maybe—" I didn't get to finish the sentence, saved by a knock at my door.

"Yo, sorry to interrupt—" It seemed Dallas also wasn't able to finish his sentence as he looked at Eve and then back to me. "What the fuck?" He reared back in surprise.

"Hi, I'm Eve." She waved her gloved hand, her attempt at a smile making her face tight.

Well then.

I guess he *hadn't* sent her.

EVE

I HAD NO IDEA WHAT I was thinking.

Never in my life had I even contemplated drawing on someone let alone permanently etching something into their skin. It was insanity. And I blamed my current state of mind.

Kitty had said Josh Logan was gorgeous.

Her description was tall, athletic and covered in exquisite wearable art.

With jet-black hair that was cropped short except for the top which he wore longer and combed back. Sort of like Elvis, but a thousand times hotter, and without the retro clothes.

So, I had been mentally prepared for a decent looking guy. But I had *just* shipped off all of Oliver's stuff and scruffy guys with tattoos weren't really my thing. Besides, I was here for a purpose, and that was not to get a date. I was a professional and this was New York, and gorgeous men were everywhere. It's not like I was a bag of hormones incapable of using her head.

Yet all it took was a single freaking smile.

How it was even possible was beyond me, but Kitty severely understated.

Josh Logan was well over six-foot and built like a South American soccer player. You know the kind—hot, toned, and looked fabulous in their underwear on the side of a building. Sadly, Josh was wearing clothes—a fantastic pair of jeans and a black fitted T-shirt that hugged his arms and chest so lovingly it needed a standing ovation.

And those eyes? Wowzas. Perfect cerulean blue.

Tattoo Jesus was freaking HOT.

And another thing, his tattoos were insane. Each perfectly toned arm was covered in intricate designs that went all the way up into his sleeves where they were tragically hidden by his T-shirt. Then the color reappeared, snaking up his neckline. I wasn't sure if I wanted to lick his skin or hang it on a wall. *Oh, that sounded bad.* Yeah. Hanging it on the wall sounded creepy. Licking. Licking was better.

I had been a locked vault. Kept it together and pretended he wasn't the hottest man I'd seen. I'd even managed to carry on a conversation, completely hiding the fact my panties had disintegrated the minute he'd walked into the room. That, my friends, was where the real talent was.

Instead, I kept talking, vomiting out words so I was distracted from looking at his beautiful face. I needed to keep my objective in my sights—I was there for a purpose. Plus surely the longer I spent in his presence the more desensitized I'd become.

And lucky I hadn't seen Josh before I'd paid off Matt, or I'd have easily offered a thousand.

I blamed my mental impairment on hormonal imbalance or maybe we just stick to my original diagnosis—insanity. Because there I was, less than a minute away from actually picking up a tattoo machine and giving it a serious try.

Idiot.

"Wow. You're beautiful." The man who walked in and saved me from making a huge mistake blinked at me. "Josh." He tilted his head but kept his eyes on me.

He—the new guy—was tall too, but a few inches shorter than Josh. And while he didn't measure up to Josh's level of panty melting, he could easily set off a smoke alarm or two of his own. Who knew all these hot men were hiding in tattoo shops in Queens? That's something the city should put in their travel brochure or something.

But for all my *keeping it together,* I had now frozen, like a deer in headlights. Words? Who even knew what they were anymore or how to use them. Because I had zero explanation for what I was about to do, or why I was acting like an absolute lunatic.

"She paid Matt to take a walk, said she was an artist," Josh answered when I didn't, his voice rumbled out of his throat. Lord, he was sexy. "I thought she might have been a friend of yours."

"Oh no, I'd remember a friend who looked like *her*." New guy's eyebrow rose and gave me a very suggestive smile. "Especially those tits."

And thaaaat was all it took, snapping me back from la-la land to the man who was undressing me with his eyes.

"I'm standing right here, you know." I waved; the attention the second guy was giving me making me feel defensive. "And my eyes are up here." I pointed in case he had a hard time locating them, most of his focus being on my breasts.

"Dallas, apologize to Eve." Josh swung his legs around from his fancy chair, letting his heavy boots drop to the floor. "And considering you've been on my ass about hiring another set of hands, I would hope you'd keep it polite."

"Whoa." Dallas held up his hand in surrender, taking a step back from both of us. "You're a tattoo artist?" A mixture of shock and surprise flashed through his eyes.

"No, I'm not." It shot out of my mouth instinctively. "I'm an *artist*," I tried to annunciate it clearly to try to show the distinction. "Singular but my mediums are varied—paper, canvas, sometimes ceramic—"

"Wait a minute." Now it was Josh's turn to hold up his hands and wear the look of surprise. "You aren't a *tattoo* artist? Why would you agree to give me a tattoo?"

"WHAT!" Dallas's booming voice spun the attention back to him. "She was gonna *tattoo* you? I mean I saw she had gloves on and you were in the chair, but I assumed you were going to . . . you know, get freaky or something."

"No! What kind of girl—" No point adding *do you think I am* to the end of that sentence because they had no idea who I was. Hell, at this moment I didn't even know who I was.

"I wouldn't have done it." I shook my head, locking eyes with Josh. "You just seemed so convinced that I could and I guess . . . look, it has been a really strange week."

Strange week would be the understatement of the century.

"Dallas, can you give us a few minutes." Josh shot a meaningful glance to the man who had been ogling my breasts.

"Dude, I want to hear this." He tried to protest, not making any moves to leave.

"I said, get out." Josh left no room for interpretation.

"Fine," he grumbled, rolling his eyes as he stepped out of the room. "But I want to hear this story later." He closed the door behind him.

"So, Eve." Josh nodded to the stool I had been sitting on before I'd leapt to my feet. "You want to help me understand what this is all about, because I'm a little confused."

"Okay." I blew out a breath, knowing it was the kind of conversation that needed at least three visual aids and probably a testimonial. Hell, where to even start. "I walked in on my boyfriend getting a blowjob from Kitty."

Probably not my best start, but oh well, I guess I had committed now.

"Kitty, your *friend?*" he clarified, his eyes squinting like he was having trouble following. "The Botticelli back piece?"

Yeah, so maybe this was going to take four visual aids.

"Well, she wasn't my friend when that happened, we sort of became friends after," I clarified, which didn't really explain anything other than I was possibly mentally imbalanced.

"After the blowjob, interesting." He lowered himself back onto the chair but surprisingly didn't show judgment. Which was odd because if this were the other way around, I would definitely be judging.

"I know, I know." I felt the need to explain further because . . . really who became friends with the girl your boyfriend cheated with. Oh, that's right. Apparently I did.

"But, really, it wasn't her fault. She didn't know he had a girlfriend." And she was probably doing me a favor. What kind of guy cheats on his girlfriend, in her own house? "And then we started discussing art."

Weird segue, but I figured I needed to get to the point.

"O-kay." More squinting, more trouble following.

Wow. I *really* sucked at this.

"Actually, I should back up a bit." Perhaps a little bit more information would be helpful, even if it wasn't really relevant to why I was here. "The reason I wasn't completely freaking out about the boyfriend thing was because my career was basically in the toilet." The truth. And it got no easier no matter how many times I'd said it. "I'd had my first show, and I was massacred by critics." The hurt and anger still raw. "Like epic level carnage." Pause. "In print." Pause. "On the internet." Pause. "Everywhere."

Strangely his expression was vacant of pity, which was usually the reaction that I got. And I really liked its absence considering I'd seen so much of it from everyone else.

"Go on." He nodded when I stopped talking.

"So then we discussed art, like good art and bad art, personal preference." I skipped over how I'd basically blamed everyone but myself because I figured I'd make my point quicker. "And then she took off her dress and showed me her back."

"Hold up." He laughed, his hands held up as he watched me closely. "I'm not trying to be an asshole, but were any kind of drugs consumed that day?"

Did I even bother telling him that we hadn't even started drinking the wine yet and confirm the insanity? Better not.

"I know it sounds crazy." Hopefully by telling him I knew it wasn't normal behavior I'd demonstrated I still had some cognitive reasoning. "That I was standing in my kitchen with a half naked girl who had previously had my boyfriend's penis in her mouth, and I was then staring at her boobs." The words rushed out of my mouth in one breath. Another breath needed before continuing. "She promised me there was a point to all of it."

"She wanted you to be Jack, and to draw her like *all of his French girls*?" He smirked as he folded his arms across his chest.

"No," I laughed, amused by his comparison. "To show me the Botticelli. Which," my head tipped in his direction, "as I have already said, is amazing. I've seen the actual painting, yours was breathtaking."

"Thank you." He smiled, the light hitting his eyes.

Crap.

That blue.

He was so freaking hot.

Don't get off track now, Eve.

"You're welcome." I quickly recovered. "So after that, we started talking about you." *Shit, that sounded creepy.* "About your talent, I mean." Better. "And not that the naked stranger in my kitchen wasn't a reliable source or anything, but I Googled. You're quite impressive." *And now I was back to creepy.* "Your work, I mean. *Your work* is quite impressive."

Seriously, it wasn't my exhibition that was the train wreck, it was my life. And possibly that long and convoluted explanation.

My mouth was the other causality.

"As much as my ego likes to hear that." That smile of his almost as amazing as those eyes. "I'm still not really sure what brings you here, and why you were pretending to be a tattoo artist."

"I wasn't pretending," I fired back quickly, not liking the inference that I was deceitful. "I said artist, you," my finger pointed at him, "assumed."

"We're in a tattoo studio." His arms spread wide indicating the space. "And you said you wanted to work for me. Not a lot of work here for anything other than tattoo artists."

"So, I should have clarified," I added, still only willing to take half the blame for the misunderstanding. "But the reason I wanted to work *with* you is because, despite us having different mediums, your work comes to life. So much emotion is translated in your pieces. That is difficult to do on a page, but on a living canvas, it's even harder. Somewhere along the way, I've lost it. That ability. Who knows, maybe I never had it? But the biggest complaint about my work was while it was technically fine, it had zero emotion. I was called *soulless*. I have a freaking soul, goddamn it. But I don't know . . . I guess I need help putting it into my work. Like you do."

It was like I was spewing out every thought and couldn't stop.

That was what desperation did to me, and I wasn't even sure he was the answer.

Why was I even here?

Why didn't I lock myself in a room and starve myself for days, let exhaustion and hunger motivate me like Edgar Allan Poe. Okay, terrible example because he died broke under mysterious circumstances, but still. There was something about that Botticelli. Venus's eyes. I was drawn to her and to the man who created her. And while irrational, for which I had no solid basis for it, in my gut I *knew* this was the right path.

Because I was crazy.

Clearly.

"Eve, while I'm honored that you think that." He shook his head, the *but* sure to follow. "But," and there it was, "I'm not a life coach. Hell, I'm not even a teacher. And even if I was, what the hell am I supposed to teach you?" He ran his hand through his hair.

He did bring up a very valid point.

I wasn't looking to give up fine art and start a promising career as a tattooist.

Repeatedly putting a needle into someone's body part sounded like a special brand of torture, and if I didn't understand it, then I should damn well not be implementing it. Could have used that kind of wisdom a few moments ago *before* I'd contemplated tattooing the hot man in the chair.

"Let me observe you," I suggested. "You have the X factor. I need it. Help me get it." I moved closer, hoping whatever *it* was could be absorbed like osmosis.

"I'm not some art Yoda. You know, I have no formal training." He looked me dead in the eye. "Sure, I finished high school, but the rest of my education I got at the bench."

"Which is why this is so remarkable."

I hated those words the minute they flew out of my mouth. They sounded so arrogant, so elitist. And regardless of where my address was, I wasn't one of those people who believed money or education made you a better person. It was offensive, and if I'd been on the receiving end, *I* would have told myself to get fucked.

"Because I don't have a degree hanging on my wall?" He tilted his head, waiting for me to continue—the irritation, offense and rudeness lacking in his voice. He was just simply asking.

"Yes, because I bet half my graduating class couldn't draw with as much passion and emotion as you, and I went to Yale," I breathed out.

And not one of those classmates would have listened this long without calling the cops, or laughing me out the door. He was different. He was soooo different and maybe that's what I needed.

It wasn't about him being hot.

Honestly, it wasn't. Well, not entirely.

It was about the electricity I felt when I looked at his walls.

At all his drawings.

At a plain outline of a Japanese fish.

I had been led here. The gallery sending me home early. Oliver cheating. Meeting Kitty. Her being naked in my kitchen. The tattoo. It all had to be for this, right? The universe closing the door but opening a window.

"Eve, you seem like a good person." His face softened, treating me to a wonderful smile. "A little crazy, but nice all the same. And I'm going to be honest with you, because you were honest with me. Even if I knew how to get you where you need to be, I have no time. Illustrated by the fact that no one returned your call. Along with the five thousand other calls I haven't had time to return and the work I need to turn down." He shrugged and I knew what came next.

Thanks for stopping by, good luck or some other bullshit that was supposed to make me feel better. The gentle let down. And I wanted none of it.

"I'll answer your phone." It fired out of my mouth.

Desperation.

There could be no other reason why I would offer to become a secretary.

"What?" He laughed, probably knowing the idea was as ludicrous as it sounded and I couldn't be serious.

Except, I was.

"I already took leave from the gallery." Which also explained why I was able to be in his shop on Friday during business hours when I should have been peddling ridiculously priced artwork to people who had more money than taste. "Technically they asked me to take it." There was no point lying about my sudden departure from my day job. "I think the embarrassment of having me there while the debacle was so fresh was more the issue. It's hard to sell art when the person who is selling to you was basically called a fraud."

"Ouch." He winced.

"Yeah, and that was from one of the nice ones." They'd said so much worse. "Feel free to Google me, it seems like everyone else seems to have an opinion."

"I don't know." He didn't seem convinced.

"Seriously, what have you got to lose?" As far as I could see, he was the one who had the upper hand. What was the worst that could happen? I forget to write a message down? They'd still be better off than they were currently. "You need help. I need help. We help each other." I gestured between us. "I can work with people, trust me. You haven't seen the type of characters I had to deal with at the gallery."

"There'd be other stuff." He was considering it, I could tell he was. "Helping out around here."

"I'm totally good with whatever, within reason. I'm not going to have to shave someone's balls or anything like that, am I?" Because ewww, and I was positive no one wanted me to accidently slip and cause an injury. I didn't have the strongest stomach when it came to blood.

"Err no. If there are balls that need shaving, I'll get Dallas to do it." He smiled, and if I were reading between the lines—which I totally was—it sounded like he might have agreed.

"So it's settled?" I wanted him to say the words, for there to be no confusion he was agreeing to help me.

"I can't pay you what I'm sure you're worth. Minimum wage probably isn't the kind of cash you are probably used to." He looked genuinely sorry, his eyes watching for my reaction.

"It will be fine, I promise." Little did he know I didn't need the money. "Besides, you're doing me the favor, I should be paying you. So when do I start?"

"I'm not really sure what the hell just happened." He took a step closer and stuck out his hand. "But I think I hired you."

"Oh, thank you. Thank you so much." I bypassed the handshake and threw my arms around him.

Wow, he worked out.

A lot.

Shit.

I was hugging a stranger who had recently become my boss.

My arms quickly released and I took a step back out of his personal space. Thankfully he didn't look mad and/or disgusted.

Small mercies.

"Don't get too excited," he warned, holding up his finger and politely not mentioning my full-body press against him. "This isn't going to be a walk in the park. I'm going to pay you, and while you sort through this—whatever it is for you—I'm going to need you to work."

"I promise." I crossed my heart. "I will be your number one employee."

"Considering your competition is Dallas, I'd say that's not going to be hard to achieve."

"Even still, I'll work so hard you'll wonder how you guys ever managed without me."

He wouldn't regret this.

I would make sure of it.

JOSH

"IF YOU WANT TO FUCK her, you should just fuck her. Offering her a job seems like a lot of effort for sex."

The man was like a heat-seeking missile, walking into my room the minute Eve had left. And in true Dallas style, he wasn't subtle and he was thinking with his dick.

"This isn't about sex." I shot him a look that made it clear that hadn't been my intention. "I didn't offer her a job to get her into bed."

"So you're blind? Or not interested? Just so I know what I'm working with." He smirked, knowing the eyes in my head worked just fine and I could see Eve was beautiful.

Beautiful was actually an understatement; she was more than that. Stunning would be one word I'd use. Eve was the kind of gorgeous that knocked you straight onto your ass. And those curves of hers, dangerous in all the right ways.

"No, of course I'm not interested." I lied. Had no choice, if I fessed up and told Dallas half of what I was thinking, I'd never hear the end of it. And that would be bad for everyone. "I don't have sex with employees." And that part was definitely true. I preferred to not get involved in a sexual harassment case, thank you very much.

"But *I* can, right?" His eyebrows sunk into a deep v. "Because seriously dude, someone needs to." His arm waved to the door she stepped out of.

"No, you can't, and more importantly you won't." I walked over to him, my finger jabbing him in the chest. "She isn't a toy for you to play with and I don't need the kind of trouble your dating life brings in my shop."

"Fuck, you're moody." Dallas took a step back not dumb enough to challenge me. He might be a decent fighter but I easily had thirty pounds on him and he didn't want to find out what those extra pounds felt like if I got angry. "Fine, fine, I won't do anything." He backed off, hands in the air. "But if she makes the first move, I'm letting you know I'm going there."

"She's not dumb enough to make a move on you." Or at least I hoped she wasn't. "And even if she were to develop some kind of illness—where all her brain cells literally fell out her ear—you're still going to keep your hands to yourself and your dick in your pants." And I wasn't kidding around. "Do I need to remind you why we no longer have someone answering our phones?"

My strict no-sex-between-employees policy was less about Eve and more about our ex-piercer/front desk person, Tess. Tess wasn't the kind of gorgeous Eve was, but she knew how to turn heads. Which she did with Dallas, and I caught them banging in his room one afternoon.

So, I sat them both down and tried to talk to them like adults, which considering Dallas was involved was probably my first mistake. I'd told them I didn't have a problem with them dating except they needed to do that shit on their own time and their own fucking space—the health violation alone enough to shut me down. And it was all happy families until Dallas decided he was more a buffet kind of guy, and Tess found him balls deep in some other girl. Naturally Tess was pissed, and not only shattered the front window of my shop in an epic battle of crowbar versus glass, but also took off with hundreds of dollars worth of stock. There was still a warrant out for her arrest, but I was almost positive she'd skipped town.

And there wasn't a chance in hell I'd make that mistake again.

"She was crazy, J." Dallas pulled his usual it-wasn't-my-fault routine. "That had nothing to do with me. Besides, it was probably more your fault than mine."

"Oh yeah? How do you figure?" I had no idea how in the hell any of it could have been turned back on me.

"She came here with a sob story, about needing a chance and all that, and like usual you were a sucker. For all we know she was just looking for an excuse to blow town and take your shit, you need to be more selective on who you let through the door." Smug ass bastard dished out excuses like he did smiles. I swear, how he hadn't landed in any serious trouble up to this point was a damn mystery.

"She was very freaking sane until you two started seeing each other." I eyed him hard, reminding him that her affliction happened very quickly after his indiscretion. "And more importantly she was a good worker. And I'm not a fucking sucker, it's called compassion, maybe you could try it sometime." I didn't like the implication that it had somehow been my doing.

Sure she had been down on her luck when she walked in the door but she was more than qualified, and if I could help her get back on her feet then what was the harm in that. And we hadn't had any issues until Dallas had gotten involved.

"It's my name on the door and I'll hire whoever I want." Friend or not, I wasn't going to take his shit especially not when it called my business into question. "And I am not looking for a repeat, we clear?"

"Yes, yes. Whatever, man." He shoved his hands in his pockets, the argument done.

"Okay then, looks like it's settled. She starts tomorrow and your next appointment should be here soon." I folded my arms across my chest. "Anything else you want to *chat* about? I've got to get a transfer ready for my next client."

"Nope, you made yourself clear." Dallas laughed, saluting me and walked out the door.

He might have said I'd been clear but there was never any way to know with him. And had he not been a damn fine artist and a really good friend, I would have shown him the door a long time ago. Besides, other than Tess, it had never affected the business before and I was sure he'd learned his lesson.

At least, I'd hoped he had.

I SPENT THE BETTER PART of the night wondering whether I'd made a huge mistake hiring Eve. I was a fairly good judge of character and usually went with my gut, but this had bad idea written all over it.

Firstly, she had a fucking college degree from a fancy school, so kicking it down to be my phone answerer was fucking ridiculous. Besides, I still wasn't sure what the hell I could teach her that they apparently hadn't.

Also, I got the feeling—and maybe I was back to being a judgmental ass—she hadn't had a lot of people tell her what to do. She was going from working at a gallery and painting, to answering phones and setting appointments. How it wasn't going to be mind numbingly boring and repetitive for her was beyond me.

Plus, there was the issue of where her head was at. Yesterday after I'd closed the shop for the day, I'd opened my computer. Curiosity got the better of me and I'd Googled her as she'd suggested.

Her description of how it had all gone down had *not* been an exaggeration.

Wow.

Article after article calling her out for her lack of talent, vision and emotion. One dude from *Time Out* had likened her exhibit to a McDonald's cheeseburger and I quote, *"Leads you to believe you are getting something substantial when in reality you are getting second rate meat and the chance of irritation of the bowel."*

You didn't have to read too far between the lines to see it was universally regarded as shit. Which was also puzzling, because wouldn't you have to be halfway decent to get a degree from Yale in the first place? Surely they weren't handing out those things to the highest bidder regardless of talent? And if they were, there was something incredibly wrong with that.

So, was she talented but stumbled, losing her way and churning out shit? Or was she always shit, delusional and she'd hoped I was going to wave my magical marker and transform it and her into something less shit? The exhibition pieces online did *not* look promising. And truth be told I was too tired to look any deeper and attempt to find anything else.

Still, I'd made my decision and I was going to see this thing through.

Four weeks.

That's how long she'd been instructed to take leave in the hopes that all the noise blew over. It sounded a little extreme if you asked me, like surely after you got a bad review, you moved on. But apparently that wasn't the way it worked in her world. And in those four weeks she needed to cleanse her aura or whatever the hell she was supposed to do so when she went back to the gallery she no longer wore the stain of bad. It was also the length of time I'd committed to having her looking over my shoulder, trying to inspire her or something.

Fuck.

I really had not thought this through.

Maybe Dallas was right, I *was* a sucker for a sob story.

"Hey!" Eve walked in ten minutes earlier than I'd asked her

to, holding a tray of takeaway coffees. "I didn't know what everyone wanted, so I guessed." Her smile bright as she strode her way into the store.

Unlike yesterday, she wasn't wearing heels or the tight dress. Instead she'd shown up in a pair of jeans and flats, and a T-shirt that hugged her breasts like it was its job. Even dressed down she was still knockout material.

"Oh, I hope this is okay?" She caught me not so subtly checking her out. "I thought casual would be more appropriate. Sorry, I should have asked."

"It's perfect," I coughed out, reminding me to look at her eyes and *not* at her tits. "You look great." Lame. "Part of the team." Even lamer. "Wear whatever is comfortable, things are pretty relaxed around here." My mouth did its best to salvage the situation.

"Great." She moved over to the front counter and lowered the tray of coffees. "They're black, but I got sugar and cream in case anyone wanted it."

"Black is fine. Thanks." I pulled out a cup from the holder and took a sip. *Mmmm delicious* and I wasn't talking about what was in the cup. I swallowed the words along with coffee. "So, let's get started."

"Dallas not here yet?" She looked around, the two of us the only ones in the shop.

"He comes in a little later, mornings aren't really his thing." And for the first time in a long time I was grateful he wasn't here. "He does a couple of late nights for me so it evens out."

"Oh, okay." She smiled, pulling out a coffee for herself. "I need stuff in mine." She screwed up her nose a little before adding cream and sugar.

"Better," she moaned, moving the cup away from her lips. They were red and plump, and I'd bet they'd taste just as sweet as they looked.

Great. She'd been in the place two minutes and I'd already

stared at her and imagined what her lips would taste like. *So much for keeping it professional.*

"Alrighty." I moved behind the counter and pulled out the appointment book. "It's a little old school, but I don't lose anything if the computer crashes." I tapped the book. "We just put the name, phone number and what tattoo they're getting as a quick reference. I have a spreadsheet, as does Dallas, of all their particulars, but this way you can see at a glance when we have a free slot."

"So, do I just book someone in?" She moved from where she was standing to behind the counter with me.

"Just thirty to forty-five minute consults, we book the ink session after meeting with them and have the sketch worked out." I nodded, trying not to notice how amazing she smelled. The mix of sweet shampoo and coffee was difficult to ignore. "But as you can see," and as I told her yesterday, "we're booked solid until December."

"Wow, six months? And people still wait?" She flicked through the filled pages, all the appointments taken.

"Yeah, they do."

"They must *really* want you." She smiled, the admiration seeming genuine. "Must feel pretty amazing to have so many people chasing you."

"I think it's my work they want," I coughed out, "but thanks for the vote of confidence."

Thank Christ, Dallas wasn't here because I would never hear the end of it. Even I could see that what I was doing was dangerously close to flirting.

"So, if the appointments are mostly booked, what do I tell them?" She looked at the flashing light on the phone indicating the dozens of unanswered messages.

"Ah well, part of this job is sort of being diplomatic." I wheeled over a desk chair and offered it to her. "So you let them know that their business is important to us and we take our time with each client." She listened intently as she took a seat. "We know that their time is valuable but most importantly that their bodies are. I'm not going to rush something just so I can fit an extra person in. Usually what I put on someone's skin is staying there for a really long time, it's important that it's done right."

Yeah, it sounded like a line, but to me it was personal. *All* of it was personal. And people trusting me was not something I took lightly, which is why I would rather lose the extra cash and give the person in my chair something we could both be proud of.

Eve's eyes beamed with respect I wasn't sure I'd earned yet. "Wow, that's really admirable."

There was something about her that I found hard to ignore, and that was going to be a huge problem.

Keep it professional, asshole.

"Did I miss a staff meeting?" Dallas smirked, strolling in two hours earlier than he usually did. "What are we talking about? You need any help setting up?"

It was a miracle. And unless the man in front of me was an imposter, Dallas Rodgers was bright-eyed and bushy-tailed before nine a.m. and ready to work. Wonders would never cease.

"A little early isn't it?" I made an exaggerated display of checking my watch. "You get lost on your way home?"

It was a Saturday morning, which meant a late Friday night for Dallas. While we weren't strictly nine-to-five, I preferred the mornings while Dallas did the Thursday and Friday night closes. Which meant the earliest he'd surface on a Saturday would be noon.

"Very funny." He looked over at Eve and the coffee still siting on the counter unclaimed. "Is this for me?" The charm thick in his throat.

"Yes, it's black, but I brought—"

"I like it black." He didn't let her finish, taking a big mouthful and licking his lips. "Delicious." And then came the moan. "Mmmmmm."

"Knock it off, Dallas." I gave him a pointed look. "And since you're here so early, I can put you to good use. Mindy has been begging for an appointment if either of us got a cancel. I'll let her know you're free this morning."

His face paled, the very name enough to smack the smirk right from his mouth. She was the one woman Dallas was terrified of.

"Anyone but her." He shook his head backing away slowly. "I'll do anything else. Anything."

"Oooooooo." Eve's eyes danced with excitement. "Who's Mindy?" Dallas's reaction obviously piquing her interest.

"Mindy Coles has been getting inked from the minute I first opened the door." I didn't hesitate to fill her in despite Dallas continuing to shake his head. "She is addicted to the process rather than the actual art, likes the feel of the needle on her skin. And all of that is fine, except she's taken a shine to Dallas. It seems the only thing she likes better than the buzz of the machine is touching his—"

"You'd think cock, right?" Dallas interrupted, unable to stay silent. "Ass even? Which I know isn't right for me to be okay with, buuuuuut I would be totally okay with it." He didn't even try to hide how much of a sick puppy he was, the idea of a strange woman grabbing his junk not an issue for him.

"But she touches my fucking hair." His eyes widened pointing to the side that had been buzz cut. "She rubs it like it's a freaking pet or something."

Eve coughed out a laugh, "Your hair?" Not what she was probably expecting to hear.

"Just the one side." He screwed up his face in confusion. "I even grew it out thinking it was the sensation of the clipped hair. Nope, she just continued, giving me hand action like she was buffing a bowling ball."

"She's specific about which head she is buffing too," I added, a little more thrilled than I should be that I wasn't the target of Mindy's fetish. "While she's happy to let me tattoo her, mine—doesn't cut it."

"That's the funniest thing I've ever heard." Eve threw her head back as an adorable laugh bubbled up her throat. "Why don't you tell her to stop?"

Which is exactly the same question I asked when Dallas skulked into my room with a weird look on his face after his first encounter.

"She gives me an extra big tip."

"Because he's a whore." Dallas and I both responded at the same time.

"I might not be kosher with it while it's happening, but the fifty she slips into my pocket kind of makes it worth it." He shrugged not even trying to hide the lack of disgust most people would feel.

"You let her do it for a fifty?" Eve chewed on her lip, her eyes going wide.

"I don't even feel bad taking the money." Dallas laughed before dropping his voice. "But sometimes when I'm on a date and the chick I'm with touches that spot, it weirds me out."

Eve laughed, the sound echoing around the empty shop. "Sorry to say, but you sort of bring that on yourself. Is Mindy's number in the book or do you have it on file?" She looked at me picking up the phone. "I'd be more than happy to place the call for you."

"God, you're just as bad as him." Dallas pointed accusingly. "I'm in my room." He turned, disappearing down the hall, taking his coffee with him. "Do not call her." The last words we heard before he shut his door.

"So, that was fun." Eve turned back to the appointment book. "Anyone else I should *know* about?" Her brow rose, shooting me a devious smile.

I couldn't help but laugh. She'd been in the shop less than an hour and whatever doubts I had about hiring her were starting to ease. Still didn't know what I was going to teach her, or what purpose it would serve, but I was really liking the idea.

"I think you'll do great here."

EVE

LIKE ANYONE, I HAD THINGS I wished I hadn't done.

Eating four Levain's Bakery chocolate chip and walnut cookies in one sitting wasn't my smartest choice. Buying a car when I lived in the Upper East Side and spent most of my time in the city was also questionable. As was lining Oliver's Calvin Klein's with Icy Hot before I'd packed them neatly into a box. No, I take that back, I enjoyed that.

But the one thing I knew I would never regret was being an artist.

I accepted the sideways glances and the mocking, *"that's not a real job, is it?"* Or that most people assumed it was somehow easier than *regular* paid employment. Ignoramuses—the lot of them. But for me there really wasn't another choice. It was the only thing I had ever wanted to do.

My parents had been supportive, but made sure I understood it was a difficult hill to climb. They sent me to the best schools and paid for trips to Paris and Rome. But they didn't hide the fact they assumed I would more than likely end up a curator or something similar. Because they loved me, and would do anything they could to stop the very thing that happened, from happening.

But I was stronger than that, or at least I thought I was. And couldn't allow someone else or their opinion to completely destroy me as a person. Not without a fight at least, even if it meant swallowing my pride a little and asking for help. Thankfully, the *help* was incredibly attractive. I couldn't believe my luck. Or maybe it was a curse, I hadn't yet decided.

"So, here is where we keep additional supplies." Josh led me to a small storage closet at the end of the hall. "It could probably use some attention." He chuckled as my eyes traveled over the haphazardly stocked shelves.

It looked like the closet had vomited supplies, with no way of being able to find anything in that mess, it was going to need more than just *some* attention.

"Yeah, I can do that." Tidying might not be my favorite thing to do but I wasn't a diva either. "Can I change things around a little? Like around the shop?"

I might have been asking politely, but in my head I'd already decided. Their system—if you could call it that—wasn't great. And if it was one thing I'd learned from working at the gallery—besides walking on high polished floor boards in heels and not landing on my ass—it was organization.

"Sure, if you think you can find a better place for things, then do whatever you want. As long as you don't rent out the space for a nail salon or something crazy like that." Josh's face lit up with a panty-melting grin. "So that's it, the grand tour." His outstretched arms filled the narrow hallway.

It had been a busy hour or so walking around and exploring the shop. Josh did a wonderful job providing commentary, and I listened intently to every single word. Like discovering the secrets of the Illuminati, I was hypnotized, and I couldn't look away. The way his mouth moved so seductive, that voice of his should have been illegal.

It was sooooo *manly*. Deep, and rough around the edges, like a piece of hammered heated steel. He didn't get hung up on articulating every syllable, his words more relaxed in his throat. I liked the cadence, and the tone—it was both hard and soft all at the same time—and it made my skin tingle when he said my name.

"Eve."

I spun around, unsure if he'd asked me a question or if I'd been caught with my tongue hanging out of my mouth. Possible, considering his blue T-shirt looked like it had been spray-painted on. No one should look that good in cotton. No. One.

"Hmm?"

You're not here to learn every hard plane of his body, Eve. You're here to learn from him.

"I asked if you need me to go over anything again?"

A reasonable question, pity I wasn't feeling very reasonable.

"No, no. I think I got everything." I nodded. "Phones, tidy, talk to walk-ins and notify both you and Dallas when your next appointment arrives." I listed my daily tasks on my fingers like a moron. "I think I can manage."

"Well, I have my first client coming in about thirty minutes so I'm going to go set up. You good?" He checked again, obviously not convinced by my stellar reassurances.

"Yep, all good." It wasn't the job I was worried about.

"Great." His face lit up with another smile. "Yell out if you need anything."

"I've got this under control." My fist lamely pumped in the air. Although, to be honest, I wasn't sure if I actually had anything under control.

He hesitated like he wasn't sure if he should leave, probably wondering if he was handing over control of the shop to a crazy person. Not far from the truth. But with nothing more to say, he nodded and turned. And holy ass, Tattoo Jesus!

I had snuck a peek earlier but hadn't been prepared for all of its unhindered brilliance. Those jeans were definitely fantastic.

It wasn't like I was intentionally checking him out, like a pervert with a zoom lens through his drapes. But I honestly couldn't help it. The course of the tour had completed at the supply closet at the end of the hall, with his room further toward the front. So unless he had special abilities to travel through walls or there was an escape hatch in the floor, he had no choice but to walk back down the corridor from which we'd come. Which meant *I* had no choice but to watch as his long powerful legs and firm ass took him in the opposite direction. My admiration extending to his back, his muscles flexing under that superb T-shirt. Cotton was my new favorite fabric.

Crap.

I needed to focus.

After making sure the coast was clear—Josh's sexy ass and the rest of him safely in his room—I took the journey myself down the hall to the front of the shop, mentally making a list of what I was going to tackle first.

Their over-packed message bank wasn't an issue. It wouldn't take long to listen in and transcribe them onto paper. Even if I did it slowly, I would be done in a few hours. There'd be one less message to worry about considering mine wasn't going to need a call back. And because I knew it was going to be my least favorite thing to do, I decided to do something more interesting to start with. My first order of business was the walls.

While they were covered with gorgeous and breathtaking pictures of both Dallas's and Josh's work, the groupings made no sense. Photo-realism was butted up next to cartoonish looking characters. Flowers mixed in with portraits. And scripts and lettering littered all over the place. There was no flow, no cohesion to any of the display. It looked like the ceiling had vomited, and tattoos had randomly splattered across the walls. Don't even get me started on the pictures not even being mounted straight. It hurt my eyes just to look at them.

So without wasting time, and accepting Josh's carte blanche permission to change things—no danger of a pop-up nail salon—I got to work. I turned on the laptop at the front counter and got a crash course on the various styles of tattoos, which was facilitated by the university of Google. Style was one thing I understood.

In less time than I'd anticipated, I had a good handle on what was what and then started to group the pictures from the walls.

Some styles were easily identifiable as their roots were in traditional styles, like typical art. But the other stuff wasn't too hard to grasp either. And by the time the first person walked through the door I had already stripped the walls bare and was ready to start over.

When Josh said he and Dallas were fully booked, he wasn't kidding. Person after person walked in, most needing to take a seat and wait before their appointed artist was ready.

Appointments, I came to find out, were really just loose time frames with the previous person sometimes running a little over.

But not one person complained. Sitting happily in reception with me until it was their time to be led down the hall. Every single one of them was polite and courteous, which wasn't what I was expecting. Not because my head was up my ass and I was profiling. I hadn't expected assholish behavior because I was at a tattoo shop in Queens, but because customer service generally had the capacity to be miserable.

At the gallery, where the people who walked through the doors had more money than God, was the worst. If they had to wait a minute, they were tapping their foot and shooting you the evil eye. But here, every single person smiled and said hello, some even made small talk and asked me how I was. Their positivity made me smile as I reattached the art to the walls. It was catchy, like a cold and before I knew it, my general mood—and future outlook—didn't feel so dark.

"Whoa." Dallas was the first to emerge, the steady stream of people dwindling a little after one in the afternoon. "You rearranged the walls?" He looked over at my various groupings.

The original photos that had graced the walls were gone. And in their place were high definition scanned copies that were printed on to high gloss paper all uniformly shaped and sized. I may have Amazon Primed a little in the morning, which meant within an hour or two I had acquired a few new pieces of office equipment. It's not like anyone would be mad, right? I used my own credit card.

"It didn't make sense before, you had New School with American Traditional," I went on to explain, hoping he liked my improvement.

"Listen to you." Dallas laughed, possibly even a little impressed. "Didn't think you'd know the difference."

"Well, I do." I walked out from behind the counter and admired my work. "And now the walls tell a story, it's easier on the eye and you don't feel like you're about to have an aneurysm when you look at them."

"Wow." Josh's voice appeared from behind us, I'd been too distracted to notice he'd emerged from his room too. He turned slowly as he inspected the walls. "You've been busy."

"It wasn't that hard," I admitted, proud that I had been a quick study. "I grouped them according to style as I scanned them in, and then I just printed folder by folder. Layouts always came naturally for me."

My brain just saw patterns easier than it did other things. Which is why a job that might have taken someone all day to accomplish, I was able to do in a morning.

"Not that I don't appreciated the change, because I do." Josh rubbed his hand at the back of his neck. "But they were grouped according to artist, chronologically."

"Oh, I guessed that when I couldn't find another pattern." I smiled, assuming that there had to be a method to the madness.

"And when I pulled them off the walls, there were dates and names on the backs. But if you see here," I walked over to the closest wall and pointed at the bottom of the photo, "I added a small box border around the edge so it not only acts as a frame, but gave me space to notate the date and the artist on the front. So now when someone looks at the three Trash Polkas, they'll know they were all done last year by you."

He looked at the photos and then to me, confused. "How long was I in my room? How do you even know what that is?"

A small thrill ran through me that I'd hopefully impressed him. *Thank you, Google University.*

"I know that it's not *true* Trash Polka unless it was done in Germany at the Buena Vista Tattoo Club by Simone Plaff or Volko Merschky." I wowed him with details that had fascinated me when I'd discovered them. Art history was more than just a slight passion of mine. "But I meant the style." I walked over to the wall where they were and examined them closely. "It's almost Banksy, but with more noise and distortion, which I guess is the point. That's what you were going for, right?"

"Yeah." He joined me at the wall, the smile edging at his lips.

"Annnnnnnd, to answer your question about how long you were in there, all morning. I cleared the messages as well while these were printing." I turned toward him, the look of disbelief still evident on his face as I pointed to the neat pile of notes sitting on the counter. "Did you want me to order lunch?"

"It's like she's a robot." Dallas laughed before turning serious again. "If you're looking for John Connor, I'm totally him. Unless you're the T-1000 who's been sent here to kill me. In which case, *he* is John Connor." He pointed to Josh.

"Eve is not a robot, you moron." Josh smacked Dallas across the back of the head. "And what you are seeing is called efficiency. It's how competent people work."

Dallas ignored his boss, his attention back on me. "He's cranky.

We should feed him, robot Eve."

I laughed, feeling slightly ridiculous at how pleased I was they both seemed impressed. It's not like I was performing brain surgery—but as conceited as it sounded—I loved the ego boost.

"Okay. So do you have a preference or do you want me to choose? I'm starving, and you both have a break until two." I looked directly at Josh, waiting for him to respond.

"There's a deli up the road, they deliver." Josh didn't even give me a chance to pick up the phone before he turned to Dallas and added, "Order whatever Eve wants and pay them when they get here."

"I don't mind ordering."

"Why do I have to do it?"

Dallas and I drowned each other out.

"It's no trouble, I can do it," I added quickly. It had been my suggestion and I was happy to do it.

Josh held up his hand either to stop my protest or Dallas's, giving his friend a loaded look. "For once in your life just do what I tell you to do and don't argue."

"Fine." Dallas rolled his eyes before turning to me. "Let me guess, you want a salad, dressing on the side."

"Are you saying I'm fat?" I responded, planting my hands on my hips. While my ass would have probably appreciated his suggestion, dry salad made me want to barf.

"Hell no, your body . . ." His eyes rolled over the length of me from my toes all the way up.

"Dallas," Josh warned.

"Is great." I'm not sure what his original word was going to be but *great* felt like a substitution. "It's just what girls usually order."

"Then maybe you should stop dating Jessica Rabbit, because real women eat." I smiled sweetly, probably being bitchier than I needed. "I'll have a turkey sandwich."

"Make that two," Josh called from behind me. "And while

we're waiting, can I see you back in my room?"

He was looking directly at me.

Shit.

Back in his room meant alone, and alone didn't mean good things.

Firstly, because I'd spent all morning successfully acting like an adult and not a fourteen-year-old girl each time I saw him and I didn't want to ruin my track record. It was going to take a while before I didn't need to remind myself to suppress a groan whenever he walked by, but that would come with practice and it was only my first day.

But more importantly, *alone* meant someone could talk to you without an audience. Which is what happened when the gallery asked me to take leave.

"Sure." I kept the smile on my face as I followed him down the hall back to his room.

He didn't look angry. Surely he wasn't annoyed about the walls? I guess I should have probably clarified, but he had said I could do whatever. I wasn't going to ask for permission every single time I had an idea to improve things. Not small things like that. Besides, he'd called me efficient. I'd shown initiative. Those were good things.

"You want to sit?" His head tipped toward his big fancy chair, a rolling stool beside it.

"Did I do something wrong?" I'd never been patient.

"What makes you say that?" He closed the door behind us, my feet undecided if they wanted to stay standing or see what that comfy chair felt like.

"Because you want to speak to me alone. I figured you needed to say something but didn't want Dallas to hear."

Unless I wasn't alone in the fantasies about pulling each other's clothes off and making out. Wild sex before lunch sounded like a good way to work up an appetite. Extra employee benefit maybe?

Stop it.

What the hell was wrong with me?

"You haven't done anything wrong. Why don't you sit down."

It was the second time he asked, so I walked slowly to the chair. Might as well take a seat, it meant there was less chance of me doing something stupid. Like asking him to peel off his T-shirt so I could categorize the tattoos on his body like I'd done to the wall.

Ugh.

I needed a new vibrator.

Pushing *those* thoughts aside, I let my butt sink into the soft leather of his fancy chair.

"Wow, this is better than my couch." My legs lifted off the floor as I relaxed further, easing into the softness of the leather. It was like a beauty salon's chair on steroids. "No wonder Kitty was willing to sit here for hours." I was momentary distracted from the suppleness of the leather as Josh lowered himself onto the stool beside me.

"Usually I'd say the chair is probably worth more than your couch but with you, I'm not so sure." His lips twitched at the edges, "In the early days, I may have slept in it one or two times."

Great. A sleepy, half-naked—I was guessing, maybe fully na-ked—Josh wasn't a visual I would be forgetting in a hurry. Defi-nitely needed a new vibrator, maybe even investing in one of these chairs as well.

"I'm really impressed, Eve." He leaned forward, his sexy man scent interrupting my thoughts before they got too dirty. "The walls look really good."

"Thank you." *Do not lean in.* "I actually enjoyed it, and I have a good eye for detail. Some of those tattoos must have taken forever, all that . . . detail."

Did it sound as dumb out of my mouth as it did in my head?

"That's what I wanted to talk to you about." His hand rubbed the back of his neck. "The details, I think you should see them up close this afternoon. I was going to wait a little longer, let you settle in but honestly, with what you did out there, I see no reason to wait."

"Huh?" The control I'd had over my mouth was gone as every dirty thought I'd had about him jostled for position in my mind. "Wait for what?"

"I want you to sit in on a session. Only if you want to, no pressure and we can wait till next week if you'd be more comfortable." His fingers raked through the longer part of his black hair. "But I have a regular, Bob. And he is solid as a rock. The man doesn't flinch and is a dream to work on. I'm doing a shoulder piece and it's going to take a couple of hours." He paused, his smile got a little wider. "And I'd like you to watch."

Oh. My. God.

I squeezed my legs together pretending him asking me to watch didn't turn me on. Or that the sentence wasn't laden with innuendo.

"I'd love to watch." It sounded just as pervy when I said it out loud. "As long as Bob doesn't mind, I think I'd really enjoy watching you work." *Among other things.*

Maybe he could work with his shirt off. By his own admission it was a couple of hours work. It could get hot in here.

"Bob won't mind, he'll probably enjoy the attention." He gave me a wink. "Okay, great. That's settled. Let's have lunch, and then I get a few hours with you back here."

Why was I being punished? With everything coming out of his mouth sounding like a dirty invitation my body was more than willing to RSVP to.

"Sounds like a plan." My body moved to get out of the seat. "I'll tackle the supply closet tomorrow."

"I can't wait to see its fate in your capable hands." Another wink.

Jesus. This man was trying to kill me.

"My hands can't wait to get all over it." My fingers waved either side of my face. The *it* I was thinking about not his messy supply closet.

"Great. Let me get the transfer done, and we can get lunch." His heavy boots hit the floor as he moved off the stool.

"Is there a reason you brought me in here?" I asked, joining him at his drafting table. "You probably could have asked me out there." Where I wasn't so close and tempted to kiss him.

"Because I didn't want you to feel pressured in front of Dallas." His hands moved to a beautiful sketch of a fob watch, the chain wrapped around an hourglass. "He has a habit of baiting people, and if you wanted to say no, that would have been okay."

"You were worried about me?" My voice rose about two octaves. His concern so incredibly sweet, I could barely stand it.

"Not so much worried." He shrugged, a slight smile playing on his lips. "I think you have demonstrated today that you can more than hold your own. But I didn't want you agreeing to prove a point. I get the feeling proving a point is important to you."

"Are you a fortune teller too?" I laughed, surprised how obviously transparent I was. "Yeah, I probably would have agreed even if I didn't want to." Too many memories of questionable decisions made on the other side of a dare flashed in my mind. "But I do want to, I can't think of anything I want to do more than to do you." Wait. That's not what I meant to say. "I mean, watch you do . . . what you do. With you." And now I was butchering the English language as well. "Crap, I mean. I want to do this."

It was the best I could do. I blamed low blood sugar and the lone coffee I'd had hours ago as not being substantial enough to make me more articulate.

He let out a huge laugh, thankfully ignoring my lame ass verbal spillage. "Good. I'm glad. Now let's get back out there before

Dallas eats our food."

IT HAD BEEN THE BEST first day ever.

As promised, after lunch I followed Josh and Bob into the back room and watched as Josh worked.

Bob had been exactly as described. A large man, who was probably in his late forties, and who by the look of his colorful skin, had been through the process a few—or twenty—times before. He was funny and a little bit flirty but had no problem with me sitting in and spectating.

I couldn't look away. My eyes following Josh's hands to the point where I had completely zoned out. The rhythmic buzz of the machine and swipes of color lulling me into some kind of trance as I watched the image literally materialize. Depth, shadow, light. It was all there in brilliant color.

"You still with me?" Josh looked up, wiping away the residual ink with a rag.

"Yes, it's fascinating." I reassured him that, despite my mental vacation, everything was kosher. "Bob, you should see it. It's really, really good."

"That's why I keep coming back." Bob laughed, his head resting on his bent arm. "Although next time, I might make my appointment with you." Flirty Bob shot me a wink.

"Oh, you wouldn't want to do that." I laughed, "Josh is the best, you should stick with him." I neglected to mention that since my lapse in judgment where I'd considered tattooing Josh, my days of picking up a machine were over.

"Pity, you have nice hands." Another flirty wink.

"You're making me a little jealous, Bob." Josh chuckled. "I thought we had something special and now you're looking to replace me?"

"Sorry, bud. Your hands will do I guess if the lady's aren't on offer."

"Wow, Bob. Cuts me deep." Josh placed a gloved hand over his heart, pretending to sniff away a tear. "Real deep."

And before I knew it, Josh was wiping the last of the excess ink off and spraying Bob's skin. Once it was clean, he let Bob inspect his newest addition with a mirror and then affixed a bandage.

Bob—as I had been—was extremely impressed and was anxious to make another appointment in the new year for another piece. He again suggested I should do the next one, trying to convince me at least three more times while I processed his payment and booked him in for January. Little did he know when he came back, I'd be long gone.

"You need any help cleaning up?" I poked my head into Josh's room, having flipped the closed sign on the shop door.

"Dallas still finishing up?" he snapped off his gloves, tossing them into the trash.

"Yeah, he has at least another hour." I'd checked in on him on my way back to the rooms. "He said he'll close for you when he is done."

"Cool, well I guess you can go home then." He stopped packing things away and smiled. "It's Saturday night, I'm sure you have plans."

"I can stay back longer if you need me," I said a little too quickly. "I don't mind. Today has been really fun." While I was a little tired—my muscles aching from hanging the photos earlier—it had been such an amazing day. "It's not a word I'd usually use to describe work."

"That's a big problem then." He shook his head, his cerulean blue eyes flicking over to me. "You *should* enjoy it."

I meant the gallery, not the work I did for myself. The job was intended to help me build connections in the art world and also give me a place to continue to learn. At least that was what I had told myself when I accepted the job there twelve months ago. Though it seemed more about sales than about art and it bored me to tears some days. But I didn't want to seem like a quitter, which was why I turned up every day even though I was sure the last time my boss cracked a smile was in 1999.

"You're right. I should." Nod. "I do. It was a bad word choice." Nod. "I think I'm just tired." The words jumbled as they fell out of my mouth because I didn't want to admit I actually did hate my *regular* job.

I think he knew I was full of shit but thankfully he didn't say anything, his smile easy as he looked me over with those amazing blue eyes.

"Okay then, enjoy the rest of the weekend. We're shut tomorrow and Monday, so back Tuesday?" He asked like he wasn't sure I would.

"Yep. Tuesday sounds great." I stretched my neck, my shoulders a little tight from sitting hunched over while I was watching him work. "Thanks, and have a good night." I gave him a quick wave before heading back down the hall.

Grabbing my bag from behind the counter, I pulled open the glass door. I debated going back and saying a proper goodbye to Dallas but then decided against it. Josh's words still rattled around in my head and I'm not sure why they made me feel uncomfortable.

That's a big problem. You should enjoy it.

Why had it made me so edgy? I had a great job and I should love it. It could be so much worse. I was just annoyed at the situation. I had no idea why I was acting so ungrateful.

Shaking my head, and hopefully my mood, I stepped out onto the sidewalk.

He was right about one thing.

It was Saturday night, and it was the first time I'd been single in a long time. I might not be ready for another relationship, but a little fun never killed anyone. Besides, Oliver was probably screwing everything with a pulse by now. Not like us being together had stopped him. Kitty had probably been one of many. And maybe that's what I needed. Go and be reckless for a change and have some casual sex to burn away some of this stupid sexual frustration. I'd never know unless I tried, right? And if there were a time to start, it would be now.

Yes. That was definitely the way to go.

I pulled out my phone and started dialing.

"Hey, Eve." Heather answered almost instantly. "You hanging in there, doll? We've been worried about you."

Heather, like the rest of my friends, had been concerned about my mental state. They'd taken turns to check on me, making sure I hadn't gone Tarantino and Kill Bill'd every asshole who'd written a bad review. It wasn't a stretch to be honest, and if not for Kitty's intervention I'd probably be wielding a sword across Manhattan. Not a yellow jumpsuit, though, because yellow wasn't in my color wheel.

I hadn't bothered to tell her or the rest of our friends about my new job, the news probably enough to confirm I had gone off the rails. But as *my situation* wasn't going to be changing anytime soon, I should probably fill them in about my committing to working for Josh. That was a conversation that needed to happen in person, and hopefully somewhere there was a lot of alcohol. So why not kill two birds with one stone.

"Doing great, Heather." I put on my best smile, hoping it would translate into my voice. "I need you and the girls to meet me at a bar in a couple of hours. I just need to get home and change, but I'll text you the details."

"A bar? You sure you're up for that?" Heather's voice dipped with concern. "We can have a quiet night in if you'd like? I'll make my famous cocktails."

"Thanks, Heather, but I want to go out." I wasn't going to find a sexy man distraction underneath someone's couch. No, we needed to outsource that search, so bar it was. "I'll explain every-thing when I see you."

Saying a quick goodbye before Heather could ask any more questions, I ended the call and hailed a cab. *A cab*, which was ridic-ulous considering I had a shiny red Tesla sitting in my undercover garage.

Ugh.

I should probably sell that car or start driving it more, I didn't want to live with any regrets even if they were minor.

Okay, I needed to get my head in the game and stop acting like a fruit loop. But tonight I was going to blow off some major steam. And screw regrets.

EVE

"SO, HOW DO YOU KNOW Eve?" Lana shouted to Kitty over the music, sipping on the straw of her cocktail.

"She works with Oliver," I answered, even though the question hadn't been directed at me. "We shared some mutual interests. She's an art lover." I winked at Kitty, her invitation to join my night out came soon after Heather's.

"Well, Kitty, it's nice of you to join us." Heather managed a stiff smile while she shuffled out of time to the music. It was a poor attempt at dancing but we loved her too much to tell her to stop. "I'm just surprised we haven't met you before."

"I'm from Queens," Kitty yelled over the music. "I don't come into the city much outside of work."

"Oh my God, these drinks are good." Kristen pulled the glass from her lips. "I don't even know what this thing is called but the bartender keeps giving them to me." She leaned in, lowering her voice as much as the surrounding noise allowed and still be heard. "And I think the bartender is flirting with me or something because I haven't paid for one of these glasses of deliciousness yet." She smiled proudly, turning and giving the bartender in question a cute wave.

"He's not flirting with you, silly." Heather laughed, taking a sip from her drink. "Eve has her card at the bar and is running a tab."

Bar 53 was a swanky bar in Midtown and the destination for our little get together. It was just popular enough that the place was always packed, but not so much that we needed to wait in line. Besides, Heather's brother was dating the promotions manager which meant even if it got busy, we were always waved through. It helped having friends in high places. And on a night like tonight I didn't want to wait on the street.

"Don't be jealous, Heather." Kristen ignored her while taking another sip of her drink. "I know flirting when I see it." She nodded to the bartender who unsurprisingly winked back. I was guessing it might have been the tips she was slipping him after each drink, and we were at least five cocktails in.

"So, Kitty." Lana tugged lightly on her arm ignoring Heather and Kristen. "You need to tell us. Is Oliver miserable without Eve?"

"Ugh. I don't want to talk about him." I downed what was left in my glass and signaled to the bartender I wanted another. The drinks weren't cheap but they kept them coming. It was a fair trade and one I would happily pay for. "I'm so done with him."

Heather, Lana and Kristen had gotten the edited version of our break-up. Oliver was a cheating manwhore who needed to go, and therefore I sent him packing. It was all the important parts anyway.

We had successfully avoided all talk of me and Oliver for the initial part of the evening. Kristen's tale of being pulled over by the hot State Trooper on the interstate had given me a small reprieve but I assumed it was only a matter of time before they asked. It seemed that time had arrived.

"How can you just be done with him?" Lana asked, not willing to accept I'd already moved on. At least not without a full explanation, post mortem and flip chart on how was I planning to proceed from here on out. "You were together forever, you lived with him.

Don't you feel anything?"

"I'm soulless, didn't you read the review?" I laughed reaching across the bar and getting another drink. Amazing how after a few drinks and used in a different context, those words lost some of their sting. "Rather convenient in times like these."

"She Icy Hot'd his underwear." Kitty cleared her throat, giving me a secretive smile. "I overheard Oliver telling one of the guys from work. Said his balls were still on fire, and he was worried his dick might be broken." She threw her head back and laughed. "He had to take a day off sick to go to the emergency room, he thought he was going to die."

"Oh my God!" Kristen smacked me across the arm, my drink sloshing all over Heather. "You Icy Hot'd his underwear? Girl, I am never pissing you off."

"I cannot confirm or deny such a thing." I sipped what was left in my glass. "But maybe he should be more selective on where he puts his penis and bad things won't happen to it."

"It's really not that impressive either, I've seen way better." Kitty shrugged as four pairs of eyes whipped around and landed directly on her.

Seriously, if they'd been lasers, she would have been incinerated.

Choruses of "What?" "Whoa?" that filled the air were joined by "But he's so tall, how can he not be huge?"

The last one was from Kristen.

We were probably going to need to cut her off.

"Shit. Sorry." Kitty bit her lip realizing her faux pas. "You've just been so cool about it, I keep forgetting."

Ugh.

Maybe we needed to cut everyone off.

"It's fine, Kitty." I sighed, the abbreviated version of how I knew Kitty no longer sufficient. "So." My fingers twisted the stem of my now empty glass. Well that sucked, this was exactly the conversation that needed a drink. "Kitty works with Oliver but was also *working* over Oliver when we first met." I giggled, the ridiculousness of it all seeming so funny. Maybe it was the cocktails. "But it's fine, we're fine." I extended my arms and twirled. "Everyone's fine."

"Except for Oliver's penis, apparently." Kitty laughed, the two of us the only ones who seemed to find the situation amusing.

"Kitty blew Oliver and you're okay with it?" Heather's extra thick mascara'd eyes widened to maximum capacity. "Eve, I love you, honey, but I think we have to accept the very real possibility you may have had a psychological episode."

"See, here's the thing." I tried to make sure I didn't slur my words, needing the important stuff to come out clear. "I don't think I really loved him. We were together so long, I think it was just a convenience thing."

Heather rubbed my arm, the conversation sobering me as I went on. "Like it was expected we'd get married, he'd fill my uterus and we'd grow old and boring. It is a little depressing when I think about it, that I would have just stayed and been content." I shrugged wondering if maybe my passion wasn't just lacking in my artwork. Maybe it had been lost in me too.

"He left the gallery early the night of my exhibit, and I didn't really care." I vividly remembered kissing him goodbye, waving him off and enjoying my night without him. "I *should* have cared that he wasn't there and he *should* have wanted to be. Yeah, he cheated, but I think he did us both a favor."

"We need more drinks," Kristen helpfully added.

"Lots more." This time from Lana.

"Yes, more drinks." I waved to our favorite bartender, signaling we needed another round. "And then I'll tell you about my new job at a tattoo studio in Queens."

⁕⁕⁕

"HOW HOT IS THIS GUY? Did he take off his shirt?" Kristen was asking all the important questions.

"Soooooo hot." Kitty fanned herself. "He's got the most amazing smile and his eyes are so blue, they don't look real."

My concern about telling my friends about my recent career change was a non-issue. While there had been some initial concerns about my mental well being—to be fair, I'd had some myself—the more I spoke, the more they agreed.

I needed to shake things up, find my zen or something, and if a hot tattooist in Queens could help me find my mojo, what was the harm. Besides, women with money weren't as conservative as most people thought. The higher their bank account, the crazier they usually were. Heather just assumed I was finally embracing my net worth. It was no secret that my trust fund was in stratosphere territory.

"You never answered if he took off his shirt." Lana leaned back against the chair, her tongue fighting to grab the straw as it swirled in her drink.

We'd moved our drunken party of five to a booth when one became available; wisely deciding that remaining vertical was going to pose a challenge. It also meant we got table service too, which was handy, the drinks seeming to appear like magic. I was really going to have a headache tomorrow.

"He has not removed his shirt." I swished my hand through the air, the admission slightly disappointing. "Sadly, there really isn't a need for him to strip down so I doubt I'll ever get to see."

"And you're not having hot rebound sex with this guy, why?" Heather asked, solidly on Team Josh.

I held up my hand and listed the reasons on each finger.

"Because he's my boss. And if there's a chance he can help me I don't want to screw this up. And he's probably not into me. And he's my boss."

"Not great reasons if you ask me." Kitty's head rolled loosely to the side. "I bet *his* penis isn't disappointing."

"We need to stop talking about him," I droned, my head falling into my hands. "I need to find someone else to lust over, at least for tonight."

"And have hot rebound sex with," Heather added, in case there was any doubt.

"Yes and that." I scanned the club looking for a suitable and willing victim, my search so far being fruitless. Surely it wouldn't be too hard to find someone to have casual, emotionless sex with? I needed to get more serious about my efforts.

"Well guys, I need to wrap this up." Lana yawned, her butt already shuffling out of the booth. "I've got breakfast with the in-laws tomorrow and I have a hard enough time not puking from my mother-in-law's shitty cooking. I can't do it hungover as well. I'm not that talented."

"Yeah, I should probably go too." Heather sighed, following her out. "I have barely spent any time with Tom this week and he flies out to D.C. on Tuesday."

"Noooooo," I wailed dramatically. "You can't leave. I haven't gotten laid yet." My pout as exaggerated as my voice.

"You haven't been trying." Kristen rolled her eyes, she too moving out of the booth. Obviously done for the night as well. "All you have to do is go to the bar and say, *hey there Mr., you want to play with my hoo-hah tonight.* Not sit here with us."

"Please tell me that's not your pick up line, because I will disown you." My head shook, praying to God she was kidding.

"No," Kristen mused sarcastically. "I say vagina when I'm talking to a man."

"I am so glad I'm married." Heather laughed.

"Me too," Lana added.

Everyone was so freaking unhelpful.

"The direct approach works best." Kitty was the only one who hadn't attempted to leave. "Seriously. Just tell the guy what you want, they like it when you're bossy."

"Ugh, all your dating advice sucks." I threw my hands up in defeat, my night of hot rebound sex slipping further away. "We're going to have to reconvene and try this again."

Yep, that's what I needed to do. Get back on the horse and try again. Maybe wear something sluttier. It couldn't be that hard to get laid in New York.

"Can we make it next Saturday night instead? I can't do back to back nights." Lana winced, her job at the law firm seriously hindering my social life. "And as much as I hate to admit it, weekdays kill me."

"I second." Heather raised her hand.

"Motion passes. Saturday night it is." Lana high-fived Heather, their stupid rule meaning I'd have to wait.

"Fine, next week then." I waved them off, conceding I was outnumbered. "You too, Kitty. This is going to be a team effort."

"I'm up for anything!" Kitty smiled, my newfound friend a well of enthusiasm. This was good. I needed that kind positivity, made me seem not so crazy, as selfish as that sounded.

"Then I guess I'm going home." I joined them on my feet, my buzz already starting to wear off. Alone. Frustrated. And still no closer to knowing what I should do. "See you all next week."

"Bye."

"See you."

The chorus of goodbyes started, hugs exchanged and all of us ambled to the exit. It seemed settled but once our faces had hit the night air, Kitty had a change of heart and decided she hadn't had her fill yet. She gave us all another sloppy hug and after repeated assurances that *yes, she was fine on her own* and *yes, she would make sure she got home safe,* and *she did this all the time, so stop worrying,* she retreated back into the dark noisy bellows of the club.

I was almost tempted to follow her back in, but I knew my head was already going to hate me tomorrow and figured I should try to be semi responsible.

Heather and Lana flagged a cab, deciding to share the commute and cheerfully waved goodbye as they disappeared up the street.

And then there were two.

"I still say you sleep with him, boss or not." Kristen smirked, blowing me a kiss as she hopped into a cab that had stopped by the curb. Her destination of Brooklyn meant I was going to find my own ride home.

"No offense, but you give terrible advice." I laughed; she had been the one who had initially introduced me to Oliver, and we all know how that turned out.

"Suit yourself." The door closed, the cab only getting a few car lengths into traffic before it was stalled by the row of taillights in front of it.

Suit myself.

If only.

I would have liked nothing more than to throw that big man down and ride him. Because *that* would solve all kinds of problems. Gah. I didn't need any more additional complications.

It had been an intense few days, and maybe I had no idea what the hell I was doing, but making a bigger mess wasn't the answer.

Vibrator it was then.

But I *was* going to think all about my hot new boss while I was doing it.

It would be a decent compromise.

Or at least one that would hopefully be the least amount of trouble.

JOSH

THE WEEKEND—WELL MY VERSION OF it, Sunday and Monday—had been uneventful.

I'd wrapped up Saturday late afternoon after saying goodbye to Eve, and met up with some friends for a few drinks. There was a bar not far from the studio, which was also conveniently close to my house. This was a good thing because, rather than keeping track of how many beers it was going to take before I could no longer keep my car between the mayo and mustard on the road, I could walk home and enjoy the summer night.

It had subconsciously been my intention to hook up. And I say that because I was hard, and had a burn through my body that only a good session of sex could extinguish. But as I turned down blonde after brunette, I knew as much as my dick was happy to take what was on offer, my brain gave me a good case of the is-this-what-you-really-want? So all those intentions—subconsciously or otherwise—didn't really amount to anything as I went home alone.

Strangely enough, my hand proved to be an adequate solution. Not even close to a substitute for the real thing but it reduced the fire to a low simmer and didn't make me feel like a complete dick—Ha! Nice choice of words—in the morning.

What did give me a slight case of the awks was that while my palm and I were getting intimately acquainted, I was picturing Eve. Her mouth, her tits, her pussy—all of it—on offer for me to explore like my own adventure park. Made me come harder than I had in months. Whoever said jerking off peaked at sixteen obviously hadn't been doing it right. And because I was dedicated to testing the theory, I did it a few more times. All in the name of science, right?

So Tuesday morning when I got to the shop early, I had to psyche myself up a little. Get ready to look her in the eye and not descend into pervert territory. Or at least not give off the vibe. Beggars couldn't be choosers at this point.

"Hey!" She pushed open the door, tray full of coffees like she had last week. "How was your weekend?" Her bright smile gave me all kinds of warm and fuzzies.

She's not here for you, asshole. So unless you can reincarnate yourself into Michelangelo's David, she's not interested in your dick. And let's face it, the man wasn't packing much, so not sure I wanted to go that route either.

"Weekend was great. Was good to power down for a few days." I took my coffee like a good boy and took a sip, the hot black liquid a welcome distraction for my mouth. "How about you?"

"I was so hung over Sunday. A few friends and I went out drinking to drown my sorrows, or commiserate or whatever." She shrugged, dropping her handbag behind the counter and took a cup of coffee for herself. "Retail therapy would have been less painful the next day. I think I'll stick to a glass of wine and online shopping next time. At least then I don't have to wear pants."

Two things flashed through my mind.

The visual of Eve relaxed, drinking and having a good time, was hotter than was decent to admit. It was something I *really* hoped I had the opportunity to see. I wasn't even going to touch the *no pants* part of the sentence.

And the other thing that got my attention was the commiserating/drowning her sorrows. That it seemed like part of her still bought into the bullshit other people had said about her.

"You still thinking about those reviews?" My mouth chose *that* option rather than tell her how I could show her how to have a good time minus the hangover.

"It's hard not to." She shrugged, taking another sip. "It still so fresh and everyone who knows me has read them." There was a quite sigh. "I have fantasies where I'm Kate Beckinsale from Underworld, and I go from house to house of my enemies and seek vengeance."

Yeah, because that image—her suited up in a tight black leather cat suit—was something I was never going to get out of my head. She had unwittingly given me jerk-off material for the next twenty years.

"Interesting choice." I coughed, stopping short to ask if she had the outfit, and if she didn't if it was going to be something acquired during those pantless online shopping sessions.

"Artists are allowed to be dramatic, right?" She grinned, firing up the computer. "And what happens in your head is not admissible in court."

And thank fuck for that.

"So, tell me what else goes on inside your head?" Even though I hadn't meant it to be, it sounded sexual. Hadn't helped that my voice was low and I was still thinking about her in that tight black outfit.

"Well, it's weird." She lowered her coffee, and if she'd got the unintentional sexual undertones, she wasn't letting on. "My mood swings really wildly."

"Between?" I rested my coffee on the bench, giving her my entire attention.

"God, listen to me." She caught herself, suddenly realizing

she was going to divulge something personal. "Sorry, I should probably go sort out the supply closet. You have more important things than listening to my problems." She turned, pulling out the appointment book and using it as a bullshit excuse to stop talking.

"Let me ask you this?" I pulled the book away from her and forced her to look at me. "Did you stop talking because you're worried about what *I* might think or because you're scared to say it out loud?"

I knew avoidance when I saw it, and I had a fairly good idea that Eve needed to talk to someone who wasn't going to give her the usual BS response. Friends were great for telling you it was going to be fine, and it would all work out in the end. But sometimes, shit wasn't fine and you needed to be okay with it. And yeah, I wasn't qualified to give her advice in any area but I sure as hell didn't judge her. The thought she'd censor herself for anyone was mind blowing, but doing it because of me, wasn't acceptable.

"You're my boss, not my therapist." She laughed, the light-happy-funny missing from her voice. "And I had to almost beg you to hire me. I'm sorry, I really am here to learn not bore you with my silly first-world problems."

"Eve, you seem like a smart girl, but never assume you know what people are thinking." I kept my voice level as I watched her eyes go wide. "If I asked you a question, it's because I want to know the answer. I'll tell you if I'm bored, and being your boss doesn't mean anything."

"Promise you'll tell me if you get bored." She narrowed her eyes, measuring my response.

"Scout's honor." I held up two fingers though I doubted anything she had to say would be boring. I wasn't even sure if she had the *capacity* to be boring, and I was more than a little interested to test out that theory.

"Or if this is crossing the line or something. I don't want to seem unprofessional," she added, either further stalling or trying to convince me that she took the job seriously.

"Have you met Dallas?" I tipped my head to his empty room down the hall. Illustrating he wouldn't be gracing us with his appearance anytime soon despite my boss status. "I think you've displayed more professionalism in your first day than he has in the entire time I've known him."

She laughed, some of the tension easing out of her shoulders. "Then why does he still work here?"

"Because he is a damn good artist and despite being arrogant and sometimes annoying, he cares about what he puts onto people's skin." The answer one of the easiest I'd ever had to give. "We share the same vision, there are no short cuts when he works, and it's more than just a job for both of us. I'll take that over someone who's punctual and who calls me sir."

She stood silent, taking a minute before she opened her mouth.

"I want to be a good artist." It was like it killed her to say those words, each one of them so full of doubt where possibly there hadn't been any before.

"Maybe you already are and you're distracted by the noise." I wanted a chance to find out if this was a confidence issue or she really lacked the ability. And I figured it was time I probably found out. "Here's an idea, my first appointment isn't until eleven, right?"

She flipped open the book and confirmed what I already knew. "Yep, a sugar skull for Bea on her upper thigh."

Perfect, gave us plenty of time to conduct my little experiment.

"So come back with me into my room, we've got time."

"For?" Her face scrunched in confusion.

"I need to show you."

I could see she was curious, and not the kind of girl who would back off when challenged, which is exactly the attitude I was counting on. And with a little more than a tip of my head, she followed me down the hall to my room. My hand automatically closing the door when we were both inside.

"What are we doing?" She looked around, nothing revealing itself. "I hope you're not going to ask me to tattoo you again."

"No," I laughed, having learned that lesson the first time. And as much as I wanted to prove a point, I'd rather not be stuck with a jacked up tattoo. "Let's leave that part to me, shall we?" I pulled out a sketchbook and turned it to a blank piece of paper. "You're going to draw."

"Well, that's easy." She relaxed taking the sketchbook, her smile making a reappearance. "Can I draw anything I want?"

"No, that would be too easy." And we weren't there to make things easy. "You need to draw me."

"You? As in a portrait?" She didn't seem concerned, wrongly assuming this was going to be like all the other things she'd drawn.

"Yes, but you need to pretend that your portrait is going to be the only thing anyone is ever going to know about me." My head tipped to the direction of my drafting table. The pencils and everything else she was going to need lying on top. "Like your version of me is the last one anyone will ever get to see."

I knew what I was doing, and I couldn't help but grin as I hopped up onto my tattoo chair, turning it so she would have a better view. She'd wanted me to show her something different, that's why she came to me in the first place, right?

"That's crazy. I don't know you that well to interpret—"

"Don't interpret." I raised my hand stopping whatever overused art crap she was going to sprout. "Your job isn't to sell me, it's to show everyone else what *you* see."

"But what if my version isn't what you really are, and the one everyone is stuck with is inaccurate?" She tapped a pencil against her lip.

I wasn't sure if it was fear, maybe it was apprehension, but she was giving this too much thought. And that was the problem.

"I'm not asking for accurate, only for honesty. So draw me, Eve. Unless you're not up for it, and want to go back to the gallery selling other people's work."

"Wow, that was a cheap shot." She smirked, obviously taking my dig in the spirit it was intended. Not because I was an asshole, but because I knew it would give her the extra incentive. She tossed a pencil through the air in mock annoyance, hitting me in the chest before it bounced to the ground.

"So, you going to do this thing? Or are we going to analyze it until my appointment comes? Because the supply closest still needs attention." My head hit the headrest as my hands folded behind the back of my neck.

Her confidence might have taken a rattle, but she wasn't a quitter. Evident by the fact she was here in the first place. So, it was with silent pride that I watched her pick up another pencil and start.

"Knew you would come around." I couldn't help gloating, or wipe the smile from my face.

"Stop talking," she hushed, her hands busy all over the page.

It was weird for me to be on the other side of this, to sit in my own chair and let someone else work. Sure, I knew it wasn't the same thing but I was super curious about what ended up on the page.

It didn't take long before I relaxed a little more. My arms rested beside me and I watched her as she studied me. Her eyes rolled over me and then went back to her page, the to and fro making me feel a little like a zoo animal. Strangely, I didn't mind half as much as I would have thought, loving her attention on me as I sat still while she worked.

And before I was ready for it to be over, she had lifted the pencil for the last time and gave her work one last once over. Her face, a locked vault.

"Let me see." My butt shuffled off the chair, my boots hitting the floor.

"It's not my best work." She hugged the sketchpad close to her chest, her mouth screwing up into a pout. "Can I have a do over?"

"That wasn't the deal, show me." My feet took a step closer.

"Nooooooooooo." Her head shook as her grip on the sketchbook got tighter. "Let's say it's a practice run." Her fingers quickly tore the page out before I got anywhere close.

"Eve." My hand was out, waiting for her to pass it over.

"Nope." Her mouth popped off the p as she quickly took a step back and folded the page.

"You know I'm going to see it, right? I'm standing between you and the door and you're going to have to pass me."

Unless she was planning on vaporizing herself out through the air ducts, there was only one way out. I could see the cogs in her head turning as she saw there was no way out.

"Come on, it can't be that bad." My hand shook, waiting for the paper to hit my palm.

I was convinced I'd seen her worst work already when I did a search online. And while I knew I could be constructive and still be honest, I wasn't going to tear her apart. Besides, judging by the concentration on her face while she was drawing, I'd bet it wasn't even close to bad.

Her eyes went to my hand as I took another step closer.

It happened so fast, me planning on backing her into the corner and commandeering the picture and her seeing my advance and shoving the folded picture of me down the front of her top.

My likeness was now nestled somewhere in between her tits. Boom.

Instant fucking hard-on.

Up to that point, I'd done a good job of keeping shit on lockdown. I'd noticed the way her top had clung to her tits and that her jeans did a nice job of curving her ass. But with some choice imagery—the hairy trucker who wanted a tramp stamp above his ass—I'd managed to keep the big guy in my pants under control. There were a few times he'd shown interest, her eyes on me something we both enjoyed, but it wasn't like I could hide a boner while

I was sitting in the chair. Standing up was even worse.

Now, all bets were off as my dick gave me the you're-on-your-own-buddy, and inflated in my pants.

"Oops." Her lips twisted into a smirk. "It just fell in there. I hate it when that happens."

She clearly hadn't noticed things in my crotch were getting tight as I could barely pull my eyes away from her chest. We no longer had to worry about *her* being the one who was acting unprofessional.

"You know I could just reach in there and get it."

I hadn't meant to say it. Because hello, sexual harassment anyone? But those were exactly the words that shot out of my mouth as I stalked closer.

"And I'm standing right here." She shoved her hands on her hips, her feet rooted on the floor. "Do I look worried?"

Was she fucking flirting with me? I mean, most of the time I got the vibe when a girl was interested. The hair flick, the giggle, the over enthusiastic touching—but she hadn't done any of that, so it wasn't clear what the fuck we were doing.

What I *did* know was my offer to reach in there and get it wasn't an innocent one. I no longer cared what was on that piece of paper, which had made the whole exercise redundant. But touching her, that was something I was very interested in.

My feet moved me, one in front of the other until I was toe to toe with her, a couple of inches the only thing separating us. A bomb could have gone off two feet away and I wouldn't have even blinked. My focus completely on her.

"You want to play dirty, Eve? They teach you *that* at your fancy school?" It was like my dick had its own heartbeat.

"You think I don't know *how*, Josh?" Her brow rose, her lips parting as she took a breath. "It wasn't something I needed to learn."

I'd never wanted to kiss a woman as much as I did right then and there. She looked like she wanted it too, her chest heaving up and down as our eyes locked.

Fuck.

My brain was screaming to back the hell off. We absolutely could not do this. And if we did, it would be bad ju-ju. Unfortunately the rest of me didn't fucking care what my mind had to say.

"Yo, J. You around, man?"

Motherfucker.

That bomb I thought I would have been able to ignore, just fucking detonated. And it was about to leave one hell of mess.

Goddamn it, Dallas.

"Sounds like we have company." I took a step back, a big dose of reality kicking in. "You lucked out." I laughed, pretending like I hadn't been about to kiss her.

"Practice run it was then." And if she was disappointed, she wasn't showing it. "I'll go get things started out front."

What the fuck?

I was beginning to question my own sanity. It was as if the whole thing didn't happen. Her breathing seemed normal, no hint of embarrassment and she wasn't awkward or running out the door. Just the same knockout smile that sucked me into a vortex of questionable decisions.

"Good plan," I coughed out, giving her a thumbs up. "I've got to set up."

"I'll let you know when your appointment gets here."

"Great."

All so fucking polite. And with a wave of her fingers she was out of my door and gone. Dallas's voice boomed a welcome as she passed him in the hall, the hi-how-are-you's not waving any red flags.

The kicker, I wasn't sure if I was relieved or disappointed.

"You hiding?" Dallas poked his head through the door not bothering to wait for a response or an invitation. "Eve got me coffee." The cup lifted in case I was blind.

"If I'd known that all it was going to take was coffee in the morning to get you to work early, I'd have done it a lot sooner." I flipped him off, able to get behind my desk in just enough time to hide my hard-on.

Not that Dallas was usually perceptive, but I didn't need the dude to suddenly have a moment of awareness when my dick was bulging and Eve had just left the room. That was a whole new set of complications.

"I'm not here for the coffee." His eyebrows danced smugly. "But I'll admit it's a nice touch. Only if Eve does it though, I'm particular."

"I'm sure you are." I wondered how long I had to pretend to be interested before I could toss him out of my room. I was still hard, and actually contemplating jerking off at work. It was a new low for sure.

"You're acting weird." He stopped short, giving me a head-to-toe I wasn't comfortable with.

Great.

"Didn't get much sleep last night." My ass sunk into my chair while my hands shuffled papers. "I was working from home."

"Dude, seriously." Dallas rolled his eyes. "You're boring me to tears. Stop working, and go get laid."

"Thanks for the advice, I'll take it under advisement." I flipped him off even though getting laid was what was actually on my mind. "Go set up."

"Aye-aye, captain." And with a two-finger salute Dallas removed himself from my doorway.

All I had to do was concentrate on getting my work done and ignore how hot my new employee was.

It was only a few weeks.

It would fly by and then she'd be gone. Hopefully *before* I chafed my cock raw.

EVE

THE DRAWING HE'D ASKED ME to do was intense.

I'd felt his eyes staring back at me from the page, his lips parted like they were about to call my name, and it's how I imagined he'd look above me while we had sex. There was *no way* I was showing him. There was also the added bonus that I'd neglected to add a shirt, *Picture Josh's* chest spectacularly naked. My imagination filled in the blanks, and if I was even halfway right, he looked amazing with no clothes. Lord, I could only hope to find out. For accuracy, if nothing else.

Just before Dallas interrupted, our eyes had connected in a way that wasn't platonic. He'd been so close to me I could feel his breath and my heart felt like was about to stop. My skin literally tingled from the heat radiating between us, and if he had touched me, I would have combusted.

Josh. Logan. Was. As. Hot. As. Fuck.

I'd never really gotten behind the phrase tossed around the Twitter-sphere, but I had a new appreciation for it. It efficiently described the man in a way three paragraphs couldn't.

And those few words had been stuck in my mind on repeat

all day long.

I did my best not to dissolve in a puddle of hormones as I went about pretending it was business as usual. Got through the entire day successfully without any major incidents. We said goodbye with neither of us mentioning the exchange in his room or my picture. And maybe that sketch had been put to good use that night—don't judge me—but I was still able to look him in the eye the next day when I waltzed in with three coffees like I always did. And that had taken some talent.

Ignoring the voices in my head that chanted how delectable he was, I did my best not to moan my thoughts—even if I couldn't stop thinking them—while I kept busy.

"Hey, Josh, your twelve o'clock is here. Want me to send her in?" I tried to hide the fact he made me spontaneously ovulate by giving him a bright cheery smile.

"Thanks, Eve. I'm almost ready." Hot as fuck head nod followed by a hot as fuck wink.

"Josh, a supplier called and said your delivery is delayed but I got them to refund the freight cost." I'd also been considering wearing heat-retardant clothes in case they accidently combusted in his presence.

"You're amazing, thank you." Hot as fuck smile with an added hot as fuck look of approval.

And building on his hot as fuck exercise from yesterday—drawing without trying too hard to interpret—I'd also grabbed a spare sketchpad and some pencils and drew while I worked.

Nothing in particular came to me. No light bulbs of inspiration struck. But as I doodled on the page while I answered the phone and spoke to customers, I felt calmer and a little more connected. Or maybe I was just going further down the rabbit hole, it would give the papers something different to write.

Eve Thorton now completely off the rails, hiding out in a tattoo shop in Queens.

"You need more cowbell." Dallas chuckled over my shoulder. I'd been so involved in what I was doing I hadn't heard him approach.

"More cowbell?" I looked at the reaper caped figure I had inadvertently drawn. I put the blame on the wall I'd been staring at mindlessly. The skulls and demons featured on it obviously seeping into my brain.

"Please do not tell me you do not know that SNL skit?" He looked at me horrified. "Christopher Walken?" He looked at me with expectation. "Will Farrell?"

"Nope." I had no idea what he was talking about.

"Lordy, lady, you are in some serious trouble." He laughed, smirking as he leaned against the desk. "You let J take care of the art BS and Dallas here will take Comedy 101."

Funnily enough Dallas was not ugly. His dark hair fell to his shoulders, one side shaved to almost zero. With multiple piercings—lip, eyebrow, nose, and who knows where else—and more tattoos than I could count, somehow it all worked to make him look good. And while he was shorter than Josh, he still towered over me. His body also looked like it was impressive under his black-on-black uniform he always seemed to wear, but I had no desire to find out.

Dallas, my funny and extremely flirty co-worker, did not make my skin tingle. He was not *hot as fuck.*

"Hey, Eve." Josh's hot as fuck hand—seriously, I had a problem—ran through his hot as fuck hair. "Want to sit . . ." *On your face? Sure "* . . . in on the next client? You've been stuck at your desk all day."

I'd avoided close proximity for all of the morning and most of the afternoon. Obviously I spoke to him—categorizing all his hotness—whenever it was needed, and as far as I could tell, I'd acted normal. It was an effort I will admit that took a lot of energy. But shit was faaaaaar from fine when you considered the condition of my underwear. And that was not a good way to be when I still had another two hours to go. His hotness, the almost kiss yesterday, my imagination—all reasons for my situation.

"Of course, I would love to." I smiled sweetly as I rose off my chair even though sitting there watching him would be the equivalent of watching porn. "See you, Dallas, I'll add jingles or whatever later."

"Cowbell." He laughed, watching me as I walked to where Josh's next appointment was.

"Michelle, you're up next." I ignored Dallas as I directed Michelle down the hall where we walked into Josh's room. It was no doubt going to be pleasurable and painful for both of us, and only one of us was getting a tattoo.

"Oh, I love it!" Michelle's face morphed with delight as she looked at the filigree butterfly that was about to become permanently part of her body. "It's exactly how I imagined."

Please don't let this be a back tattoo, please don't let this be a back tattoo. My whispered request hoping that Michelle's position on the chair wouldn't eliminate visual contact. I figured we'd do better if there were a pair of eyes on us, acting as a referee.

"So glad you like it." Josh grabbed the transfer paper and directed Michelle to a weird looking chair. Strangely not the huge reclining one he usually worked on. "It's going to look great on your back."

Crap.

Well, there went that theory.

Michelle slid off her shirt, remaining in her bra as she sat on what looked to be some kind of therapy stool. Face first into a cushioned doughnut for her head, she wiggled to get comfortable so there wouldn't be a chance she'd see a thing. Yep, I was pretty much on my own as I grabbed one of the rolling stools and sat adjacent to Josh.

"You ready?" he asked, preparing her skin, ready to accept the stencil.

"Yep, go for it," Michelle responded, her arms flopping either side as he rubbed the paper just above her bra line in between her shoulder blades.

"If you need to stop at any time, let me know." Josh reached for a machine, looking at me as he placed his hand on Michelle's back.

Why did it feel so erotic when he was talking and touching someone else? This couldn't be right. I would need to investigate side effects of mental trauma; maybe this was some weird thing I was going through.

"I won't need to stop," she responded, not bothering to lift her head.

Funnily enough I wasn't able to say those words with any conviction.

It wasn't a huge tattoo, but Josh took his time as he inked in solid black outlines. While the needle was against Michelle's skin, his eyes were on his work, but when he took a minute to wipe off the excess stain, they found their way back to mine.

Curves and swirls, his steady hand moved, and I was both captivated and mesmerized. He watched me, watching him, as the air around us seemed to crackle.

I wondered what it would feel like if he did that to me, and surprisingly I got wet. The thought of his gloved hands on my bare back and the buzz of the machine got me more excited than I thought it should. Was it the combination, or was it just because it was him? It intrigued me, and maybe it was something I'd consider. Or maybe it was the thought of him doing *anything* to me that was the turn on. I silently contemplated as he worked, his eyes on me at every available opportunity. My breath started coming out in slow exhales, the draw in and then out, deeper. It was ridiculous that a moment that had nothing to do with sex was so overtly sexual.

There was something wrong with me because surely this wasn't normal.

"We're done." The buzz of the machine cut off as Josh wiped

Michelle's back one last time. "Let me clean it up and then I'll grab a mirror so you can see."

Putting his previous tools aside, he cleaned the reddened skin and then let Michelle have a look in the mirror.

"It's perfect." Her body turned, the butterfly seeming to move as she twisted. "Thank you so much." Genuine happiness exploded across her face as she reached out and hugged him. "I love it. It's exactly what I wanted."

A pang of jealously echoed through me. Not because I thought Josh was interested in Michelle, or vice versa. But because unlike her, I had no reason to hug him, and I wished that I could.

"Here's some info on after care." He unwrapped himself from the hug, handing her a leaflet and a small tube of ointment. "Make sure you keep out of the sun and keep it moisturized, it's going to take at least a week to heal."

"I will, I promise."

After she was done inspecting and admiring her new back adornment, he rubbed in some of the ointment and then added a bandage. At each step he was slow, careful and considerate, not rushing just to be done and get her out the door.

And I couldn't look away.

I saw a slight smile on his lips each time his eyes met mine but it wasn't like I didn't know he would notice. It was odd how even with another person in the room it still felt like there was only the two of us.

With Michelle's shirt back on, I got to my feet ready to walk her out so Josh could clean up. Once the tattoo was done, I'd lead them out to the front where I'd usually process their payment and check if they wanted another appointment. Today it would give me a minute to catch my breath and give my vagina a break.

"I've got it, you can stay here if you want." Josh nodded, as my butt froze halfway off the stool, he and Michelle walking out.

I wasn't sure why he'd decided to handle it himself. Maybe

because it was the end of the day and he wanted to wrap it up. Or maybe he had felt the zap between us too and needed the physical break. I know I sure did, my body so wound up that if I put my hands into my panties I could probably make myself come with the sweep of my thumb.

There was a goodbye and then heavy footsteps came back into the room. Could he see how aroused I was? Could he feel it? Did he want to rip my clothes off as much as I did his, the idea of putting my mouth on his slowly making me crazy.

Sitting idle wasn't something I usually did, so I saw no point in starting now. If I wanted something, I needed to go get it or at least make it clear that's what I wanted, right? Sure there were lines that maybe shouldn't be crossed but wasn't part of the fun breaking the rules? But I wouldn't risk another interruption. No, I needed him somewhere where it would be just the two of us alone. Hopefully naked.

"Thanks for letting me sit in, I love watching you work." I eased into it, wading into the water a little before taking the dive headfirst. I was all for going out and getting what I wanted but had no intention of making a fool of myself.

"I'm glad." He smiled—which was sexy as fuck, of course— studying me like he knew I was up to something.

"So Michelle was your last appointment." I did my best not to sound too eager, off-the-cuff and unrehearsed more of what I was hoping to achieve. "Maybe we can go out and get something to eat."

It wasn't as confident as I usually was, and I should have omitted the "maybe." It sounded too desperate, too unsure, which I was neither, even if I really, really wanted him to say yes, I wasn't going to throw myself at him.

"I'd love to, but I can't." A slow breath pushed out past his lips. "I'm sorry."

It might have been a nice brush off, but it was a brush off nonetheless. So, either I was feeling all of this on my own, or he had other reasons. Who knew what they could even be.

"Okay, maybe some other time." I quickly recovered, flashing a smile so he didn't see how disappointed I was.

"Yeah, definitely some other time." He nodded slowly.

His body was a mass of contradiction; his mouth was saying no but other parts—the heat in his eyes, the tightness in his shoulders—was saying otherwise.

And what did "some other time" mean? Was that a no? Maybe? Later? Could all of it be a timing issue? I was confused because surely he'd felt the connection between us. Didn't he at least want to explore the possibility of what it could be?

"Sounds good. Well, I'm going to get going unless you need me for something else." I tried to ignore the double entendre I hadn't intended.

"Nope, all good here." He started to pack things away. "Thanks for all your help today."

"My pleasure. See you tomorrow." He turned, his attention on packing up and cleaning.

Like nothing had ever happened.

Maybe he was just super sexy, friendly and intense with everyone, and I was just reading more into it. Maybe I needed to sit in on a tattoo with Dallas and see if the same sexual tension sliced through the air. It was either that or there were some funky pheromones in the ink that acted as aphrodisiacs. Honestly, I had no idea.

I guess it was going to be a learning experience on a few different levels, and I was really, really going to need to find another distraction.

JOSH

TWICE.

Motherfucking twice she'd been so close I could almost taste her and didn't.

Oh, I knew why I didn't. Me and my fucking bright ideas about keeping the lines from blurring. I had no one to blame but myself, because from all the signs she was throwing, it seemed like she wanted it too.

I wasn't even sure why I was still fighting it. But I'd made the stupid decision that I was going to wait until she was back at the gallery before I asked her out, and I was going to stick to it. Just so there was no confusion. For one, I didn't need the liability if this all went pear-shaped. Dallas and Tess had been proof enough that you shouldn't mix business with pleasure. And there was another part of me that wondered if this wasn't some knee-jerk reaction and a way to get her confidence back. Not that I was worried this was her version of slumming, but I didn't think I was her usual flavor. What was even worse was that I was totally okay with that. Happy to be used.

So, day after day we did this stupid dance, where we both

seemed to ignore the attraction and pretend like there was nothing going on.

Shit would start with her bringing coffee in the mornings. Big smile, happy to be there, and I'd force myself to take the cup, thank her and not kiss that beautiful mouth.

Then like a pussy, I'd give us the buffer of space for a while. She'd do paperwork or some other job I hadn't asked her to do but had discovered needed doing, and I would work in my room with an erection that could cut glass. It was a great system, so productive and pleasant for everyone, especially for my balls who were threatening to go rogue if they didn't stop being ornamental.

It was usually around lunchtime when I'd delude myself we could be in the same room and none of the sexual tension that had been there earlier would still be there. And every fucking time, like a revelation, there it was. Front and center, waving a pair of semaphore flags SOSing from my dick.

And yet I didn't stop the torture, loving her eyes on me while I worked.

Another thing, while I still hadn't seen the original drawing she'd done of me, she'd taken to drawing in every spare minute. She didn't catch me sneaking a peek but I saw the pages and pages she'd worked on during the last few days.

Flowers, faces, buildings—there didn't seem to be a theme, just restless hands keeping busy while she was at the front counter or streamlining the point of sale program at the desk.

"Water lilies?"

It was noon, so about time to end my room seclusion. She hadn't heard me approach, the temptation to look over her shoulder too great.

"Shit, you scared me." She grabbed at her chest, her tits getting pushed together for an even better view.

S-O—Fuck.

Every single time.

"Let me see." I didn't give her the chance to shove this one down her top as I spun her sketchpad toward me and got a better look.

It was in grey scale, shadow and light the only thing used to hint at depth, texture and color. But what I was looking at was a pond, full of reeds and water lilies; tiny ripples breaking the water's surface.

"Eve, this is fucking beautiful." I picked it up, bringing it closer to inspect. "It feels like I'm looking at a dream." It was both peaceful and surreal.

"That would be because it's Monet." She laughed, "It's not my original work."

"Neither was the Botticelli." I smirked, reminding her that it had been my version of a different master that had made her walk through my door.

"It's actually what prompted the picture." She shrugged, tapping her pencil on the desk. "That, and what you said earlier in the week about just drawing what I see. Not trying to sell it."

"You know this is good, right?" She looked surprised as I placed the sketchbook back in front of her, a smile spreading across her face. "That even though it's not your idea, it's still your skill. Unless you dug up Monet and he's hiding under the desk."

It was so different to the stuff I'd seen online from her exhibit. Literally like night and day. And not just because it was in a different style.

"Nope, there was no grave digging involved." She spun around the page and looked at it herself. "Just me."

"Full disclosure, I Googled you," I admitted, having done so on her suggestion. "And your other stuff . . . well, it wasn't great." I winced, not wanting to cut her down further when so many people had already done that.

"I know," she groaned, throwing her head back and closing her eyes. "That's probably the kindest thing that has been said about it."

"That stuff felt like I was looking at a picture. 2D. It felt like reading a phone book." I saw the flicker of hurt in her eyes when I said the last part. "But this one felt like you captured a memory." I pointed to the page. "It's not just what's there, it's like there is something I can't see as well."

"Well, that's great." She mock laughed, my compliment obviously missing the mark. "Maybe I should be an art teacher or reproduce other people's work. Because unless I can do this with my original pieces, there isn't much point."

"You're missing the *point*." I shook my head. God, she was beautiful but she was so freaking defensive.

"Which is?" The words dripped with sarcasm as her hands moved to her hips, her head tilting to the side.

"There is passion and feeling in this, all the things you said you needed. So it's in there." I tapped the side of her head, both loving and hating the excuse to touch her. "What were you thinking about when you drew this?"

"I wasn't thinking." She rolled her eyes. "You told me not to think about it, so I didn't. I just . . . I don't know, it just happened. I started with water and then before I knew it I was looking at a Monet."

"I'm still a little in shock that you listened." I barked out a laugh. "I know how much you looooooove being told what to do."

"I listen." She elbowed me before adding, "Sometimes." Her lips twitched into a smile.

"Good, then I feel privileged to be one of the few." And wasn't that the truth. Glad something I said had left a mark.

"I thought only Dallas gloated." She smirked folding her arms across her chest, another smile making its appearance.

On cue, the man in question emerged from his room, his Beats slung around his neck.

"I heard my name, we talking about how awesome I am?" He grinned at Eve, the bastard showing her more interest than I liked.

"We were talking about whether you had anything blacker in your wardrobe." Eve bit her lip, eyelashes batting at him playfully. "You always look like you're going to a funeral."

"Maybe I am." He imitated Johnny Cash perfectly, making Eve laugh hysterically.

Great, now they were both flirting with each other, the day couldn't get any worse.

The asshole pulled up a chair and started flipping through Eve's sketchpad. "So, what are your plans for tonight? Nice water lilies."

"Thanks." She gave him an unconvincing smile before addressing his earlier question. "And yeah, I'm meeting up with friends tonight."

"Hot date?"

Dallas's question was the exact same thing I'd been thinking. Of course I'd never ask so maybe having him around wasn't such a bad thing after all.

"God, no," she said quickly, my mood suddenly improving. "Just some of the girls."

He leaned over the counter, chin on his fists as he smirked at her. "Oooooo, I like the sound of this. Can I come?"

"You are not a girl. So, no, sorry." She grimaced, shuffling all her papers into a pile and then packing them away.

I'd never been so glad to hear Eve's company that evening was going to be female.

"Well, there you go, Dallas. Either schedule a sex change or find your own party tonight."

Dallas rolled his eyes, throwing his hands in the air. "Fine, be like that. Josh and I will hang tonight without *you*." He pointed in her direction. "It's going to be so awesome, you'll be jealous."

"Me?" I laughed at Dallas, shaking my head. "Sorry, new phone. Who is this?"

Which just made Eve laugh harder.

I liked the sound of that, liked the way her eyes lit up and how her shoulders relaxed. And I was glad I had been the reason.

"Okay, okay." She wrapped her arms around her sides, struggling to breathe. "I need to order lunch before your next appointments arrive. I found a place that does Korean barbeque down the road, who's game?"

"Hell yeah."

"Absolutely."

Dallas and I both answered at the same time.

She picked up the phone and started dialing. "You boys are so easily pleased."

If she only knew how easily she could please me.

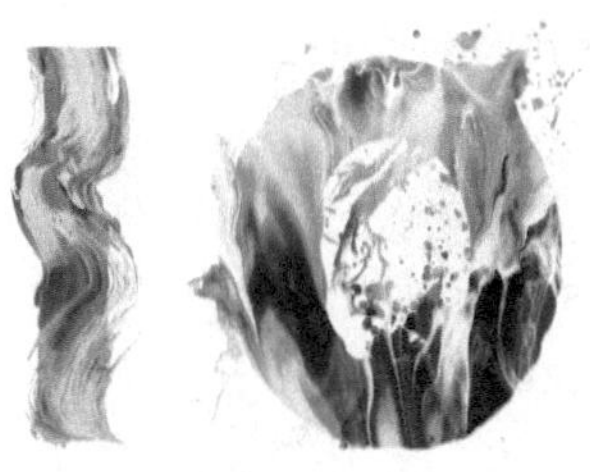

EVE

TIME HAD BOTH RACED AND stood still, which I knew was impossible and yet there was no other way to describe it. But as days had turned into the end of my first full week, I felt like digging in my heels and trying to slow it down. At this rate I'd be back at the gallery in no time and I wasn't ready. Even if I'd wowed Josh with my mindless doodles, it wasn't like I'd done anything real or tangible. It was just messing around.

The other side of that coin, the one where I felt like I was dragging ass? Was that every single minute I spent looking at him and not touching him felt like an eternity. Our thirty-minute lunches where we'd sit and eat, felt like they lasted hours. Thank God Dallas was there most of the time, breaking up the weird staring contest we always seemed to get into.

We didn't even have to be alone. The times where I'd watch him work in his room were the hardest. He'd be so close, and yet so unattainable. Always keeping his distance so there wasn't even the possibility of kissing.

It was driving me crazy.

Which is why I was so thankful when my prearranged Saturday

night arrived. Kitty, Lana, Heather and Kristen had met me as promised. Same bar, same time, same mission. And this time, I was definitely going to get laid.

"All right," Heather set down the shots on the table. "Let's get this party started."

"We're doing shots now?" Lana picked up the glass and sniffed the clear liquid. "Jesus, Heather, tequila? Are you trying to kill me?"

"Oh, stop being such a baby." Kristen swallowed hers without waiting for the rest of us. "I know for a fact you used to do like ten of those in college."

"That's right, college. I'm not twenty-one anymore." She sipped the shot, screwing up her face as the tequila hit her tongue. "Give me a cocktail, I can't drink this shit. It makes me want to gag."

"I'll do it." Kitty took care of Lana's shot before following with her own. "Happy to take one for the team."

"Kitty, you are not allowed to get drunker than me." I swallowed the tequila quickly, the burn traveling down my throat. "It's my turn to be irresponsible and I can't compete with you."

"Then drunk you shall be," Heather insisted, waving over a waitress. "Is this about your lack of sex, the critics or the fact you want to sleep with your hot boss?" She took her shot, slamming her glass on the table. "Just so we are all on the same page."

Stupidly, I confessed I might, *might* think Josh is *hot as fuck*. See what I mean, I was basically a walking hash tag. My friends— whether they would remain so by the end of the night was still debatable—decided to take that part of the conversation and run with it. Totally ignoring how I was still trying to find my groove again, and how I was a little freaked out about returning to the gallery. You know, ignoring the *important* parts of the conversation for the more trivial ones I couldn't control. My need to have Josh's hands all over me, the biggest one.

"I say you go in there early," Kitty weighed in with advice. "Lay on his chair naked."

"Yeah, because he said no to dinner a few days ago but he'll be *totally* cool with sex in his place of business." I shook my head refusing to leave myself so exposed. Both literally and figuratively. There was no way I was drunk enough to even consider it.

"Fine. Then lust him from afar." Kristen laughed, the next round of drinks being delivered to our table. Thankfully they were cocktails this time so Lana didn't complain.

"Ugh, I need to get laid. It's been almost two weeks since I broke up with Oliver. How long have I got where it's no longer rebound sex? I don't want to miss my window."

"I think after a month it's sort of just sex, Eve." Kitty laughed, her timeline freaking me out.

"One month!" I reared back in horror, almost able to hear the tick-tock of the clock breathing down my neck. "Maybe we need to move back to shots, I'm not leaving here until I find someone."

The idea was stupidity at its finest. And one that I could only believe was perpetuated by my growing sexual frustration—I honestly couldn't ever remember being this worked up—and the drinking.

The smart thing would have been to stop the drinking.

But clearly I wasn't interested in being smart.

"What about the other guy?" Heather asked, I'd lost count on how many drinks I'd drunk.

Drinks I'd drunk. Hehe. That was funny.

"Dallas?" I laughed. "There is literally zero sexual attraction to him. I mean, I tried," I admitted, those shots, cocktails and lord knows whatever else I'd consumed clouding my judgment. "But there is not even the tiniest spark."

I'd even tested the theory, imagining peeling off all those black clothes and trying to visualize what that tongue ring would feel like on my clit. All I got was a sore hand and an elusive orgasm. The minute I'd flipped my mental pictures to Josh, I came so hard my legs shook. And like Survivor, the tribe—in this case my body—had spoken. Dallas had to leave the island.

"Let's talk about something else," I groaned, feeling slightly lightheaded and frustrated beyond belief. "I know, Kristen, tell us about the hot mechanic who needs to rebuild your transmission."

That was all it took, deflecting the attention to someone else while I drank more, listening to the girls talk and laugh while I scanned the bar for anyone who would spark my interest. I felt like I was a lioness in the wild, looking for a suitable lion to mate with. It was totally happening tonight, my mind and body perfectly primed for sex without strings. At least, the alcohol haze convinced me so.

"Hey, it's you!" A well-dressed man I didn't recognize pointed at me and smiled. "Fancy meeting you here."

In another time and place, I would have probably been into him. He was good looking, his sandy hair and dark eyes lighting up his handsome face. But there was something about his recognition that sparked caution in me. Like I didn't know him, and was concerned that he knew me. That was not a good thing.

Sadly, my disastrous show had given me the wrong kind of publicity. And while to the average person I was still a nobody who had nice hair, every once in a while I stumbled on someone who "recognized" me. It had been difficult the first days, and one of the reasons I'd been asked to take leave. And on the few days after there had been a couple more occurrences. I'd even had the lady who did my dry cleaning give me her two-dollar's worth. And of all the nights I wanted to fake smile and listen to *helpful* suggestions, tonight wasn't it.

"Sorry, I think you have me confused." I tried to be tactful, slowly turning my body to the side. I leaned in, like I was listening to something being said, but my friends who had been talking and laughing minutes ago, were now silent and staring.

I needed new friends.

Sitting on the end of the booth always had its dangers, being accosted by people you didn't want to speak to, the biggest.

"No, no. It's definitely you." He shook his head, his finger still waving insistently. "I never forget a face."

Oh, he was one of *those*. How lovely for him. *Never forgets a fucking face.* Why every asshole felt they were an expert was beyond me, or why they thought I needed to hear it was even more bewildering. Didn't these people have lives? And seriously how shallow was their existence when they needed to criticize me to inflate their level of self-importance.

I really should have stopped drinking.

"Let me guess." The rudeness I'd been keeping at bay crept in. "You just saw me here, relaxing having a few drinks and thought it would be the perfect time to tell me how ineffective I used the space on the canvas."

He blinked, shocked I'd had the audacity not to sit there and take it. Smile, like a *good girl* and thank him.

"Or was it something else?" I held up my hand, positive I knew where this was going. "How there weren't enough *feelings*, your chest not fluttering like a heart patient with arrhythmia when you looked at my work."

"Eve," Heather coughed, her fist hitting my thigh in the universal sign of shut-the-hell-up.

"No. Screw this." Something inside me splintered and I couldn't make my mouth stop. "All I wanted was to go out, get drunk and get laid. But noooooooooooo." I waved my hands crazily in front of my face. "Even in a fucking bar, on a Saturday night, some asshole in a thirty-five-dollar shirt needs to tell me how he didn't get the *right* kind of hard when he looked at my pieces. So yes, yes it's me, Mr. I-never-forget-a-face. Did I cover everything?"

"Ummmm." He had the decency to be speechless, hopefully embarrassed enough to leave. "I'm Matt." He shifted awkwardly on his feet. "You paid me two hundred dollars last week. You know, for my spot? With Josh?"

Dear God.

Why?

Hadn't I suffered enough?

"Oh, Koi Matt?" The embarrassment all mine as I squinted, his button down and slacks making him look different from what I remembered. "Hiiiiiii."

I was not doing a good job of humaning lately.

When he'd walked into the studio last week he looked completely unremarkable. Wearing jeans, a T-shirt and a baseball cap pulled low, it could have been Ryan Gosling and I wouldn't have known.

I had been too busy paying him off, concerned about getting face time with Josh to pay any real attention.

"I just saw you over here and . . ." He looked over at the open-mouthed audience sitting with me and blinked. "Never mind." His head shook as he made a move to turn.

"No!" I stood up quickly, my feet slightly unsteady as I tried to retain balance. "No, I'm sorry." I felt terrible, my misdirected tirade uncalled for and more importantly unwarranted. "I was a complete bitch. I thought you were someone else. Honestly. Please. Stay. Have a drink with us." Words tumbled out of my mouth hoping one of would be the right one to say.

"Yes, stay," said Kristen, shuffling along in the booth to make room. "Eve needs to make it up to you." Her encouragement probably for less noble reasons than mine.

"Um, I was just going to say hello." He looked at the faces of my friends—their overenthusiastic smiles and bright eyes probably not helping—and then back to the bar where I assumed he'd left a friend or two. "We were about to leave."

"Boooooooo," Heather jeered, her arm waving dismissively. "It's still early. It's not even ten o'clock."

"She's right," I agreed, the bar still not even at capacity. "It's a Saturday night, and I'm sure there is a law about leaving early.

Lana?" I looked to our resident attorney who was probably the most sober.

"It's a relatively unknown administrative code but I believe Eve is correct." She smiled, giving me a nod. "Midnight in Manhattan and not a second before."

"And it would be very irresponsible if we didn't report you." My hands moved over Matt's arms, maybe the night hadn't been a bust. "We'd be accessories and I do not want to go to jail." My smile hopefully looking as coy as I'd intended. "You have friends with you?"

"Yeah," he answered, his hand tapping his thigh nervously like he had when I'd met him.

"And I have friends." My arm waved dramatically to the seated posse of inebriated women I was with. "So, why don't we share our friends."

"I like this plan." Surprisingly it was Kitty this time. "I just met these ladies last week but I can tell you they're awesome. It's a guaranteed good time." She clicked glasses with Kristen and Lana.

"See, verbal testimony." I tugged on his arm. "Besides, you have to let me buy you a drink for being rude or I'll never forgive myself."

Truth be told, while I did feel terrible for the tongue lashing I'd given him, my motives weren't entirely honorable. I still had my quota of rebound sex I needed to fill, and while Matt wouldn't have been my first choice, it was too soon to rule him out entirely. That ticking clock and all. He wasn't Josh-level hot—which we'd established was its own level of insanity—but I didn't cower away in horror either. And who knows? He had friends; maybe one of those guys would fit the fictional brief I'd assembled in my mind of what my one-night stand should be like.

This is what it had come down to.

I was categorizing whether or not I would sleep with someone based on if they *fit the fucking brief*.

My downward spiral had been epic.

"Well, I want you to forgive yourself," he relented, his need to leave slowly easing as he smiled. His eyes settled on me with a look that hinted he was interested. "Let me go get my friends."

MATT WAS CUTE.

Not because I was drunk—I was under no delusion that I wasn't plastered—but because he was being genuinely sweet. His friends were nice too, Darryl and Charlie sandwiching themselves between Kitty and Kristen.

Lana and Heather had husbands—enough said.

And it seemed everyone was enjoying themselves with the new situation. Kitty was lip locked with Darryl and was possibly giving him a hand job—it was too dark to say definitively. And Kristen was showing Charlie how she could tie a cherry stem into a knot with just her tongue. He was suitably impressed, needing to adjust *himself* after she'd performed the feat three times successfully.

Lana and Heather had abandoned us temporarily, the siren's call of the dance floor too great. Heather still hadn't found any rhythm but at this point was to drunk to care what she looked like. Just as well because it wasn't pretty.

And as for me, I was having a blast. The drinking, the laughing, the flirty hands moving under the table—what wasn't to love?

"You thought this shirt only cost thirty-five dollars?" Matt breathed in my ear, my hand tightly around aforementioned shirt as I leaned against him. My words from earlier being tossed back at me. I deserved it. It hadn't been a nice thing to say even if it were true.

"I was annoyed, it is a very nice shirt." My cheek rubbed against the fabric; okay maybe it was a fifty-dollar shirt.

"There were some other interesting things you said." His hand moved suggestively down my back. "About wanting to get drunk and." His eyebrow rose. "Other things."

"Laid, I wanted to get *laid*." I batted my eyes, subtlety no longer in my repertoire. "Is that something you're interested in?"

It was more direct than I was usually, and while I had no problem with casual sex as a theory, it hadn't been my usual go-to. Relationships tend to stop those kinds of things. That, and the fear of someone stealing my credit card and running up twenty thousand dollars on internet porn like the loser did to Phoebe McKay. It happens.

"Yeah, it is something I'm into." Matt lowered his mouth and kissed the corner of my mouth.

It was a chaste kiss.

Something like what you'd give your Aunt Myrtle after she'd stuffed ten dollars into a birthday card and you had to say thanks. She had that mustache that gave you the creeps so always went for the cheek. But she'd turn at the last minute and you'd catch the edge of her lips. THAT is the kind of kiss Matt gave me.

Ewwww.

And now I was thinking about kissing my elderly aunt instead of the guy whose hand was dangerously close to my boob.

"You okay?" Matt asked, his other hand brushing over my cheek when he felt me tense.

"Mm-hmm," I mumbled, too nervous to open my mouth in case I puked.

To be fair, the puking wasn't just kiss related, I think I'd pickled my liver with the amount of alcohol I'd consumed.

"You sure?" He wasn't convinced.

Or maybe I was turning as green as I felt?

Either way, I wasn't a quitter. And if I was going to go through with my casual rebound sex and work out my frustration from hot tattooed Josh, then I needed to give it the good old college try.

Which is when it came to me.

Hot. Tattooed. Josh.

Just thinking his name gave me tingles in all the right places and a tug in my lower gut.

He was gorgeous. Those eyes. The way his hair flopped in front of his eyes toward the end of the day. His big broad shoulders and those freaking amazingly toned arms.

"Mmmmmmmmm," I moaned out loud, shamelessly imagining one guy while I was with another. And yet, I didn't want to stop, desperate to feel good, even if it was with a substitute.

"I want to try that again." I moved my hand onto his thigh, sliding my fingers seductively up toward the fly of his pants. I didn't know if it was *actually* seductive, but that's what I was attempting.

"Really?" He looked surprised, as the corpse he'd been *aunt kissing* seemed to reanimate. "Well, okay then."

He moved in, lowering his head as he attempted round two, but I needed to take the lead. I wasn't sure if he was a bad kisser or it had been first time bad luck, but I couldn't risk another shitty kiss again.

No, I needed to take control and kiss the pants—literally—off him.

The hand that wasn't hovering near his crotch reached up and bunched his fifty-dollar shirt, my fingers gripping the fabric tight.

"Eve." It might have been Matt's voice but I no longer saw him, *Josh's* perfect lips parting as I brought mine crushing down on his.

"I want you," I growled as I thought about those strong heavily inked arms hauling me onto his lap and grabbing my ass. "Grab my ass." It tore out of my throat as I deepened the kiss.

It was dark, noisy and no one was paying attention. Or maybe they were and I didn't care, but I was willing to bet the pair of Jimmy Choos I was wearing I could fuck this guy right here and no one would notice.

Yet, despite my rather explicit instructions, it was a tentative hand that came to rest on my lower back. Fingers skirted at the top of my ass before moving quickly to my hip and that's where they stayed.

There was no hauling onto his lap either.

Extremely disappointing.

"Someone might see." Or something to that effect was mumbled against my mouth. "We could go out to my car? More privacy?"

His car? I wasn't going to make out in someone's car like I was a teenager, the gearshift getting lodged in my ass. No. It needed to happen here, in the dark where I could conjure up images of that wide torso that was probably covered in color.

"No one can see." My grip on his shirt tightened as I looked over at Kitty still fused at the mouth to Darryl. She wasn't even coming up for air let alone worrying about what I was doing. And Kristen and Charlie were noticeably absent, so they'd either gone to join Lana and Heather on the dance floor or were doing a tango of a different kind.

Again, taking control I lifted my butt from the leather of the booth and shifted into his lap. I wanted to straddle him, to grind up against him and soak my panties in a frenzy of dry humping, but I settled for sitting astride him.

"Eve." My name on his lips as I shifted my weight back, feeling his hardening cock beneath my ass.

"Yes." *Josh*, I finished in my head as I imagined him sliding his hand under my dress and pulling aside my panties. "Touch me." A voice so needy and primal came out of my mouth it even surprised me, my core on fire with want.

I felt a hand—oh thank you, Jesus—move closer to the hem of my dress. Encouraged by the fingers working their way up my leg, I deepened the kiss, my tongue exploring every inch of his mouth hoping he wouldn't stop.

Please don't stop, Josh, I'm so close.

"Wow, I can't believe you paid *me* two hundred dollars and I get to kiss *you*, this has been the best two weeks ever."

"Oh my God, stop!" I all but threw the words at him as I scampered off his lap. My world tipping upside down as his words sobered me like ice water hitting my skin.

"What? What?" Matt looked at me confused. He was probably wondering why the woman who'd been riding his cock for the last few minutes, demanding he touch her, had leapt from him like he was on fire.

Why did he have to talk? I had practically gift wrapped myself and then he had to go open his mouth, insinuate that I paid him to kiss me.

Like a prostitute.

Holy shit. Was that what I'd done? Was he kissing me because I'd paid him?

Fuck.

I was so angry.

Mainly at myself, because what the hell was I thinking?

"I'm sorry, Matt," I said, any pretense this was going anywhere shattered. "I think there's a line somewhere, and I'm pretty sure I crossed it."

I didn't bother with any further explanation. I mean, what was the point? I was up for almost anything, but paying for sex—even in the most vague insinuation—I would *never* do.

"Shit," he cursed under his breath, "if I did anything that you didn't want, I'm sorry."

Huh?

He was apologizing to me?

"No, no. You did nothing." *Well other than reminding me there had been a monetary transaction that had made it icky* but I didn't mention that.

Besides, I had been kissing him and pretending it was another guy. My boss. Who I'd met just over a week ago, and had a crazy sexual attraction to. If it were a competition, my sins were far worse.

"Hey, you want another round?" Charlie and Kristen were back, his hand suggestively draped across her shoulder. His head tipped to our empty glasses.

"We're going to go." Kitty had finally taken a breath, her mouth puffy and swollen from her marathon make out session. "Darryl is going to split an Uber with me and share the ride home."

Darryl didn't answer, just wore a silly satisfied smile like he knew the *ride* wasn't going to end at her front door. Kitty was getting lucky. And so was Darryl.

"Yeah, I think I'm going to go too." My head clearer than it had been all night. "It's been a long day."

"Oh, do you want me to come with you?" Kristen looked at Charlie, his face deflating a little at the suggestion. "I can get Heather and Lana, see if they are ready to go?"

"No, stay," I insisted, preferring to make the trip back to my apartment solo. "Have a good time and we'll talk tomorrow. Can you tell the girls I left?" I gathered my clutch and steadied my feet on the floor. Good, I didn't fall down. Awesome, the body was still solid even if the mind was scrambled.

"Of course." Kristen smiled, her eyes floating to Matt to see if he was going to be following me out. He wasn't. That ship had sailed.

"Well, thanks Matt. It's been real." I punched him lightly in the arm, arms that were nowhere near as fabulous as Josh's. "I'll see you around."

Thankfully he spared us both and didn't follow as I turned, allowing me to fight my way out through the crowd and the noise by myself so we didn't have to prolong my suffering.

Two hundred dollars well spent, Eve?

Idiot.

And as the warm night air hit me, I breathed in deep and let my shoulders sag. The relief instant once I'd stepped out of the noise.

This wasn't me.

I was forcing something I wasn't, and maybe that was a bigger problem than my unsuccessful attempt at casual rebound sex.

How long had I been doing it? Following a path because some screwed up part of my brain dictated it was what I needed to do. Were my thoughts so heavily saturated by a need to please that despite me believing I was confident and independent that I'd created this alternate version of myself. A watered down version of someone I thought I should be?

No. This wasn't me. No wonder people thought my art lacked depth—*I* lacked depth. And what was worse is that I hadn't even seen it.

Ugh.

I needed to go home.

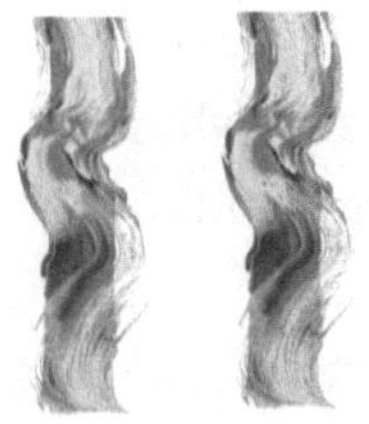

JOSH

I DON'T KNOW WHAT THE hell I was thinking.

Letting Dallas convince me to go out drinking with him didn't usually end well. And last night had been no exception.

The plan had been simple. Have a few beers, maybe sink a few balls at the pool table, and get my mind off the smoking brunette who'd given me a hard-on for the better part of a week and a half. Because if it was one thing I needed, it was a distraction. It was either that or go home and jerk off for hours like a teenager who'd recently discovered porn.

Not to say the jerking off part wasn't going to happen anyway, but I'd hoped to take the edge off at least. So I didn't feel like a complete pervert.

"Oh my God, I'm going to die," Dallas moaned, his hand wrapped in his T-shirt stemming the blood from the cut above his eye.

"You are not going to die," I said for the hundredth time in an hour. "Maybe the next time you decide to be stupid. But, unfortunately it won't be tonight." Unless I choked him out myself, which given the level of drama I was having to deal with, might not be such a reach.

"You are so heartless, man," Dallas hissed, his lip curled up in disgust. "I might have a severed aorta and you're giving me shit. Some friend you are." More mumbling as he shifted in his seat.

"Your aorta is in your heart, Einstein." I laughed, the cut—more like a scratch—was nowhere near anything vital. "You're going to need a few stitches and maybe a tetanus shot, stop being such a baby."

I should have gone home and jerked off.

Instead I was sitting in the ER of Mount Sinai, Queens, with a man who glassed *himself*. He didn't even have the excuse of being in a bar fight, the dumbass juggling beer glasses trying to impress a woman. His ability had been grossly exaggerated, as had his coordination. I still couldn't believe he'd been so freaking stupid.

"That thing just shattered . . . on my head." He reared back in surprise, like he literally couldn't believe it happened. "That can't be right, it must have been faulty. Or had an existing crack."

"Funny thing about glass, Dallas, is it's not meant to be tossed. In a bar. Full of people." I shook my head, still bewildered the statement was necessary. "You're lucky all you hurt was yourself and not that redhead you were trying to impress. I doubt she'd be too pleased if you'd taken out her eye."

It could have been so much worse.

We had been drinking but neither one of us was anywhere close to being drunk, especially me considering I'd driven in. Of course, alcohol never accounted for Dallas's lack in judgment, he had plenty of that even without the booze.

And just a few inches either way, he would have either done more damage to himself or possibly been up for an assault charge. It really had been stupidity at its finest.

"I was all over it, J." He gave me the usual relaxed Dallas reassurance, his hand pulling away from his face to inspect his blood loss. "Some bastard knocked me." Cue the absolute shock, like the possibility hadn't even entered his mind.

Fucking Dallas.

"Because you were in a fucking bar. Full of people." Again I was being Captain Obvious, questioning my own judgment considering I hadn't stepped in to stop it. We needed to get him a minder because I sure as shit didn't want the job.

"Still got the redhead's number though, so it wasn't a total wash." He flashed me a smug grin. "Plus, girls like scars," he added, calmer now the bleeding had slowed and he no longer felt he was dying. "I bet she even offers to kiss it better for me." He took cockiness to a new level.

"Then maybe you should have had *her* drive you here so I could be in bed asleep already." Not even kidding either; it would have probably saved me the headache he was giving me. Both literal and figurative.

"So you could have sex dreams about Eve?" Another cocky smile, his eyebrows dancing like the smug bastard that he was.

Man, I was never going to hear the end of it. Sure, I'd thought about it, I'd imagined it plenty. Most of the week in fact, in every position imaginable. But how could I not? She was smart, beautiful, sassy and most importantly talented. Add in that she was single and I would be insane not to be attracted to her. And I didn't have anything regular happening at the moment, my status matching hers.

But *thinking* was as far as it was ever going to get. At least until she no longer worked for me.

"How many times do I need to tell you?" I met him eye to eye so he knew I was serious. "I'm not going there."

"Tell *yourself*, man," he chuckled, not buying it. "I saw the way you've been looking at her." He sat up a little straighter, nudging me with his shoulder. "And don't think I don't notice all those private talks you two have in your room. With the door closed. Yeah, nothing suspicious about that." He barked out a laugh, his health crisis obviously over as he found a new distraction. Me.

"It is work related." I shook my head; annoyed he'd baited

me. "She sits in while I tattoo. I'm trying to help her see the connection between the person and the art. There are other people in the room with us, what the hell am I going to do? Screw her with an audience?"

Although, given how I'd been feeling lately, I couldn't have given a fuck who was in that room with us. Which is why I made a point of never touching her, even though my hands were dying too.

"Surrrrre." The sarcasm dripped from every letter.

I should have just told him to mind his business and kept my mouth shut.

"Whatever." I pushed myself to my feet, done with the third degree and the conversation. "I'm going to see how much longer it's going to be."

Saturday nights / Sunday mornings in any emergency room were busy. There were kids crying, people moaning in varying degrees of pain and the occasional code being blasted on the PA. And as Dallas's *injury*—and I use that term in the loosest possible way—hadn't been urgent or life threatening, we'd been triaged down the line when two road accidents came in. Which meant we'd been there awhile. And there was no indication how much longer I was going to have to endure before someone threw in a stich, slapped on a Band-Aid and sent us on our way.

Leaving the thorn in my side back on the benches, I wandered over to the nurses' desk with a sea of activity going on around it. Almost everyone was busy, either on a phone, scribbling on a chart or interacting with someone else, but there was one nurse who was sitting by herself at a computer screen. She looked equally as tired as I was, her light brown hair pulled into a ponytail away from her face which was free from makeup. She was pretty, understated, and in another time and place, the kind of girl I might ask out. She also seemed to be a little bored which suited me perfectly, because I was too.

"Hi, I was wondering if you could help me?" I tried not to

come off as an asshole knowing how much shit these poor people had to deal with. "I'm here with my friend." My head tipped in Dallas's direction. "He came in with a cut to the temple, and I was wondering if I can get some drugs?"

"Oh, is he in a lot of pain?" Pretty nurse looked up at me slightly alarmed.

"No, the drugs are for me." I smiled, my new view a lot more impressive than Dallas and his big ass mouth. "To knock me out so I don't have to listen to him anymore."

She laughed, her face animated as she glanced down at the row of seats where Dallas was camped out, shirtless, playing with his phone. "He's next, it shouldn't be too much longer."

"Thanks." I leaned in, checking her out a little closer. She had a nice smile and I wondered if that had been the first time it had been on display tonight. "So that's a no on the drugs?" I grinned back.

Was I fucking flirting? In an emergency room? Maybe I should get my head checked out while I was here too.

"As much as I would love to help you." She leaned over the counter, her *kittens in space* scrubs showing barely a hint of form as she lowered her voice. "I could get into a lot of trouble if I did."

"Thanks anyway." I nodded, giving her a smile. "Wouldn't want to get you into any kind of trouble."

"No problem." She fiddled with an invisible piece of hair, her fingers fidgeting nervously. "I'm Sasha by the way." She held out her hand stopping me from leaving.

"Josh." I reciprocated with a hand of my own, our polite handshake slightly weird given the circumstances.

I had no problem meeting women. I'd had girlfriends, casual hook ups and everything in between. Sometimes they broke it off, sometimes I did and I'd made it through twenty-nine years with no major heartaches or any crazy exes. Actually, I was still friends with most of them. But it had been a while since I felt an immediate strong attraction to anyone, someone who really got my attention. And as much I would have liked for it to be this cute nurse, it wasn't her.

Shaking hands with her didn't give me the same jolt to my balls as when I looked at Eve. Which was a problem because how could I be so fucking interested in a woman I barely knew?

"Dallas Rodgers?" a voice called out from behind me, cutting our little interaction short. Probably for the best, because I was thinking about Eve, and Sasha probably had more important things to do than talk to me.

"That's us," I called out, turning to wink at Sasha. "Enjoy the rest of your shift."

Her cheeks turned an adorable shade of pink as she gave me a little wave, our goodbye over as I turned to walk to the other woman in a white coat.

And just as quickly as Dallas recovered, he had suddenly re-gressed, clutching his eye again. No doubt knocking at death's door.

"Over here, doc." I shook my head, meeting Dallas half way. "Seriously, dude. You're embarrassing."

"Fuck you, Josh," he hissed under his breath. "You had your chance with the nurse, I'm calling dibs on the doctor."

"She's all yours, buddy," I chuckled.

Dallas was good—I'd give him that—but he had a snowball's chance in hell in winning her over.

"I'm Dallas." He gave her his best smile, shirt bunched up against his face in case there was any confusion as to which one of us was the patient.

"I'm Dr. Susan Wilks. Let's get you into an exam room and check out the eye." She gave us both a tight smile and then turned. Her soft-soled shoes barely made any sound as she led us both through double doors toward a curtained off area.

"Take a seat." She nodded to the hospital bed shoved up against the wall, slapping on some gloves while Dallas got situated. "You can stay if you like." She nodded to the chair as her eyes landed on me.

"Thanks, I'm Josh by the way." I sunk into the chair as Dallas shuffled onto the bed.

"Good to meet you," she responded, her smile more business than pleasure. "So how did this happen?" She pulled out a light and started the exam.

Dr. Wilks was probably in her late thirties and had a strong Queens accent. She was polite but you could tell she had probably seen a thing or two in her time in the ER. Which is why when Dallas relayed the story of his mishap, she didn't bat an eye. Nor was she affected by his charm, going through the motions oblivious to the effort he was putting in.

"It needs some stitches but it shouldn't be too big a scar." She thumbed over the cut. "Did you black out at any time?"

"No," Dallas responded, grinning as she moved in closer to inspect.

"Any headaches? Blurred vision? Dizziness? Nausea?" She didn't seem to notice his eyes were on her tits as she flashed the light into them.

"Small headache but nothing else."

"Okay, well." She clicked the light off and scribbled on his chart. "It doesn't look too serious, but a concussion can take a few hours. Do you have someone to stay with you tonight?"

"Are you offering?" Dallas smirked, the bastard having no shame.

"Ignore him." I rolled my eyes. "He's an idiot and sadly, he's always like this. I'll stay with him," I offered, wondering if giving him a concussion might actually be an improvement. I'd happily put my hand up for the opportunity to knock some sense into him.

"Great." She didn't react to his ridiculous request. "Let me suture this up and we can get you on your way." More writing on the chart. "I'll be back in a minute."

"I'll step out and make sure the paperwork is good so we can get out of here." I stood up watching the doctor leave. "I'll wait for you outside."

"Sure." Dallas nodded. "She's not into me anyway, so the quicker we get out of here the better."

"Yeah, better for everyone," I agreed, thankful Dallas had seen the light and was hopefully going to cool the Romeo act.

I made my way back through the double doors to the nurses' desk. Sasha wasn't there which was a shame, but someone else was more than happy to help me out. All very efficient which was great because I was ready for the night/early morning to be over.

My empty bed had never been such a welcomed destination.

"Josh?" A female voice called from behind me as I was assuring the nurse I knew what the signs for concussion were.

"Hey." I whipped around to find a petite blonde with messed up hair and smudged makeup standing behind me.

Well, shit.

If it wasn't the Botticelli back piece, in the flesh.

"Kitty." I smiled, the name and the story of her meeting with Eve not something I was going to forget in a hurry.

"Wow, you remembered!" Her eyes lit up as she sauntered closer. "I've been meaning to call you." She stopped before quickly, adding, "To make another appointment I mean."

Kitty had been a dream to work on. She didn't whine about being in the chair and let's face it, was really nice to look at. I'd had my doubts about her being able to take the amount of ink it was going to take to finish the piece. But she not only sat in my chair for hours, but did it with a smile.

"Sure, would love to do something else for you." I meant it too, she'd been an amazing client. "And thanks for referring me to your friend."

While the thanks was sincere—honestly, I *was* grateful—the opportunity to find out a little more about Eve proved too tempting. It was just talk, right? And it would be rude not to acknowledge the connection. I wasn't interested in being rude.

"Oh, I'm so glad everything worked out with Eve." Her smile exploded across her face. "Isn't she the best? We're kind of new friends, I haven't known her for long, but I just love her."

Yeah, I knew the details unfortunately. It takes a special kind of woman who could be friends with her ex-boyfriend's *whatever*. Still, who was I to judge? And in a weird kind of way, I'd somehow benefitted, Eve seeking me out. Kudos to the piece of shit who couldn't keep his dick in his pants.

"Well that's great." I grinned, the secret knowledge staying under wraps. "Are you hurt?" The venue for the conversation overlooked initially, but it was hard to ignore we were in a hospital.

"Me?" She shook her head, smiling. "Oh, no. The guy I was with." She chewed on her bottom lip, her eyes darting either side of her as she leaned in to whisper. "We got a little carried away with ass play . . ." She trailed off. "Something got stuck."

And that was waaaaaaaaaaaaaay more than I needed to hear.

Ever.

Fuck.

Who even says that?

"Wow," I coughed out, not sure how to respond. *I'm sorry? That blows?* Nothing seemed to fit. Literally. Now I couldn't stop thinking about it. "Unfortunate," was what I eventually went with, trying not to laugh.

"Yeah, it really was." She sighed wistfully, her shoulders giving a little shrug. "Anyway, I'm just heading home. He doesn't want me to stay." She gave another shrug before looking me up and down. "Are you sick?"

"Not me, Dallas." I wasn't sure if she remembered him from the shop, but calling him dumbass, while more accurate, wouldn't have been helpful.

"Poor Dallas, is he okay?" Her face morphed, eyes clouding with concern.

I swear I didn't know which one of them was worse. Kitty—who was more preoccupied with Dallas than the guy she'd come in with and who-knows-what stuck up his ass. Or Dallas—who had a legion of dedicated fans despite no claim to fame. Unless you counted stupidity, and then he was the motherfucking king.

"Nothing major, he should be done soon." I smiled, not feeling the need to elaborate. Although I was tempted to mention he had something up his ass too, surely driving him to the hospital and the hand holding gave me permission to have a little fun with it.

"Good, I'm glad everyone is okay." She looked genuinely re-lived. "Do you want to split an Uber?" Her voice hopeful.

"Thanks, but I have my car." I watched her smile slip at the rejection of her offer. "I can give you a ride if you don't mind waiting until we're done."

Usually I didn't offer rides to random women, especially not at two in the morning. But Kitty had been a good customer and I vaguely remembered her address not being too far from my house anyway. Besides, it would mean Dallas would be distracted on the ride home and I wouldn't have to listen to his complaining. Plus, apparently I had a thing for a damsel in distress—Dallas's words, not mine—so I wouldn't feel right about not seeing her home safely.

It had absolutely zero to do with the time in the car giving me an in to find out more about Eve. Hadn't even crossed my mind.

Not.

One.

Bit.

"You would?" Her eyes shot to mine, smile coming back full force. "That's so nice of you; I would love one. Are you sure you don't mind?"

"No problem at all. You're in Astoria, right?"

"Yes, sure am, right near Astoria Park."

That was like ten minutes away at that time of the morning, hardly any time to get anything solid. Still, better than no time and it really wasn't that far out of my way.

"I'm in Long Island City, not far from the shop." I rationalized dropping Dallas off first but that would probably raise a few too many questions. "I can take you home and then head to my place. Dallas needs to crash at mine so I can keep an eye on him."

"That sounds great." Her hand reached out and gave my arm a squeeze. "Thank you so much."

"Happy to do it."

Well, things just got more interesting.

We both took a seat and parked it while we waited. Figured I might as well use the time here to my advantage since the drive wasn't going to be long.

"So, big night?" Shit. I immediately regretted asking and prayed she didn't elaborate on how and what had been big.

"We were out drinking in Midtown." She thankfully went with the PG version, hopefully keeping away from the evening's eventful finale. "Eve invited me out with some of her friends."

And that didn't take too long at all.

I knew Eve was planning on going out with her friends, she'd told us as much at lunch. But she hadn't named names so I was guessing as to whether Kitty had been on the invite list. Of course after seeing her here, I'd been hopeful.

"Really?" I tipped my head in mock surprise. "Well, that sounds like fun."

"Oh, it so was. We all got hammered." Kitty laughed. "Then this guy—Matt—came up to talk to her." Another chuckle. "She totally lost her mind at him, I mean, really lost her mind. But then she apologized, and she really was sorry. Then she made out with him, so I think he forgave her."

It was like someone threw some words in a blender and turned it on without putting the lid back on.

"She yelled at a guy and then made out with him?" I clarified, irrationally annoyed. The thought of her kissing some other dude made my blood boil.

I wasn't even sure why, I had no fucking right to have an opinion either way. She could see, argue, and kiss, whoever she wanted. Clearly it was the sleep deprivation making me antsy because there could be no other reason why my fists were clenched.

"Yeah, it was a misunderstanding though. He was some guy from your shop that she paid off or something, but she thought he was trying to complain about her exhibition." She threw her hands in the air. "It's all good now though."

Wait.

Matt, Matt? The guy who I was supposed to tattoo the day she walked in?

She made out with fucking Matt from *my* shop?

What. The. Actual. Fuck?

It wasn't bad enough she'd paid this dude two hundred dollars, but she had to kiss him too? What was that for? A thank you card when she ran out of fucking stationery.

"Sounds like I should have been out with you guys." My jaw so tight it hurt. "My night wasn't half as fun."

"Oh, you should come out with us next time." Kitty grabbed my thigh, her hand lifting quickly when she realized what she was doing. "I would love that."

"Maybe next time." Yeah, maybe not. Especially not if I was going to have to watch Eve make out with random dudes. What was she even thinking?

I knew I was acting like a jerk—being angry for no good reason—and I needed to stop. After all, what was she supposed to do? She was young, single, beautiful, so of course men would be interested and vice versa. She wasn't a freaking mind reader, and had no idea of my intentions. Didn't have a clue I was waiting until she went back to her job at the gallery before I gave myself the green light to ask her out. Assuming she was interested. And I had been pretty clear that I wasn't making a move.

I was still simmering, trying to rationalize my own stupidity when Dallas finally emerged, a small butterfly bandage across his upper right eye and a look of bewilderment on his face. I'd assumed it was the newly acquired company that had him looking at me so strangely, but it could have easily been the lidocaine.

"You ready to go?" My ass rose out of my seat. "We're going to give Kitty a ride home."

"Say what?" His eyes narrowed. "You're going to ride her *kitty?*"

Ordinarily I would have smacked him across the head and reminded him to watch his mouth. I didn't even care about the possible head injury. But my mind was still mulling over Eve playing tonsil hockey with Matt and how that ended. If Kitty had gone home with someone, it stood to reason Eve might have done the same. And I'm sure that cocksucker Matt would have just jumped at the chance. Dallas was right about him, he would have totally been a pussy in the chair. She could do so much better.

"Nooooo." Kitty giggled, her cheeks getting pink. "My *name* is Kitty, don't you remember me, Dallas?"

"Head trauma. Don't take it personally," I coughed out, my mind still elsewhere.

"Ohhhhhhhh Kitty." Dallas smiled, and I knew he still had no idea who she was. "Of course I remember you." He sidled up to her, his eyes falling to her cleavage.

She giggled, squeezing her tits together to give him a better view.

Clueless.

Both of them.

"Well if everyone's set, we should make tracks. I would like to see my bed before Monday." My mood had gone from bad to worse.

"Yep, good to go." Dallas grinned, outstretching his arm. "Ladies first." Gesturing to the door.

And it wasn't about manners either, it was so he could check her out from behind.

"Oh, you are both so nice." Kitty smiled as she twisted, hips swaying toward the exit.

"Careful, D," I whispered under my breath when Kitty was just out of earshot. "The last guy she was with ended up in the ER with something lodged up his ass. Just so you know, that happens to you, you're on your own."

"It's just been the week for hot crazy chicks it seems." Grin spread across his face. "I say we go with it."

Yeah.

Or maybe we don't.

EVE

I HAD SPENT TWO DAYS in a sea of paper, paint and charcoal.

No, I hadn't set fire to my apartment, but I had decided to get back to basics and sketching had been my first love.

It hadn't been pretty on Sunday. I was hungover and still feeling pretty nasty about kissing Matt, it seriously had been a new low for me. I had been so hung up on meeting some arbitrary timeline for a stupid fling, I'd forgotten why I was in this mess in the first place.

No, it wasn't because my boyfriend cheated on me. And it wasn't because I had a strong attraction to Josh. Those were by-products of the disarray in my life. And while yes, I wanted Josh to kiss me and possibly do every other dirty thought I could imagine, it wouldn't change things for me. And as much as my hormones were screaming for the release, all of that would have to wait. Besides, I'd done almost everything but throw myself at him and he still hadn't cracked. There was the very real possibility he wasn't interested.

I didn't need a man; I needed an overhaul.

But if nothing else, it was one of the many wake-up calls I'd received over the past week. All turning me back to the direction

I needed to be. Finding my passion.

Like a mad scientist, my hand moved over the pages, fluctuating between simple doodles to full-blown shaded portraits. I forgot to eat, to sleep, to shower. And the more covered in black smudges my face and body became, the more energized I felt. The light bulb had finally been turned on.

Tuesday couldn't come soon enough, I was itching to get back to the studio and soak up some more inspiration. And sure, possibly some of the excitement was seeing Josh and to share it with him. And maybe partly because his face had been one of my favorite things to sketch. My interest was purely platonic and artistic. At least that was the lie I told myself and even if he wasn't interested in me, we could still be friends.

It had been weird getting to the shop a little after nine with coffees in my hand and finding the door still locked and the lights off. Josh was always there early. No matter what time I arrived, he always looked like he'd already been there for hours. So much so that I assumed sometimes he must have spent the night on that fancy chair like he joked he had in the past. So as it got closer to ten, I was contemplating calling the police, concerned that he was still a no show.

He must have slept in, I rationalized. Or had car trouble. Or a family emergency. Any one of those, reasons for him to be late. Surely nothing bad had happened, I was just acting paranoid.

"Hey!" I jumped to my feet the minute I saw him walking toward the door. I was so grateful he was okay, I forgot myself and threw my arms around him. "Hey," I repeated lamely, not able to say all the things that were really going on in my mind. Most importantly it wasn't about the artwork I had initially wanted to show him.

"Hey." He gave me a tight smile, his arms hanging loosely by his side while mine were around him. The hug was entirely one-sided.

Quickly, I dropped my arms, slightly embarrassed about my initial reaction. And in an effort to keep my hands from getting into more trouble, I picked up the tray of coffees that were now probably cold sitting by my feet. My smile no doubt fake, as I watched him twisting his key in the lock to open the door.

"Hope you haven't been waiting long, I slept in and I wasn't sure you were going to be back." He didn't wait for my response, pushing open the door and tipping his head in the direction for me to go through first.

"Why wouldn't I have come back?" I half laughed, not sure if he was kidding as I entered the shop. And why was he acting so weird? "I still haven't fixed the supply closest yet, so at the very least I have to do that."

It had been our running joke, the menial job always getting pushed back for something I deemed more important. And usually it made him laugh, today it seemed he'd lost more than just his sense of humor.

"Hmm." He made a non-committal grunt, tossing the keys behind the counter and opened his appointment log. Me and the coffee I was holding, ignored.

"Is everything okay?" I asked, feeling a strange vibe in the room as I lowered the coffees onto the counter. "You seem a little off."

The lack of smile—not counting the halfhearted effort at the door—was my first red flag. His beautiful warm smile had been the first thing I'd noticed about him when we first met. Plus he would barely look at me, flicking on lights and keeping busy—anything other than make eye contact. The air was definitely frosty for July, and it had *nothing* to do with the outside temperature.

"Nope, just a busy weekend. Tired." He didn't look up, clicking on the computer.

Something was off and I didn't know if it was me, or the situation, or something else. Things had been fine when I left him on Saturday afternoon. Well as fine as it could be if you didn't count the crazy sexual tension.

We had tried something new for lunch, laughed a lot, and had a productive afternoon. Nothing that could lead me to believe his current mood had anything to do with me. Maybe he was just tired, he had been putting in a lot of hours lately.

"Well I can relate." I tried to be cheerful, convincing myself that I was imagining things. "I hardly got any sleep this weekend either." I couldn't wait to show him all my work. "Not that I'm complaining, I haven't had that much fun in a long time."

"Good, happy for you." Another fake smile, and this time I *knew* it was bullshit, his eyes narrowing in distaste. "If you want to get started on the supply closet, I'm going to head back to my room and get set up. Let me know when my eleven o'clock arrives." He was so cold and completely disengaged as he turned to walk away.

"Josh, have I done something wrong?" I refused to let it go, unable to handle the way he was looking at me any longer. He stopped, keeping his back to me as I added, "You seem mad at me, which seems ridiculous because I haven't seen you in two days."

I strained my memory, trying to remember anything that could explain why he was acting so weird. If I'd done or said anything offensive before I'd left on Saturday night. Or if I'd accidentally forgotten to do something, put stock away or return a phone call—anything that may have upset him.

But nope.

I came up with nothing.

"If there's something bothering you, I'd really just wish you'd say." My hand moved to his arm, pulling him, slightly hoping he would turn around. "I thought we were friends."

"Look." He whipped around, the action making my hand drop from him immediately. "I wasn't going to say anything, but since you've brought it up, I figured maybe I should."

He didn't yell, but there was no warmth to his voice, like he was trying to hold himself back from saying something.

"Okay, what is it?" I wondered what I could have possibly done to warrant his reaction, and deep down hating the way he was looking at me.

"You paying my client Matt in the foyer, that was one thing." He shoved his hands in his pockets, his eyes staying on me. "I don't care how you spend your cash or what floats your boat. But I told you straight up that I didn't appreciate it from a business standpoint, but obviously he took the money so there's not much point being pissed about it."

"O-kay . . ." He was bringing up Matt? The guy I had coincidentally just seen on Saturday night and had picked *now* to be mad about it? The timing seemed too strange not to be intentional.

"But what I am not cool with, is you dating customers. It's nothing personal. I have the same set of rules for Dallas. And I probably should have mentioned it upfront, but I honestly didn't think it would be an issue. Anyway, if you can make sure you don't cross that line while you're still working here, that would be great. Thanks."

What?

What!

Did he have me under surveillance? How could he even know I'd hooked up with Matt? I mean, the club had been dark, so who knows who was there to see. Surely I wasn't that drunk and I would have noticed if he'd been in the shadows watching my sorry attempt at casual sex. It's not like my body didn't go off like a fire alarm whenever he was in a two-mile radius; he wasn't easy to ignore. And if he had seen me, why wouldn't he have said something there? At the club. Instead of bringing it up now.

"I'm not dating Matt." I laughed at the absurdity of it all. I could barely stomach kissing him without conjuring up some hot stand-in—which ironically had been him—so the idea of dating him obviously ridiculous.

"Whatever, Eve." My reaction seemed to annoy him further.

"Your personal life isn't my business." His shoulders squared off as he breathed out. "I'm just saying, if someone walks through those front doors, they aren't someone you should consider for extra curricular activities. Not until after they are done here."

Was he serious? Surely this was some kind of stupid joke.

"I already told you, I'm not dating Matt." I tried again to explain, hoping to reassure him that whatever he thought he knew, he was wrong. "I saw him on Saturday, briefly, but that's it. It was a pure coincidence, in fact he approached me and I wasn't even nice to him."

Besides the obvious—me not addressing how he knew—his inference was starting to bug me a little. Sure, it would have been poor judgment to sleep with someone I could potentially see at the shop, but it wasn't a stoneable offense. I was temporary, and chances are Matt and I would never even see each other in a professional sense. I doubted he would even be back. He seemed way too upset about something so minor.

"I'm sure if I ask *him*, he'd say different," he baited, not so subtly hinting he knew more than he was letting on.

"Did he say something to you? How do you even know I saw him?" I asked, wondering if Matt had decided that because I'd left him with a case of blue balls he would be vindictive and tell my boss some bullshit as payback.

It seemed unlikely, but nothing about this whole situation seemed to make sense, so I couldn't rule anything out. Besides, this had stopped being comical and ridiculous and was now starting to feel a little offensive.

"It doesn't matter what was said or how I know." He met my eyes for the first time, their lack of warmth startling. "If you want to work here, you follow the rules." He looked away, avoiding me again. "There aren't many, so it shouldn't be hard. If you want to argue then you know where the door is. I've got to get set up."

He turned, his heavy boots echoing off the floor as he walked to his room.

What just happened?

Well, *now* I was pissed.

There was a difference between telling me he didn't condone employee / customer relations—something well within his rights—and making me feel cheap and insignificant. Which is exactly what he did when he spoke to me like that.

If you want to argue then you know where the door is?

Yeah, I did and I'd slam it on his rude judgmental ass when I told him to go to hell. No one spoke to me like that.

"Are you kidding me right now?" I yelled at him, not giving a shit about his need to set up or his general bad mood. "You think it's okay to speak to me like that and then dismiss me?" I ran after him, storming into his room like a lunatic. "Am I supposed to kowtow for you too? Get on my knees and kiss your fucking feet?" I waved my hands in the air wildly in case he hadn't gotten my point. "You, Josh Logan, are an asshole."

It clearly struck a nerve. Probably more than it should have, but I had been at my limit for people making snap judgments about me and believing they had me all figured out. I was done being dismissed, written off based on bullshit and inaccurate perceptions.

He took a step back, his eyes popping open like he wasn't sure he'd heard me correctly. "What did you say?"

"I said," I didn't bother lowering my voice, no longer possessing the capacity to control my volume or my temper. "You," I shoved my finger right into that firm, muscular chest of his, "are an asshole."

I sneered it.

Like a villain in a Disney movie. Because let's face it, considering the size difference, the idea of me trying to be intimidating was laughable.

But I didn't care. No, logic had no place here. And I was so fired up on adrenaline and agitation that I was liable to scratch his eyes out like a raccoon.

"Did you sleep with him?" he asked, his dark pupils almost filling the perfect cerulean blue iris. Ugh, those freaking eyes. "Saturday night, I know that you kissed him." He moved closer, his body coiled tight like a spring. "How far did it get?"

"Not that it's any of your business." My hands pushed against his chest. Mmm. Those pecs were waaaay nicer than I'd imagined, my brain reminding my hands I was too angry to enjoy them. "But no, I didn't sleep with him. I couldn't even kiss him until I imagined it was you, and I almost threw up in his lap."

I tossed caution to the wind as I spewed out the truth. He wanted to know what happened, if I'd had sex with Matt? Fine, then he could hear the whole truth no matter how uncomfortable it made him. Who cared anyway? I doubted after our "little" outburst I'd still be working here tomorrow.

"You imagined he was me?" His voice low, a rumble.

"Yes, because in case you're too freaking blind to notice." I didn't bother sugar coating it, keeping my eyes locked on his. I was no longer embarrassed or concerned about what he thought. "I wanted it to be *you*, to kiss *you*."

His feet were lightning quick, closing the few feet that separated us until he was on me. *On me.* His mouth, his hands, his body—pressed against me while my brain tried to catch up.

Kissing me.

Touching me.

His lips pried mine apart as his tongue sought refuge in my mouth and there wasn't a chance I wanted it to stop.

"Josh." My hands gripped the back of his T-shirt, clawing at him to get closer. I needed more—more contact, more lips, more him—the reality so much better than what I'd imagined. His mouth, hungry for mine.

"Fuck," he hissed, his hands grabbing my ass as he lifted me off my feet. The hard ridge of his cock hit me between my legs as he pinned me against him.

"Yes, God, yes," I moaned, rubbing my body to seek more friction.

I tried to think, to work out what was happening and what it all meant, but my thoughts stalled as my body took over. Thinking was for losers, and right now I was having the kiss of my freaking life.

"I've wanted to do that for so long," he moaned against my mouth, his slipping down to my neck as he sucked on my skin. "Wanted to see what you tasted like."

"Then why didn't you?" My fingers dug into his back, grazing him as they traveled down toward his ass.

Was screwing him so soon out of the question? It wasn't like I'd just met him; it was totally fine.

"Work for me. Didn't. Take advantage. Trying. Right thing." His words not making sentences as he tried to talk but gave up in favor of using his mouth for other purposes.

Oh, and how wonderful that other purpose was. His lips and mouth were demanding, moving all over me in what felt like a calculated dance of domination.

"I want to touch you." My hand reached out without waiting for permission, palming his cock as his hand cupped my breast.

"Eve," he warned, my fingers working his length. "You keep doing that and I'm going to blow my load in my jeans."

"I don't want to stop." My breasts rubbed against his chest, trying to remember what time his first appointment was and how much time it gave us.

"We need to stop." His hand moved on top of mine, not giving me a choice other than to freeze. "While I still can."

His heavy breathing matched mine, our chests heaving as we stood still. It wasn't easy, not when my hands were still on him and I could feel how hard I'd made him.

"Does this mean you won't kiss me again later?"

I needed to know if the stop was permanent, if he was going to pretend it didn't happen. Because I will tell you right now, that would not fly.

"The reason I didn't want to start is because I knew I wouldn't be able to stop." He thumbed over my lips, his mouth curving at the edge. "So, yeah, I am going to be kissing you later. That okay with you?"

"Yes." I grinned, wanting to ask how soon *later* was. "Maybe we can try without the yelling at the start."

Not that I cared about it now. If the end result required the verbal gymnastics at the start, then I would happily raise my voice again.

"Yeah, about that." His hand moved to the back of his neck, rubbing it as he took a step back, giving me space I hadn't asked for. Most of all, space I didn't want.

"Not my finest moment." He gave me a tight smile. "But I've just spent the last couple of days thinking about you and Matt and it was driving me crazy. I shouldn't have spoken to you like that though, that was out of line."

"You were jealous? Of Matt?" A silent thrill ran through me, it hadn't been my intention but I was sort of glad I hadn't been the only one suffering.

"Of course I was. He got to kiss you and I didn't, it pissed me off." His thumb traced along the edge of my jaw. "Dallas is probably going to have to do his tattoo if he ever comes back. I don't trust myself with a machine in my hand." His lips twisted into a smirk.

"So firstly, how did you even know about that?" The mystery yet to be explained. "And if you were so worried about it why didn't you call me? You have my number." Which might have meant we came to this realization sooner. Like possibly on the weekend, where we could have done something about it.

"I saw Kitty in the ER on Sunday morning, more like, she

saw me. She told she'd been out drinking with you and that you'd kissed Matt. She'd said some other stuff but that's what stuck out the most."

"Waaaaaaaaaaaaaiiiiittttt a minute!" I held my hands up, pausing a beat to understand what he had said. That first kiss had been pretty amazing so maybe I was hearing things too. "*You* were in the hospital? And Kitty was in the hospital? Why didn't I know any of this?"

He didn't look sick or injured and the parts I'd touched felt fine. And Kitty? She'd left just before I had, splitting an Uber with whatever his name was, which I was positive was going to result in sex. I should have checked on her, I was a shitty friend. Although she had sucked my boyfriend's penis, so I obviously had some leeway on the shitty friend criteria.

"I'm fine." He outstretched his arms, displaying the *fine* in case I wasn't convinced. "Dallas was an idiot at the bar and ended up cutting himself on a beer glass. He got a couple of stitches, which is why he hasn't waltzed in this morning."

Honestly, I hadn't noticed Dallas's absence. Josh had been late and then acting weird and that was where my attention had been directed. Of course then it was all about the kissing and once again, he hadn't been a priority. We had already established I wasn't thinking. Although the amount of times he'd interrupted an almost kiss between Josh and I, I had to wonder if he'd been here if it even would have happened.

"And Kitty?" The other part of the puzzle still not making sense.

"She was there with the guy she'd left the bar with." He winced like he suddenly remembered her reason for being there. "Trust me, you don't want to know why he was there, but suffice to say she was fine, and he was probably going to be singing high notes for a while." He leaned in closer. "I don't hold up much hope for their future, both her and Dallas were flirting with each other when I drove her home."

"So, let me get this straight." The importance of articulating this out loud understated because . . . It sounded crazy. "You're both in an emergency room but neither of you are hurt, and you talk about me?"

I wasn't sure if that inflated my ego—that Josh was obviously thinking about me so much that he hadn't been able to help but talk about me—yeah, that probably wasn't it. Or if it made me incredibly tragic, that my name and ER were obviously synonymous because I was such a disaster.

"I may have steered the conversation in that direction." He didn't even try to hide his grin. "Don't look so shocked, Eve. I've been trying to be good but I'm not dead. I was hoping that after you left the shop, we might go out."

"You know I've been flirting with you, right?" It hadn't been my best work but it had been an effort nonetheless. "And you were going to wait?"

"I didn't say it was a good plan." Josh laughed. "I just said it was *the* plan."

Thank God, the *plan* had other ideas. I doubted I would have lasted another couple of weeks.

"So, how's Dallas now?" I looked around, no inconvenient interruption breaking up our connection. The man whose head injury contributed to the catalyst was still missing in action.

"Milking it for all it's worth," he groaned. "He is fine, but he needs a day or two. To recover."

"Well, that's good I guess."

Was it wrong that I was too concerned about what was happening with Josh and I to care about Dallas's wellbeing? I know I asked, but once I'd heard he was fine, it wasn't a big priority for me. I know, I know, I am a terrible, selfish person. But Josh had kissed me, I couldn't help it if I'd lost the ability to think straight.

"I've got someone coming in soon." He moved in closer,

cupping my face with his hands. "And then after today is over, I'm taking you out on a date." He lowered his lips and kissed me softly.

"Just like that, you're not even going to ask me?" My fake annoyance completely betrayed by my huge grin. "I don't know, Josh. Maybe I have plans."

"If you do, you'll cancel them." Another kiss, not as soft and hell of a lot sexier than the first. "We have unresolved issues we need to deal with, and they can't wait."

"I don't have plans," I admitted, wanting nothing more than spending time alone with him.

"Good, makes it easier." Another kiss, his strong arms locking around me. "Eve." He pulled his lips from mine.

"Yes?" I debated not answering, hoping he'd kiss me again.

"Keeping my hands off you today isn't going to be easy, try not to torture me too much." His eyes glanced down to my low neckline, the swell of my breasts peeking out from under.

"I think you deserve a little punishment." I took a step, allowing him to get the full effect. My wardrobe choice had been completely accidental, but I wasn't above using it to my advantage.

"I suppose I do deserve it. I'll look forward to the exquisite agony."

JOSH

SO MUCH FOR NOT KISSING her.

I didn't even regret it, wanting to immediately do it again. The only thing stopping me was knowing we weren't going to be alone for much longer, and I would have considered cancelling every appointment I had for the day, if Dallas hadn't been off sick.

Coming home after dropping off Kitty had been bullshit. Dallas complained his head hurt—no fucking surprise there—so I pretended I was a good friend and let him hang out in my apartment. Truth was, it had less to do with him and more to do with me not wanting to be alone with my own thoughts.

Her.

Him.

Together.

Doing fuck knows what.

The shit rolled around in my head and my gut for two days, knowing I would have to eventually see her. And then when I did, she would be all smiley and satisfied. It stoked an irrational anger in me I couldn't contain. Because even though she wasn't with me, I didn't want her with anyone else. I didn't even care that it didn't make sense.

Which is why I acted like an asshole.

Which is *also* why the minute she'd mentioned she'd needed to picture me just to kiss him, I snapped. She wasn't going to have to do that mental substitution ever again. I was going to let her know exactly how it felt.

"I'll reschedule Dallas's appointments for the day." Her lips were still puffy, the pink gloss she'd been wearing no longer on them. "Will he be back tomorrow?"

"Yeah, he'll be back tomorrow." I nodded, struggling with not kissing her again. It hadn't been enough the first time, holding out for later was going to be a challenge.

"Great, I'll go get started." Her smile hinted she knew exactly what was on my mind. "And I'll send in your appointment when they get here." She hip swayed her ass out of my room.

Fuck.

Between being annoyed, all up in my own head and Dallas's company, I hadn't jerked off since Friday.

It was going to be a long day.

Lucky for me, business was good and the day was out of control busy, which meant there would be limited time to get into trouble.

And while I worked, Eve finally took care of the supply closest, which not only meant it was easier to find shit in there but she was too busy to sit in on any sessions in the afternoon.

Two birds.

One stone.

And I was saved from the perpetual hard-on I usually had whenever she was in the room.

"What do you think?" I watched as Jack checked out the new addition to his sleeve.

"Seriously, Josh. Not sure how you do it." He moved and twisted his forearm, the space looking like flesh had been torn, revealing an exoskeleton underneath. "This is seriously badass."

"Glad you like it." I admired my handiwork, happy to have another satisfied client. "If you want to do the other side, it will have to wait a few months. We're kind of booked."

"Yeah, I heard," Jack laughed, "local celebrities now."

"I'm just doing my thing, I can't help some asshole showed up with a camera one day and all of sudden everyone knows about it." I finished putting on the bandage to cover up his new piece. "Not that I'm complaining, it's great but yeah, not a lot of down time."

"So, who's the new Tess?" Jack's head tipped to the door, the smirk on his face meant he was talking about Eve. "New *and* improved I might add."

Irrationally it annoyed me he'd noticed, and that his interest in her was more than her job description. He wasn't wrong about her though, and it was more than just her looks.

Eve was stunning; anyone with a pair of eyes could see that. But she was also smart and confident, and even though I had just started to see it, she was incredibly talented as well.

"Eve isn't the new Tess," I corrected him, reminding myself it was both stupid and unnecessary to get territorial. "She's just here filling in for a few weeks. She's actually an artist in her own right."

"Really, she tattoos?" His eyebrows shot up his forehead, and if I wasn't wrong, looked a little more interested.

"Not yet, but you never know." The idea of Eve holding one of my machines and permanently inking me with one of her designs, turning me on more than should be normal. "She's more traditional, the pencil and paper kind."

"Is she . . ." He bent his head, lowering his voice. "Single?"

Of course *that* would be his next question. And how in the hell was I supposed to answer that. If I said yes, he would no doubt try his luck on the way out. I was fairly confident he wouldn't be successful, but there were no guarantees considering it had been only a few hours since I'd kissed Eve for the first time. We hadn't even worked out what the hell we were doing. So, did I roll the dice and hope she turned him down? Or did I lie? Tell him that she was taken and effectively pissing on her like a fire hydrant.

"Nope, she's got a boyfriend."

Lying it was.

"Well, that sucks." He stood up, running his hand along the bandage I'd just finished. "Still, lucky guy, huh?"

"Yeah, he is."

"Hey, how are we doing in here?" The lady in question poked her head into the room, her hand holding the door she'd just opened. "Oh, it's already wrapped?" Her smile dropped when she saw Jack's arm already covered.

"Yep, we're just finishing up." I eased back, giving myself a chance to look at her. I didn't think I'd ever get sick of it. She was really, really beautiful.

"It looked good, Josh did a great job." Jack smiled, probably loving the attention. "I'll email a photo later if you want."

"I would love that, then I can add it to the wall in the foyer." Eve stepped a little further into the doorway. "Do you want me to finish up with Jack?" Her beautiful light brown eyes on me. "Everything else has been done for the day."

Instinct was to tell her no. That I would handle Jack, process his payment and walk him out. That would also stop that stupid grin he had on his face, which I knew was there because of her. But I didn't want to raise any red flags or drag this out longer than it needed to be. Besides, Jack might be all smiles but he didn't seem like the kind of guy to go after a girl who was off limits. At least, I didn't think so.

"Sure, I'm just going to pack up. That would be great, Eve."

Jack jumped up out of his chair like a dog looking for his treat, tossing a "catch you later, Josh," over his shoulder as he followed Eve down the hall.

Predictable.

Pushing it out of my mind, I packed up my working area and listened to their voices carrying down the hall. I heard Eve's laugh and murmuring, but nothing I could make out. And then it stopped, the click of the deadlock being engaged as footsteps returned back to my room.

"How are you doing in here?" She moved slowly, pulling her hair out of the ponytail it had been tied in all day. "Almost ready to leave?"

I stopped what I was doing and met her half way. "Almost. You have somewhere you need to be?"

"Hot date." She slung her arms around my neck and the tension in my muscles bled out. It felt so natural, I had to remind myself it was new.

"Really. Do you think your hot date will mind if I kiss you?" I cocked my head to the side, pulling her in closer.

I didn't wait for an answer, putting my lips where they'd been dying to go all day, holding her while I tasted her.

She kissed me back, her hands raking through my hair. "He would definitely mind."

"God, it's been killing me." My mouth begrudgingly moved from hers. "I haven't touched you all day."

"Would you like me to remind you that you used to get through all your days without touching me?" She fluttered her eyelashes, acting cute.

My hand dropped a soft whack on her ass. "Wiseass. So where do you want to go on our first date? Dinner? Movie?" *Back to my place where I can worship you all night?*

"Actually, I wanted you to come back to my place?" She bit her lip suggestively. "There's something I want to show you."

Thank you, Jesus.

"Oh, I am sooooo there." I lifted her off the ground, planting a kiss on her neck.

She rolled her eyes. "No, not like that, although, I think you will probably find first-date rules won't apply to you."

"I hope you mean in a good way." I couldn't decipher if she meant that despite knowing me, I would not be getting to second base. Or she would go back to rubbing my cock through my jeans and I got to touch her tits. It had been magical the first time but way too rushed. "But seriously, we don't have to do anything you're not comfortable with."

"I was rubbing your crotch this morning, are you really worried about what I'm comfortable with?" Her eyebrow popped, her body demonstrating exactly what she was comfortable with.

"So, would you rather me toss you onto my chair and peel those pants off you with my teeth?" I grabbed her ass, only half joking about the hypothetical.

"God, yes." She arched against me, my dick immediately looking for the ejection handle on my jeans. "I would love that, but I still need to show you something first."

"So let's get out of here." My room wasn't as clean as I would have liked, but at this point I didn't care. There was nothing urgent that couldn't wait until tomorrow. Not unless you counted the rod in my pants. "My car is back at my apartment but it's walking distance from here."

"Oooooo, I get to see where you live?" Her eyes lit up with excitement.

"Seems fair since I'm going to see yours. And we better go before I change my mind about that chair." I dropped another soft whack on her ass and spun her around. "Let's go."

She chuckled as I hit the lights, shutting the door to my room as we walked down the hall. She grabbed her purse from behind the desk as I waited for her, my full attention on her as she did one last check around her work area and collected her sketchpad.

"You staring at me?" She hip swayed over, her sketchpad tucked under her arm. "Sort of creepy if you are."

"Then I won't admit I've been staring at you since day one, it can be my little secret." I unlocked the deadlock and pushed open the door.

"I said it was *sort of creepy*, I didn't say I didn't like it." She walked out onto the street and watched as I locked up behind us. "And full disclosure, I've been watching you too."

"I like this game." I nodded to the sidewalk in the direction we needed to go, my place not far. "Full disclosure, I told Jack you had a boyfriend."

"Well, that's interesting." She fell into step beside me. "I don't remember falling into a relationship recently. I hope my new boyfriend is better than my last one." She side-eyed me before adding, "Because, full disclosure, I'm done being with someone out of habit."

"Noted. And I wasn't assuming, by the way." I laughed, pressing my hand against her back as I guided her around the corner. "But full disclosure, if you were with me, it would be for a lot of reasons, and *habit* wouldn't be one of them."

"Full disclosure, that's pretty freaking hot." She shot me a grin, her feet continuing to move. "And I'm really hoping I find out."

"Full disclosure, that option—if you want it—is on the table."

I wasn't the kind of guy who liked to play games, or bullshit women with crap I thought they wanted to hear. And maybe that was why I hadn't settled down for a while. Who knew? Yet that other stuff, wasn't in me and if I had to fake it, it wasn't worth it to me. But even saying all of that, I'd never been so honest with a woman and laid it all out on the line. Still, couldn't make myself regret it.

"I really, really like this game too." She leaned into me, fitting perfectly under my arm. "Maybe we should skip my place and stay at yours."

"Nope, I want to see what you were going to show me." We got to my apartment and walked to where my Jeep was parked. "You won't get out of it that easily, get in."

Get in? That's what we've been trying to do, screamed my balls, wondering why the hell I was turning down her offer to go upstairs. And I couldn't say that I didn't agree with them, and that my decision to not, wasn't a bad one.

But I liked this girl, and for reasons I hadn't fully explored yet either. So I wasn't going to blow it by treating her like a sex toy. And if I were lucky, I'd get to see what made her tick *and* have her body. It was all or nothing, and I wanted the package deal.

I jumped into the driver's seat and started the car, the engine under the hood rumbling to life as I pulled out from my parking spot and onto the road.

"This is exactly what I thought you'd drive." She smiled, looking around at the interior. "It's so rugged. Manly."

"Thanks, I guess." Not entirely sure if that was a compliment. I'd never given that much thought to the car. I had the Jeep because I liked it, what people thought about it didn't really factor into it.

"And you?" I looked over at her as I changed lanes. "What do you drive?"

Call me curious, and I wasn't even sure she had a car. But if she thought a Jeep was typical for me, then I imagined something red and flashy was her go to.

"Um, just like a regular sedan." Her smile told me there was nothing regular about the car she drove.

"Like a Ford?" I baited, knowing there wasn't a chance in hell it was. "Or do you mean *regular* like a BMW?"

"It's a Tesla." She bit her lip, side-eyeing me. "It's environmentally responsible."

"Eve, you have a massively warped definition of regular." I laughed, those cars on the serious side of eighty K. "Let me guess, it's red?"

"No." She coughed nervously, meeting my raised eyebrow. "Okay, fine it is."

"This is good. Talking. Getting to know each other." I nodded, my eyes back on the road. "First date stuff."

We had kind of done the relationship thing ass end around. I knew about her insecurities, her dreams, bits about her family and of course the disaster that was her boyfriend, but I didn't know the normal stuff. Like her address or what set of wheels she drove, so it was good to get caught up.

"Yeah, I guess it is."

So we talked, filling in the blanks as we made the commute. It was the first time I hadn't cared we were stuck in traffic, the time in the car giving us an opportunity we hadn't had before. And it's not like we could do anything else. I hadn't mastered the art of making out while still keeping my hands on the wheel, so that would have to wait.

Driving through Manhattan, it was obvious how different we were. And it was more than just real estate. But while she wore nice clothes and had gone to a fancy college, she didn't seem as pretentious as I thought someone who lived on the Upper East Side would be. She had a realness to her that was so freaking endearing. And while there were some moments of privilege I saw poke through, for the most part she wasn't the spoiled princess I would have expected if I'd seen this world before getting to know her. Sure, I was stereotyping, but we all did it. I'm sure she had her own ideas on me.

"I'm here." She pointed to a flashy high rise, the shiny glass windows catching the afternoon sun.

I had expected nice, given where we were on the island. But her apartment building was really, *really* fucking nice. I hadn't even seen the inside yet, and I could already tell.

She directed me to the undercover garage and I pulled into an available guest space. The existence of the spot in that part of town was a massive giveaway about how much she was probably paying in rent. I didn't bring it up though, just eased the Wrangler in between the two white lines and killed the engine.

Next was the elevator, she leaned into me and I kissed her neck as we climbed the floors, the lights on the display board getting higher until we almost reached the top. Yeah, her apartment probably cost more for a month than I made in a year.

"You live here by yourself?" I asked as we walked to the front door, her hand wrestling with the keys and her sketchpad under her arm. She hadn't mentioned a roommate, but then again I hadn't asked either.

"Yeah, just me. I was living with Oliver before he turned out to be a bastard, but now it's just me."

I didn't like the idea—her living with another guy—but it had nothing to do with me. I reminded myself if not for his epic fuck up, I wouldn't have met her. Besides, I was still coming to terms with her address.

Do not bring up money.

Do not bring up money.

Opening the door was like being slapped in the face with the dissimilarities between us. And it wasn't just about the money, even though that was a big part of it. It was her furniture style, her framed pictures, the way she neatly placed her keys into a crystal bowl that sat on a side table by the entrance. Walking in there felt like I was at the ballet, the dancers knew what they were doing and made it look effortless—but not everyone was going to be able to get on their toes or look good in a pair of tights.

"You okay?" She cocked her head to the side trying to read my reaction.

"Yeah, I . . ." *Do not mention money.* "You have a really nice place."

"It's a lot, isn't it?" She kicked off her shoes and pulled me into the living room. "I know what it looks like, the big apartment in the nice part of town. But it belongs to my parents, and I rent it." She looked at me, her eyes fierce with determination as she kicked up her chin. "I know I'm lucky and I'm not going to pretend I'm poor, but money doesn't mean everything was easy for me. Or that I haven't had to work for things."

Like I said, honesty. She constantly surprised me, and now was no different. She might have been a product of it all—the flash and cash—but something told me she wasn't going to let it define her.

"You don't need to explain yourself or apologize for having money." I pulled her in close, wanting my hands around her.

"I know and I'm not." She pressed her palms to my chest. "But I see that look in your eyes and I know what it means."

"I'm sorry, I didn't mean to give you *a look*." I kissed the top of her head. "I just didn't realize that there was all of this." I gestured to the space around us. "It was a little more than what I was expecting."

"Yeah well, it's just an apartment." She shrugged. "Now let me show you what we came here for."

"I can't wait."

She tugged on my arm leading me to her massive leather couch, pushing me down on it as she joined me on the other side. The coffee table in front of us was covered in paper, some in various stages of completion, alternating between gray scale and color.

"What's this?" I picked up one of the sheets, the face staring back at me like looking into a mirror.

It was really good too, not only in likeness but I could tell she'd put a lot of work into it. And both of us, the guy on the page and the one holding it, seemed really fucking pleased.

"Some guy's face I like." She laughed, taking the picture back. "Full disclosure, I've drawn *him* a lot."

"Just his *face*." I snapped the picture up and held it beside my head for comparison. "Or are there other things as well? And full disclosure, that's kind of a turn on."

Turn on was an understatement. The thought of her drawing me made me so hard, my dick was losing circulation.

"Well, all I've really seen has been his face." Her mouth pulled into a frown. "Although I'd really like to see the rest of him."

"I think that can be arranged." Getting naked right now was too soon, right? Because I would like nothing more than to play show and tell with her. "And I'm done talking about myself in the third person."

Her tongue parted out of her mouth, flicking across her lips and I knew what she was thinking.

We were alone, together, with no chance of interruptions.

And whatever reasons we had for keeping our hands to ourselves didn't seem so important anymore.

It was dangerous.

"Tell me, Eve, what do you want to show me?"

EVE

BEING ALONE WITH JOSH WAS harder than I thought it
would be. And by harder, I didn't mean the sizeable erection I
could see when I looked down.

Crap.

He caught me looking at it.

"Something you want to see?" His eyes followed mine down,
the bulge straining against his jeans.

What were we here for? Oh, that's right. The watercolors.

"It was easier to think when you weren't so close." My hand,
completely of its own accord, reached and touched his thigh.

"Do you want me to leave?" He leaned back moving his arm
to the back of the couch, allowing me room to get closer. "We
could go somewhere public?"

He was being a gentleman, trying to do the right thing and
be a nice guy. I knew it and should have appreciated it. That even
though he was obviously aroused, he wasn't pushing me. Problem
was, gratitude wasn't what I felt.

"No, don't leave." My fingers gripped the denim of his jeans,
stupidly fooled in believing their hold alone would have been

enough if he chose otherwise. "I want to be alone with you. I *really* want to be alone with you."

"This wasn't how I wanted this to go down, honestly." His nose grazed the side of my face. "I wanted to take you out, talk. But being this close to you." He sucked in a breath. "Fuck it."

His mouth was on mine as he hauled me into his lap, my legs straddling him as we kissed. It wasn't soft, his lips demanding as mine opened with a mewl, wanting him inside of me any way I could.

I felt his hard length pressing against my core, my jeans and his providing too much of a barrier, and I needed them off. I wanted to be naked, feeling his skin on mine while we kissed.

It was crazy, a symphony of lips and tongues, and breaths stolen from each other as our hands roamed out of control. I couldn't get close enough.

"Take off your shirt." My fingertips gripped around the hem, peeling it off him with or without his permission. Lucky for me he didn't seem to mind, yanking it over his head and tossing it aside, his perfectly chiseled chest completely bare for me to see.

Wow.

"Wow." I thought and said it at the same time. Most of his toned skin covered with a landscape of color that only enhanced his amazing torso. A six-pack didn't come close. It was more like an eight-pack, with his waist thinning into the most delicious V that not even sitting down could hide.

"This is amazing." My fingers traced the lines of the eagle, wings outstretched in flight, which sprawled from the top of his left pectoral to his right. "It's beautiful." My hand ghosted across the delicate feathers, down to the powerful talons in the middle of his chest.

"The art or me?" he laughed, moving his mouth to my neck. "And is it wrong that at this point, I don't care which."

"All of you," I moaned, my fingers exploring every curve and hard line, craving more contact. "You're so beautiful."

"That's what I'm supposed to say to you," he eased my head to the side, sucking the skin at the curve of my neck. "Not the other way around."

I felt his hand move to the hem of my top, his fingers slipping underneath as he cupped my bra. "These have been taunting me all day."

"Take it off." I arched into him, sacrificing his mouth for more of his hands.

He didn't hesitate, his hands getting busy wrenching off my top to reveal my lacy bra. "Now *this*," he kissed the swell of my breast, "is beautiful."

Moving his fingers to my back, he flicked the clasp as the lace gave way. His eyes locked on mine as he pulled the straps from my shoulders, slowly revealing my naked chest.

"I don't have any pretty pictures on mine." I watched as his hands moved to my skin.

"Anything on there would be a distraction."

He lowered his head, his lips curling around one nipple as his fingers tightened around the other. "God. You're perfect."

I couldn't concentrate on what he was saying, my mind so lost in the sensation as he closed his mouth and sucked.

"Josh." My hands threaded through his hair as he moved his mouth to my other breast, giving them both equal attention. "Don't stop."

He didn't, showing me how talented his tongue was as he moved it back to my mouth.

My body rocked against him, the pressure between my legs building as my hips bucked. My body was so primed, so ready, I would probably come the minute he got my bottom half naked.

"Josh, please." My hips ground on his lap, his hard length teasing me to insanity.

"Eve, I'm not fucking you on the first date." His hands stilled my hips, his breathing labored as he tried to rein it in.

What?

What!

He couldn't stop. Not when I was so close, my body so desperate to come. Now was not the time to be polite.

"No. No, it's okay." I kissed his chin, the stubble covering his jaw scratching my lips. "I want to and it's not really our first date. It's fine." My lips continued to kiss him as I tried to find traction in his lap. His hands locked around me refused to let me find my release.

"You're not making it easy for me," he groaned, his body tense.

"Good." My hands lowered to his belt as I started taking matters into my own hands. "Please, I need you."

It was tricky with our bodies so close but I managed to unlatch his belt and then start on his jeans, my hands feeling how hard he was as I worked his length.

"No." His feet planted on the floor as his legs rose off the couch taking me with him as he stood. "Not like this, not now."

My body froze, his voice like a kill switch, stopping all movement.

Seriously, what was the problem with me and men?

All I wanted to do was get lost in an orgasm with a guy I thought was incredibly sexy but noooooooooo, he had some moral code or something.

"O-kay." I attempted to unwrap my legs from his waist, dejected and extremely frustrated. I had already begged, there wasn't much point of continuing. "Put me down, Josh."

He didn't release me, his hands locked on my ass, keeping my legs around him.

"Okay, so you can put me down and I'll get dressed." My body bucked, accepting nothing was going to happen and seeing no reason to continue the mortification.

"I said I wasn't going to fuck you on the first date, Eve." His eyes locked on mine, his face so full of need I had no idea how he could say no. "I didn't say I wasn't going to make you come."

"What?" The word squeaked out as he turned and lowered me back onto the couch, my brain not comprehending what was happening.

My back hit the soft cushioned surface, freeing up his hands to unbutton my jeans and strip them off. My legs fell open as he dropped to his knees in front of me. His hands wrapped around my underwear and tore them off. I was completely bare, exposed as he looked at me with hooded eyes.

If he wasn't going to have sex with me, what the hell—OHH-Hhhhhhhh. Pleasure shot up my spine as his mouth sealed around my pussy, my arms and legs tingling as his tongue flattened and stroked me.

"Oh. My. God." My back arched, unashamedly giving him better access as he sucked on my clit and continued his tongue assault. The frustration I had felt two seconds ago had completely evaporated as tension pooled between my legs.

God, he was good, slipping in a finger on another sweep of his tongue, my eyes rolling back into my head as every cell in my body woke up at once.

And then he slid in another, stretching me a little further as his fingers pumped, his mouth not stopping as he alternated between licking and sucking, the sensation both amazing and maddening.

"Josh, I'm going to—" I didn't get to finish, the sensation slamming me from behind and engulfing me as my entire body shook. The crest of my orgasm rolled over me again and again as he slowed but didn't stop, teasing every last pulse out of me till I almost begged him to stop.

"I-I—"

I was going to need a minute to find where my brain had been tossed and collect what was left of my thoughts.

Sex with Oliver had been good. Other than not being able

to keep from sharing his dick with others, he hadn't left me disappointed in bed. And sure he'd gone down on me, as I had with him. But this, this was something different. I wasn't sure if it was technique, or pace, or if Josh AKA *hottest man alive*, wasn't the orgasm whisperer.

"You still with me?" Josh slowly slid his fingers out of me, bringing them to his mouth and sucked. "You tasted exactly how I thought you would, sweet."

"That was amazing." I still couldn't move, my spine feeling like a shuffled deck of cards as I lay exactly where he'd placed me. "I don't think I can move."

"So don't move, I like the view." He grinned, easing back onto his knees so he could get a better look.

I should have been embarrassed but I was too relaxed to care, endorphins ricocheting through my body responsible for my blissed out mood. He could have robbed me at that point, and I would have probably thanked him for the privilege.

"It's not fair that you got to see me, and I didn't get to see you." I pointed to the pants he was still wearing and the hard-on that was still extremely evident. He might have taken care of me, but it was going to take a hand or two to get that monster down.

"If I took off my pants, I wouldn't have been able to stop myself from being inside of you. It was a judgment call."

"And now?" I glanced at the anaconda—no seriously, how big had it gotten—in his pants and wondered if he still stood behind his *judgment call*.

"I still want to be inside of you." He didn't hesitate, his voice gravel, as he looked me up and down.

"Take them off, Josh. I want to see you."

He toed off his boots, pulling off his socks before his hands moved to his waistband. The belt had previously been loosened—by yours truly—as had the button, so his jeans hung low on his hips. He slowly rose to his feet, towering above me as he slid his jeans down, letting them drop to floor. The thin cotton of his boxer briefs, the only thing restraining him.

"Everything, take everything off." I nodded to his underwear, smirking, as his fingers looped around the elastic and hesitated.

"You sure about this?" He waited, watching for my nod before he slowly eased them down. "I meant what I said about not sleeping with you tonight."

"I know, but there is a whole bunch of gray area we could explore."

I sucked in a breath. "Wow."

It was the second time I had said it, this time more enthusiastic than the first. His long hard cock jutted out from his hips, framed by strong muscular thighs, every inch of him a paragon of man. I had imagined it, dreamed and even fantasized about it, but his body was insane. Insane. Lines and hard edges defined every muscle with pops of color traveling up and down his torso and down his arms. I'd seen thousands of documented examples of the perfect male form, and none of them had come close to him. I could stare at him for days.

"Now what?" he asked causally like he wasn't standing in front of me naked with the biggest erection I'd ever seen.

"I want to make you come." My thighs pulled together as my feet lowered to the floor. My legs accepted my weight as I came to stand. "I mean, I'm *going* to make you come."

"Really, and how are you going to do that?" He arched his brow, smile curving on his lips as he watched me with interest.

"Well, there is a combination of things actually." My fingers reached out and wrapped around his girth. It was a struggle, my hand not able to close fully.

"Tell me more. I'm intrigued." His jaw tightened as I slowly stroked his shaft.

"I'd rather show you." I sunk to my knees in front of him, an audible hiss escaping from his lips the minute I took him into my mouth.

"Fuck."

His eyes dropped to me, watching him as I hollowed out my cheeks, sucking him while my hand worked his length.

He was so hard, his ab muscles tensing as I drew him in further, smacking my lips as I pulled him all the way out with a wet pop.

"Feels so good." The words rushed out on a breath. His hands fisted my hair as I moved to licking him, my tongue twisting up the side of his cock and circling the head, my hands picking up the tempo as I pumped.

I didn't stop, moving slowly and then faster, alternating the rhythm with my hands and my mouth.

I loved feeling his grip on my hair, sensing his desperation as I watched him. It was a power play and I wasn't sure who was in control. And at that moment, I didn't care—so turned on I almost came again.

"Eve."

I wasn't sure if it was a warning or a plea, but I loved the way it sounded, reedy and unhinged.

His body tensed, and I could feel he was close as I continued, wanting to make him feel as good as he made me feel.

"Eve."

His hand tightened in my hair as I felt the rush, his beautiful toned abs rigid as I watched him come undone. My mouth continued to suck as my hands gripped him tight and I swallowed hard.

"God, your mouth is magic." He pulled his cock from my lips, his thumb replacing it as I sucked. "So freaking good."

"Likewise." I grinned, lifting off my knees and rising to my feet. "I've wanted to do that for a while."

"Yeah, me too." He chuckled, pressing my chest against his. "I'm not going to lie, I've thought about going down on you way too many times to be normal. And just thinking about my dick in your mouth gets me hard."

"I really like that." My flat palms traveled up the wide expanse of his chest, feeling the ripples under my fingertips.

"What?" He lowered his head, meeting my eyes. "That I think about you so much, or that you can get me hard?"

"Both."

It should have been a whole heap of awkward. I was standing in my living room, naked, with my boss essentially. But oddly enough, it didn't feel so weird at all. And the fact that it wasn't, should have been the tip off. God, please don't let me screw this up.

"We should get dressed." I bent down and collected my clothes from the floor. "I actually did want to show you something other than my stellar blowjob skills and I don't think I can do that while you're naked."

"Yeah, that's probably a good call." He grabbed his jeans, boxer briefs and T-shirt. "I'm already second-guessing my decision not to take you to bed."

"I'll be right back." I held my pile of clothes in my arms, deciding to go into my bedroom to change. "There's a bathroom down the hall if you want to freshen up."

"Thanks." He glanced down the hall in question. "I might do that."

I didn't run or hide my body as I scampered away. Instead, I turned calmly, giving him one final look before striding to my bedroom.

I couldn't stop the massive grin from spreading across my face as I closed the door. Today had been most unexpectedly awesome.

While the weekend had been fruitful creatively, the only orgasms I'd received were the ones I had given myself. Mostly with the image of Josh in my mind and sometimes—okay, mostly—with the multiple renderings I had done myself. It was like I had created my own porn.

Draw him.

Think about him.

Touch myself.

It wasn't an efficient method but an enjoyable one nonetheless.

I had no way of knowing that the new day would have forced the confrontation, which inevitably revealed my true deviant feelings. Feelings where I thought about Josh in every sexual position known to man.

Come to find out the reality was hotter than the fantasy, blowing my mind the minute he got me naked, without even the use of his impressive cock. And make no mistake, it was impressive.

I giggled like an idiot as I freshened up with a washcloth and changed into clean panties—the ones I had been wearing destroyed—and a slip dress. And oops, I just happened to choose a dress that unfortunately didn't allow for the wearing of a bra. Completely coincidental that it also hugged my body and sat halfway up my thigh as well. A dress was a dress, right?

It had been a deliberate effort not allowing him into my room. Not because I didn't want him there—because I did—but because I wanted to show him what I had ultimately brought him home to see. The artwork he had unintentionally helped to inspire. And the bed would have proven too much of a temptation. No, I needed a buffer. At least until I said what needed to be said, because clearly I couldn't be trusted keeping my hands to myself.

I didn't bother with shoes, strolling back into the living room where he had also redressed and was sitting on the couch.

"I thought we were going to talk?" His eyes narrowed when he saw the dress. "That doesn't look like an outfit conducive to chatting, Eve."

"What, this?" I ran my hand coyly over the fabric. "It was the first thing that fell out of my closet."

"Yeah, I believe *that.*" He laughed, turning his attention back to my drawings strewn all over the table. "These are really, *really* good."

"Thank you." I went and sat down beside him, the praise

feeling well earned. "And this time it's my own work, but this is what I really wanted to show you."

In a folder by themselves I had a series of watercolors. While they had the traditional markings of the style—the blurred line and blended color—I amplified the pigment in the paint so they were brighter, more vibrant. And to mix it up a bit, I added a focal point on the page that was crisp and clear—a paradox.

"It's like a dream." He squinted his eyes looking at the next.

"Exactly, it got me thinking when you said it about the Monet. How it felt like I captured a memory? And I thought about what that might look like." I moved closer, feeling excitement prickle my skin. "And the thing about memories are, there is usually a point that is clear, focused and precise. You remember everything about it. What you were wearing, what it smelled like, how it tasted—all of your senses are razor sharp in that moment. But the other things, in the periphery, they aren't as clear, blurred into that memory."

"Eve, these are really freaking amazing." He looked at each of my prints, each focal point positioned differently so that when the prints lined up together, they formed a wave. "Each one is the same, but different."

"That's what I was hoping for. That by looking at them, you see my moment, the one that I have provided. But in the edges, you bring your own baggage. You feel your own sadness, or happiness, or emptiness. You have your own interpretation of each piece, so no one person will have the same experience."

It had been late when I'd come up with the concept. I had drawn one of the many Joshes and accidentally spilled my drink on the page. I was able to soak up the water before it seeped too much into his face and I assumed the picture was done for. It was only in the morning after the paper had dried that I saw his eyes had remained as I'd drawn them, but the aperture had changed. The fuzziness on the lines of his face and his hair made it seem like he was under water, and just part of him had broken the surface.

It made me think of summer, of happiness, of swimming in cool water, the ripples of the waves kissing your skin as you moved through its resistance. And if I could feel all that, then maybe someone else would feel it too.

"Eve, this is what you should be working on." His attention turned to the picture that started it all, *Swimming Josh*, my heart thumping as he looked at it. "This is what your next exhibit should be."

"It's too soon to even think about another exhibit." I shuffled the pages in some kind of order. His idea had been one I'd tossed around as a possibility, but couldn't even dare to think it so soon. "It would take months to prepare enough pieces and then to apply for a space. Assuming they would even take my application, some people have long memories."

From the corner of my eye I could see him, his smile dropping a little as his attention moved from my pictures to me. "Sounds like an excuse, and I thought you were done with those. I didn't take you for a coward, you trying to prove me wrong? Because if that's what you are doing, sure keep making excuses and hide away like the talentless hack they accused you of. "

I winced, his words a little hard to hear and not what I was expecting. "Wow, tell me how you really feel." I didn't bother trying to make it sound polite.

"Come on, Eve." He shook his head, blowing out a breath. "Why did you even come to me in the first place? I'm not going to sugarcoat it and you know that. So if you are looking for someone to tell you to play it safe, I'm not him."

In an instant, the air had changed.

Gone was the euphoria, the excitement, both from the sex and about the future. Instead, anger was edging into the room, making me feel like showing him any of it had been a huge mistake.

"I'm not asking you to sugarcoat it, but you could maybe be a little nicer." Heat prickled my neck as agitation bit into my voice.

"Jesus, Josh, it's just been a couple of weeks."

"You're mad at me?" he asked, actually surprised his criticism hadn't been welcomed with open arms.

"Noooo." The word dripped in sarcasm, my face not able to hide how I really felt. "What gave you that idea?"

God, I'd been an idiot.

I'd gone from one bad decision to the next. Sure he was good looking, and sexy and extremely talented with his hands—both on me and in his craft—but I had no idea who this guy was. So what did I do? I'd thrown myself at him, told him to train me like some padawan. And what was even worse, I was totally going to sleep with him. Thank God, I'd dodged that bullet.

"Okay, so you're mad. That's cool." He turned, facing me, a smile on his lips. "It's healthy to fight in relationships."

"Fight in relationships? Healthy? We aren't even dating. And considering it's been twice today you've pissed me off, I'm pretty sure that it is never going to happen."

God, the nerve of this guy.

Maybe I should throw him out too, it seemed to be a theme for me of late. Tossing men out of my apartment after they proved what douche canoes they were. I was going to stop inviting men home.

"Let me ask you something?" His finger stroked his chin, unperturbed by the change in my mood. "How many times did you fight with Oliver?"

"Oliver? Why are you bringing him up?"

Was he seriously trying to piss me off? Because I couldn't think of one good reason why he would bring him up, unless it was to illustrate all men were pigs.

"In case you forgot." I lamented my lack of ability to shoot lasers from my eyes. It sure would have come in handy right about now. "We had a pretty big fight when I threw him out on his ass for cheating on me."

"Oh, I remember. I'm talking before that." His chin tipped, rolling his hand to demonstrate. "You guys obviously dated for a while, lived together." His arm waved to the living room, which had previously housed things that belonged to Oliver. "How many times did you argue? Disagree?"

"We didn't," I snapped, agitated. "We always got along, and if he hadn't put his dick where it hadn't belonged, he would have been the perfect boyfriend."

Take that, asshat. Bet he didn't think that was going to be my answer.

"Because he told you what you wanted to hear?" The stupid grin still plastered across his face. "Or because he didn't care enough or wasn't invested enough in the relationship to challenge you, even if you were wrong?"

"I wasn't ever wrong."

"Well, considering the shit you hung for the world to see, I'd say there were a few occasions where you were." His words felt like a slap in the face, a wound that had just started to scab over was ripped open so he could pour salt on it. "And yeah, it's harsh. But that stuff you displayed, after seeing this, we both know it was shit. And if he was half a man or cared half as much as he should have, he would have told you that too. I sure as hell would have."

My mouth slammed shut, my brain getting stuck in idle as Josh's words soaked in. I knew I hadn't loved Oliver and that he hadn't loved me. Hell, I even knew that our "wonderful relation-ship" had really just been friends with a side of sex. So it's not like Josh dug up some deep hurt that Oliver wasn't the soul mate I'd wanted him to be. No, that wasn't what shocked me into silence. It was the words *"I sure as hell would have."*

That was what stumped me. What did that even mean.

"What do you mean?"

"It means, Eve. For whatever reason, our paths crossed." His hand touched my arm, his fingers moving across my skin giving me goosebumps. My brain too confused to know if I even wanted to be touched. "Maybe it's just so you can yell at me and tell me to fuck off. So you can go on to succeed in spite of me, in spite of everyone. Or maybe I get to stick around for a while. I don't have a crystal ball so I can't tell you which it is." His eyes softened, his lips spreading into a smile. "But I do know that you're smart and you're talented and it's a fucking tragedy if you waste a minute of that on a half-assed effort. Whether it's on a page or on a person. You're not looking for someone to enable you and you knew you wouldn't get that with me. And as crazy as it sounds, I care. So let me serve my purpose."

Mouth open.

Mouth closed.

Words missing.

I couldn't even think in complete sentences, let alone speak them.

"How do you do that?" My eyes widened with genuine wonder.

"Do what?" he asked earnestly, his fingers still feathering over my skin.

"Know what to say?" A nervous laugh bubbled up my throat. "It's like you're a psychiatrist or something. I don't know whether I should be laying down on a couch and paying you, or begging you to be my friend forever."

Every time I thought I had him worked out, he pulled something else out of his bag of tricks, just like Mary Poppins. And every single time it warmed my heart, the heat radiating through my body in a way I hadn't felt before. It was insanity that my mood could swing so fast in opposite directions, and that with a few words he could change my whole outlook.

"I'm not a doctor." He chuckled, those eyes slaying me. "Although if I was, I'd say that the impulse to pay men is a problem."

"Low blow, asshat." I grabbed a pillow from beside me and whacked him across the chest. That beautiful, sexy chest that I would hopefully have the chance to lick soon, and which happened to belong to one of the smartest people I knew.

"You love it when I get you angry." He grabbed the pillow from my hand and returned the favor with a soft thump on my arm. "Because unlike some of your friends, I'm not afraid to tell it how it is."

"So we're friends who argue?" I bit my lip, our relationship still defying categorization.

"Ouch, you're friend zoning me already?" He clutched his chest in mock hurt. "I guess I had it coming." His smile reappearing. "I did call your work shit."

"No, I'm not friend zoning you." I pushed playfully against his chest. "I clearly have unresolved sexual feelings for you, so at the very least we're gonna have to be friends with benefits."

There was no way we weren't going to have sex, I think we both had unresolved sexual feelings. And if the orgasm he'd given me before was anything to go by, then I was definitely going to enjoy exploring that.

"Yeah, that wasn't much better." He screwed up his nose, grinning. "But seriously, Eve. I like you. So let's try this and see what happens. The only condition is this." He grabbed my hand, intertwining our fingers. "I get the *real* you, and you get the *real* me. Even if we argue." He brought my hand to his mouth and kissed my knuckles. "Even if sometimes we piss each other off. You think you can do that?"

"Like as in actually date?" The idea thrilled me more than I wanted to say. I bet Josh was an amazing boyfriend.

"Sure, why not." His eyes clear of any doubt. "Unless you want to hold on to your earlier statement when you said I pissed you off and it was neeeeeeeever going to happen. I don't know you well enough to know if you're easy to sway."

"Again with the sarcasm, you know it would be easier if you just charmed me." My body moved closer, shifted so I was nestled under his shoulder. *I could get used to this*, our bodies fit so well together.

"I already told you the conditions." He accepted my weight, wrapping his arm around me. "Sometimes I'm charming, sometimes I'm not. Lucky you, you get the whole package, baby." He chuckled in my ear.

"I've already seen your package, it was pretty impressive," I responded on reflex. It was also the truth, and since that was what we were going for, I felt compelled to tell him.

"You're making dick jokes now?" His arm pulled me back so he could kiss my mouth. "I'd say we should be more worried about *that*, than you dating me."

"Yes, I'm going to date you." The words got lost in a kiss. "But how is the boss thing going to work?"

I still had another couple of weeks before I was due back at the gallery. And even though I didn't need the money, I really liked working at Ink Addiction. Dating the boss, however, was never a good idea. Not that I ever let a bad idea stop me in the past.

"Another thing I'm under no delusions about." He rolled his eyes, cinching me in closer. "You've been doing your own thing since you got there, I can't remember a day where I told you to do something, and you did it. So I wouldn't say we have a traditional working relationship, would you? Besides, you'll be back in your old job in a couple of weeks, so that problem is an easy fix."

I loved we were on the same page. That he didn't automatically see what could be a challenging situation and decide to file it away as too hard. I know he had his reservations, which was why it took a while for us to get here.

"What about Dallas?" It needed to be asked. Our being together undoubtedly raising a few eyebrows, I wasn't sure if he would end up resenting me or being an asshole to Josh because of it.

"Well, I'm straight, so not interested in him." He grimaced. "And trust me, you don't want to date him. He is waaaay high maintenance."

"So a threesome is out of the question?" I laughed, not because I was interested but because I knew it would get a reaction. For some crazy reason, I loved pushing Josh's buttons.

"Yeah, I liked the dick jokes better. That one isn't funny." He playfully bit my shoulder. "But Dallas isn't going to be a problem. He not so subtly hinted he knew I had feelings for you at the hospital over the weekend. It was part of my whole come to Jesus moment, first him and then when Kitty showed up. He gave me shit about it most of the weekend. I doubt anyone is going to be surprised."

He was right about that.

It had been no secret I had thought Josh was hot. My friends had actively encouraged it, even if I had maintained, "nothing was probably going to happen."

There was no reason why this couldn't work, and like he'd said, there was obviously a purpose for all of this.

"I'm going to date you *and* I'm going to compile another exhibition. There are plenty of galleries in the city." My resolve setting in, and I felt more determined than I had in forever.

"That's what I wanted to hear when we started this conversation." He nodded, his grin widening. "And I can't wait to be there on opening night."

JOSH

IT WAS EASIER TRYING TO avoid sleeping with Eve *before* I'd seen her naked.

My imagination had been pretty vivid, filling in the blanks on what I thought she looked like underneath her clothes. But reality was like a right hook, flat across my jaw.

She was fucking perfect. With peaks and valleys in all the right places, I doubted I was ever going to get enough. But as much as I wanted nothing more than to take her to bed and have her scream my name, it wasn't going to happen last night.

It was a bone—no pun intended—of contention between my dick and I, but it was the right choice. I didn't want her to be a one-time deal, a quick lay, or for me to be her rebound. She was girlfriend material, and I didn't want to screw that up. I wanted a little more time before we went down that road, so she understood it was more for me than just sex. She deserved more than that, and I wanted to give it to her.

So, we spent the night talking. She showed me more of her drawings and I listened to how excited it made her. Seeing that spark inside of her was even sexier than the dress she'd been wearing. So,

I may have taken it off before I left and gone down on her again. Hey, I wasn't a saint. But that's where it ended. I left sometime in the early morning after she fell asleep beside me on her bed. I hated leaving without a proper goodbye, but there was no way I could spend the night with her and not be inside her. I only had so much restraint.

"Hi." She walked in bright and early, her hands filled with coffee. Weird how even though I'd only kissed her goodbye a few hours ago, it felt good to see her again. "I must have fallen asleep on you, I'm sorry." She pouted, lowering the coffees onto the front counter and wrapping her hands around my neck. "You could have stayed, I wouldn't have minded."

"You were tired and needed the rest." I planted a kiss on her neck, loving the feel of her in my arms. "And when I do spend the night, you won't fall asleep."

"What. The. Fuck?" Dallas walked in pulling his sunglasses from his face as he took in the view. My lips on her, her hands on me, and not in a way that looked like we were just being friendly. "How hard did I hit my head?"

"Hi, Dallas." Eve spun in my arms to greet him. "Are you feeling better?"

"Don't try to change the subject." He pointed wildly between the two of us. "You two were fucking on the counter."

"We were kissing, moron." I laughed, my hands staying exactly where they were around Eve's waist. "*Fucking* looks a little different, and is generally done with other parts of the body."

"Kissing, fucking—we all know where *that* was leading." He continued to wave as he approached us. "And I'm not saying it's a bad thing." He tossed his shades on the counter and wriggled out a cup from the tray Eve had carried in. "Far be it for me to cock block anyone." The cup lifted to his lips. "But when I was sitting with this sad sack on Sunday and Monday, this," his head tipped to the two of us as he took a drink, "wasn't happening. Man, this coffee is good."

"Not that it's any of your business, but it happened yesterday." I figured now was as good as time as any to do the debrief. "And we're dating, not fucking, so be respectful." The warning, one I would be reinforcing a little later just to be sure.

"Yes, yes. Dating. Whatever." He rolled his eyes and took another drink. "I approve in case anyone was wondering. He needs a decent woman, hopefully you can straighten him out."

"I'll do my best," Eve chuckled. "And thanks for your blessing, I know we were both worried sick about it."

"Barely got any sleep last night," I added, which technically wasn't a lie but not for the reason I admitted.

"I know sarcasm when I hear it." He narrowed his eyes. "And I'm going to choose to ignore it on account my head still hurts."

"Hey D, if you're really in pain, you can go home." All jokes aside, I wasn't a complete asshole. "We can juggle your appointments another day."

"Nah, it's not that bad and I was bored at home." He shrugged. "I'm better off here."

"Well, if you change your mind, let me know." I shot him a stern no-fucking-around look. "We can deal."

"Yeah, thanks dude." He gave me a nod, a silent dialogue bouncing between us. "I'm heading to my room."

He tossed us a wave and with coffee in hand, walked down the hall. His door closed soon after.

"That went easier than I expected." Eve glanced down the hallway like she couldn't quite believe the conversation was done.

"I did try to tell you it wasn't going to be a problem. You should listen to me." I moved my mouth back to her, wanting to give her the kiss I had intended before we were rudely interrupted.

Her lips opened for me without protest, feeling her warmth as I let my tongue explore. I loved being inside of her mouth, all hot and sweet. My cock bucked against my fly, concurring with my assessment and immediately wanting a piece of the action. *Not yet, buddy.* My hand wrapped around the back of her head as I got in deeper. Maybe Dallas was right, because I was minutes away from putting her on the counter and getting inside of her in another way. The reasons why I was waiting, not so clear now.

"You give the best kisses." She took a long breath. "I like the ones you give me in private too."

"Yeah, sort of what I was thinking about." I glanced down at my pants, Mr. Happy not so subtly making his presence felt.

"I know you said we should wait, but I'd really like you to stay over tonight." She quickly tacked on, "We don't have to do anything."

"I wanted to do everything." I brushed the hair off her face, never having wanted to be with a woman more than I wanted to be with Eve. "I'm trying to be good, wait, so you know you aren't just a fuck to me. But I really, really want you."

"I know I'm not just a fuck, Josh. I hated waking up with you gone." Her eyes gripped me tighter than her hands around my biceps.

"Then I'll stay," I said, with no more argument. This girl, she could probably ask me for the world and I'd find a way to get it for her. "Anything you want."

What had Dallas called me? Sucker. And I didn't even care. All I knew was I wanted more with Eve than I had wanted with any girl in a long time.

"I should go set up, you okay out here?" I looked around the empty shop, my appointment bound to show up soon.

"I think I'll manage." She smirked, pretending to ignore me and clicking on the computer screen. "I need to troll prospective venues for my next showing, see if I can find one who doesn't have a stick up their ass."

"Don't ask Kitty for advice." I chuckled. "And if you need help, let me know. I know a few people who can help."

"Thanks, but no offense." She looked up, meeting my eyes. "I need to do this on my own."

"None taken, and I completely understand."

And if anyone got the need to do things on your own, it was me. It was one of the reasons I was running my own shop and not punching someone else's clock.

"Let me know when my appointment arrives." I gave her a final kiss before disappearing down the hall.

Once in my room, I laughed at how quickly shit had changed since she walked into my shop. Me, with my head up my ass, denying what was an immediate attraction. Couldn't even explain why, but it was more than just her face. Maybe it had been the way she'd spoken about art? Or that she would reach out to a stranger for help because improving herself was more important than pride? That shit would get my attention one hundred percent of the time. And probably why deep down, I was so intrigued by her. It was what dominated my thoughts all morning and into the afternoon.

One of the reasons I hadn't initially pursued something with Eve was because I thought things might have been awkward between us at work. I also didn't want to get into a situation where she agreed to something under duress. But the more I was getting to know Eve, the more I was seeing she was stronger than she gave herself credit for. Maybe stronger than a lot of people knew. And if it ended sometime down the track, I couldn't imagine a scenario where shit would get ugly. Maybe I was delusional, stuck in the feel good early stage. But there was something about this that was different. I wasn't sure how, but it was.

"Hey, it's lunchtime. You haven't been out all morning." Eve appeared at my door, her smiling face a very welcome distraction.

"Yeah, I got caught up in stuff." I rolled away from my table, my last appointment having left twenty minutes ago. "I was trying to squeeze something in between jobs." I flipped closed the cover on my sketchpad, my work not ready to be shared. "A bit of a secret project."

"Oooooo, can I see?" She strode in with a face full of mischief. "Is it for a client?"

"You did hear me when I said it was secret, right?" I shook my head, probably should have known better than to mention anything at all. "As in, can't talk about." I folded my arms and watched her with interest. Seriously, I probably enjoyed pressing her buttons a little too much.

"But you didn't mean me, did you?" She didn't even try to hide her grin as she sauntered over to where I was sitting. "I'm the best at keeping things a secret. You don't even have to tell me, just leave it lying around for me to see, we don't even have to discuss it."

"I love that you are trying to find a work around, very resource-ful of you." I pulled her into my lap, the project safely covered from nosey artists for the time being. "But the answer is still no. I promise I'll show you when it's done. You'll be the first to see it."

"Fine." She pretended to be annoyed. "I can take the hint. But it's going to cost you."

"And what's the going rate for pissing you off?" Little did she know she could probably ask for anything and I would agree.

"You need to go with me to the gallery night on Friday. I had originally RSVP'd before . . . well *before*." The word enough of an explanation. "So I was just going to cancel, but now I sort of want to go."

While we had discussed her "other" life, I had only seen a peek of it when I saw her apartment. At the shop, things were on my terms so to speak but it would stand to reason that there was a whole other part of her than what I saw here. The part that wore the fancy dress and high heels like she'd worn the day she first came in. The part who owns a Tesla she barely drives.

"You want me to go with you to your fancy gallery thing?"

I pulled her hair aside and kissed her neck. "As your date or as a friend?"

Honestly, I would have gone either way, but like most men, I was hoping she wanted me there in a date capacity. Because, even though I pretended to be cool about it, I wasn't interested in just being her friend.

"As my date. But I understand if you don't want to," she added quickly, spinning around in my lap to face me. "It's a big deal and press will probably be there so if you want to just go as a guy friend, I understand. The attending part however, is non negotiable. I need a wingman, and we've already established you owe me for not telling me your secret."

"I would love to go as your date, and for the record I'm going because I want to, not because I owe you." I gave her a squeeze, the bribery not needed.

"That's great, does that mean I get to choose something else as payment?" Her eyebrow rose, her ability to bargain, absolutely astounding.

"How about I repay tonight. In bed. With any part of my body you want," I offered, knowing it was a win/win situation. No hardship on my part, that's for sure.

"Your terms are agreeable, I will allow it." She shuffled in my lap, looking pretty satisfied with herself. Not half as satisfied as she was going to be tonight.

"I'm so pleased." I reminded myself that Dallas was just next door, and we didn't have the time or the privacy to get started on that promise early. "Now tell me something, before we go out there and need to deal with Dallas. And know whatever your answer is, I am totally fine with. No judgment at all."

"Just ask, because now I'm getting paranoid." She cut in, impatient as ever.

"Do you want to go to this gallery thing because you feel like you have something to prove or because you want to go?"

It hadn't escaped my attention that this was the first I'd heard about it, and when she'd previously spoken about the gallery, it hadn't been complimentary. So the change of heart could be a big fuck you—to which she was entitled—or she may have just really wanted to go. As I said, I would have supported either.

"Honestly, both." She looked at me, so much emotion in her eyes I could never understand how anyone could have called her soulless. "I hate that I was made to feel like a fifteen-year-old unwed mother from the 1950's. Hidden away for the shame of it all. I hate the gallery insisted I take leave, which whether they want to admit or not, supported the view that I was crap and should be embarrassed." I could hear the hurt in her voice, but there was an edge there too, like she wasn't going to take it lying down.

"So yeah, I feel like I need to go in there and hold my head up high and not be cast into the shadows like a pariah." She kicked up her chin proving she wasn't going to take their shit. "But I also want to go because it was so much a part of my life before and I honestly loved the events. Oliver wasn't a fan, so I had to drag him along half the time. But dressing up, being around the art, talking to the artists—I really enjoyed it. Besides, usually there's an open bar. What's not to love?"

"Then we go and we'll have a good time. And fuck everyone else, and their opinions of you." I meant it too. I wasn't going to let some asshole's view dictate her good time. She was going to be with me, and she was going to smile all night.

"Fuck everyone." She agreed, laughing. "But you're going to have to wear a suit." Her previous happy face turning concerned, probably expecting me not to own one. "It's formal."

"I can do a suit." I laughed, reassuring her that while I didn't wear a jacket and tie most days, I still had one or two hanging in my wardrobe. Might even be time for an upgrade, the idea of looking my best for her something I'd happily shell out money for. "It might not be designer, but it will do."

I wasn't deluding myself. She probably paid more for one pair of shoes than I did my entire wardrobe, but I knew I could make it work.

"I don't care if it's designer." She waved me off. "But if you want to buy something, we could go shopping. My treat, I could even get a new dress." Her eyes lit up at the prospect.

"Yeah, that isn't going to happen. You aren't buying me clothes."

There were some things where I wasn't willing to bend. Her spending money on me, buying me clothes was a hard limit for me. Maybe I was more old school than I thought, but there was more chance of her trading in that fancy car for a truck than her buying me a suit.

"It's just money, Josh. It's no big deal." She lowered her voice, not understanding why I would say no.

"It's a big deal to me."

"Okay." She shook her head, a whole lot of I-don't-get-your-issue-but-I'm-not-going-to-fight-you-either. "Whatever you want."

"Good, now let's go get lunch while we still can."

FOR THE REST OF THE day I was spared questions about what I was working on, and we didn't talk about money either. It was something that no doubt would come up in the future, but we'd jump off that bridge if and when we came to it.

Instead, I focused on my work, both human canvases, and the stuff on regular paper. My secret project was not so surprisingly a gift for Eve, something I hoped might make her smile. But I wanted to finish it before doing the unveiling, which was going to prove challenging given we spent so many hours together.

"Hey, J." Dallas walked in without knocking, the open door clearly an invitation. "You want to go get some dinner tonight?"

The bastard looked unreasonably smug. "I'm buying."

"As much as I hate to turn you down." And Dallas offering to pay was something that rarely happened, so the regret was real. "I have plans." My plans of Eve and her body, something I had been thinking about all day.

"She can come too." He rolled his eyes, stupid grin on his face. "I assumed you were a two-for-one deal. Besides, she's better looking than you, and it's possible I might even like her more than you too. So this is a roundabout way of me getting to have dinner with her. Like dating by proxy."

"You realize how messed up that makes you sound, right?" I shook my head, his brutal honesty not at all surprising even if it was ridiculous. "And that you're basically admitting you're interested in the woman I'm seeing?"

"Dude, how long have we known each other?" He had the nerve to look offended. "You know no matter how interested I am, I would never make a play for someone you were seeing. *But,* I'm still allowed to look." Dallas cracked a grin.

"Fine, as long as Eve is cool with it, we'll go to dinner." We still had to eat, right. And I'd waited this long, what was another hour or two. "But she gets to pick the place so be prepared to spend big."

"Oh, she already said yes, I asked her first." And now the smug ass grin made perfect sense. "I figured she had your balls in her purse anyways, but if you did say no then the two of us would have an enjoyable dinner."

"You are such a shit." I threw my head back and laughed. Had to hand it to him, he was fucking slick. No wonder women loved him.

Dallas planted his butt on the chair opposite me, looking pretty freaking pleased. "Yeah, but your girlfriend thinks I'm sweet, so there's that."

"I never said she was my girlfriend, by the way." My head did a quick look around to see if she was in earshot. Not that I didn't want to call her that, but I understood it was probably too soon. And I probably should discuss it with her before Dallas.

"Oh, come on, dude." He didn't even try to be subtle. "Don't insult my intelligence or hers. If she's not your girlfriend then what the hell is she? Some girl? Your receptionist? Actually, let's clear it up right now." He turned toward the open door, giving his voice more volume. "Eve, sweetheart, can you come here a minute?"

"You, my friend, are asking for trouble." I wasn't sure if I wanted to let this play out—part of me curious—or whether to just put him out of his misery.

"Did you just call me sweetheart?" Eve looked at Dallas like he'd sprouted a second head as she entered the room.

"Yes, but more importantly, I need you to do something for me." He waved her in closer, not having the decency to let this stupid issue go. "Are you Josh's girlfriend?"

"Is this a trick question?" She looked at me and then back to Dallas confused. I didn't blame her, it didn't make a lot of sense out of context.

"Dallas seems to be hung up on labels." I decided to man up and just tell her the freaking truth. It's not like he wouldn't enjoy giving her his version of it. Something told me, mine would be better.

"He called you my girlfriend. I pointed out that the term wasn't something we'd discussed yet. He decided he needed to make an issue of it. Feel free to ignore him."

"Oh, well in that case." The confusion eased out of her face, smiling as she turned toward Dallas. "Yes, I'm Josh's girlfriend."

"See, I told you so." He tipped his chin, satisfied. "Be ready to go in ten, kids. Josh, you're driving," he called over his shoulder as he walked out the door.

"That doesn't freak you out, does it?" Eve moved closer, her eyes catching mine. "You're not one of those guys who panics about the C word are you?"

"Nope, was just looking for the right time," I admitted without hesitation. "I had unofficially claimed you the other day if you remember, I'm just giving you the illusion it wasn't a done deal." My hand ran down the side of her arm, the need to touch her too great.

"Well good, because I didn't want to be like all those people who have Facebook statuses of *it's complicated*. I always called them douchey, my friends would never let me live it down if I became one of them." She laughed. "Besides I like that I get to call you my boyfriend. It's less wordy than *the guy I have sexual fantasies about*."

"They're not fantasies if I make them happen." I planted a kiss on her neck, a promise of what was going to happen later. I'd enjoy hearing all about those fantasies too, and check them off one by one.

"I said ten minutes, people. What are you doing? I'm hungry," Dallas called from the front of the store.

"We're coming," I shouted back, wondering if it was too late to change our minds. Dinner with Dallas no longer seemed appealing.

Eve giggled at my choice of words and tossed back at me, "Not yet," before she went to my door, waiting for me to join her.

"Let's go." I hit the light and slung my arm around my new girlfriend's waist. "The sooner we get this over with, the sooner I can get you home."

EVE

"SO, YOU WERE JUGGLING? IN a bar?"

I was hearing Dallas's account of how he ended up in the emergency room and even though I had heard Josh's version, it was no less ridiculous the second time around.

"And I don't know any woman who'd be turned on by juggling, Dallas, sorry. I think you need a new party trick, maybe something with less chance of injury." I took a sip of my draft beer, something I didn't usually drink but surprisingly it wasn't so bad.

Even though the venue for dinner had been my choice, I was conscious to keep it low key. I knew both of the guys would feel more comfortable at a local steakhouse in Queens than a fancy bistro someplace else. But even though it had seemed simple and understated, dinner had been amazing. The food was perfectly cooked, the service had been impeccable and the company—outstanding. Interestingly enough, I'd preferred the local steakhouse to the bistro as well. I was sensing a theme, and it had little do with dinner.

"What? So you're an authority on all women now?" Dallas argued, amusement peppering his voice. "I would say my track record speaks for itself."

"I think what Eve was trying to point out," Josh played the diplomat. "Was the caliber of woman you would attract with the juggling wouldn't be as high as something else. *Anything* else." His throaty laugh made my skin tingle.

He had a really awesome, manly laugh that conjured up visions of wood chopping and camping in a forest. I didn't even like camping, let alone in a forest, but that laugh would probably be enough to convince me.

"Well, not everyone wants fancy. I'm happy playing in my end of the pool. No offense, Eve." He took a swig of his beer, hiding his smirk.

"Okay," I laughed, not offended even though usually I would be. It was obvious he was baiting me looking for a reaction. "And what end of the pool would that be, Dallas? The shallow end?"

"You want some ice for that burn?" Josh smirked, draping an arm around the back of my chair and giving me a kiss. "Nicely handled."

While I knew he was joking, people threw out innuendo like that all the time. That because my family had money, that it somehow made me conceited. And it was just not true. We all had preconceived ideas to overcome; no one got a free ride despite outward appearances.

"Well, anyway." Dallas pretended to ignore me, making an exaggerated display at tipping his beer at Josh. "I wanted to thank you for saving my life last weekend. This could have ended with a much sadder ending, one where I didn't make it." He lifted his beer. "You're a true friend."

"There was no danger of you dying, you moron. It was a cut." Josh grinned, clinking his glass despite not agreeing with the toast. "But anytime, dude." It was heartwarming to watch.

"So have you done anything *interesting* for a girl?" My attention turned to Josh, my interest at an all-time high. "Made a fool of yourself to impress someone?"

"Nope, not a thing." He hid his grin behind his beer as he shot Dallas a funny look.

"Oh, now I know there's a story." I shuffled in closer, curious to hear how Josh, who always seemed in control, had unraveled for a girl.

"He has the *worst* tattoo I've ever seen on his left shoulder," Dallas volunteered, moving in closer, grinning as he dished the dirt. "It's supposed to be a crow, but it looks more like two storm clouds fucking, flanked by a pair of wings. It's so saturated, there's no chance of saving it either."

"It's not that bad." Josh rolled his eyes. "It was a first attempt, and it's not even that big. I barely even know it's there."

"I'm assuming you let someone else do this to you?" I couldn't help but cast my mind back to when I had held a tattoo machine in my hand, my effort probably a thousand times worse than the one they were talking about.

"Jade, my girlfriend at the time." He rubbed the back of his neck, coy grin told me it probably was as bad as Dallas implied. "She wanted to learn, we went through the basics and then when it was time, I offered myself up as a canvas."

"He broke the golden rule, don't ever mix ink and women," Dallas weighed in, passionately trying to sell his point. "Ends up badly for everyone. Do you know how many dudes get some lame ass tattoo because of a girl and then end up breaking up? And women aren't any better either, getting Billy Bob on their freaking arm and then end up shacking up with Brad Pitt."

"I'll remember that next time Angelina Jolie walks in." Josh laughed. "Oh, wait, she probably doesn't give a shit what two no-names from Queens think."

"So, after you let her—Jade—do it, then what?" I was curious about the story of Josh, the crow tattoo and the girl. It sounded like a suspense movie, and one I was dying to hear the conclusion to.

"So, I picked the design, thinking the crow would look badass. And she practiced on paper, sketched it out and everything." He shook his head as if it was playing back in his mind. "But when she came to the actual piece she freaked. Then she got nervous and didn't want to tell me she wasn't feeling good about it, and figured it was better just to finish. End result wasn't great. It scarred pretty badly and like Dallas said, it's too saturated to even consider a cover up. I mean, it would have to be a really, *really* good artist. So I just left it there as a reminder that I don't always make great decisions."

I hated Jade.

Ridiculous, because it was before I knew him, and she was no longer in the picture. But I hated she had gotten a chance to draw on him when I hadn't. Which was again ridiculous considering I didn't know how to tattoo and my effort would've probably been worse. It was dumb, I was jealous. Dumb, dumb, dumb. And yet, there I was. Annoyed they'd shared something I knew was important to him and I never would.

"Well I hate to agree with Dallas on this, but he has a point." I tried—probably unsuccessfully—to keep my agitation out of my voice. "Not a smart move. Such a shame to ruin perfectly good skin."

"Yes, Eve sided with me." Dallas raised his hand, waiting for me to high-five. "Someone write that on a calendar or something."

"No real harm was done." Josh shook his head, shrugging. "It's not like I put anyone else at risk."

Well, that was a matter of opinion. He'd put himself at risk, and that was enough as far as I was concerned.

I wondered if there were other times he had sacrificed part of himself for someone else. It was evident he had a big heart, so many little things he did hinted to that. The way he'd allowed me to come work with him even though he probably had his doubts. That he allowed me to sit in with him while he worked, an extra set of eyes probably adding pressure he didn't need. Taking Dallas to the hospital, and staying with him over the weekend, making sure he was okay. Driving Kitty home from the hospital after her date had gone south. Not telling me how he felt because he was trying to do the right thing. Agreeing to go to my gallery thing even though he probably didn't want to. So many little things that I hadn't really noticed, yet put together showed me what an amazing, considerate and caring man he was.

Jade had taken advantage of that, and I'm sure other women had too.

"Hey, you still with us?" Josh's hand had dropped to my shoulder giving me a slight shake. "You zoned out on us."

"Yeah, I don't know where I went," I joked, tapping my head lightly with my fingers and forcing the smile. My thoughts, not something I wanted to share.

"We can go, Eve." Josh focused on me. "If you're tired, or whatever, we can call it a night. Dallas is cool with that." His head tipped to his friend sitting across from us who was nodding.

"Totally, just let me grab the check and I'll hitch a ride with you guys." Dallas pushed away from the table and flagged a waiter.

The waiter, Pete, ended up being someone Dallas and Josh knew, so after a quick introduction, Dallas walked off to the counter to chat and settle the bill. The two of them made plans to catch up on the weekend as they left Josh and I sitting at the table.

"I was okay with staying, honestly." I leaned my head against Josh's broad shoulder, which was on my top ten places to rest it. "I'm not a party pooper." Nor did I want to seem like the reason to end their night.

"Did you think maybe I was using that as an excuse so I can get you home and alone?" Josh bit back his grin. "It's a lot more polite than telling Dallas I need to get back to my place to have sex with my girlfriend."

"Well, in that case, I am tired." I faked a yawn, wanting to be alone with him too.

Dallas returned to the table so we said a quick goodbye to Pete and returned to Josh's black Jeep. The conversation on the ride to Dallas's house was easy. The guys talked about the shop, tattoos they had coming up and even asked me for input. I interjected enough conversation so I didn't seem rude but my mind was on Josh. On how lucky I had been to find him. Not just because he was gorgeous and talented, but because he had an amazing heart and I was going to be a better person for knowing him. He was exactly the person I needed right now, and I thanked God, Kitty, my wayward boyfriend and even my shitty work for creating the storm so our worlds collided.

"See you both tomorrow."

When we got to his apartment, Dallas hopped out of the Jeep and waved goodbye. Josh waited for him to disappear before turning to me. "My place okay with you?"

"Yep, more than okay." I smiled back, giving him a reassuring squeeze.

I had briefly seen the outside of his apartment when we picked up his car yesterday but was excited to see his personal space.

He lived close to the tattoo studio in a row of apartments in what was the artsy part of the city. Galleries, art institutions and studios—it seemed a melting pot for inspiration and I immediately understood why anyone would choose Long Island City as a place to live and work. It didn't have the stiffness of the Upper East Side, the streets living and breathing as much as the people in them.

"This is a really nice neighborhood," I said as he pulled up to the curb, parking the Jeep in front of his apartment building.

"Yeah, I like it here. It just feels right." He shot me a quick wink and stepped out of the car.

I joined him on the sidewalk as we made the short trip to the security door. Josh pulled out a set of keys and unlocked the outer door that opened up into a narrow hall with a set of stairs.

"No doorman." He squeezed my hand as he led me to the

stairs. "There's no elevator either. But I'm only on the second floor."

"I don't mind, it will help work off dinner." I followed him up the carpeted stairs to the second floor.

"This is me." He unlocked his front door and opened it, waiting for me to go through.

The light came on as he stepped in behind me, closing the door with a thud. Inside was not what I expected at all.

Everything was tidy. The pale blue couch matched the pale blue drapes, and the coffee table was stacked with two neat rows of magazines. It was small, but cozy, with the kitchen and living room all visible from the front door.

"Let me give you the grand tour." He pulled me further inside, our feet hitting the carpet just a few feet away.

"This is my living room. And over there is the kitchen." He pointed it out even though it was easy enough to see. "There is the dining room." His finger moved to a small nook off to the side, which had a wooden kitchen table and four chairs. "And through the hall is the bedroom and bathroom."

"It's great." My body turned, taking it in from all angles. Honestly, I was surprised how neat it was and how homely everything felt. If I'd walked in without knowing who lived here, I'd never guess it was a big tattooed guy.

"Not as impressive as yours, but it's mine." He wrapped his arms around me. "You want to see the other rooms?"

"Yes," I answered with zero hesitation, unaffected by the comparison of our apartments or his statement. I followed him the few steps that it took to enter his bedroom.

Like the rest of the house, it was small but neat. While the living room had been styled with cool hues of blue, his bedroom was a mix of charcoal and different shades of gray. The small lamp he'd switched on threw a muted yellow wash across the room; it was bright enough to see everything without the harshness of halogen.

It was obvious there were differences between the places where we lived, but to me it didn't matter. Sure, I loved my apartment with its two bedrooms, large closet space and terrace but I could have just as easily been happy in his place trying to find places to stuff my collection of shoes.

"You're not having second thoughts are you?" He mistook my silence as nerves, lowering his head to look at me as those kind, perfect, blue eyes studied me. "Because we can wait, Eve."

"No, no second thoughts." I slung my arms around his neck, stretching on my toes to kiss him. "And because we're at your place, I don't have to worry about you sneaking off in the middle of the night."

"Is that so?" He grinned, tipping me back so he could kiss my neck. "Neither of us are going anywhere."

The rumble in his voice was like a jolt of electricity up my spine, my skin prickling as warmth spread across it. And I was no longer thinking about the apartment, the neighborhood and where I could store my shoes.

"Take your clothes off for me." I unwound myself from his body and lowered myself onto his large mattress.

"Funny, I was going to ask you to do the same thing." He stood with his feet shoulder width apart as he looked down at me, all that delicious skin still covered.

"I'll make you a deal." I kicked off my ballet flats and wiggled my toes. "I will take off everything while I watch you strip. Think of it as an exercise in efficiency, you said you liked that." I glanced at him under my lashes, taunting him with my hand hovering at the hem of my shirt.

"I like a lot of things." His fingers curled around the bottom of his T-shirt and yanked it off, tossing it aside. "You naked—is currently at the top of my list."

Josh's chest when he was wearing clothes was hot, but naked, it was spectacular. The explosion of color snaked up his torso, down both arms as each muscle flexed under his movement. I'd already seen it, but it was no less impressive the second time around.

"Uh-uh." Josh shook his head. "You don't get any more until I do. This was your deal, remember?"

Slowly, I unbuttoned my shirt, my fingers blindly moving down as I kept my eyes locked on him. Pushing the sides open, I shrugged it off my shoulders allowing it to drop onto the comforter behind me. His eyes heated as they latched on to my white sheer bra.

"Take it off," he enunciated slowly, his jaw tight as his tongue slid across his lips.

"I could say the same." My hands reached around my back, waiting until he unhooked his belt and lowered the zipper of his jeans.

"Now, Eve." He toed off his shoes and pulled off his socks. "I want to see you."

With a flick of my finger, the sheer material went slack, my hands holding it against my body as he bent down and kissed my lips.

My hands dropped and so did the bra, my arms lifting around him as his tongue entered my mouth with so much urgency it pitched me back onto the mattress.

"That didn't last long." He moaned into my mouth as his fingers circled around my breast, his weight pinning me below him.

"It was a stupid idea," I mumbled against his mouth as my hands went to the waistband of his jeans and tried to push them down over his hips. "I was trying to be seductive."

"Are you kidding me?" He lifted his hips, freeing his jeans and kicking them off. "Everything about you is seductive." He captured my mouth again while his hands traveled down my belly until they got to the fly of my jeans. "I don't think I've ever wanted a woman as much as I want you now."

My hands joined his, working in the tight space between our bodies to shimmy my pants down my legs while his hard length, still in his boxer briefs, moved against me.

"That feels so good." I arched my back, kicking off my jeans, loving the sensation.

"It will feel even better in a minute." He lifted off me again, his feet planting themselves on the floor as he stood.

He watched me as my eyes stayed glued to his fingers pulling down his boxer briefs and freeing his erection. His thick length swelled as his hand moved up and down the shaft, moving closer.

"Now you." His fingers unwrapped themselves from his cock and landed on my underwear, sliding them down my legs until I was laying in front of him, bare.

"I need to touch you." My fingers reached out needing the contact. He didn't give me the chance, capturing my hands and raising them above my head.

"Not so fast." His body pressed against mine, the delicious weight exciting me even further.

"But I want—"

His mouth sealed mine, forcing me to swallow the rest of my sentence. The kiss felt desperate, unrestrained as his hands slid down my arms, where they'd been holding me still, down to my body.

There weren't any more words, ours mouths fused together as he reached down further, his hand cupping my center.

Oh. Yes.

Tingles spread across my skin, the heat between my legs almost unbearable and he'd barely touched me.

I couldn't wait.

I had no idea what his game plan was, if he was going to tease me one microsecond at a time or work me up until I begged, but I was at my limit and I needed him inside of me.

"Josh."

The word tore from my throat. Part frustration, part desire, and all impatience.

He chuckled, lifting off me just enough to knee my thighs apart. I was so wet, so slick and needy for him that foreplay would be redundant.

"I wanted to play a little longer." His thumb rubbed against my clit as my hips lifted toward him. "But if you want this." His hand was replaced by his cock, its firm length sliding against me. "I'm not going to deny you."

"Yes. Please." My hands no longer restrained pressed against his body and roamed all over his delicious chest.

Again he moved away, this time reaching across to his night-stand and pulling out a row of condoms. "We're going to need more than one unless you plan to leave soon." The smile curled on his mouth.

"I'm not going anywhere." I shook my head, watching as he opened the foil packet and covered his cock in the latex.

He was huge, his body looming above me as he shifted back onto the bed, my hands wrapping around him the minute he was within reach.

"You don't get to jerk me off, no matter how good it feels." He unwrapped my hands and pinned them back above my head. Holding them there with one hand, he lowered his head and sucked on my nipple, the pink peak raising the second he made contact.

"That feels so good."

He moved to the other breast, circling it with his tongue as his cock moved against my entrance. He was so close, teasing me with the head, without allowing it to enter me.

I couldn't take it anymore, tilting my hips as I bucked against him, taking control as he slipped into me.

"Fuck." His jaw tightened, holding himself still as I lifted toward him. "You want this, Eve?" He inched in a little more, giving me just enough to drive me more insane.

"Yes." I moaned, wild underneath him, wanting all he had to give me.

Every muscle in his body was tight as he released my hands and grabbed my thighs. His abs rippled as he leaned back and thrust all the way into me, filling me completely as I sucked in a breath.

"What? Nothing to say?" He taunted me, his grin widening as he pulled out and then pushed in again.

"More," I groaned, lifting my hips to meet his as he stretched me, bottoming out as he thrust in again.

It was the last word I was able to say, Josh taking over the tempo as he rocked against me.

Faster.

Harder.

Deeper.

Pounding into me, our bodies fused together as our breaths raged out of control.

Sweat broke across my skin, the heat combining with the friction of our bodies and the unrestrained passion.

It had never been like this with Oliver. Hell, it had never been like this with anyone, the connection between us more intense than I'd ever felt before. A line had been crossed where *want* was tossed to the wayside and *need* took over.

"I'm going to come." I'd barely gotten the words out as the sensation slammed into me, every cell of my body fracturing into a million pieces as warmth spread across my skin.

"Yes, Eve. God, that feels so good." He didn't stop, continuing to move as my pussy gripped him tight as wave after wave of ecstasy washed over me.

"That's it, baby." He thrust one last time, exploding inside of me as my body shook. "God, Eve." He collapsed, covering me as his cock continued to pulse.

"Stay." My arms wrapped around him, holding him in place when he tried to move, his weight blanketing my body. "I love the feeling of you, stay on me."

"I'll crush you." He dropped a soft kiss on my lips, pushing onto his elbows to support himself. "You're so fucking beautiful." He kissed me again.

"I could say the say about you." My hands moved up and down his slick skin. "I love your body."

"Well, good." He grinned, rolling onto his side, disposing of the condom before pulling me back into a hug. "You're going to get more of it in a few more minutes."

"Not a hardship, Josh Logan." I shuffled in closer, my back against his chest. "Besides, you pulled out all those condoms, it stirred my competitive nature. I'll bet you tap out before I do."

"Ha. Not a chance." His hand strummed against my skin. "I want you to spend the night. All night. With me."

"I thought that was the plan." My body turned, rolling toward him so we were facing each other. "And if you recall, last time it was *you* who left."

"I know, I didn't want to rush you. Or cheapen this." His fingers traced the edge of my shoulder. "This isn't a one night thing for me."

He didn't say rebound, but I think maybe he thought it.

"Me either." It was crazy how safe and content I felt in his arms, like all the other stuff that had been tumbling in my head before just didn't matter right now. "I'm spontaneous, and often impulsive. Which is why I didn't think twice about tracking you down." I laughed, knowing how badly it could have all turned out. For all I knew, Josh could have been a serial killer who tattooed on the side.

"But when it comes to relationships, I'm usually pretty cautious." It had been three months before I finally agreed to sleep with Oliver. "It's different with you. I can't explain why, but it feels *more*. I *really* like you, and I feel that waiting would be wasting time. Time we could spend together. God, I'm not making any sense." I laughed, burying my head in the crook of his neck, my mouth saying way more than I'd intended.

It sounded ridiculous in my own head. That I had developed feelings—and not just sexual ones—for someone so fast, so I could only imagine how crazy it sounded out loud. Stage-five clinger, anyone?

"It makes perfect sense." His fingers wrapped around my chin, forcing me to look at him. "It feels right, and sure it's sort of soon but we're both adults. No one else gets to be an authority on how much time we should wait. Fuck." He threw his head back and let out a throaty laugh. "I tried and failed miserably, so I'd say we stop worrying about stuff like that and start worrying about us."

"Us," I repeated, the word barely a whisper. "I like that."

"Good, I like it too. Almost as much as I like you." He tapped me on the nose.

His words should have reassured me, proven I wasn't alone on the USS Crazy and celebrated I'd seem to have found a decent man. But of course, my ego and my self-esteem had recently taken a battering, so my confidence wasn't as high as I would have liked. And what happens when I feel slightly inadequate? I compensate. And sometimes, not in a good way.

"Do you like me enough to let me tattoo you?"

Because I couldn't leave well enough alone, I had to bring up Josh and what he'd done with another woman. Jealousy, insecurity, or maybe just the general feeling that I wasn't "enough." Even though we'd just had great sex and discussed our feelings. Or maybe it was because of that, and now I felt exposed?

"Is that a hypothetical question or are you asking for the opportunity?" His brow furrowed, and I couldn't tell if he was choosing his words carefully or he just genuinely couldn't work out why I'd brought it up. It made two of us, I guess. I wasn't entirely sure what I was trying to accomplish either.

"Hypothetical of course." I forced the smile, perpetuating the façade that this was just pillow talk.

"Well considering I was going to let you do it before, I guess

I'd let you do it." He shrugged, not seeming to have any real hesitation. "But only after some serious instruction from me, and maybe some practice on Dallas." He laughed.

"Can I see the crow?" I bit my lip, pushing a little further because obviously his reassurance wasn't enough. No, I needed the reminder of another woman in my face. "I was too distracted to look before."

"Sure." He shifted, loosening his hold around me, and twisted to his side. "It's not great, and don't tell Dallas I agree with him, but it does kind of look like two storm clouds fucking." He laughed, tapping his shoulder as he moved back so I could see.

It was smaller than what I'd expected. No strong lines defining the shape of the bird, and no texture to indicate the feathers or where there was a beak. Not only did it not look like a crow, but it didn't look like anything else. Just a bunch of flat black color on a back that was otherwise covered in beautiful artwork.

"Wow, it's a mess." I ran my fingers along it, the space around the two-storm-clouds-fucking vacant.

"Tell me how you really feel." He chuckled, not acting like he was at all surprised.

"You left room?" My palm flattened against it, my hand able to entirely hide the hideous mess. All that was left visible was the untouched skin around it, looking a little naked considering the rest of his back.

"I assumed that later I'd cover it with something." He shrugged again. "But as you can see, it's so dark and scarred, I'm not sure it's worth it. It would need to be a really on point design to hide it and not make it look worse. It's not just the design, you'd need a damn good artist too. I didn't want to make the same mistake twice, so I left it."

"Yeah. It would be a challenge for sure." And looking at it, I made a silent vow to never even consider tattooing him or anyone.

Sure, it would be easy to convince myself I could. I'm sure

Jane or Jade or whatever her name was, probably convinced herself too. But my two-week crash introduction showed exactly how much skill was involved.

"I would never want to be responsible for a mistake that someone would have to live with forever. Even if you would be willing to take that risk with me, I will never allow it."

"Don't you think that's *my* choice to make?" He twisted back around, his arms locking around me. "And one bad tattoo isn't the end of the world."

"Don't you see? It's not about the tattoo." I snuggled in closer, loving the feel of the thump of his heartbeat against my skin. "It's how much of yourself you give. What you sacrifice for someone else. I'm concerned you are too busy worrying about other people, and no one is worrying about you."

It was more honest than I wanted to be, but I had a hard time keeping up the walls around Josh. I really had to concentrate, and when I didn't—words tumbled out whether they were welcome or not.

"You got all of that from one tattoo?" He kissed me, so soft it was almost like a feather brushing against my lips. "Nothing we ever did would be a mistake. And that you're worried about me is so fucking sweet, but unnecessary. Sometimes a bad tattoo is just a bad tattoo. And as long as you learn from it, it's not really a mistake."

"God, I wish I could be more like you." My hands ran over his chest. "I want to be a better person. To know what it feels like when I close my eyes and know I was the best I could be. And, I'm really trying."

"Eve, you are the most proactive person I've ever met." His eyes were fierce, like he needed me to believe him. "You haven't laid down in a heap and given up. I don't know why you can't see that."

"I have a long way to go, Josh." I kissed his chest and then his shoulder, working my way up to his neck. "But I know I am capable of more, and I owe it to myself to do better. Wow, I am such a buzz kill." I laughed, the conversation way too deep. We were supposed to be talking dirty to each other, or I could be categorizing his muscle groups with my tongue. That was the kind of stuff we should be doing.

"I love that you talk to me." His fingers knotted in mine. "Trust me, the conversation is refreshing. I know it's not easy for you to say those things, so the fact you trust me makes me feel like I'm a hundred feet tall. So think of it as good for my ego." He grinned, the only man I'd ever met who could smile and immediately make me smile.

"You are such a dork." I laughed, the previous self-doubt being pushed to the side. "And for the record, I'm sticking to paper and canvas. And my next exhibit is going to be badass." And for once, I really believed it.

"I have no doubt." His fingers wrapped around my hip, and his grin morphed into something a little sexier. "Now, is there anything else on my body you want to see?"

"We've got all night, right?" My hands floated down his amazing toned chest. Licking it was definitely going to happen. "Show me everything."

JOSH

IF YOU HAD TO WAKE up early in the morning, doing it beside a beautiful woman was definitely the way to go.

We had spent the entire night getting to know each other, and by that I meant *really* getting to know each other. There wasn't an inch of her that I hadn't explored, and every single part of her had been perfect.

Yes, she had a knockout body. Toned but still looked like a woman, with my hands loving the feel of her curves. And yes, she was stunning. Her light brown eyes looked almost gold in the dim light of the lamp, and that smile was the kind a man would go to war for.

But she was more than the surface stuff, the inside more intriguing than the outer. I loved that she was going through her own evolution, and letting me be a part of that. Fuck, that was a kind of bravery that most people didn't have. Throwing themselves into the unknown with not much more than a wing and a prayer. Eve—whether she knew it or not—was fucking fearless. And that turned me on more than her perfect body.

"Eve." I kissed her shoulder, her face covered by a mane of

hair. "Time to wake up, sweetheart."

She mumbled, nothing I could really understand, with a hand flapping in my general direction. I assumed that was her way of telling me she wasn't ready to wake up and probably to fuck off. It was adorable to watch, and something I could get used to very easily. The more I learned about this girl, the more I was convinced she was my freaking dream girl. There wasn't a chance us meeting hadn't been fate.

"Come on, gorgeous." My hands slid up her body and cupped her tits. I loved the way they felt in my hand, and now that I had permission to touch them, I did as much as I could. "I hear your boss is a tyrant, he'll be pissed if you're late."

"Ugh," she mumbled underneath the hair. "I think he should give me the day off, considering it's his fault I'm so sore this morning."

I wasn't surprised she was sore. Even though I worked out, my muscles felt a little tight too. She had bent her body into positions I didn't think were possible, her sense of adventure not restricted to the parts of her life where she wore clothes.

"I hope the pain was worth it." I kissed along the back of her neck. "And I hear the best way to relieve sore muscles is light exercise and heat."

"Does that mean we're staying home?" She flipped onto her back, pushing the hair out of her eyes. "In bed?" Her eyes looked so hopeful, it almost killed me to say no.

"Nope, it means you're getting your sexy ass into the shower and then tonight, I will give you a full body massage." My fingers slipped down to her thigh muscles to demonstrate, gently working them. "With my hands, and other parts."

"That sounds like heaven," she moaned, the sound shooting straight down to my balls.

"Good, so let's get moving." My dick not pleased that I'd taken my hands away. *Trust me, buddy, neither am I.* "I'm assuming you want to stop by your place and pick up clothes. It's going to take a while to get into Manhattan and then back out. I strongly suggest you pack a bag, you won't be sleeping at your apartment tonight either."

That part was non negotiable.

While I was happy to play taxi, and go back and forth between her place and mine, she was sleeping in my bed tonight. And as many nights after that as I could convince her to. Of course I didn't tell her that up front, but I was confident she'd see it my way. I'd even crash at her place every once in a while just to shake things up. Location didn't matter so much, but the end result was going to be the same. Me. Her. Together.

"Two nights in a row, aren't you worried you'll get sick of me?" Her lips twisted like she knew that wasn't a possibility while her hands moved up and down my chest.

"Not even after ten nights, stop stalling."

Without giving her a chance to argue, I hauled her off the bed and into my arms. She yelped as her body hit my skin, my strides taking her into the bathroom.

"You can go first." I lowered her down, her feet hitting the bathroom rug. Her face was slightly flushed; her eyes wide as I took a step back to admire the view. "Towels and everything you need are under the sink. Don't argue." I dropped a kiss on her lips and closed the door behind me.

As tempting as it was to get into the shower with her, I didn't. Mainly because I didn't trust myself. Seeing her wet and steamy would be something I wouldn't be able to ignore. And as much as I wanted to have sex with her against the tile, I wasn't kidding about the traffic. We'd be lucky to get back in time to open. Thank God I always scheduled my first appointment thirty minutes to an hour after I flipped the sign.

So after we'd both showered, and after a not so quick commute into the city, we arrived at Ink Addiction a few minutes later than I was hoping.

"I'll go get us some breakfast and coffees." Eve kissed me as I opened the door. "Is there anything in particular you feel like?"

"You, but I don't think they serve that at the deli." I pushed open the door and waited till we were both inside, then pulled out my wallet to hand her some cash. "Surprise me."

"Uh-uh." She scrunched up her nose at the bills in my hand. "You pay for lunch and I do breakfast. That's our system. You can't change it now."

"You pay for coffee, not breakfast," I clarified, curling open her hand and placing the money inside. "So meals are still mine. And you're delusional if you think I'm going to let my girlfriend pay for breakfast the first time she slept over. What kind of savage do you take me for?"

"You know what decade we're in, caveman, right?" She laughed, waving the money in front of my face. "There was this whole movement of female empowerment, maybe you missed it? And maybe *I* want to buy my boyfriend breakfast." She did her best to give me her pissed off face, but it didn't cut it. The grin told me she wasn't as mad as she was pretending to be.

"Did you ever buy Oliver breakfast?" I watched her face deflate at the mention of his name. And as much as I hated mentioning the douche, it was to prove a point.

"Yes, all the time." She kicked up her chin. "You know we were together awhile."

"Yeah, I just figured as he had a job and was living in *your* apartment, he would have covered other things. Like food." Not so subtly hinting that Ollie boy had probably been more interested in a free ride than supporting her female empowerment. The dumbass seriously couldn't be any less of a man if he'd tried.

"He offered . . . sometimes." It was obvious she hadn't given it much thought, habit would do that to a person.

"And when you go out with your friends, do you usually pay

too?" I asked even though I knew the answer. Kitty had been very vocal about Eve picking up the tab for their famous nights out. Something told me they hadn't been isolated incidents.

"Maybe." She shrugged. "It's just easier if I use my card and then we can work things out later."

I highly doubted anything had ever been worked out. I would even go so far as to doubt it was even mentioned again. And while I also didn't think her friends were using her on purpose, I could see how easy it was for them to fall into a rhythm of letting someone else pick up the tab. No harm, right? From what I saw—the car, the apartment, the fancy clothes and shoes—Eve was loaded, not like she was hurting for cash.

"I know you mean well, and it's obvious you're generous because you care about these people. But you're not an ATM. Do you think your friends are going to suddenly not hang out if they have to pay for their own drinks?"

"Of course they'd still hang out. We've been friends forever." Her voice was surprisingly neutral, not defensive like she usually got. Probably—because as I suspected—these people weren't bad, they were just conditioned.

"You have money, I get that. But it's not going to work like that for us." My fingers curled around the fist that still held the fifty I'd handed to her. "So, take my money and go buy us breakfast."

"Fine, as long as you concede that it's not always going to be you paying. Your theory could also be said in the reverse, I'm not interested in taking advantage of you either." She rolled her eyes, not thrilled she'd given up but not interested in arguing either.

"I would love for you to take advantage of me." Her lips proved too great a temptation as I moved closer and kissed them. "We'll take turns tonight."

"Mmmm." She made a satisfied noise in the back of her throat. "Okay."

"Go, I'm starving." I gave her a soft whack on her ass as she turned and walked back out the door.

First up today, I had a consult, which meant I didn't have to set up right away. I had done some prelim drawings through the week but we were hopefully going to hammer out the final design today. So, while I was waiting for Eve and breakfast to return, I went over some of the stuff I'd already worked on. I was leaned up against the front counter with my sketchpad when I heard the door.

"Well, well. If it's not the Tattoo King of New York." A voice almost as big as the man who owned it stepped up to the counter. "I saw the article they did on you in *Ink Magazine*." Big grin spread across his face. "I was disappointed they didn't let you wear your tiara for the photo. Let me guess," he rubbed his fingers along the base of his chin. "It was laundry day, and it didn't match the outfit."

"Come on, Troy. You know it's a fucking crown and not a tiara." My grin matched his as I stuck out my hand. "And unlike you, I like to be humble."

The big guy exploded into a laugh, his whole body shaking as he returned my handshake.

Troy Harris was a few inches taller and definitely a few pounds heavier. He was also the drummer for international rock band Power Station and the only thing he had more of than money, was talent. Oh, and I had also dated his wife for about five seconds before they were married.

"I heard you've got another kid on the way. Congrats." I gave a nod of respect. Not that he needed my approval, but I was genuinely happy for him and Megs. They were both good people and despite my earlier jibe about him not being humble, he actually was a decent and very grounded dude.

"Yep, number two is due in a month." His pride beamed brighter than the lights of MetLife Stadium. "I think we've got a least a few more in us too, I want my own drum line."

"Holy shit." Eve stood at the door, her hands filled with paper bags and a tray of coffee, wide-eyed and open-mouthed. "Are you

Troy Harris?"

"I am." He turned around giving her a big million-dollar smile. "Most people just call me Troy though. You don't need to use my last name."

If I didn't know he was happily married I'd be convinced he was flirting. Guys like him couldn't help themselves, being charming was part of the job. But just because I understood it, didn't mean I liked seeing how impressed Eve was with him. That I even felt threatened proved how up in my head I was with this girl.

"Hiii, Troy." She moved toward us, gently lowering the coffee tray and the paper bags onto the counter. "I'm Eve." She put her hand out.

"Pleased to meet you." He gave her a polite shake before turning to me. "You finally decide to replace Dallas? Good move, it was time you cut the dead wood."

"Fuck you, Troy Harris." The man in question waltzed in, shades still shielding his eyes. He flipped him off for good measure before I had a chance to answer. "You come to steal another one of Josh's girlfriends? What happened to the last one? She get wise and dump your big, out of time ass?"

When I said Dallas had my back, I was not joking. Even though the guy was five-nine and one hundred and fifty pounds soaking wet, he'd go toe-to-toe with anyone he thought was a threat. Unfortunately even with my assurances that it had been water under the bridge between me and Megs, Dallas liked to ride Troy's ass whenever he came in. Lucky for Dallas, Troy took it in good nature and gave it back to him just as hard.

"Dallas, bright and early I see." I was barely able to suppress the grin. "Eve got you breakfast." I nodded to the coffee and food on the counter, hoping to defuse a full-blown assault between the two of them.

"Thanks, Eve." He nodded to Eve whose look of admiration had turned into what-the-fuck. "Don't be impressed by the rock star." He put a protective arm around her. "He's only just recently stopped dragging his knuckles on the ground."

"Have you graduated from paint by numbers, yet?" Troy deadpanned, looking bored. "Or does Josh still do your outlines?"

"Ummm, what the hell is going on here?" Eve ignored both Dallas and Troy and looked to me for an explanation.

"Troy, can you head back to my room and give us a minute?" I tipped my chin to the hall knowing he'd be fine to see himself down there.

"No problem, bud." He slapped me across the shoulder before turning to Eve. "It was nice meeting you." The sly bastard gave her a wink and a smile before heading down the hall to my room.

"Well, that was fun." Dallas pulled off his shades, grinning like an idiot. "You need to ask him if we can get in on his poker game. I'll bring snacks." He gave us a two-finger wave before also disappearing down the hall.

"What the hell was that?" Eve pointed in the direction of the two closed doors. "You know Troy Harris? And why does Dallas hate him? What was with all that girlfriend stealing stuff?" The questions tumbled out of her mouth in a hushed voice.

"I met him a while ago, the girl I was dating at the time was friends with the band. Troy ended up marrying her." The story a little shorter than what actually happened, but the core elements were there.

"Troy Harris stole your girlfriend?" Her eyes looked like they were about to pop from her head as her mouth dropped to the floor.

"Nah, Megs was great, but she wasn't ever mine for him to steal. I think we had like three dates tops, and those two had history. They were always meant to be together, I was the rebound in between." I laughed, no bad blood between any of the parties. "Everything is cool though, and I've done a couple of tattoos for the guys. All of them are super cool. And Dallas likes to get into a pissing contest with Troy because he is a sick puppy who gets off on it."

"Wow. Okay. Wow." She contemplated, her hands resting on her hips as she chewed on her bottom lip. "Well, you should take the food and coffee, and get to work. I'll drop off Dallas's in his room and then go back to the deli and get some more for myself."

Like water off a duck's back, she shook off any weird. Thankfully also losing the stars in her eyes she'd had when she seen Troy. Because even though I categorically knew there was no chance of anything happening between the two of them, I was still a jealous shit who didn't like his girlfriend being gaga over another dude.

"You don't have to do that, I can call and get some more delivered." I had hoped we'd have time to eat together, but I had seriously misjudged time.

"Don't be silly, I enjoy the walk and besides I still have your change." She wrapped her arms around my neck, cheeky grin on her face. "Just doing my part in spending your cash."

"That's what I like to hear." I planted a kiss on her forehead. "I promise we'll do breakfast tomorrow."

"You'll make it up to me with more than just food." She gently pushed against my chest. "Go. Go work."

Grabbing a couple of breakfast burritos from the bag and a couple of coffees, I headed back into my room. Troy was already situated in the chair, playing with his phone, looking up when I walked in.

"You want some breakfast, man? Coffee?" I offered him one of the bundles in my hand, and tipped my head to the coffees in the tray.

"I won't say no to food." He took the wrapped burrito and grinned. "But you can keep the java. Can't drink the stuff, thanks anyway."

"So that's what's wrong with you." I unloaded the tray of coffees onto my workbench and sat down on the stool. "You know you're not normal, right?"

"Yeah, so I've been told." He took a bite out of his burrito, chewing for a bit before adding, "So you and Eve, huh? Good for you."

"Is it that obvious?" I laughed, taking a bite of my breakfast. Mmmmm. It was so good, only thing missing was eating it with the woman Troy had just mentioned. I didn't even care he'd picked up on it, deep down it sort of pleased me.

"Yeah, it was a dead giveaway when you looked like you wanted to rip off my balls for smiling at her." He took another bite. "I'm familiar with the look, might have worn it myself a time or two," he added with a chuckle.

"Yep, was fortunate enough to have witnessed it." I laughed, rolling over to my desk while trying to finish the rest of my breakfast. "Let me grab the sketches I've done and we can go over them."

Troy and I sat in the room and finalized the design. He'd really liked the work I'd already done so it was just a matter of tweaking what I already had. I was able to show him the finished product before he had to leave, which meant that when he came in for his next appointment we could get to work on the actual ink.

The rest of the morning was consults as well, which wasn't usual but actually convenient since I was still pretty tired. I was going to need another shot of caffeine before the afternoon sessions for sure.

"Hey, sexy." Eve appeared at the open doorway, my last client having left a few moments before. "I've got a turkey sub with your name on it." She waved the bag seductively between her fingers.

"You are a goddess." The pencil in my hand dropped onto my drafting table, whatever I was doing no longer important. "If you're not careful I'm going to hold you hostage when it's time for you to go back to the gallery. As far as I can see, the bastards don't deserve you anyway."

Part of that statement was true. The gallery didn't deserve her. Anyone who would make someone feel like crap was a poor excuse for a human as far as I was concerned. Reviews aside, that they'd treated her like she should be ashamed or something, well that was just the icing on the shit cake.

But I would never force her to stay anywhere. Even if deep down, I hated the idea of not having her with me every day.

"Please." She sauntered in, her personal brand of food delivery blowing Uber Eats right out of the fucking water. "In about another week everything is going to be so organized, you won't even need me. You should definitely hire another tattoo artist though." She took a seat opposite me and dropped the sandwich on the desk.

"You've been talking to Dallas, huh?" The sly grin told me she hadn't come to that conclusion on her own even if it was accurate. "You sure I can't convince you to learn? Think of how much fun we could have. Lots of skin on skin practice before we even get to the machines."

"I've already told you, we do not want me going anywhere near someone's skin." She smirked. "But nice try, you should be in recruiting with a pitch like that."

"I'd like to point out that pitch was personalized." I leaned across my table. "No one else is getting that kind of training."

"You say all the right things, don't you?" She schmoozed, her eyelids batting like crazy.

"So, not that I don't appreciate the personal delivery, but don't we usually have lunch out front together? And it hasn't escaped my attention there's only one sub here. I wasn't sure we were at the sharing food stage of the relationship."

"Actually, I was hoping to take a few hours off." She smiled, her voice a little hesitant. "I wanted to pick something up to wear for Friday night and there wasn't going to be time between now and then. Both you and Dallas only have two people this afternoon. And all the messages have been cleared, stock levels checked with low items reordered and everything else is done." She blew out the sentence, almost out of breath.

"Of course you can have the afternoon off." She'd more than earned the time, effectively doing what most people would do in three days, into one. "Do you want to take my Jeep?" I reached into my pocket for my keys.

"Thanks, but no." She screwed up her nose, her head shaking. "Even thinking about parking that thing makes me want to barf. I'm going to go get my car, it's easier to drive."

"This isn't your way of weaseling out of spending the night again?" I was only half joking. "I thought I made myself clear this morning."

"Relax, I'll drive back tonight." She rolled her eyes, rising back to her feet. "I may even pick up something else to wear tonight, especially for you." The suggestion backed up by a wicked grin.

"Don't get anything on my account, I prefer you naked." I stood up and rounded the desk, my hands finding their anchor around her waist. "But by all means, enjoy shopping."

"Predictable." She reached up and kissed my lips. "Don't forget to eat." Her eyes dropped to the sandwich on my desk. "You'll need your stamina for when I get back."

"I wasn't the one who was complaining this morning," I reminded her. "You should go," I warned, being so close to her and remembering last night not giving me an incentive to let her leave. "Before I find something else to eat other than the sandwich."

"Tonight, you can eat whatever you like." Her body twisted in my arms and blew me a kiss. "Bye, Josh."

I watched her leave, her hips swaying unnecessarily and I knew it was on purpose. Stirred up feelings both in my chest and the other organ, the one that hung a lot lower than my heart.

This girl was going to be the death of me. She had me twisted in knots I had no hope untying. Not that I wanted to. Wherever that road we were on was leading, I was heading there willingly.

EVE

I HAD SPENT ALMOST EVERY waking moment with Josh since Wednesday. Well, really Tuesday if you wanted to get technical, pretty sure the few hours we were apart were when I was asleep and so didn't count.

It made sense for us to sleep at his apartment; it was walking distance from the shop and meant we didn't have to make that killer commute from Manhattan every morning. Funny how it never really bothered me before, but spending the extra time in bed in the morning became a huge motivator. And while I missed my huge two-person shower with its thirty-five water jets, and not having to compete for bathroom time, I was slowly becoming a fan of cramped spaces. It led to lots of touching. Most started innocent enough, a hand on my hip while he tried to scoot by. But soon that incidental touch would turn into something else. Which made me forget about what I was doing in the first place.

Which is why even though work was so close to where we were spending our nights, we were usually there right on opening time. Funny thing was, neither of us seemed to mind.

The gallery showing had been something I contemplated

intermittently. I wasn't so much nervous—no longer willing to hide behind someone else's veil of shame—as I was anxious. Sort of like hitting the gym after a hiatus. You were sure your body would know what to do, but it would also feel awkward until you got back into the rhythm.

There were people I hadn't seen in a few weeks, some of which I actually missed. Not the gallery director though, Mr. Ashton could go suck a big bag of dicks. We'd never really gotten along, and his reaction to my show sealed the deal for bad feelings. He was the one who suggested I take personal time, who snickered when reviews came out the next morning. I was mad at myself for not being stronger and telling him to shove his *personal time* right up his ass.

Still, like a stack of dominoes it had all brought me to where I was. So I couldn't be totally angry. I was more motivated and inspired than I'd ever been and I had an awesome new boyfriend as well. Some might say I'd hit the jackpot, and I wouldn't argue.

I was excited to walk in there tonight with Josh and show him my world. One, because fuck them, I wasn't out for the count. And two, because I loved the art. Seeing it on the walls, walking around and contemplating it. Drinking it in and trying to imagine the artist's thoughts. It's what I hoped people would do with my pieces, and to be fair, they kind of did. It wasn't their fault my mind had been stuck in bored-and-going-nowhere so naturally my work chose to follow.

"Hey, baby," I crooned into the phone while I finished my makeup. As the gallery was on my side of town it made sense to get ready at my apartment and have Josh meet me. "You on your way?"

The idea of getting ready and surprising him had also played a part. We had missed out on the whole dating thing, so I wanted to take the opportunity to experience that opening-the-door-and-seeing-him buzz whenever I could.

"I'm in the car as we speak." His voice echoed out of the

speaker and bounced off my tiled walls. "You need me to pick anything up? Whipped cream, chocolate sauce, condoms?" His chuckle peppered the air.

"Oh, baby." I could barely contain my smile. "You got confused. It's an ART show, not SEX show. Easy mistake but sadly the nudes we'll be seeing won't be sucking anyone's dick."

He laughed, the sound making my body tingle. "Well this *is* awkward. I'm assuming my leather codpiece and chaps probably wasn't the way to go. Too late now, you'll just have to be cool with turning heads tonight."

"Well then I better get into my pearl G-string and dominatrix boots." I added extra lashings of black mascara. "I would hate for you to have all the attention."

"I'll be there in ten."

"You said you just left, you can't make it across town in ten minutes." My hand paused mid stroke, the mascara wand still in my hand. Unless he had a helicopter—which he didn't—and even then it was dicey. Manhattan's airspace was almost as crowded as the roads.

"I can," his voice rumbled out of the phone, "if I know all you're going to be wearing is a G-string and a pair of boots."

"Pervert." I laughed, shaking my head. "Drive carefully and I'll see you when you get here. I'd like you to be in one piece as well, and no outstanding warrants for excessive speeding either."

"Anything for you."

I believed him too, the heat radiating across my entire body as we said our goodbyes and hung up.

It was some time later—not ten minutes like he had threatened—when he knocked at the door. His name had been given to my doorman, but he didn't have a key so I was expecting the knock. But I still had butterflies in my stomach as I walked to the door and opened it.

"Oh. My God."

The air was knocked out of my lungs as I stood in front of a black-suit-wearing Josh.

He looked amazing, the jacket framing his shoulders perfectly as it buttoned up in front of his narrow waist. His long legs in black dress pants made him look impossibly tall, with the crisp white shirt making his blue eyes pop.

"Wow." He seemed to be oblivious that I'd become a statue at the door, my eyes about to pop out of my skull as he walked into my apartment. The invitation to come in not extended because I couldn't speak. "You look beautiful."

The dress I'd picked was cobalt blue. I'd fallen in love with it before I'd tried it on, knowing how much it reminded me of his eyes. It was satin and fell all the way to the floor. The two thick straps from the front crisscrossed on my back leaving mainly exposed skin, the liquid material clinging to my body and rippled as I moved. It was old Hollywood at its finest, my hair tamed into a sophisticated topknot. My makeup to match.

"Are you kidding?" I couldn't even thank him for the compliment as my eyes remained glued to him. "You can't go out looking like that."

Most of his tattoos were hidden. Only a few rogues peeked out of the starched shirt from the collar, giving a hint to the wild that simmered underneath. The longer part of his hair that he usually styled into a messy quaff had been slicked back neatly. And on his chin he'd left a tiny bit of stubble, playing rebel to the clean cut the rest of him was representing. And put all together, it was enough heat to incinerate not only my panties, but any woman's underwear in a five-mile radius.

"What are you talking about?" He twisted, looking at his outfit for something I might be offended by. "You said a suit, this is a suit."

"I said wear a suit, not combust my vagina." I waved in his direction, taking a step back. "I think . . . no, I know, that you are the hottest man I've ever seen."

"Wow, guess the couple of hundred bucks I spent on this thing yesterday was worth it." He adjusted his cuff. "You weren't the only one who took a trip to the mall."

"You picked that up from a mall?" I shook my head, wondering how he made a couple-of-hundred-dollars suit look like a million bucks. "Wow. Just. Wow." Words eluded me.

"Forget the suit." His hands circled around my waist. "We have more important things to discuss." He glanced down at my breasts, the tops peeking out from the bodice of my dress. "Like how I'm supposed to act respectful with you dressed like that. Makes me want to do dirty things."

Heat filled his eyes, drinking me in from head to toe like he couldn't get enough. It was dizzying, making my heart skip a beat as I tried to remember the last time anyone looked at me like that. I was almost positive, no one ever had.

"I'm pretty sure the gallery has a policy against public fornication. I think we're both going to be in trouble tonight." My fingers wrapped around the lapels of his jacket, mentally calculating how much damage I would do to my makeup and hair if I pushed him up against the wall and screwed his brains out. Whatever it was, it would be worth it.

"You looking at me like that, isn't helping." His hands slipped lower, cupping my butt as he pulled me toward him. The hard length in his pants leaving nothing to interpretation. "And yes, I've already thought about it. On the floor, on the couch or up against the wall. Any or all of those places." He rubbed himself against me, the ridge of his cock taunting me through his suit and my dress. "But it means we'll be late. Very late. Like next week kind of late. Because it's going to be that long until I'm even close to getting my fill of you."

Did I even want to go to this stupid—my earlier excitement and praise of the event now missing in action—art show? It was pictures on the wall. I'd seen it many times, could read all about it tomorrow. Seeing it in person was highly overrated.

"We don't have to stay long," I rationalized, trying to remind myself that it wasn't just the art we were going to see but some of my work friends and colleagues. I'd seen his world, time to show him mine yada, yada, yada. "An hour, two, at the most."

"Nope, we're not only going to go." His grip around my hips tightened. "But we're going to stay until the very end. Everyone is going to see how fucking beautiful you are, and then they are going to see you coming home with me."

"I think I should be offended by something in that maybe, but I can't get past how hot it sounded coming out of your mouth." I swallowed hard. "Let me grab my clutch."

Of course, in order for me to do that, he'd have to let me go. Which he hadn't.

He waited a second, his eyes steamrolling over my body again before brushing my lips with a gentle kiss. "Anymore than this and I won't be able to stop."

You're telling me. All I could do was make a weird noise in the back of my throat, which was a cross between a moan and possibly an animal dying.

Once his hands had freed me, I gathered my clutch and my keys. "There's no way I can climb into the Jeep in this dress. You mind if we take my car?"

"No problem at all." Surprisingly, he gave me no resistance. "I should drive though, seeing as I'm not the one wearing stilts." His chin dipped down to the floor, the edges of my Louboutins just visible underneath the dress.

"Yep sounds great." I tossed him the keys, his hand pressing on my lower back as we left my apartment.

I had hoped he wouldn't assume that his car wasn't flashy enough, because honestly I couldn't give a shit. And had I not been wearing a dress that gave me the leg movement range of a geisha, I would have been all about getting into his big, manly car.

He didn't mention it and I didn't want to plant a seed if it wasn't there to begin with, so with my mouth shut, I slipped into the passenger seat of my Tesla.

Josh looked at ease in the driver seat, his fingers wrapping around the steering wheel as he pulled out of the parking garage and onto the street. And if he had any hesitation of going tonight, he wasn't showing it.

"So this is where you work?" he asked as we pulled up to *Lenore West*, the private gallery where I'd had spent most of my days in the last twelve months.

"Yeah, it's small and by appointment only." I sighed, some of the old doubts coming back to me from when I originally took the job. "Not as impressive as the MET or MoMa, but I got to actually work with artists and had a chance to see some of the pieces move from our walls into people's homes."

Didn't sound so awesome anymore. Basically, it felt like I'd gone to college just to become a very knowledgeable sales person. Sure, I was oversimplifying it. I could tell you why one painting was worth a million dollars and why another was only a couple of hundred thousand, but it had never been my dream. The only art I had wanted to sell was my own. A curator—like my parents had assumed I would have become—at least had some nobility about it.

Oh. Fuck.

This was a hell of a time for the wake-up call.

"You okay?" Josh had popped open his door but hadn't stepped outside yet. I guess me sitting silently, staring through a windshield trying not have a nervous breakdown might be concerning.

"You want to go?" He closed the door, ignoring the valet standing beside the car ready to take the keys. "If you've changed your mind, we can go. Fuck this place."

"It's not the place." I shook my head, thoughts swirling wildly in an ironic moment of clarity. "It's not even the people in the place. It's me."

"What are you talking about?" His brow furrowed, rightly confused considering the person he was talking to wasn't making any sense.

"Let's go inside." The kind of conversation it required taking longer than the few minutes we had in the car. I wasn't even sure a day would cover it. "I promise we'll talk about it later."

"Are you positive?" he asked, his hand hovering at the door handle after waving off Mr. Valet Guy who had knocked at the window.

"Yep, I'm positive." I plastered my best smile on my face and opened my door.

Josh had tossed the keys to the kid and was around to my side before I had a chance to fully step out. His hand wrapped around my waist as I straightened on the sidewalk, the additional support welcome, given the high heels and the long dress.

"Eve!" Bree had already spotted me, her hand waving madly from the top of the steps. "OhMGee, I can't believe you're here." She rushed down the steps to the street as fast as her Valentino heels would carry her. "You look Amaaaaaazing."

Bree was one of the women I had worked with and one of my favorite people at *Lenore*. And while she spoke like a teenager stuck in a woman's body, intelligence wasn't something she was lacking. Unlike me, she had no aspirations to produce original pieces. She was all about the investment. Wanting to Wolf of Wall Street herself—without the FBI indictments and cocaine habit—to an early retirement. Her ten-year plan had an island in it, as well as a well-oiled European whose job it would be to please his wife. And for all its ridiculousness, she was closer to her goal than I was.

"Thank you." I smiled, able to pinpoint the exact second her attention slipped from me to the man slaying ovaries in his sexy suit.

"Errrrrrrrrrr." She blinked blankly. "Who are you?" The breath slipped from her mouth seductively. She didn't even try to hide it, her pink lips spreading into a smile.

"I'm Eve's boyfriend." Josh didn't miss a beat, keeping one hand on me as he extended the other to Bree. "Josh."

"Boyfriend?" Bree looked to me, her eyes squinting, probably confused. The last man who had worn that title was Oliver—douche canoe, not to be confused with the hot man who was standing beside me. "I'm Bree." She accepted his handshake, giving him a big smile.

"Yes, this is my boyfriend, Josh." The steps outside the gallery not an ideal location to have that conversation. "We should probably go inside."

"Yes, yes. Of course. I'll see you in there." Bree smiled, nodding to both of us as we passed her on the way up the stairs. "Have fun."

"She seems . . . nice." Josh smirked, his hand on my back as he opened the door for me to pass through. "Is she an artist too?"

"Nope, she is here for the cash. She's her own biggest customer." I gave him the condensed version, not really wanting to spend my night talking about another woman. "And don't let that smile fool you, she will cut your legs from under you if you go up against her in an auction."

"Thanks for the tip." He kissed my forehead as he joined me inside.

Lenore West might not look large from the street but the interior was huge. The old Brownstone had been gutted, with non-load-bearing walls being knocked out to create an airy open space. Then a buyer could wander through both levels, the white walls and polished floors not detracting from the canvases and prints. Tonight, like most showings, it wasn't easy to wander, people with champagne flutes in their hands congregated in front of the art, talking.

Sometimes they were nice. Complimentary. Sometimes they weren't.

"Eve." My name again, this time from my friend, Lana. She strode toward us, wrapped in a black cocktail dress with a champagne flute in her hand. Her smile was unusual given the setting.

She hated these things and the gallery as well, but her husband had Bree's school of thought. So he dragged her along to exhibits so they could nest away for their portfolio. It was how we met actually, but I wasn't sure she was coming tonight.

"Lana." I welcomed her with a hug, turning to Josh to do introductions. "Josh, this is my good friend, Lana, she's not an asshole." Making the distinction between *her* and the evil people I used to work with.

"There are a few lawyers who would disagree with you, honey, but thank you." She gave me a squeeze before turning her attention to the man waiting patiently beside us. "And you must be Josh, I've heard so much about you."

"Really." He glanced at me, giving me a grin. "All good I hope?"

"Of course." She laughed, creatively sidestepping further implication on exactly what had been discussed. Him being hot as fuck, and my crush—the usual topics of conversation when his name had come up.

"David's buying something but I'll introduce you later." She gently placed her hand on his arm. "Don't judge him, he's going through this colored suit stage and no amount of telling him it looks ridiculous will sway him."

"I'm the last person to ever judge someone on what they wear. This isn't my usual get up." He yanked playfully at his collar. "Though Eve seems to like it, so it's worth the suffering."

"I do." My hand smoothed the front of his shirt, my fingers hitting his rock hard abs. "I'm going to fill our calendar with events just so I can see you in it."

"Get a room you two." Lana grinned, rolling her eyes.

"How about I go to the bar and get us some drinks instead." His hand slipped to my hip, gripping me tighter. "It will give you ladies time to talk about me behind my back."

"We'd never do that." My hand covered my mouth in faux horror. "Not sure what you're even talking about."

"Yeah, yeah." He shook his head, not buying it for a second. "I'll be back in a second." He kissed me lightly on the cheek and then walked toward the bar.

"Wow. That suit." Lana's eyes followed his retreating ass. Her smile saying more than her mouth.

"I know, right?" I wasn't even mad, my eyes on the same journey as he disappeared from sight.

"I like you this way." Lana waved her champagne glass in front of her. "Happy, relaxed. Usually when you're here you've got that fake smile happening. Like you want to kill someone, but haven't decided who." She pulled her face into a fake grimace.

"Wow, thanks." I pretended to look hurt. "So glad you're my friend."

"Come one, Eve. You know I didn't mean it as criticism." She took a sip of her champagne, eyeing me with approval. "I just meant he looks good on you. Whatever the two of you are doing, keep doing it."

She was right on both accounts. I had never been at the gallery in an unofficial capacity. Usually I was running around, making sure everyone was having a good time and drinking enough so their wallets had an easier time opening. Tonight I had none of that pressure, my attendance purely voluntary. And while I hadn't worked out all of my issues, I knew I was going to get there in the end. Josh had been the catalyst, and I was excited to see what the future held now I was slowly giving myself permission to be me. God, he was such a good man. So good I wasn't sure I deserved him, but I wasn't stupid enough not to take advantage of what fate had thrown at my feet.

"Holy smokes. Evie? Wow."

It was probably the only voice that could sour my great mood. The man who usually had to be dragged kicking and screaming to almost every event when we'd been together, was here now of his own volition. Fucking typical.

"Oliver." There was no warmth to my voice. "I'd say it was nice to see you, but we both know that it's not." My smile curled all on its own. "How are things downstairs?" My eyes dropped to his crotch. "I heard you had some issues. Anything I need to get tested for?"

Lana snorted, doing her best not to spill her drink as she tried to compose herself.

"Yeah, I might have deserved that." He winced, the memory probably still fresh. "But I forgive you. Let's call it even." The bastard had the nerve to smile, mistakenly assuming I was looking for his forgiveness. But that wasn't enough, no. His delusions extended further, assuming that me Icy Hot-ing his Calvin Kleins somehow negated his penis being in someone else's mouth.

Jesus, take the wheel for the man, please. He was beyond any help I could offer him.

"Oh, Oliver." Any feelings of affection I'd had were replaced by pity. "You really are clueless."

"Here you go." Josh appeared beside me, champagne in his hand. "What did I miss?" His arm wrapped around my waist.

Crap.

It wasn't bad enough that Oliver's appearance had dulled my mood; I now had to introduce him to Josh. Wasn't throwing him out of my apartment and ending our relationship enough? I didn't want to continue the freaking conversation and he definitely didn't deserve to meet Josh.

"Josh, this is Oliver. He was just leaving." I glared at Oliver in case the words hadn't been enough.

"You've moved on already?" He eyed Josh's hand around my waist hard and I could almost smell the jealousy. "Didn't waste any time, did you. Maybe it's because you had him on the side while we were together."

I felt Josh's grip tighten around me. "Dude, I'm going to give you some advice. Modify your tone and walk away." His blue-eyed stare was cold, his words steady. "Because I guarantee you, you don't want to be talking like that to any woman, least not one I care about."

"Just a minute." My hand pressed against Josh's shirt.

While I loved he'd stood up for me, in this case—against this loser—it really wasn't necessary.

"Yes, I've moved on." I tried to keep my voice low, not wanting to attract any more attention than we already had. "We broke up, which means I can see whoever I want." I took a step toward him, my eyes narrowing. "And the reason we broke up is because you had your bit on the side, not me. Also because you were a terrible boyfriend and if you'd been the slightest bit attentive you would have known I was coming home early that day. So you don't get to show up here and speak to me like I'm some whore. Do what you always do, have a drink at the bar and then leave."

"But, Evie, it was a mistake,." He had freaking nerve to say, changing tactics when calling me a whore hadn't worked out for him. "Look, I'm sorry. I fucked up, okay? I know you were faithful, I'm just. . . . Give me another chance, we were so good together. I still love you."

To his credit, Josh didn't say anything and I'm almost positive it's not because he couldn't think of anything. I'm sure he had a whole bag of things he wanted to say, but he stood behind me quietly and waited for me to respond.

"You love yourself, Oliver. Maybe my money, but never me. We were never good together. So do us both a favor and fuck off."

I heard a gasp, and first I thought it was from Oliver because he was looking particularly shocked. But for all the you-can't-possibly-mean-it on his face, it hadn't been him who'd seemed perturbed. No, it was someone behind me.

"Eve Thorton." He said my name with such distaste, it made

my skin crawl. "I was under the impression you were on leave."

Mr. Ashton was not my biggest fan. While he actively didn't like anyone, I was probably on the list of most disliked.

The feeling was mutual.

"I am on leave." I smiled sweetly knowing it would bother him. "I'm here as a guest."

"Well, as a *guest*." He sneered, like it hurt him to say. "I'll remind you that we don't tolerate that kind of language in here. *Lenore West* isn't a bar."

I'm not sure what exactly happened.

Maybe I'd snapped and lost my mind entirely, or maybe for the first time in a long time, I was thinking clearer than I ever had.

Two assholes that I didn't respect nor give a shit about their opinion, tried to handle me.

Two assholes too many in my mind.

"You." I pointed straight at the asshole who used to be my boss. "Can go fuck yourself, with the *we don't tolerate that kind of language here*." My voice had become so loud, everyone had stopped and was now looking at us. Not that I cared, I was too deep into this.

"I've seen it with my own two eyes, you ignore two buyers having sex in a stairwell." A chorus of gasps and a few snickers echoed around me. "Because their purchase got *you* enough commission to buy a yacht. So don't tell me what we accept here. You only care about your bottom-line, asshole. You never once gave a shit about anyone who worked here, and you sure as hell don't care about the artists, except for their capacity to earn you money, you evil, heartless prick."

Silence.

It was so quiet you could have heard a pin drop.

Not a click of a heel on the hardwood floor.

Not a clink of a glass.

No one was moving and sure as hell no one was talking. Probably wondering if Eve Thorton, the soulless, talentless wonder had finally flipped and gone completely crazy. *Write about that,* Time Out. *Oh, and by the way, fuck you.*

I felt a hand, and I almost flinched until I saw that it was Josh's, his arm wrapping around me. It felt warm and safe, giving me the courage to continue.

"And you know what, I could buy this whole fucking building if I wanted to. Oooooh, I'd love that." I smiled at him, his beady little eyes not knowing where to look. "And the first thing I would do would be to fire your uncompassionate ass."

Without thinking, my hand with a mind of its own, I tossed the champagne from my glass onto Mr. Ashton, the wine trickling down his stunned, silent face.

"You want another drink?" Josh asked, unfazed by my apparent outburst or meltdown. I guess it depended on where you rated my mental wellbeing at the time as to what it was categorized.

"No, I think I'm done here. We can go." A genuine smile spread across my face, his perfect blue eyes were my anchor in a sea of crazy. "Oh in case there was any doubt." I glanced back at Mr. Ashton. "I resigned. The rest of my leave can serve as my required notice. Or not. I don't care." My body turned back to Josh and I nodded. "Okay, definitely done, let's go."

"Great." He grabbed my hand, bringing it to his mouth, kissing my knuckles. "Let's go."

Every single pair of eyes in the room were on us. But I didn't care and neither did Josh as he strode calmly to the front door.

"What the hell happened to you?" Oliver—the man seriously was a dumbass—called out from behind us. "When did you turn into a crazy bitch?"

I didn't turn, not bothering to give him any more attention and instead threw the words over my shoulder. "When I started realizing that I deserved better."

It was the last thing I was ever going to say to him. To Oliver. Mr. Ashton. And anyone else who thought I was a bitch. They could start a little club with matching T-shirts and burn my picture in effigy. I no longer cared.

"The red Tesla." Josh handed the ticket to the valet, not having said anything else until we'd reached the street.

"Didn't you just get here?" The pimply face man-child looked at the ticket and then back to us.

"Yes, but I need to have passionate sex with my boyfriend, so be a sport and go get our car please." My bitch mode obviously stuck.

"Okay, sure." The valet took the hint and left to retrieve my car.

"You want to talk about it?" Josh wrapped his arms around me, kissing my forehead. "Because we don't have to, but I will tell you that it was pretty fucking badass."

"I think we can safely say we know what will be included in this week's art review. *Eve Thorton epic breakdown*, funnily enough I can't make myself give a shit." I leaned into him, loving the way my body fit against his. "Guess this wasn't such a good idea after all."

"Well for one, it got me this sweet suit." His arms lifted off me momentarily as he extended them to his side. "And you love the suit."

"Yes, I do." I laughed, running my hands down the front of the jacket. "So one good thing came of it."

"And for second." He lowered his head and kissed me gently. "And the most important thing is that you stood up for yourself and know that you don't want to waste your time anymore. That is better than anything you're ever going to draw."

"Aww, Josh." My eyes were starting to get teary. "Don't make me cry, I'm not wearing waterproof mascara."

"Then don't cry. Give me a smile instead."

On command, my lips spread into a smile just for him. Because obviously he was a magician. Or a saint. Maybe when I'd called him Tattoo Jesus in the early days, I'd been close to the mark. He definitely felt like more than just a man.

Before there was anymore crying or smiling, my car pulled

up to the curb. The valet handed Josh the keys and we both got into the car.

"Let's go back to my apartment tonight." My head leaned against the headrest. "I know it means we will have to get up earlier in the morning to get to Queens, but I really want my own bed tonight, and I'd love if you were in it with me."

"Of course." He moved one of his hands off the wheel and gave my knee a squeeze. "Anything for you."

We drove down the streets in an easy silence. I'm sure Josh had questions but he was gracious enough not to ask them and I was enjoying the gentle rock of the car as we navigated through Manhattan. He'd even turned the radio down, the whatever-was-playing barely a whisper through the speakers as I stared out the window.

I loved the city at night.

I love the lights, and the noise, and the movement. That even though the sun had gone to bed, people were still on the streets. The vibrancy, the energy—it was the city's heartbeat, and I hadn't listened to it in a while.

"I should have left a long time ago," I heard myself say. "You told me I should love what I do and I lied. I love my art but I never loved the gallery. I should have left a long time ago."

"Well, maybe you needed time. It's all a journey, isn't it?"

He was so fucking wise. I wish I could be that fucking smart, have it all worked out.

How could I tell him that I hadn't even *needed* the job. That I had an obscene trust fund that if I was even a halfway decent person I'd be embarrassed about. That I could continue to live my lifestyle as I've been living it, and still leave a sizeable inheritance to whichever poor human was tragically cursed to be my child when I left this mortal earth. That I had zero excuse for staying at *Lenore* other than it gave me an excuse to not give a hundred percent to what I should have been doing in the first place.

How could I tell him that, despite everything I'd said and done,

I'd really just been a coward?
    God, I didn't think I could stand it.
    The disappointment.
    His in me, and mine in myself.
    I needed to turn this around.

JOSH

SOMETHING WAS OFF.

We'd gotten up to her apartment and into her bedroom and her hands were all over me. Ordinarily this would not be a problem. In fact, it was my preferred state whenever Eve was around. But I knew it was a distraction.

Sure, we didn't have to talk about it. She probably had enough of it running around in her head that she didn't want to share. So I would be patient, give her whatever space she needed until she would talk. Or maybe we wouldn't. The fuck you I'd seen her give to her boss and her ex-boyfriend the last I'd hear on it.

But while I was fine to leave shit in the past—move on, deal with the future and all that fun stuff—I could tell one of us hadn't.

Here's a hint.

It wasn't me.

"Yes, Josh. Yes." I slammed into her hard, her eyes closed tight. "Harder."

"Yeah? You think you can take me deeper?" I raised her legs, rested her knees on my shoulders. Her body shook as I thrust into her. "That what you need?"

We'd practically torn the clothes off each other, tossed them to the side with no fucks given to their welfare. And while I knew the sex was a Band Aid—a diversion for the underlying issue—I didn't have it in me to deny her.

"God, yes. Josh," she gasped. "I think I'm going to come."

There was no need to tell me, I could feel how primed she was.

"I want you to come on my cock, baby. I want to feel you grip me so fucking hard it hurts."

My balls were so tight up against my body, I was skating the line between pleasure and pain. I wouldn't allow myself to come though, wanted the pleasure to be hers first. She needed it and I was going to give it to her.

"Josh." Her head thrashed on the pillow, her fingers wrapped around her perfect fucking tits. "Fuck."

And *fuck* is exactly what I did, pummeling into her until I felt her pussy fisting me. Tiny pulses ran up and down the length of my cock as she came hard, her body convulsing as I continued to hammer into her. She might have thought she was done, but she wasn't.

"Oh my God." She repeated it over and over again, as I felt the tension once again building in her body.

"You're going to come again." I didn't stop my assault, watching my cock slide into her with each stroke.

"No, I can't. I can't," she panted, her eyes squeezing shut as she gripped the sheets either side of her. "Oh. Oh. Oh."

The second explosion happened. Her back arching off the mattress as the wave took her, her pussy so tight around my dick I thought it might snap off.

Watching her like that, her hair a mess and so out of control is what did me in. And I couldn't hold back any longer as the feeling jacked up through my balls and hit me from behind.

"Yes, Eve. I can feel you, baby." I spilled my load, filling the condom as we came together. My body rock slowed as she shivered underneath me.

Her eyes flung open and she focused on me, watching as I pulled out and then slid back in, little whimpers escaping her lips each time.

"That was amazing," she moaned, stretched out on the mattress as I lowered her legs and slowly withdrew.

"You are amazing." I collapsed onto the bed beside her, my own body doing the shake. "I'll give you a few minutes to recover and then get ready for round two. You said you wanted to be fucked hard and I take my responsibilities very seriously." I pulled the condom off my dick and tossed into the waste paper basket beside her bed. Thank God she had a stash of her own in her bedroom, the one rubber I had in my wallet wasn't going to cut it.

I was only half kidding. But if she needed the distraction, then I was going to give her one so good she was going to forget. Even if it was just for a few hours.

"You are a machine, I'm going to start needing to go to the gym just to keep up with you." She rolled onto her side, her hands sliding up my torso.

"Or we could just condition you using sex. Never have to leave the bedroom." My hand found her hip. "If it's a choice, I like my plan better."

She laughed, her mussed up hair covering her eyes as she repositioned on her pillow. "Me too. We should go with your plan."

I'd hoped some of the tension had eased out of her, but while she looked sated and relaxed, her eyes were a dead giveaway that whatever reprieve I'd given her was over.

"You want me to order some food? We haven't had dinner yet." I changed tactics, shuffling up her headboard as I shifted into a sitting position.

"I guess, I had made reservations for Matteo's at nine but I'm pretty sure we're not going to make it." She didn't even bother looking at the clock on her bedside table. I had a hunch it had more to do with her not wanting to leave the bed, than whether or not we had time to make the reservation.

"How about I get pizza instead, we can eat slices in bed." I offered a suggestion, happy to stay in for the rest of the night and just be with Eve.

"You are a prince, Josh Logan." She gave me a million dollar smile that made me feel about ten feet tall.

"Anything for you." I kissed her on her nose and climbed out of bed.

My phone was lying on the floor next to my discarded suit. It had probably fallen out of my pocket when I'd tossed my pants there. I picked it up and ordered pizza while I sat on the edge of Eve's big king-sized bed. She kept her eyes on me while I spoke, covering herself with the sheet.

"Thirty minutes or so." I pulled down the sheet, wanting to look at her naked body some more. "You don't seem shy, and surely you're not cold." Her beautiful body was revealed. "I don't think you need that."

"Ugh, it's a nervous habit I guess." She took a deep breath, slowly blowing it out. "As much as I don't want to, I keep thinking about things. My mind isn't where I want it to be."

"I wasn't going to say anything, but yeah I noticed." I lightly rubbed the base of her foot, my thumb circling the sole. "You know you don't have to leave the shop, right?"

It wasn't something I'd mentioned before, but the longer she was at the shop the more I wanted her to stay.

"Two more weeks, two more years—as long as you want."

It was clear she didn't need the money. Hell, the amount I was paying her would barely cover the utilities in her apartment. But if she wanted a job, I'd happily provide her one. I may have had my own agenda as well, but it didn't make the offer any less sincere.

"Thank you, that's really sweet." Another deep breath. "I don't even want to think about it to be honest. And please don't take this the wrong way, but it was always going to be temporary, I don't think it would work out long term."

I had no idea where her head was at and she wasn't giving me a lot to go on. But the *I don't think it would work out long term,* didn't make me feel warm and fuzzy. Did she mean the job or us? Did I risk sounding like a needy fuck and ask or just assume shit would work itself out in its own time?

It had been me who assured her that us meeting served a purpose, temporary or otherwise, so I wasn't sure why I was getting hung up on the expiration date now.

Maybe it was because all that stuff I'd said earlier was bullshit. The *purpose* was for us to be together, and I wasn't just going to walk away because she assumed we were done. Not happening.

"Well, the offer is there." She wasn't going to get any pressure, but I was making it clear where I stood. "I know Dallas would love you to stay."

"Just Dallas?" Her brow arched, fishing for more.

"Come on, Eve. You haven't worked it out by now?" My hands moved to the other foot, keeping my eyes on her. "Yes, I want you to stay. *I* would love you to stay."

"I'll think about it." She shrugged, not convincing me that she actually would. Part of me felt she'd made her mind up. I just didn't know if it was the shop or me she was planning on bailing on.

"Okay, when you decide what you want to do, let me know."

It might have sounded like I would have been okay with whatever, but that couldn't have been further from the truth.

I'd be patient but I wasn't going to be passive. And I wasn't giving her a chance to just walk out either.

SATURDAY MORNING WAS ROUGH.

After we'd eaten the pizza and showered together—shower sex had definitely happened—we'd spent most of the night enjoying each other.

We'd talked, but it was surface stuff. She hadn't mentioned the gallery or what'd happened last night. And if I hadn't been there and witnessed it myself, I might have questioned whether it happened at all. She laughed and smiled in all the right places, but she was keeping down her real feelings. Funny how working on people for years and watching their reactions made you a good reader of human emotions. Her grid was all over the place.

But playing the nice guy, I didn't bring it up. We got showered and dressed earlier than I would have liked, and then argued about whose car we were going to drive back to Queens. She had argued hers was easier to weave through traffic, while I told her it was ridiculous to leave my Jeep in Manhattan.

In the end we decided we would take both the cars back. She followed me in her Tesla and parked it at my place. Her reasoning was she had a car and it made sense to have it close in case she needed it. Bogus excuse, but I didn't argue. As long as we got there in the end, she could have parked a tank in front of my apartment building.

With last night's spontaneous sleeping arrangements, I was without suitable work wear. While I know she enjoyed the suit, trying to do ink in a jacket wasn't going to happen. So I took a minute to run upstairs and change before both of us jumped in the Jeep and headed back to the shop.

"I'll go get us breakfast." Eve held up her hands to stop my protest. "And before you argue, my treat."

"You don't have to do that, but thank you." I unlocked the door, deciding I'd let her have the battle because I was planning to win the war.

"Great, see you soon." She turned, her ponytail bouncing as

she walked in the direction of the deli.

I took the opportunity to turn on all the lights and get everything set up. Even though it was a Saturday, it wasn't a light day for us. No days were, and for the first time in a long time, my own grueling schedule was starting to weigh on me.

It wasn't that I needed time to get to know her, I knew who she was. What I needed was to get to know her *better*. Without the distraction of clients, or Dallas or anyone else. I wanted to take her out. Meet her parents, her friends. Have her meet mine, but being a business owner meant there was no such thing as regular hours.

There was noise from the front but it was too early to be a client, so I assumed Eve had come back, maybe there hadn't been the usual Saturday madness at the deli? It would be nice to enjoy breakfast and our last hour or so of quiet time before we got lost in the noise for the day.

"Hello, can I help you with something?"

I walked out to see an attractive, well-dressed woman standing at the counter looking around awkwardly. It was sort of reminiscent of the day Eve had walked in, except Eve hadn't look awkward. This woman, she definitely didn't belong here.

"Yes, I'm here to see Eve Thorton, if that's okay." She glanced over my shoulder to the hallway that led to our rooms. "Is she here?"

"And you are?" I was casual but cautious.

I wasn't going to tell this woman shit until she told me who she was and her purpose. For all I knew it could be one of those fucking assholes from the gallery, and those pieces of shits were not welcome in my shop.

"I'm her friend Heather, sorry." She held out her hand, her voice not at all confident. "I'm not usually this rude, I'm just a little concerned about her. She's not returning my calls and well . . . Lana told me about what happened last night."

The name was one I recognized, Eve had mentioned her as one of her friends, but I didn't know much else. Besides, it wasn't up to me to tell her anything. If Eve wanted to talk, she would. Then there was the issue of Eve avoiding her calls, so maybe she didn't want to talk. Of course I hadn't heard any calls, which hinted she'd killed her phone last night or put it on silent.

"She should be back soon, you're welcome to wait for her." I nodded to the chairs behind her. But not without adding a little condition of my own. "But if Eve doesn't want to talk, you'll have to leave, okay?"

And well-dressed woman or not, if Eve wanted Heather gone, she would be shown the door. Wouldn't lose a minute of sleep about it either.

"Thank you." She gave me a tight smile. "We all appreciate what you've done for her." She hesitated between the chairs and the counter. "I know we haven't gotten a chance to properly meet, I'm glad I got the chance to thank you before her time ended. We all thought she was crazy, but being here has been good for her."

If she hadn't had my attention before, she sure as hell had it now. If she hadn't spoken to Eve, then what could she possibly know that I didn't. As far as I was concerned, the situation with her staying or leaving hadn't been decided. She was done with the gallery, that wasn't a secret. But other than that, nothing had been set in concrete. Was she baiting me? Looking for a reaction? It pissed me off a little that she seemed to know a lot about me and I knew nothing about her.

"Yeah, cool. No problem." My response was as non-committal as my smile. "Was happy to help."

Happy to help? What kind of fucked up response was that? Obviously the only one I was capable of since Heather and her talk of gratitude dredged up the freaking doubts I'd had since last night. *Yeah, very fucking helpful, Heather.*

"Hey!" Eve walked in her arms full with coffee and food. "Heather, what are you doing here?"

She didn't look pissed, but she didn't look thrilled either. Her eyes flashed in confusion as they flicked to me like she was searching for information.

"We've met," I volunteered, walking across and freeing up her hands. "Heather was concerned you hadn't answered her calls."

"Oh. Shit." She grabbed her phone from her handbag, checking out the black screen. "I switched it off last night after we left the gallery. I didn't want to deal with the calls. I must have forgotten to turn it back on this morning."

"We've been worried sick, Eve." Heather threw her arms around Eve. "Lana called me and we have all been going out of our minds. Even Kitty was worried. And then when you didn't answer . . . well, I'm just glad you are okay." She gave her another hug, both of their eyes getting misty.

"Josh, is it okay if I take a minute." She glanced over at me, the I-want-to-talk-to-her-in-private broadcasted loud and clear.

"Sure, take whatever time you need. I'll be in the back." I grabbed my breakfast and my coffee and walked down the hall into my room.

I had no idea what either of them was going to say, but it pissed me off Eve wanted to chat with Heather, and didn't want to say it in front of me.

Of course I tried telling myself I was behaving like a little bitch, that she was probably filling her in on her version of events. But even so, the fact she wanted to talk about it when she'd remained so tight lipped with me, irked me.

Fuck, this was so unlike me. What the hell did it matter what was being said; what Eve and I had was more than some bullshit arrangement where I offered her help. I knew there were real feelings. I'd felt them, so surely she had to feel them too. I wasn't going to let this shit get up in my head and start messing with it.

In an effort to get my mind right, I pulled out my sketchpad to work on the project I'd been giving attention to between jobs. All those sketches Eve had done of me had given me an idea. I wanted her to see herself, how I saw her. The fierceness, the bravery, and of course the beauty and intelligence. But not one of those single things defined her, she was whole because of the combination. And I'd never wanted to draw anything as much in my life.

I'd hoped I'd get it colored and finished soon so I could get it framed for her as a gift. While I would give her the original, I'd get a copy made for me to hang in my room with all my other stuff. Because I could look at her all day long and never get tired of the view. And sure, maybe a little part of me subconsciously felt then I would always have her around. Because let's face it, neither of us had talked about what was happening between us.

Fuck.

I really hated this shit.

But was now really the time to have that talk? *Hey, so I know you just resigned and your future is sort of unpredictable but our relationship is good, right?* I wasn't sure whether to get my head checked or my balls.

There was a knock at my door and I knew it was her. Not a good sign since she usually just stuck her head in without permission. Of course I didn't usually close it when it was just the two of us either so it could have gone both ways. I was reading waaaaay too much into this shit.

"You're knocking now? When did we get so polite?" I called out, covering my work and waiting for the door to open.

"I didn't want to assume." Her hand still on the handle as she opened it and stood in the doorway. "Maybe you had something you didn't want me to see." Her eyes went to the sketchpad that was now closed.

"You'll see it when it's ready to be shared." My head tipped to the stool in front of my drafting table, inviting her to take a seat. "How about you, anything you want to share?"

"Heather was just worried because I didn't answer my phone." She gave me a smile that I didn't quite believe as she lowered her butt onto the stool. "Of course, she called my parents before coming over here so I had to talk to them as well. I think I need to go see them tonight. I guess I have been unconsciously avoiding them, along with some other issues."

I left the *other issues* alone and concentrated on her folks. We hadn't really spoken about either of our families to be honest. Not because I wasn't interested, but because it just hadn't come up. Now it seemed, I knew almost nothing about her.

"They live in the city?"

"Connecticut. But they've been really good about giving me my space even though I live so close." She winced, probably feeling guilt from Heather or the call to her parents. "I have a brother that lives in Zurich, and as long we both check in every couple of days, they are usually cool. But I haven't really spent any time with them since I came to work here." She looked around the room. "I should really go and see them."

It was the second time in the last couple of minutes she had said what she *should* be doing. Not once had I heard what she *wanted*.

"I could go with you," I offered, not knowing if she even wanted the company or me to meet her parents. "Moral support."

"Thanks, but I think it's better if I go on my own." She shifted in her chair. "My parents have always been supportive, I'm not worried about them flying off the handle or anything. But I don't want to turn up on their doorstep after they haven't seen me in a few weeks with someone in tow they've never met. That's not really fair to either of you."

Ouch.

She could dress it up however she wanted but those weren't the kind of words that reassured me we were on the same page. Hard to feel like we were even in the same book.

"Okay, well then you should go see your parents." Not much else I could say, at least not without looking like a needy fuck.

"Thanks for understanding." She got up out of her seat and

walked around to me. She was hesitant; her eyes clouded with uncertainty and it felt like there was a wall between us. Worst of all, she hadn't even attempted to touch me.

I knew there was more to it. It was written all over her face, the tone of her voice—the formality of it all. A contrast of how she'd been with me literally twenty-four hours before.

"Josh, I'm thinking of spending the rest of the weekend with them and coming back Monday." She might have phrased it as a hypothetical but I could see she'd made up her mind. "But I need you to understand that this isn't about us. I just need to go sort through my head and process."

Yeah, kind of sounds like it has a lot to do with us considering you won't talk to me and you're running away, was what I wanted to say. But I didn't. For too many reasons to count. Besides, at this point I wasn't sure it would accomplish anything anyway. I couldn't tie her to a chair and force her to stay. And while I wasn't giving up on her, I knew if I made an issue of this, she wouldn't come back.

"If that's what you want to do, Eve. Then you should do it." I shrugged, unable to muster up any more enthusiasm. "I'm going to be here when you get back."

It was tempting to say *if* but I forced myself to believe she would be back. That she would go see her parents and come to the conclusion I'd already come to. Me and her, we belonged together.

"Do you hate me?" She tilted her chin, her light brown eyes catching mine.

"No. I don't."

And I didn't. I didn't have the capacity to hate her even if I didn't agree with the decision she was making. I hated I couldn't fix things for her. That she'd come to me looking for answers and all she seemed to have were more questions. I hated she was leaving, even if it was only for a couple of days to see her parents. Because we were unfinished business, and there wasn't a goddamn thing I could do about it.

"I'll call you." She looked like she wanted to reach out, her hands twitching at her side. "Let you know when I'm getting back. Maybe we can have dinner on Monday night, if I don't get in too late?"

"Why don't you give me a call, see where things are at later."

I hated saying those words to her, brushing her off like I didn't give a shit. Of course I wanted to see her Monday. I didn't want her to leave. And I didn't give a fuck how late she got back. Even if she crawled into my bed and we just slept together, I wanted her with me. But the last twenty-four hours had obviously changed things. How much they had changed between the two of us was what I couldn't work out.

"That's a good idea." She nodded, forcing a grin. "You know, you are being really great about this. Thank you."

Again with the thanks.

"That's me," *sucker*, "great about things." I gave her a smile.

"Okay, well I'll go out front." She pointed toward the door. "Let me know if you need anything."

"We could probably manage, if you wanted to go now." The voice was mine but I don't remember saying it. "It might take a while in traffic, it's probably better not to drive in the dark."

"Oh?" She was genuinely surprised, like my words had caught her off guard. She wasn't the only one. "Are you sure, I could wait . . . stay until after lunch?"

I had no idea if she wanted to stay or she was just being a good employee. And that I didn't know was probably what annoyed me the most. Did I beg? Did I play it cool? Did I keep her at the shop for as long as I could in the hopes she'd change her mind? No. This was the one choice I couldn't make for her. And maybe that was my lesson to learn. I couldn't fix everything.

"Nah, we're good." I didn't bother fighting the urge and pulled her in for a hug. She didn't fight me, wrapping her arms around my chest. "Go see your parents, Eve. Text me to let me know you got there safe, okay?"

"Thanks, Josh." She whispered into my chest, her head resting against my pecs. "Thanks for everything."

I wasn't sure if it was a goodbye or a see you later. Didn't ask. But I gave her a kiss on the forehead and let her walk out my door.

It was ironic that it had been less than twelve hours since I promised myself I wouldn't let her walk away. That in my head I'd vowed to fight for her, for us.

I didn't know if that made me a hypocrite, or if maybe I'd wised up that perhaps there were things I couldn't control. I was moody as fuck, time away wasn't what I wanted, but maybe it was what we needed.

We had been in a pressure cooker, first avoiding the attraction and then diving head first into it. We'd gone from zero to a hundred so fast we'd barely had time to assimilate. And even though I couldn't make myself regret it, maybe putting the brakes on for a little while wasn't the end of the world.

At least that was what I convinced myself when Dallas waltzed into my room about an hour later.

"Dude." He gave me a chin tip, walking in to inspect the infinity symbol I was doing on a college girl's wrist. "Hey." I wiped off the excess black ink from the infinity symbol. "I'll be with you in a second." I nodded to Dallas before focusing back on my client. I cleaned the area and then let her see.

"It's perfect, thank you, Josh." She cradled her wrist, staring at the curves of the outline. "I love it."

"I'm glad." I got her situated with a bandage. "Don't forget to take care of it like we spoke about." I snapped off my gloves. "Eve—" I stopped short, remembering she wasn't at the front and instead was in a car, driving away from me. "I guess I'll hook you up with some cream on the way out and give you some more information on aftercare. We can head out to the front."

"Great, thanks again," she squealed. "It's so cool." She slid off the chair giving Dallas an appreciative smile before heading out of my room and down the hall.

Dallas reciprocated, volleying back with a flirty grin of his own, making me roll my eyes as I followed the customer out to the front. I processed her payment, gave her some ointment, and got involved with as little conversation as possible. And then after I waved her goodbye I walked back into my room and closed the door. I had a hunch I knew what he was going to ask.

"You want to tell me what that was about?" He eyed me as I walked back over to my stool.

I retook my seat, not in the mood for conversation. "It was an infinity symbol. I'm sure you've done a few yourself."

"You know that wasn't what I was talking about." He hopped onto my chair, the space vacated by the college girl now full of Dallas. "You were so mechanical with her, almost cold. And don't tell me it was about the design because you've never been like that before. What gives?"

I wanted to laugh, but I didn't have it in me, the irony of Dallas questioning me. "Is that what you came in here for, to judge my mood? I'm just having a bit of an off day."

"That wouldn't have anything to do with Eve not being here, would it? Funny how she has been here for three whole weeks and she now has mysteriously disappeared."

"She's gone to see her parents." Not a lie, that's where she'd gone. "There was some drama last night at the gallery."

"Eve telling her boss to go fuck himself. Yeah, I heard." He grinned, a little too pleased with himself.

I wondered if maybe he'd caught her at the door, before she'd left. I hadn't heard him come in so it was possible they could have crossed paths. "How do you know, did Eve tell you?"

"Nah, Kitty. I *may* or *may not* have been with her at the time Lana called." He lifted his eyebrows a couple of times. I didn't even bother asking when the two of them decided to get together.

"Those girls sure know how to call the fuck out of a phone tree. At one point they had a four-way conference call happening. And while you know I don't mind sharing my attention with other ladies, the conversation was fucking depressing."

"Well, you probably know more about it than I do." God, I wished I was kidding, but at that point I wasn't sure *what* I knew anymore.

"What are you talking about, weren't you there?" Dallas narrowed his eyes confused why Eve's date and boyfriend was apparently in the dark. Yeah, that made two of us, buddy.

My eyes shot to the closed door, the one she'd walked out of over an hour ago. "Yeah, I was. Not that it did me any good. It's like there is a fucking wall or something."

"Are you sure you're not imagining this shit, dude." He again looked at me confused. "She was fine with me yesterday."

"Yeah, she's fine with everyone else except me, and I don't fucking get it."

If Eve and I hadn't shared personal stuff before, then I would have totally understood. But that hadn't been the case, and I knew she was intentionally holding back now. Why she was doing it, I had no fucking clue.

"Do you think she was nervous to tell you about the other gallery?" Dallas shrugged.

"What other gallery?" My head snapped up, my ass lifting out of my stool "What the fuck do you know?"

"Calm down dude, the girls were talking about it on the phone last night. One chick—I think her name was Heather? I don't fucking know—anyway she said she had a connection or something. At another gallery. She was going to call Eve about it."

Was that why she was at the shop this morning? To convince Eve she needed to go work somewhere fucking else? Another place she hated, who would treat her like shit? Yeah, that was fucking smart. And why didn't she tell me? Instead she decided to take off. Was she even coming back Monday? Or was she going to take the job Heather hooked her up with and say goodbye to the shop.

"Guess a lot was covered on those phone calls then." I tried not to sound bitter. "Well, I'm sure she'll be happy at the new place."

"What do you mean, she's leaving us?" For the first time since we started the conversation, Dallas looked shocked. Like it hadn't occurred to him she would eventually leave. Funnily enough, I don't think it had occurred to me either.

Sure, she had been originally temporary, but I just assumed something would happen and she'd stay.

"What do you want me to do? Tell her not to go work at whatever shithole her friend as set up and stay with us?" *Stay with me?*

"Well, fuck if I know, Josh." Dallas ran his hand through his hair in frustration. He wasn't exactly a beacon of wisdom when it came to women, and was even worse with conflict. "You're the one who knows how to fix shit."

Man, did I wish he were right. "Not always."

"Well, that fucking blows."

Great. Now both of us were depressed. I only had enough energy to pull one of us from a mood, I couldn't deal with Dallas moping around too.

"Look, she's gone to spend some time with her parents. Let's go have a few drinks or something, blow off some steam. Maybe I'm just overthinking this thing. Who knows?"

While I didn't believe for a second I was overthinking, it didn't seem like giving it any more mental space would solve anything in the short term. Shelving it for now would probably do me some good, it sure as shit couldn't hurt. If nothing else, maybe the distance might give me some perspective and hopefully do the same for her.

"Sure, whatever you want."

I knew Dallas would take little convincing, it was one of the things that was great about him. If you ever needed a dude to hang and drink with, all you had to do was name the time and the place.

"Cool, I've got my next client coming in soon so I'll catch you later."

"No probs. I'll see if any of the boys want to join." He seemed to perk up, the promise of beers later giving Eve's departure a silver lining.

"Yeah, whatever. No juggling this time." I eyed him hard. "If you end up in the emergency room it will be because I put you there."

"Yeah, yeah, whatever." Dallas laughed. "It got you results with your girl though, didn't it? You should act more appreciative."

And that was part of the problem. I wasn't sure for how much longer she was going to be my girl.

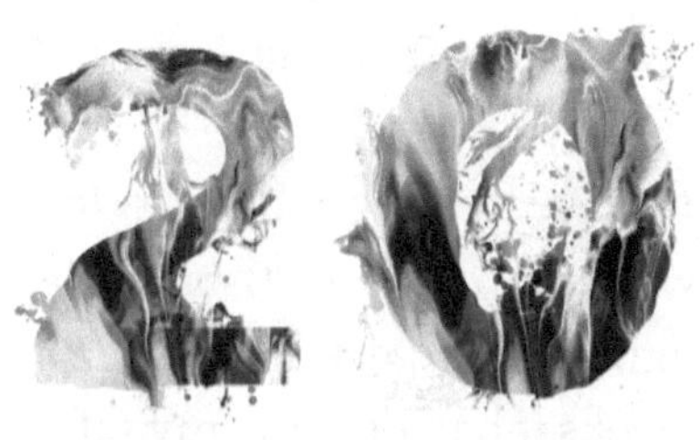

EVE

THE LAST THING I WANTED to do was leave Josh in limbo.

It wasn't fair.

And I had been prepared to stay the rest of the day, and then take the drive to see my parents. It wasn't a trip I necessarily wanted to make but the more I thought about, the more it seemed I had to.

Heather had mentioned another gallery that was interested in taking me. Who, despite the bullshit they'd read, didn't care and wanted me to work for them. She meant well, but I told her it would be a cold day in hell before I went from one gallery job I hated to another.

I couldn't go back to what I was doing before because I had changed.

It wasn't a lightning bolt realization, more an *ah-huh, well isn't that interesting.* But between my chat with Heather and the drive out to Connecticut, I'd gained some incredible perspective.

I was happy *away* from the gallery. And it wasn't just about working at the tattoo studio. Sure, it helped to be around people who seemed genuinely happy—I couldn't remember a time where Mr. Ashton had ever seemed pleased even when we made him a truckload of money—it was more than that.

No, it had been me. I had been the one who changed.

And while I was contemplating, working on what made the new Eve tick, that it occurred to me. I needed to resign for a second time.

I was going to have to say goodbye to Ink Addiction.

It pained my heart to have to think it, let alone say it, but I knew it was the right call and it was time.

In the three weeks it had become my safe haven, and not only that, but I would actually miss the shop. Josh's offer of staying on had been more than a little tempting. The customers were great, the work was fun and my co-workers were amazing. Of course, getting to see my boyfriend everyday was a huge sweetener. I loved working beside him and seeing the work he produced—it was inspiring.

But all of that had been a safety net of another kind. And while it had cradled me when I needed it, if I was going to pick myself up and get my shit together I needed to do it on my own two feet. Not because I had something to prove to anyone else, but because I needed to prove it to myself.

No one could do it for me, not even Josh.

I wanted him to be proud of me. I wanted him to look at what I had achieved and for our relationship to be on equal footing. He was either my boyfriend or he was my savior; he couldn't be both. And if I needed a hero, then I better find one in the mirror.

I pulled up to my parents' house just after noon; the three-hour drive—the pit stop in Manhattan to pack a bag had slowed me down slightly—had been cathartic. But as much as I liked the time to think, I was glad when the big brick house my parents had recently moved into came into view.

Oh, they still had our family home in Greenwich, but rather than downsize when both myself and my brother had left home, they up-scaled. Because unlike me, they didn't *do* apartment living.

A massive manor house, situated on a huge property with so many rooms I doubted either of my parents had even counted. Because two people *needed* that much space. Sarcasm totally intended.

"Eve." My mother greeted me at the door, wrapping her arms around me like it had been months not weeks since she saw me. Honestly, we'd had longer periods of not seeing each other. I could only assume she was so emotional because of everything that had been going on.

"I'm fine, Mom. Seriously, I am fine." I reassured her, knowing the things that had been said about me had probably hurt them too. And had I been less consumed with revenge and proving everyone wrong, I might have seen that.

Dad was right behind her and gave me a hug of his own. "I'm glad you came to see us."

While so many men of my dad's vintage were afraid of showing their feelings, he was too self-confident to give a shit what other people thought. Therefore he hugged tight, and often.

"Are we going to keep hugging on the doorstep or are you guys going to let me in?" I laughed, not at all annoyed I was being loved on by my parents.

"Of course, of course." My mom discreetly wiped a tear she probably didn't think I'd seen and ushered me into the living room while my dad got my overnight bag out of the car.

"You repainted." The walls had graduated from white to a light mocha. "It looks good."

"You didn't come here to talk about our redecorating, young lady." I heard my dad from the front door. "So, take a seat and let's hear it."

"You're not even going to give me time to settle in?" The soft cushions of the couch hugged my body as my butt lowered onto it.

"Baby, it's been over three weeks." The concern in my mother's voice unmistakable.

"I needed to prove to myself that I could sort out my own

mess. I didn't want either of you to feel you had to fix me, or to fix the situation."

"Eve, you know we'd do anything for you, sweetheart." My mom gently stroked my hair. It was something she used to do when I was younger and having a crisis. When I fell and grazed my knees, had my first heartbreak, when I'd underperformed in my first year of Yale. "You're stubborn just like your father, so we gave you your space. But you don't have to do everything by yourself."

God, I loved them. They were such wonderful people and I wanted to make them proud. Because despite the money, and the privilege, I had been raised with a lot of love.

"You have done so much for me already." It was hard not to get emotional. "But I have learned so much about myself in the past few weeks. I used to think I was brave, independent and strong, but I've been playing it safe this whole time. I can't do it anymore."

"Sweetheart, you have been strong. Doing what you do takes a lot of guts, putting yourself out there." My mom was the eternal optimist. No matter how badly one of us screwed up, she would always see the glass half full.

"I know you think that, and I love you for it." I guess this is why I had avoided them for so long, having to confront them and admit I hadn't done my best. "But I've been skating through for too long. I have some ideas, and I am going to do better."

My dad handed me a glass of wine he'd poured and then sat down on the big armchair opposite. It didn't matter it was early in the day, he had rightly guessed the conversation would be easier with a drink. He'd also poured himself one so I wouldn't feel lonely. "So what did you have in mind?"

My dad, while affectionate, was less emotional than my mother. He'd had to be, his success in business demanded he make decisions with facts and figures and not with his heart.

"I'm not going back to work at the gallery," I said cautiously, not having told them about my recent resignation. "Or any other gallery either."

"Good." My father casually took a sip of his wine. "Rob Ashton is a slimy prick, I couldn't stand shaking the bastard's hand."

"What?" I almost spat out my wine, my mother not blinking an eye to my dad's apparent strong feelings toward my ex-boss. I mean, he *was* a slimy prick, but my dad had never said anything.

"Eve, we were polite to him while you worked there. But make no mistake, we never liked him." This time, from my mother.

It was like I was in the twilight zone.

"You both hated him, but you told me nothing?" I looked at them blankly, like maybe I hadn't heard them right. "You both seemed so excited when I got a job there."

"What were we supposed to tell you?" my dad weighed in. "Not to do it? You were so determined to do it your way, to show everyone what you were made of. I'd have preferred you not to work at all, if he had been the only choice. But I promised your mom I wouldn't interfere. And I didn't." He nodded to her, looking for recognition that he had done well in keeping his mouth shut.

My mother shook her head, mildly amused. "You really are stubborn like your father."

"I prefer the term driven."

"Wait!" I held up my hands, still reeling from the revelation. "What else haven't you told me?"

"I just don't understand, Eve." He seemed frustrated, like maybe he'd wanted to ask me in the past but hadn't. Probably my mom's doing. "Why you put yourself through it."

"Because I love it, Dad." I took a deep breath, ready to defend my choices even though neither of them had ever challenged me before. It was a new era in the Thorton household. "The art—"

"No, I get that." He cut me off, waving his glass in the air. "You have a talent, you're good at it. Lord knows we had enough trouble keeping your original works off the walls when you were younger." He chuckled, the warmth in his voice wrapping me up like a blanket. "But you have a trust fund, why the hell would you waste your time and your talent working for someone else?"

"Dad, I've told you. I'm not going to buy my way in." Like I hadn't enough of a hard time with the socialite tag, I wasn't going to add more fuel to the fire by perpetuating the stereotype. "I wanted to be respected."

"You earn respect by doing good work, Eve," my dad snapped. "Not by pulling out your wallet. You do good work and no one cares how you got there." He put down his glass of wine and leaned forward in his chair. "Your problem was you focused too much on what other people thought. Why the hell would you apologize for an advantage?"

"It just feels like cheating," I conceded, desperately wanting to prove I could do it without my last name or my dad's name.

"So do you feel guilty about walking because you have two good legs and someone else doesn't?"

"Well, no." I laughed at his ridiculous comparison. "But *that* is different."

"No, it is the same," he dismissed with a headshake. "Money might open doors but that's all it will do. What you do with them once they're open is what counts. You going to walk through the doorway? Or worry about what someone said about your hand on the handle?"

He was right.

Money could get me where I needed to be but it wouldn't keep me there. Only my talent could do that. And why wouldn't I use everything in my arsenal to succeed. It would be like limiting myself to only the primitive tools because, well, that's all Da Vinci had.

"I'm going to walk through the doorway."

I was done tying one hand behind my back.

I was done being afraid.

I was done making excuses.

My dad gave me a smile of pride that made my heart want to burst. "Now, *that's* my girl."

I didn't need a gallery—*Lenore West*, or any other substitute. Fuck them and their bullshit rules, regulations and their invite-only policies.

All I had to do was pull out my checkbook and DIY. Because while the gallery had sponsored my first exhibit, this one would be completely bankrolled by myself.

Everything from renting the space to how the pieces would be mounted. Time, place, location, theme—every tiny detail would be mine to decide, and if I once again went down in flames, I would know I had absolutely given it my all.

With an old legal pad and pen, I sat on the floor and brainstormed ideas. Lists were created of possible venues, timelines, supplies—contacts I'd made while working at the gallery, were now being put to good use. My time there hadn't been a total waste it seemed.

Like a mad scientist I worked through the rest of the day. Despite my assurances I was okay and not wanting to stop for meals, my parents brought in food and drinks. So I didn't die from malnourishment or dehydration or collapse from low blood sugar, my mom had insisted.

"How are we doing?" My dad came in late, my mom already in bed hours ago, in his hand a bottle of wine and two glasses.

"Good." I happily accepted the glass of red he'd just poured, the caffeine wearing off hours ago. *Step aside coffee; this is a job for wine.* "Almost every gallery in the city is available for the right price, but I've decided to be more unconventional."

"Sounds interesting, like a warehouse?" my dad asked, taking a sip from his glass as he looked over my notes.

"Nah, too cliché. Fashion houses do that all the time. I was thinking a hotel." I grabbed my phone and showed my dad a listing for an old hotel that was being sold. It was in Queens—ironically not too far from where Josh lived—and while the structure was rock solid, the interior was seriously decaying. Walls needed painting, fixtures replacing and it looked more like a haunted house than a place you would want to spend the night.

"Baby, you know I always think property is a worthy investment, but this would take months to renovate. Is this something you are willing to wait that long for?"

"I would wait if I had to, but I don't." I smiled, excited to share my ideas with him. "My pieces read more like dreams, memories." I flipped onto the photo reel on my phone and showed him one of my pictures. "I thought it would be cool to display them in a place that had a story of its own. The dilapidated walls, the wonky fixtures, the scuffed floors, it makes you feel like you are actually *in* the dream. And even though the pieces are connected by a common thread; each one should be viewed on its own. People can go up and down the stairs, and depending on what order they see what in, they build their own story in their head. Each person will have their own unique experience."

"That's brilliant, Eve." His hand landed on my shoulder with a big smile spreading across his lips. "I'm really proud of you."

"Thanks, Dad." While I loved the admiration, for the first time in possibly my life, I wasn't doing it for that. "I was able to speak to the agent—amazing how they'll take your call even though it's a Saturday when you tell them you are interested in buying—but it looks like the soonest I could get my hands on it is ninety days. She's going to talk to the seller and see if they can make an exception so I can get it in thirty."

"So, not to be a downer but you know I have to play devil's advocate here. What are going to do with the real estate once you're done?"

My dad was typically cautious, and I knew he would be concerned about the investment possibilities. A hotel wasn't something you could easily flip for a profit. Not in the real world, anyway.

"I thought about that too." I twisted my body around to face him. "I want to set it up as a venue. There can be a bar in the basement, and we can run exhibits at night. Have more of a club feel to it rather than a gallery. It would not only give exposure to more urban unconventional artists, but hopefully get more people excited and interested in art."

My excitement spiked as I flipped over the pages on the legal pad, showing him my rough sketches.

"I want one of the upper floors for consignment pieces. We can rotate work in and out to give as many local artists a chance, and the other three floors can be used for exhibition space. It doesn't only have to be static art either, we can have dance recitals, plays, spoken word nights. It will be a way to keep it fresh. And because it will only be open for a few hours at night, it will give me time during the day to create. I can do two things at once, do what I love and actively do something to give back as well."

My heart was racing. Never had I wanted to be a business owner, I didn't even own the apartment that I lived in, but the idea of making this a reality made me giddy. It was possible because I had money, but it would succeed because I had talent. "And I'm going to make sure I have some of the best people in the business working for me. So, whatever I don't know, they will be able to help me with.

"This is a real smart business idea. Are you looking for investors?" He gave me a smile and I knew exactly *who* he had in mind.

"Nope, I'm going to use my trust fund and do this all without a safety net. Besides, if it all goes down in a ball of flames, at least I'll have a place to live. I'm going to convert the top floor into a residence."

"I have a hunch you won't need to worry." He squeezed my shoulder tightly. "But if anything happened, you know that your mother and I—"

"I know. I know." My hand rested on his, their support never something I'd ever question. "But I can do this and I'm not scared anymore."

"Good." My dad took a breath before looking at my pile of papers scattered on the coffee table and floor. "Tomorrow morning we'll call my lawyers and get things moving." He held out his hand to stop the protest he knew was coming. "And before you argue with me Eve, I said I would *call* them. You are the one who is going to pay their bills, so let your old man lend a hand."

"Okay, Dad, thank you." Warmth spread through my chest. "Maybe you could help me with the business side of things. I know nothing about applying for permits and stuff like that."

"It would be an honor to work with you, sweetheart. Now, are you going to tell me about this new guy you've been seeing?"

When I'd call to tell my parents I was coming home, I had casually mentioned to Mom I had been seeing someone. It was a detail I hoped would be lost in a sea of other important stuff, like telling my old boss to go fuck himself and the scene with Oliver at the gallery. But apparently while she'd given me some space, nothing had been forgotten. And she'd told my dad, which meant I was going to have to spill.

"Well . . . he's different. He's a tattoo artist." I waited for the reaction, the shock, the horror—the judgment.

It didn't come.

"And?" my father asked, his hand rolling indicating for me to go on.

Where did I even start? How could any words I used be enough to tell them all the amazing things that he was?

"And, he's a good man. He treats me like a queen, he has given me time and space even though he probably doesn't understand why. He's kind, and he's so good to me."

My dad sighed. "It's all we've ever wanted for you and your brother. We weren't thrilled with his decision to move away, hell, your mother cried for a week. But we would never stop you kids from being happy."

I felt the lump form in my throat. My emotions so frayed that even if he'd only said half of it, I would have cried.

"I'm sorry I didn't tell you sooner. I was just . . ." I didn't even know what to say.

"Well, you've told me now and that's what's important. Make sure you talk to your mother tomorrow, you know she'll want to hear. It looks like you're going to be here awhile, so I'm going up to bed. I love you, sweetheart." He kissed me lightly on the top of my head and said good night.

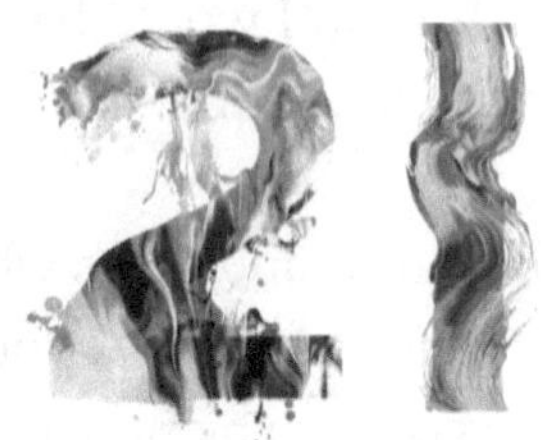

EVE

I WOKE UP ON THE floor surrounded by a sea of notes and sketches. Obviously at some point I'd fallen asleep, not that I'd remembered. My mouth was dry and my neck hurt from lying on the floor in a weird angle, but other than that I felt amazing.

A lot had been worked through during the night and I'd felt more positive about things, especially since I'd come clean about Josh.

"Good, you're awake." My dad handed me a mug of freshly brewed coffee, not even questioning I had obviously slept on the floor. "I've got George coming around this morning." He took a seat on the same sofa he'd sat on last night as he relayed the conversation he'd already had with his lawyer. "He's almost positive we can get you into this hotel within thirty days. He also said you can apply for temporary permits for the event until you have something more long term in place. It's easier to get permission for a special event, rather than an ongoing business. He plays golf with someone from the City Hall, so he'll help us with that as well."

I laughed as I took a sip of the hot, caffeinated goodness. "Wow, you've been busy. I knew it would take a little more time for the long-term goal. I thought I could have my showing in a month and then slowly work on the rest. The construction will take a bit of time too, but I'm fine with that."

"I'm glad we're on the same page." He gave me a warm smile and a wink. "He'll be over in about an hour so you might want to get yourself cleaned up."

"What?" I stretched out my hands in front of me. "Didn't you say I always looked good?" I laughed.

"I'm pleading the fifth." He wisely remained tightlipped.

I didn't need a mirror to know I looked a mess. Crumpled clothes, messed up hair—I probably smelled terrible too. So I scooted my ass up the stairs and into the shower and got dressed.

Mom appeared in my bedroom with coffee and some bagels while I finished getting ready, using the excuse of breakfast to hear about Josh. She listened as I applied my makeup, smiling as I told her how wonderful he was. Naturally she'd been just as supportive as Dad and we'd just wrapped her thirty thousand questions when George arrived.

While I had enjoyed being dressed down while I worked with Josh, dresses, skirts and heels were definitely more my style. And I wasn't going to feel bad about that either. If I wanted to wear a pair of six-inch spike heels and red lipstick, that didn't make me superficial. I was empowered, and I would dress how I wanted to dress and fuck what anyone thought about it.

"Someone grew up." George nodded to my father as I walked into the room. "I'm glad we're playing this deal from the same side of the table, Eve. You look like you could eat us for breakfast."

"I know what I want." I nodded my hello and took my seat at the head of the dining room table, the venue for our meeting. "Gentlemen, let's get started."

To his credit, my dad sat in on the meeting but made minimal contributions. I knew it was a conscious effort, both supporting my independence and believing that he knew what I was doing. I asked George lots of questions, which he answered, and both he and my father made a few suggestions of their own.

The realtor called and gave us the go ahead to inspect the property, and also miraculously—money really does talk—pending the report from the building inspector I had managed to hire that morning, the hotel would be mine in thirty days.

The rest of the day was spent with a phone glued to my ear as I put all the gears in motion. George and Dad also pitched in, either on the phone or calling in favors to ensure everything would go to plan. Assuming everything was okay with the building—gut instinct told me it would be—I was taking a massive leap of faith and planning my new show, thirty-one days from today.

It was going to be a tight turn around, probably insane to even attempt, but it was go hard or go home time, and I wasn't about to quit.

And I also had another project I wanted to work on. This time something special for Josh—

Josh.

"Shit." My dad and George jerked their heads around to look at me, my random outburst catching them by surprise. "Ahhh, I've got to make a private call." I held up my phone, the one I should have used to text or call Josh and tell him I'd arrived safely yesterday.

Or wish him goodnight.

Or check in on him this morning.

All of the things I hadn't done.

"The boyfriend?" my dad asked, the raised eyebrow hinting there wasn't much that got past him.

"Yeah. I was supposed to call him. I'm a bad girlfriend." More like the worst.

"I'm sure he'll understand, go ahead and make your call." Dad waved me off as I walked out of the dining room into the study.

"Shit," I mumbled to myself when I saw the time.

It was almost dinnertime, and I hadn't spoken to him since I left the studio yesterday. I hadn't forgotten about him. He had been in my thoughts the entire time. But I'd been so focused on what I was doing that I kept putting off sending a message, rationalizing that I wanted the time to say something important. In the end, I hadn't said anything at all . . . and that was even worse.

I was a terrible person.

My fingers hit his name on my contacts with my heart beating quickly in my chest. Would he even want to hear from me? Would he accept the call?

"Hello?" a male voice answered, the noise in the background making it difficult to hear. "Hello?"

"Hi, is Josh there?" I pulled the phone away from my ear making sure I'd dialed the right number. Even with the background noise I could tell it wasn't Josh. "Dallas, is that you?"

"What?" mystery man screamed through the phone, it was definitely not Dallas either. "I can barely hear you."

"I WANT TO SPEAK TO JOSH." I pulled the phone away and yelled into my cell. "IS HE THERE?" I was positive the people in the next neighborhood heard me so I hoped whomever I was talking to was able to catch at the very least his name.

"Oh, *Josh*." Thank you, Jesus, he had heard. "He's taking a piss."

Well at least he wouldn't be gone long. It was obvious they—Josh and this guy—were in some bar. And that was totally fine, I was glad he was out with friends and hadn't been waiting around for my call. Okay, so maybe a little part of me was hoping he'd been waiting, but that was the total irrational part that needed to shut the fuck up. I had left for the weekend, remember. Me. So he had every reason to be out. Having a good time.

"Hey. You still there?"

Shit.

"Can you let him know Eve called?" I figured I should answer the guy rather than continue my internal debate.

"Steve?" he hollered into the phone. "Hey my name is Steve

too, what a coincidence. You don't sound like a Steve though."

"NO, EVE," I shouted back, not knowing who Steve was but at least I had the name of the mystery voice.

"Yeah, I heard you the first time, Steve. I'll let him know you called, bye."

He hung up before I'd had a chance to correct him.

Damn it.

Did I call back? How many Steve's did Josh know? Would he put two and two together or check his recent call register and see it was me? Of course he would, I told myself. There was no reason at all to be worried.

Other than it was barely dinnertime and he was already at a bar.

Where there were probably women.

Who were probably eyeing him with intent.

No.

There was no reason to worry.

I wandered back into the dining room and found my dad and George had wrapped up. George assured me he would get his assistant on it first thing tomorrow when business opened and waved goodbye as he hopped into his Lexus. It made sense, there was little else we could accomplished on a Sunday evening anyway.

Mom insisted I take a break and had dinner at the table like a civilized person, so I put off the rest of my irrational thinking for a couple of hours while I enjoyed a lovely meal with my parents.

Muriel—the cook who had worked for my family for years—had prepared a beautiful dinner, which we enjoyed with a glass of wine. That one glass turned into two, and maybe I was self-medicating a little with the Pinot Noir. The small buzz it gave me eased some of the tension.

Even though Josh still hadn't called me, everything was fine.

Fine.

He would call.

And if he didn't, I would risk looking indecisive and needy and call him again . . . even though I told him I needed time to work shit out. Because I was an idiot and shut him out, and he was the one thing in my life that wasn't a mess.

"Are you going to be working much longer?" Mom asked, me and my third glass of wine headed to the living room.

"I'm going to do some sketching and then I'm going to go to bed. It's been a long day and I could use an early night. Go watch television with Dad, I'll be fine." I gave her a reassuring smile.

She gave me a hug goodnight. "Please sleep in a bed tonight, Eve. Finding your body sprawled out on the carpet like a crime scene scared me half to death this morning."

"I'm sorry." I laughed, the wine working its way through my system. I was not even close to being drunk but I was definitely on the happy side of the street. "I promise I'll go to bed."

Both her and my dad disappeared upstairs and I again took residence on the floor, wine in one hand and sketchpad in the other.

I wanted to work on my surprise. My something special for Josh to show him how much I cared about him. How instrumental he'd been in my change. How much he'd shown me in such a short time.

I wanted to tell him . . . that I was falling in love with him.

Maybe it was the wine talking, maybe it was fatigue, or maybe I'd stripped myself so bare that now I finally saw things for exactly what they were.

I. Loved. Him.

And I wasn't only going to tell him. I was going to show him. The best way I knew how.

⟡

"SHIT."

It felt like my soul had been tossed back into my body as I woke up with a start.

At least this time I had been smart enough to do it in a bed. I was still wearing my clothes though. Hey, one out of two wasn't bad; thankfully I wasn't passed out on the floor like yesterday. Small victories.

Josh hadn't called, or at least he hadn't before I'd tiptoed up the stairs and fallen into a coma.

I had just finished Josh's surprise and could no longer see straight and figured I'd just close my eyes for a few seconds before pulling up my big girl panties and calling him back.

Spoiler alert: It had been longer than a few seconds.

My hand grabbed aimlessly for my phone in the dark, and came up empty. It wasn't beside me or on the nightstand.

Shit. Shit. Shit.

I hit the lamp beside me, blinding myself momentarily as I dropped to my knees and searched the carpet and underneath the bed.

No phone.

Shit. SHIT. SHIT.

I must have left it downstairs. My sleepy wine-induced state wasn't known for its stellar decision making skills, my feet quickly exiting the bedroom and scuttling down the stairs as quietly as I could.

It was morning, barely, but the sun hadn't come up yet and my parents were still fast asleep.

"Fuck."

I swallowed the scream as I stubbed my toe on the coffee table, my little pinkie throbbing as I grabbed my stupid, freaking phone—yes, I was blaming the phone—off the coffee table and checked it.

Well.

Shit.

Josh had called around ten thirty. Not late by anyone's definition, but after the long day and few glasses of wine, I was one bedtime away from a retiree in Boca.

He'd also sent a message.

> *Hey, sorry I missed your call. Took me a while to work out who "Steve" was considering Steve was the one delivering the message. Is everything okay? Call me. J x*

And then again just before midnight.

> *I guess it wasn't urgent. Glad to hear you made it to your parents' house safely. Ok, bye.*

No.

No.

No.

God, I was an asshole. He was probably thinking I was playing games or trying to mind fuck him. Ugh! I was so mad at myself.

It was three a.m. and he would most likely be sleeping.

I shouldn't call.

But what did "bye" mean? *Bye* as in, see you later or *bye* as in, you selfish bitch I hope you rot in hell.

No. It was just a bye. It was nothing.

Unless.

Crap, it was *not* nothing.

Screw it. I couldn't help myself, dialing his number anyway because there was no way I was going to text.

What would the message say anyway? *I'm sorry for being a dumbass?* Yeah, thanks but no.

My pulse raced wildly as I waited for the call to connect, only having to wait a minute before disappointment set in.

Voicemail.

And I didn't know if I had enough of my mom's optimism to believe it wasn't personal.

Could he be punishing me for what he might figure was me blowing him off?

He had every right to be angry, but my lack of communication hadn't been intentional. And then when I did get my shit together and call him, I didn't even follow up with a text. Because I was a moron. That wine had a lot to answer for.

So of course when he tried to contact me and I hadn't responded, assumptions were probably made. Ones where he decided I was an evil bitch who was wasting his time.

No, I was acting paranoid.

I dialed again, hoping he'd been in the bathroom, in the shower, getting a glass of water, sleeping—any other scenario where he wasn't avoiding my call.

Voicemail.

Shit.

The smart thing to do would be go back to bed, wait until a more reasonable hour and then try again. Be rational considering I had missed his calls initially, so maybe his phone had been forgotten in his living room like mine had.

A problem considering I was currently not feeling rational nor smart.

Which was probably why I decided that getting into my car and driving back to Queens was a good idea.

I would miss morning traffic, I told myself. And I'd always planned to go back today, so what did it matter if I left a few hours earlier. And at least I wouldn't be in the car, stuck in traffic when businesses opened, in case I needed to make calls or something. Yes. I wasn't being ridiculous at all. Any single one of those reasons would be valid, all put together and I was appalled I wasn't already in my car.

With my mind made up, I raced back up the stairs and threw myself in the shower. I probably set the land speed record for getting dressed, ready and repacked, but I had a mission and unfortunately the clock was working against me.

Quickly I scribbled a note telling my parents I had decided to go, citing all my reasons I'd previously mentioned—traffic, needing to make calls, etc. etc.—and left it on the kitchen counter. I'd signed it with lots of hugs and kisses and I knew it was going to cost me another weekend back home to make up for it. This time—assuming he was still my boyfriend—I would bring Josh, so they could see how wonderful he was.

It was only once I was in the car and leaving my parents' driveway that I felt I was able to breathe again. In a couple of hours I would be at Josh's apartment and I would tell him everything. About buying the hotel and my exhibit and that I was in love with him and needed him in my life. And he would tell me how much he loved me too, because what other possibility could there be?

Of course there *were* other possibilities, and I probably imagined every last one of them as I crossed back into New York and headed to Queens. My mind, it seemed, had no shortage of them as I tried to drown out my thoughts with loud music.

Uncomfortable heat prickled my neck the closer I got to where he lived. The last time I had visited a boyfriend unannounced, he'd had *company* and it hadn't worked out so great. And the surprise had definitely been on me.

Problem was this time I felt a hell of a lot more for Josh than I'd ever felt for Oliver. So chances were, if history decided to repeat itself, I would not be adding the other woman to my circle of friends. *Oh please don't let him have picked up some random girl at the bar.* Even just the thought of walking in and finding him with someone else made me want to throw up.

No.

Josh wasn't like that. Even though we hadn't been together long, I knew he had more integrity than that. He wouldn't cheat on me.

Yeah, but you didn't think the last guy would either, so your track record isn't exactly great, is it?

See! My mind was a complete asshole, but I wouldn't allow it to sabotage me when I had no reason to even suspect it. I was just thinking too much.

Overthinking.

Too many thoughts.

Fuck.

When I finally arrived at his apartment building, I had argued both sides of the would-he-cheat-on-me argument so effectively I wasn't sure who had won. Either way, I promised myself I wouldn't fall apart. It would be okay, I promised myself. It would be okay.

I took it as a good sign that I found a parking spot out front, putting the car in park and taking a couple of deep breaths.

Slowly—which was ridiculous considering I'd been cursing every minute till I got to his place—I exited the car and pressed his buzzer and waited.

And waited.

No answer.

Shit.

Well, at least I hadn't caught him screwing someone else. Unless that had been his reason for not answering the door.

No.

He wasn't Oliver.

He wouldn't.

I tried his cell again while I took the short walk to the tattoo shop. Maybe he'd decided to go in early to do some work—unlikely, but I was hopeful. Or maybe after his big night drinking he'd decided to crash at the shop—even less likely considering how close he lived he could literally crawl home. It didn't matter about his early-days stories about sleeping in his chair, if I could almost sprint the distance in heels, he could get himself home.

Voicemail.

No matter how many times I dialed the number, it was always the same result and to top it off, the shop was dark.

No lights and no sign of movement.

This wasn't good.

Where the hell was he?

I was just about to give up—and possibly lodge a missing person's report, that wasn't overacting surely—when I saw something had been lodged just underneath the door. A receipt from a gas station had been folded and shoved in the small space but once I pulled it out, I was able to see it was actually a note.

Josh,
Was in town, stopped by.
Here until Friday.
Give me a call.
~ T

A phone number was scribbled underneath.

I had no idea who T was and what business they had with Josh. But it obviously wasn't of a professional nature. Last time I checked, people didn't book appointments by shoving notes under a fucking door. So I could only assume it was personal. Obviously someone he hadn't seen in a while because they'd "stopped by" his shop rather than calling him on the phone.

Maybe an ex-girlfriend?

Great.

I was back to worst-case scenario again.

Checking to see no one was watching—I probably looked like I was about to rob the joint—I stuffed the note into my purse and casually—and as quick as I could—walked back to my car.

I was riding high on adrenaline and irrationality and I wouldn't be swayed. I was going to call T and find out who the hell they were and what they wanted. Because *of course* I had that right.

Besides, I told myself, shaking off any guilt. If I would have been with Josh I would have seen the note anyway. Probably—I rationalized—returning the call for him if it was business related, which I could safely assume considering the note had been left at his place of business. It's not like I'd yanked it from his front door at home. So *technically* I was just doing my job. Yes. That was exactly what I was doing.

Trying not to attract any sort of attention or suspicion—well, no more than I probably already had if anyone had been watching—I made it back to my car and locked the door.

And with my ignition back on, I left Queens and headed back to Manhattan. I was still no closer to finding out where Josh was, but I wasn't going to sit outside of his apartment and wait for him to come home, like a stalker. All right, not perpetuating the stalker stereotype more than I already had.

Besides, I had something else I needed to take care of. I needed to make a call and find out what I was dealing with.

Yep, I had taken insanity to a new level because whoever T was, was going to have to speak to me first.

JOSH

"WE WILL NEVER TALK ABOUT this again." Dallas loaded himself into my car, slamming the door behind him. "Never. To the fucking grave."

Unlike the last time Dallas and I had gone out drinking, we hadn't ended up at the emergency room.

In fact, on Saturday night I'd called time early and decided to go home. At that point I was still hopeful Eve would call and we could talk. I assumed she'd arrived at her parents' house—of course I didn't know for sure because she hadn't sent me a text—but still had no idea where things stood with us.

And here's a hint, I wasn't much fun to be around. You know those dudes who sit at the bar peeling the label off their beer, embodying every shitty country song ever written? Multiply that by ten and you were somewhere in the vicinity of my mood.

But I didn't call her.

Even though every instinct I had was to pick up that phone and tell her to come back. Why? Because I was a pussy, trying to be the *nice guy* and give her *fucking space*. She didn't need space. She needed to hear what I had going on in my head, that I was crazy about her and going absolutely insane without her.

She wanted until Monday. Two whole fucking days I was supposed to sit on my hands and pretend like it was all-good. I did that before when I tried to fool myself into believing I wasn't attracted to her, now it was like asking for the impossible. But I fucking did it anyway. Because her fucking happiness was more important than my own.

S-U-C-K-E-R.

Fuck, I just needed to know if we had a chance.

But it was her call, so until such time as advised—because I'd clearly lost my balls at some point—we were on radio silence.

So because I was a glutton for punishment, I went out with Dallas again. This time he'd brought reinforcements so I wouldn't kill his vibe.

Then it fucking happened.

We'd passed whatever dark side of the moon Eve had predetermined and she'd *finally* called me last night. Of course life was still tossing me shit grenades so I'd missed it. It wasn't until after a serious game of drunken charades with Steve and Dallas that I even realized what had happened. Steve's insistence that I needed "to call Steve" had been chalked up to him being a drunken dick. How was I supposed to know *Steve* was really *Eve*, and the dumbass had answered my phone when I'd gone to take a piss. At least if the bastard had left it unanswered I might have gotten a missed call notification or a voicemail.

But after both a returned call and a text from me to Eve had remained unanswered, my tolerance for my drunken friends and to be in public dropped to an all time low. So I went home, with my second message around midnight also not getting a response.

Of course me being home in my bed alone didn't insulate me from drama. Especially not when I'd left Dumb and Dumber without a sober chaperone. I swear to freaking God I was going to need to hire Dallas a keeper. Although I guess if nothing else, it forced me to think about something other than Eve.

"I'm not sure why you're even making those kinds of demands, Dallas." I hadn't even bothered to start the car yet. "You are going to owe me for the rest of your life."

It seemed shortly after I left the bar, both Dallas and Steve had found two lovely ladies to keep them company. Far be it from me to stand in the way of anyone having a good time. And as long as these girls were legal and sober enough to know what the hell they were doing, it was none of my business. Until it became my business, when the "hot blonde" Dallas had left with screwed him, and then took his wallet, his clothes and left him naked and stranded at Rockaway Beach.

The police picked him up after they'd gotten calls of a Caucasian male flashing his junk trying to hitch a ride home. And once they filed the police report, laughed at his stupidity, gave him some pants and decided not to pursue a public indecency charge on account he'd probably suffered enough, they'd called me.

How Dallas was able to remember my phone number when he couldn't remember what he ate for breakfast was one of the world's greatest mysteries. But he surprised everyone—including himself—by spitting out the digits to my landline. Which coincidently was the only available form of communication to reach me after I'd tossed my cell against the wall at two in the morning when I'd woken up and still hadn't heard from Eve.

Because smashing my phone was a smart idea.

"Just fucking take me home, asshole." Dallas stewed in the passenger seat, still mostly naked except for the pair of basketball shorts one of the officers had given him. "I've got a hangover that's going to last for a week."

"Fine." I wasn't even going to pretend I was letting him off the hook. "But in case you didn't see this for the wake-up call it is, you need to stop putting your dick inside everything that moves. It's like you have a built-in magnet for crazy."

While his "date"—assuming she had used her real name, he couldn't remember it—had only gotten fifty dollars and a used iPhone out of him—which was probably the reason she'd taken his clothes—it could have been a lot worse.

"I know, dude, I know." He shook his head, scrubbing his face with his hands. "She looked so normal. How was I supposed to know?"

"The fact she drove you out to a fucking beach to fuck should have been your first clue." That I even had to speak the words was bewildering. "Please tell me you used protection."

"Of course. I'm not an idiot." Dallas had the nerve to look indignant as he folded his arms across his chest.

"No words, dude." I shook my head as I started the ignition. "No fucking words."

It was evident anything I had to say at this point would fall on deaf ears, so I figured I'd save it for later. Like when he was sober and dressed. So I saved us both the headache and didn't give him anymore shit on the drive or when I dropped him off at his place. But tomorrow, we were going to have a serious conversation.

I was freaking tired, cranky and edgy as shit when I arrived at the shop. It wasn't a day we opened but I wanted to get the spare cell I kept in a drawer. I figured I could switch out the SIM card and at least get reconnected. Not because anyone *important* was going to call. No. Not for any reason like that.

Fuck, I was in a mood as I unlocked the front door and yanked it open. I still had no idea if she was even coming back. For all I knew she could be emailing me her resignation, modern technology was wonderful like that.

Screw it, I was going to call her.

I grabbed the spare phone and loaded in the SIM from the mangled one I'd been carrying in my pocket. Even though the piece of shit no longer worked, I stupidly had taken it with me when I left the house. Habits were terrible things to break, but in this instance I was thankful.

As soon as I switched on the new/old phone, it sprung to life, lighting up with a stack of missed calls.

All from Eve.

No messages or texts, but I didn't care, the fact she'd called sent such a bolt of electricity up my spine I couldn't be sure I hadn't been zapped.

We were going to talk.

Fuck being the nice guy.

Fuck being understanding.

Fuck being patient.

This was bullshit, and whatever she needed to work out, she was going to do it with me. It had been barely two fucking days and I was ready to seriously cause some damage, there was no way I'd survive if she wanted to make our hiatus permanent.

I hit the call button and brought the phone to my ear, one way or another, this shit was getting straightened out today.

"Oh my God, Josh," she breathed into phone as soon as it connected. "Please tell me that's you?"

"Eve, are you okay? What happened?" The desperation in her voice cut through me like a knife, and all the shit I needed to straighten out took a backseat to making sure she was safe.

"I kept putting off texting you because I wanted a better time, and then it got late, and then I had a few drinks, and I fell asleep and, then you missed my call and I missed your messages." She inhaled sharply, her interrupted sentence taking every ounce of air she'd had. "I couldn't find you, you weren't home this morning."

"You came by?" I was mentally kicking both my own ass and Dallas's for missing her visit. "Where are you, baby? I need to see you."

"I'm at my apartment, I can come to you."

"No, stay where you are." I grabbed my keys and was already locking the front door. "I'm getting in my car now and I'm coming to you."

"Okay. I'll be here."

"Eve." I yanked open my car door and hopped into the driver's seat. "I should have never let you walk out that door, I'll be there as soon as I can."

I didn't wait for her response, killing the call, putting the car in gear and hightailing it to Manhattan.

Man, the traffic sucked. I cursed every freaking mile between here and there as I weaved in and out of traffic like the assholes I usually flipped off. I didn't care how many times someone beeped their horn or shot me a dirty look, I needed to get to her and the longer it took, the more it was driving me insane.

Finally I arrived at her building, inputting the code to gain access into her undercover parking garage and put the Jeep between two white lines. I didn't even care if it was the designated *guest* spot, too concerned with getting into the elevator and seeing her.

My skin was almost humming by the time I'd made it onto her floor, my fist only making contact once before the door swung open and she flung herself on me.

I didn't even blink.

My arms engulfed her, pulling her onto me.

It felt so right, her weight against me as she wrapped her legs around my waist.

"Josh."

I didn't care what came after, putting my mouth on hers as I walked us back into her apartment and slammed the door. I had a sick need to be in her, cover her with my body and mark her so she knew she was mine.

Mine.

It took her leaving for me to really understand what that word meant but it was more than a throwaway. We were going to be together and I refused to accept an outcome that was any different.

Her mouth was hot as I invaded it, my tongue exploring every inch of her inside. I wanted more. To be closer, to be deeper, but for now it was going to have to do.

She moaned, the noise going straight to my cock as her hands clawed at my shirt.

"You wouldn't answer the phone." Moan.

"I didn't know." Moan.

"I was going crazy."

She spat out half sentences as I moved my mouth to her neck and carried her into her bedroom. I hadn't asked her if that's where she wanted to go, and honestly at this point I didn't care. I needed to get closer and standing up wasn't cutting it.

No words.

All that shit I had said about needing to talk to her, and I had nothing that I could even contemplate saying. My mouth was so desperate for her, there wasn't a syllable that was worth wasting a breath over. It could wait.

All of it could wait.

But I couldn't.

"I need you, Eve." I lowered her onto the mattress, my eyes rolling over every inch of her sexy body.

She looked similar to the day I'd first met her, wearing those ridiculous heels and a dress that thankfully flared out from the waist.

"Would it be incredibly irresponsible for us to have sex right now and then have a conversation later?" Her eyes speared me, licking her lips as her shoulders lifted from the mattress.

"In my opinion I've been too responsible, I'm no longer interested in it." I kneeled on the bed as I hovered above her. "I want you."

"I want you, too." I heard her shoes drop as she parted her legs. "Take me."

My mouth slammed onto hers as I took exactly what she was

giving me. She'd used me as a distraction before but this time it was different.

We were different.

I was different.

I kissed her like I couldn't bear to stop, my hands trailing up the sides of her body as my cock hardened in my jeans.

It wasn't soft. Or romantic. Or loving. I was so jacked up with all kinds of emotions I couldn't decipher what was which. The sheer need of it all spiked up my spine like I no longer needed my bones to hold me in place.

"We are going to talk about this later." My mouth moved away from hers as my hands roughly yanked the zipper to her side. "I'm not letting you get amnesia, so in a week you leave again."

"I won't leave. I promise." Her hands were at my belt, yanking and pulling in an effort to get it off.

"This will not be temporary." My fingers gripped the bottom of her dress and pulled it over her head. "Whatever I said before doesn't count. We are meant to be together."

She stilled for a second, her hands pausing on the fly of my jeans. "There is nowhere else I want to be."

"Fuck." I yanked off my shirt and kicked off my boots.

She'd probably just said the sweetest words I'd ever heard, and yet I couldn't find it in me to be sweet. I pulled at her hair, moving her head to the side as I sucked on her throat. "I need you naked."

"Yes." She arched her back, her fingers unhooking her bra, and flinging it aside. "I want to see all of you. I want you in me."

It was a mess of uncoordinated limbs, arms and legs being bent and twisted as we stripped each other while remaining fused by our lips. I wanted to taste her everywhere, my mouth closing around the peak of her nipple and sucking hard.

"Ah," she hissed, her neck bending back as I circled her nipple. "Josh," she moaned as her hands scraped against my skull.

God, I loved the way she said my fucking name.

Loved how the breath pushed out between those sweet lips of hers and made it sound like a plea.

My mouth moved lower, my tongue swirling down her flat belly until I got to the cleft of her pussy. I hovered above it, the heat of my breath covering her bare skin as I pressed the flat of my tongue against her.

She was so wet—slick and warm, ready for me—the thought alone making me want to come. But tasting her, that was a torture all of its own as my body bargained with itself over which part of us got to have her first.

"Josh." Her hips tilted as my tongue pushed into her, my hands parting her thighs so I could get better access. "Oh my God. Yes." She bucked against me, grinding herself against my face as I alternated between sucking her clit and fucking her with my tongue.

"Fuck me. Please. Just fuck me," she demanded, her nails scraping against my shoulders as her legs seesawed under her. "I want to come on your cock."

I could have kept going, up until *that* point. Licked her long and hard until I teased out the orgasm I could feel was building. But the minute she'd told me she wanted my cock in her, I didn't have a hope. My body overrode any plans I had as I lifted off of her and moved further up her.

"I'm not wearing a condom, Eve." I became painfully aware we'd skipped a step as my mouth moved back up to her tits. "I need to get—"

"No, I trust you." She grabbed my hair, pulling my head back so we were eye to eye. "Do you trust me?"

Our stares locked and I said the only words I was capable of. "With my life."

"Then you, just you. Please." She tilted her hips, the ridge of my cock hitting her right between her legs. "It's fine, I promise."

I didn't ask any more questions. Didn't check to see if she was sure or get butthurt over the innuendo that I would fuck someone else. All I wanted was to feel myself inside of her and make her scream so loud the neighbors would call the cops.

"Fuck." I gritted my teeth as the entire length of my cock entered her.

I had intended to be gentle, ease in an inch at a time. But once I felt her warmth around me, I couldn't stop, needing to be so deep into her I bottomed out.

"Yes." She arched into me as I thrust again, the slow drag in and out giving her a chance to adjust.

"God, you feel so good." My hands wrapped around her waist, my hips swinging deeper and faster with each rock. "Like fucking heaven."

She lifted her legs, locking her ankles at my back as her hands gripped my shoulders. "Want you," she breathed out. "Want you so much."

My self-control disintegrated at the sound of her voice and the need in her eyes. I drove into her, my hips smashing against her as my shoulders bruised under her fingertips. Her nails bit into my skin as I rocked harder, filling her completely with every thrust.

"Josh," she warned, the telltale shiver of her body cluing me in she was close.

"Come for me, Eve." My jaw locked as I gritted out the words. "Come for me, baby. God, I want to feel you."

One of my hands moved from her waist and punched the mattress to steady myself. The leverage it granted me was all I needed as I slid my fingers across to her pussy and thumbed her clit. She was so fucking wet, whimpering with each stroke of my thumb.

"Josh!" she screamed, exploding against me as the tight pulses ran up my shaft. Each squeeze sent me deeper into the sweet agony.

"Eve." I cursed out her name as the heat spread across my skin. "I need to come."

There was no holding back; jets of my hot load filled her as I rocked against her. Every shudder, every squeeze, every movement amplified as I collapsed against her, our bodies slick with sweat.

I whispered into her shoulder, my lips against her skin as I repositioned onto my elbows. "God, I missed you."

It wasn't just about the time she'd been gone either, she had checked out *before* she walked out the door.

"I missed you too." Her fingers feathered up and down my back as her breathing slowed. "I didn't realize how much until I was back."

I could have stayed like that forever.

Just me and her in the bedroom, with nothing else, and I would have been happy. But I knew there was more to it than that. And awesome sex—monumental sex—did not fix everything.

I rolled slowly, my back hitting the mattress before tucking her back into my arms. There wasn't a chance I was letting her go—physically or otherwise.

"Where were you?" she asked softly. "I thought you might have been with someone else, now I know you weren't, but why didn't you answer the phone? Why weren't you at your apartment? Were you punishing me?"

"No, Eve. I'm sorry, baby, but I was never punishing you." That she even thought it killed me. The last thing on earth I ever wanted to do was hurt her, even if part of me was hurting. "I smashed my phone when you didn't call, it was dumb. I was so frustrated by the situation and I had no idea what the hell was going on, it was making me crazy." I kissed her forehead, almost not believing she was back and I was able to tell her exactly how I felt.

"I'm sorry, honestly I got sidetracked and then I called, I'd missed you." Regret clouded her beautiful whiskey-colored eyes.

"I almost killed Steve when I found out it had been you." I cursed under my breath. "I thought he was yanking my chain. He kept saying *Steve called* and then laughing like an idiot. I swear I need better friends."

Her face softened, hopefully knowing there wasn't a thing

that would have kept me from her call if I'd known sooner. It was hell those hours in between.

"And then Dallas got into some trouble and I had to pick him up from the police station." Her face screwed in horror. "Don't ask and he's fine." I was in no mood to relive how Dallas's poor choices snowballed into my night from hell. "I'll tell you all about it tomorrow. Or next week. Or next year. We have time."

There would be time for all of it, but what I needed now was to hear from her. To know what was going on in that beautiful head of hers.

"Talk to me, Eve."

"I've made so many mistakes." She shook her head. "Part of me was embarrassed that I was such a mess. I mean, I have had more opportunities than most and in a lot of ways, I still fucked it up."

Instinct was to tell her she was wrong, but now she was talking I wasn't taking a chance she'd stop.

She took a deep breath, and like the floodgates had opened, she told me everything. About the choices she'd made and why she'd made them, about how she'd been fighting the shadow of her family's money—my estimation of her net worth, wasn't even close—and how despite being a badass and having confidence for days, she'd always felt she had something to prove.

There hadn't been a chip on her shoulder so much as a boulder.

For hours she talked. About her insecurities. About her idea for her exhibition. About a hotel she was buying—no seriously, my girlfriend had the kind of capital where she could just decide to buy a fucking hotel like it was a game of Monopoly.

She talked until her voice got hoarse, telling me more about herself than I'm sure she was comfortable with. But she did it anyway.

"Aren't I a catch?" She snuggled up closer, her laugh lighter than it had been before.

"Nothing you could ever say to me is ever going to scare me

away." My arms locked around her. "There isn't a thing that you or *anyone* could do that would change my mind. We belong together, Eve. I'm not saying it's going to be easy, but nothing worth having ever is."

She buried her head in the crook of my neck. "Good, because I didn't want to have to tie you up and hold you against your will . . . but I would have."

"Wait now." I pulled her head back and gave her a kiss. "I might actually like being tied up. Let's not rule anything out until we've given it proper consideration."

"Then I will." She brought my fingers to her mouth and playfully bit them. "And no more holding back."

"Nope," I agreed, knowing there would never be another woman for me. "Not for either of us."

EVE

I PROMISED JOSH THERE WOULD be no more secrets between us. I had cut myself open and bled in front of him—not literally because that would be gross—but emotionally every part of me had been exposed.

That was some hard shit.

I'd rather face a million art critics picking apart my fucking brush strokes than risk the man I loved thinking I was a basket case.

Okay, so maybe I hadn't told him everything.

The L word hadn't left my lips just yet. And it wasn't because I was scared. I had reasons for holding onto it just a little while longer. Because when I finally said it out loud, I wanted him to know it wasn't just a knee-jerk reaction to me jumping off the cliff.

There was something else I hadn't told him either.

Fine, so maybe my track record for keeping secrets sucked, but I was a work in progress and the ones I was holding onto were for good reasons.

But I needed to tell him everything soon, or I was going to explode.

"Hello, beautiful." He looked up from his desk, his perfect

smile still making me weak in the knees. "You want to get me lunch for old time's sake?" He laughed, pushing away from his work and wrapping his arms around me.

"Maybe *you* should be getting *me* lunch." I looped my arms around his neck and brought my mouth to his. "You never did get me a parting gift from Ink Addiction. You think at the very least I would get a cake. I gave you three of my very best weeks."

After our epic chat three days ago, I had resigned as I had planned. I hated leaving the shop, but if I was going to get an exhibition together and get the hotel/gallery up and running, I needed to dedicate every minute I had to it.

Josh completely understood and supported my decision, but it meant we only got to see each other outside work hours the past few days. Except today when I surprised him at lunchtime.

"You want a cake, sweetheart?" His brow arched with mischief. "I'll let you eat it off me, if that will make you happy. The rest of my afternoon is design work, no clients until tomorrow."

"Seriously, how is it we never screwed in your chair?" I eyed his fancy tattoo chair with wonder, the thought of me tonguing cake off his abs almost too much to take. Incidentally I knew about his free afternoon, which is why I had picked today for my impromptu visit.

"Health inspections." He laughed, kissing the top of my head. "So what brings my amazing, talented girlfriend to my shop? Something on your mind?"

Honestly, I was still surprised I had held out as long as I had but I didn't want to ruin his surprise. Josh was more intuitive than any person I knew, and he always had a sense when I was holding back. It was one of the things I loved about him the most, his ability to *know* me. But it made occasions like this extra difficult, which is why I was glad I could finally come clean.

See, what he didn't know was, on the day we'd both spilled our guts and decided we belonged together, I had intercepted a message that was intended for him. Okay, maybe it was less *intercepted* and more *stolen,* but there was no reason to get hung up on semantics.

And in my panicked madness of not being able to find Josh—insecurities completely messing with my head—I had wrongly suspected it had been a woman. Possibly an ex-girlfriend who'd come to her senses and discovered that yes, Josh was the most awesome man alive. That shit would not fly. Not while I still had breath in my body. Did I mention I had been more than a little irrational?

But like a few instances where I'd assumed, I had been wrong.

Like really, *really* wrong.

And in a weird and twisted way—sort of like how I'd met Kitty when she was blowing my boyfriend, but not quite so twisted—it had been fate that I had got the note instead of Josh.

"So, I have an idea." I bit my lip, both excited and terrified at the same time. "Something I decided while I was away at my parents' house about something I wanted to give you. A surprise."

"That's two *somethings*, and you look nervous." His hand dropped to my ass and squeezed. "You want to tell me what it is?"

"Your tattoo. The crow." My finger circled over the cotton of his T-shirt that hid the offending monstrosity on his shoulder. "I want to give you a do-over."

"Wow. Okay." I saw his face pale a little, a slight flicker of fear flashed through his eyes. "Maybe we should get you to practice a little first. Holding a machine isn't as easy as it looks."

"Do you trust me?" I gently pulled his arm guiding him to his big fancy chair that a few moments ago I had considered defiling.

"Of course I trust you, baby." He allowed me to push him down into the chair, his butt hitting the cushion. "And if you really want to do this, I'll let you, but I need you to really think about it. A regular tattoo is difficult, a cover up? Eve, that's seriously advanced."

"I have thought about it, Josh." I walked over to a box of black gloves and pulled them on. "I really want to give you this tattoo."

"Okay." He scrubbed his face, shaking his head for a minute

before turning his eyes back to me. "Then let's do this."

"Seriously, dude, you really are a sucker." Dallas waltzed in, shaking his head and taking a seat on a stool. "Didn't you learn from the last time?"

Of course, I had told Dallas my plan. I mean, I had to tell someone and figured it would be easier if I brought him in from the beginning. Plus he knew Josh's tattoo so he could give me a second opinion if I needed it.

"I'm not a sucker, asshole." He flipped off Dallas and stripped off his shirt. "But seeing as you're here you can help. You can be Eve's assistant."

Oh. Shit.

He was going to actually let me do it.

Was he insane?

"Are you sure?" I looked at Josh, my heart beating so hard in my chest I was positive it was going to crack my rib cage.

There was no hesitation.

"Positive."

"How about I do it instead?" Tommy poked his head through the open doorway, not able to hide his huge grin.

"Tommy Vaughn?" Josh leapt out of his chair, looking between me and Tommy in confusion. "T, what are you doing in town?"

"Got here Sunday night," Tommy threw out his hand, smacking Josh across the shoulder. "I left you a note, but someone else decided to call me instead." He tipped his chin at me, his smile inching wider.

Okay, so Monday, when I'd called *T* ready to give her a piece of my mind, I had been pleasantly surprised that T was actually short for Tommy. And that Tommy was a man who had no designs on my boyfriend. It was a double win.

What I also found out through the course of the conversation was that Tommy—a tattooist from Las Vegas—had been voted one of the best artists in the entire country. He and Josh had met a few months ago at a convention and Tommy had promised to check out Josh's shop if he happened to come to New York. And guess what. Tommy happened to be visiting New York.

"I drew the sketch while I was away. I worked out a way where we could use the texture of the wings to cover the existing tattoo, and there's enough negative space around it." I nodded to Tommy who handed me back the sketch I had emailed him after our initial conversation. "I just needed an artist who was good enough to pull it off. Because, as much as I love you, I can't be the one to put it on your skin."

"What did you say?" Josh's head whipped around, his eyes not even looking at the crow I had drawn.

Well. Shit.

The right time I was waiting for to tell him I love him? Yeah, I guess it was kind of now.

While he had his shirt off.

With an audience.

"Guys, can you give us just a minute." I turned, hoping Dallas wouldn't make a big deal of it and Tommy didn't think I was a complete nutcase asking him to walk out when he'd barely walked in.

"Yep. No problem." Dallas nodded to Tommy, the two of them walking out of the room and shutting the door.

"I." I placed the sketch on the chair and wrapped my arms around his neck. "Love you. I love you so much, Josh."

"God, I love you." His hands moved to my jaw, cupping my face as he kissed me. "So much."

"Well, that kind of worked out for the best." I laughed, my hands moved down the ripples of his beautiful colored chest. "Would have sucked if you had another tattoo on you from an ex."

"Yeah, that's not going to happen." He kissed me again. "But I am super excited to have yours. Let me see the sketch."

I let Josh inspect my version of the crow while I went and got Dallas and Tommy. They both walked in and got busy setting up.

Dallas prepared the transfer while Josh got situated in the chair, his face so excited you'd think he'd just been given a puppy, and ice cream and a year's supply of free cable.

"You good, dude?" Tommy pressed the stencil onto Josh's shoulder, the purple lines on his skin the same ones I'd drawn on a piece of paper.

It was so surreal, my work being on someone's skin forever. It wasn't something I had on my bucket list, but now it was happening, I was secretly thrilled.

"All good." Josh gave him the thumbs up as he laid on his side, ready to get inked.

"I still can't believe you got *Tommy Vaughn* to tattoo Josh." Dallas shook his head, talking about the man like he wasn't in the room. "This shit is so unfair."

"She was very convincing." Tommy smiled, continuing with Josh's black outline. "I just couldn't say no."

"Yeah, been there, done that." Josh laughed. "It really is easier if you just agree."

"I'm right here, you know. And for the record, it didn't take a lot of convincing." I rolled my eyes, not at all annoyed.

"To be honest, I wanted to see these two storm clouds fucking." Tommy stopped the machine for a second and laughed. "I'm so glad we're fixing this for you, even if it's not my design."

"You know if you want to toss out one of your designs, I'm happy to take one for the team." Dallas raised his hand. "Dude, I'd let you tattoo my dick if you wanted."

"Ewww, Dallas." I popped him as hard as I could in the arm.

"Seriously, D, you need to put it away." Josh chuckled trying not to move. "All it's ever done is get you in trouble."

"Thanks for the offer, but I'll pass." Tommy smirked as he continued.

I'd only ever watched one tattooist up close, and that was Josh. I'd checked in on Dallas from time to time but never sat and observed. Part of me felt I didn't want to share it with anyone other than Josh, the feeling in the room almost too personal. But strangely as I watched Tommy work, it didn't feel the same way.

He was incredibly precise. His hand moved with skill and purpose from the darkest black to almost translucent, all in the way he worked the needle. And as it started to take shape, it looked even better than I envisioned, the original crow slowly being hidden underneath.

But the spark wasn't there.

Watching Tommy didn't excite me. There was no chill up my spine as the machine buzzed, and it was safe to say my earlier questions about whether it was isolated to one particular artist were confirmed.

It was Josh.

And only Josh.

"So you getting some ink any time soon?" Tommy lifted his head and smiled. "Being around them usually gives you the itch."

I shook my head. "I don't think so. But you never know."

I wasn't ruling it out entirely, but if I ever did it, there'd have to be a purpose behind it.

"She's perfect the way she is," Josh answered turning to face me. "There isn't a tattoo that would do her justice."

He caught me staring and smiled, the same smile I remembered from when I'd first walked in. He was so incredibly perfect, my eyes hurt. And he was all mine.

I reached for his hand and he didn't hesitate to link his fingers with mine, and that's how we sat while Tommy worked.

Slowly, everything in the periphery faded into the background and it was only the two of us in that room.

Just the way it had always been with us.

And the way it would always be.

EPILOGUE

JOSH

"GOD, I'M GOING TO PUKE."

Eve wouldn't stop pacing, her hands locked on her hips as I sat watching. "Tell me again why I invited those jackasses to come tonight?"

"Because you don't care what they think," I reminded her. "And because they are doing their jobs and like it or not, while you don't need them, *Art Addiction* does."

My beautiful, smart, talented and ridiculously wealthy girl-friend had bought her hotel. Put her money where her mouth was and bet everything on black. And if things hadn't been awesome enough, she'd decided to call it *Art Addiction*, as a nod to the shop and I guess to me as well. I had told her she didn't have to, that she should name it whatever she wanted, but she insisted her mind was made up. And the thing about Eve was, once she decided something there was very little you could do to change it.

Secretly I was fucking ecstatic and incredibly proud for whatever small part I played in it.

She had done an amazing job of pulling her pieces together, her *Midnight Moments*—the dream-esque watercolors with sharp focal points—looked amazing. And when construction started next week, she was going to do an outstanding job on the hotel. Oh, and in case I hadn't mentioned it, it was exactly two blocks from my shop and apartment. Seemed like Santa was handing out presents early this year.

"You're right." She smoothed down the front of her tight red dress with her palms. "It will be good for business."

"Hey, can we come in?" There was a voice from the doorway. "We know the owner." Heather smiled as she walked in with her husband, followed by the rest of her posse. Lana and Dave, Kristen and some guy I hadn't met, then finally Kitty who was surprisingly dateless.

"Hey!" Eve screamed excitedly, taking turns to hug everyone.

"This is so great."

"I love the space."

"Your pieces are amazing."

All of them fawning over her as they took in the view.

It was good to sit back and watch her have her moment; it was something she'd worked hard for and she had every right to enjoy it. All that praise had been hard earned, and I knew after tonight she was going to be getting a lot more of it.

"Hey, asshole." Dallas tipped his chin, walking in to join the growing crowd. "How does it feel to be the *second* most famous artist in the room?" He smiled and waved to Eve. "Incidentally, she's prettier than you too."

"You are one hundred percent right my friend." I cupped the back of his neck and shook him. "And I couldn't be happier if I tried."

Kitty sidled up next to Dallas, the smirks on both of their faces answer enough as to why they both arrived stag.

"No fucking in public," I warned both of them. "This is Eve's night and if either one of you screws it up, you'll have me to deal with."

"Yes, yes." Dallas waved me off as his other hand did something to make Kitty giggle. "We'll be on our best behavior."

Yeah, not likely.

Still, at least our location offered a lot of rooms, most which still had locks on the doors. I'd hoped one of them was smart enough to use them.

"What are you doing over here by yourself?" Eve found her way back to me, her friends helping themselves to drinks at the makeshift bar.

"Just waiting for you." I wrapped her in my arms and kissed her. "Can I steal you for a few minutes, I have a hotel warming present."

"Is *hotel warming* even a thing?" She narrowed her eyes, looking at me skeptical.

"If I say it is, then it must be. Come on, I've stashed it up stairs." I pulled gently on her arm as I led her to the staircase.

When Eve had been getting ready earlier, I took the time to come to the hotel and deliver my gift in preparation for tonight. Of course it wasn't as badass as the gift she'd given me. The *Eve Thorton* original inked into my skin by Tommy Vaughn wasn't something I thought I'd ever be able to top. Not unless I figured out a way to reanimate Rembrandt.

"The first thing that needs repairing is the elevator." Eve's heels echoed off the stairs. "And I should wear flats whenever going above the third floor."

"Do you want me to carry you?" I offered, only half joking. "Come on, one more flight."

"You know if you haul me on that big body of yours we'll end up having sex." Eve laughed, her feet continuing to move. "And my parents are going to be here soon."

I'd had a chance to meet Eve's folks a couple of weeks ago. We'd gone to Connecticut and had dinner with them and we'd all gotten along surprisingly well. Despite her parents having the wealth to rival a small country, they were awesome and down to earth.

Her dad had wanted to hear all about the shop. It seemed that business was business, and he respected anyone who worked hard. That I was self-made—got me extra points.

And Eve's mom was amazing. Super nice, and made a point of telling me how thrilled she was for both of us. She asked a lot of questions, but seemed genuinely interested in my answers, which was a nice change. Parents weren't always so *thrilled* when their daughter brought me home. Mr. and Mrs. Thorton, couldn't have been more welcoming.

And while initially the money had freaked me out a little, I realized how moronic I was being. My stupid hang up was basically bullshit, the idea of my girlfriend having more money than me meaning absolutely nothing.

"Okay, we're here." We paused in front of the door of the biggest suite in the place. Eve was going to eventually turn the whole top floor into a residence but for now was using it as an office.

"My office?" She looked at my hand on the door handle.

"It's inside, silly." I twisted the knob and pushed open the door.

It was dark inside so I hit the switch, light flooding the floor and the previously blank wall that now wasn't so blank.

"Josh." Eve gasped, the sketch I'd been working on now framed and hung on the wall. "Oh my God. It's beautiful."

"Just like the person who inspired it." I wrapped my arms around her, pressing her back against my chest. "And that sketch doesn't even come close to how amazing you are."

"The detail in this is amazing." She walked closer, her hand hovering over the glass from the frame. "It looks like a photo."

"This tattoo artist from Queens did it, I hear he's pretty good," I whispered against her ear.

"Oh yeah?" She laughed, the sound of it filling the room

with the most amazing sound in the whole world. "I've heard that rumor too."

"Have you heard the other one about him?" I gripped her tighter, my lips skating against her neck.

"What would that be?" Her hands moved against my arms.

"That he is crazy in love with his girlfriend and wants her to move in with him."

"What?" She spun around, our little game of talking in the third person obviously over. "What did you say?"

"I know your place is bigger, and has a doorman and is like five thousand times nicer. And if you would rather move there, I will follow you in a heartbeat. But since we both work on this side of town, I figured it made sense to live in mine. It's your choice, Eve, but I want us to live together."

Having two places was ridiculous; it was a rare night we didn't spend together. And with almost all of her cash now tied up in the business, it made economic sense to downsize and consolidate. But even with all those practical reasons, there was only one I cared about.

I was selfish and I wanted her with me.

Every night and every morning.

"Yes!" she squealed, pulling me in closer, her eyes gleaming with the soft shine of happy tears. "Yes to anything you are ever going to ask me."

We barely got time to kiss when my phone buzzed. Heather had sent a text notifying us that our presence was required downstairs.

I linked my fingers with Eve, unable to wipe the grin from my face as we returned to the group. While the doors hadn't officially opened, there had been some VIPs who were making their way in.

"Where have you been?" Heather grabbed Eve's arm the minute we'd reentered the group floor. "Someone has made an offer."

Eve looked at me before turning back to Heather. "What are you talking about? Bidding doesn't start for another hour."

"Yeah, well the buyer doesn't give a shit." Heather seemed to be struggling at keeping her voice low. "He offered twenty thousand dollars."

Eve tightened her grip on my hand as her eyes widened. "Are you shitting me? Twenty grand for one watercolor? Which one?"

I had a hunch I already knew, but the minute Heather's lips started moving it was confirmed.

"*Train Wreck.*"

While it was hard not to love every single one, we both shared a favorite.

It was one of the larger canvases, the focus on two trains colliding head-on with the cars derailing into a sea of color. It was loud and chaotic but incredibly beautiful.

And its significance multi layered.

Obviously partly representing us, and our own collision. But also how she'd drowned out the noise, and found beauty in her personal disaster.

"It's not for sale." Eve had gotten the words out just before I had.

If I had to cough up the twenty K myself to keep that one piece, I would.

"Are you insane?" Heather looked at both of us. "Twenty. Thousand. Dollars," she repeated, like we hadn't heard her the first time.

Ordinarily, cash like that would have been pocket change for Eve, but all that had changed with the gallery. And twenty grand would have given her a hell of a lot of breathing room.

"I know, and it's the one piece that isn't for sale." Eve's eyes stayed on me even though she was answering Heather.

"Fine." Heather dropped her arms dramatically. "I can't work with crazy. But you might want to consider opening up bids sooner than later, there are people circling those canvases like piranhas. And the writer from *The Times* is about to blow his load over *Water Lily*."

I pulled Eve into my arms, planting my lips on her mouth. We'd get to the crowd in a minute, but not before I demonstrated how incredibly proud I was.

"Wasn't he the one who said you had *no passion, no emotion and originality?*" I pulled my mouth away from hers.

"Yep." She grinned, every part of her positively beaming. "Come on, let's go out there. I'm going to enjoy this."

THE END

To keep up to date with all T Gephart's news, appearances and releases, please subscribe to her mailing list. Link available on her website: *www. tgephart.com*

ACKNOWLEDGEMENTS

SPECIAL THANKS TO GEP, JENNA, Liam and Woodley—so much love for you all. So. Much. Love.

Thank you to my amazing family and friends, most who have been ignored the last few months. Forgive me, I'm sorry and I love you. All catch up dates will be redeemed soon, I promise.

To MK #EverTheRomantic and Danielle #Weird #Burrow-Furrow. You guys rock my world.

Thank you all the amazing authors I get to hang out with either online, in between the pages, or in person. I will find you and I will HUG you.

Hang Le—THIS COVER. I CAN'T EVEN. A million thank you's and ninja hugs.

A HUGE thanks to all the bloggers and blogs who have, and continue to support me. I have so much love and appreciation for all of you. I try to make sure I comment and like all the posts and shout outs but I know I miss some. I beg forgiveness. I am incredibly thankful for all of you who share my covers, releases, sales.

Thanks to the T Gephart Entourage.

Thank you to my editor, Nichole Strauss, from Insight Editing Services. I was all panic station with date changes and you were like, "I've got you." Hugs, I worship at your feet.

Thank you to my proofreaders, Rachael B. and Rosa.

Massive thanks to Christine Borgford from Type A Formatting. You are a goddess, my books are stunning and you are a dream to work with.

And as always, thank you to all my readers. You allow me to keep doing this.

THANK YOU.

ABOUT THE AUTHOR

T GEPHART IS A USA Today and International bestselling author from Melbourne, Australia.

With an approach to life that is somewhat unconventional, she prefers to fly by the seat of her pants rather than adhere to some rigid roadmap. Her lack of "plan" has resulted in a rather interesting and eclectic resume, which reads more like the fiction she writes than an actual employment history. She'd tell you all about it, but the statute of limitations hasn't expired yet. But all those crazy twists and turns have led her to a career she loves—writing romantic comedy.

When she isn't filling pages with sassy and sexy characters with attitude, she's living her own reality show in the 'burbs of Melbourne with her American husband, two teenage children, and her fur child—Woodley.

She loves adventure, to laugh, travel, and strives to live her life to the fullest.

CONNECT WITH T

www.tgephart.com
Facebook
Goodreads
Twitter

BOOKS BY
THIS AUTHOR

The Lexi Series

Lexi

A Twist of Fate

Twisted Views: Fate's Companion

A Leap of Faith

A Time for Hope

The Power Station Series

High Strung

Crash Ride

Back Stage

The Black Addiction Series

Slide

Sticks

Stand

#1 Series

#1 Crush

#1 Player

#1 Rival

#1 Lie

#1 Muse

#1 Love (coming 2019)

Collision Series
Train Wreck
Car Crash (coming soon)

Standalones
The Fall

www.ingramcontent.com/pod-product-compliance
Lightning Source LLC
Chambersburg PA
CBHW021503110726

47899CB00001BA/275